FIRE ON THE WIND

He was consumed by the impulse to make long, sweet love to her. It was wrong. It was wicked. It was dangerous.

He had only to stand up and walk away. But he couldn't bring himself to leave her scented warmth and the comfort she offered his shattered soul. "If you don't stop me, Sarah, I'm going to make love to you."

Instead of the disgust he expected, a smile transformed her features into heart-stopping beauty. "The *Kama Sutra* describes so many positions. Which way will you do it?"

A chuckle of astonished delight swelled his throat. Damn the consequences. The world had turned upside-down, and life was short.

"My way," he said.

Critical Praise for
FIRE ON THE WIND

"*. . . an exhilarating, exotic,
and adventurous love story . . .
enthralling . . .
Barbara Dawson Smith's
most powerful romance yet.*"

Kathe Robin, *Romantic Times*

If you've enjoyed this story by
Barbara Dawson Smith
be sure to read

DREAMSPINNER
SILVER SPLENDOR
STOLEN HEART

And don't miss this other
AVON ROMANTIC TREASURE

DANCE OF DECEPTION
by Suzannah Davis

Other **AVON ROMANTIC TREASURES**
Coming Soon

LADY LEGEND
by Deborah Camp

ONLY IN YOUR ARMS
by Lisa Kleypas

RAINBOWS AND RAPTURE
by Rebecca Paisley

FIRE ON THE WIND

BARBARA DAWSON SMITH

An Avon Romantic Treasure

AVON BOOKS ◢ NEW YORK

To my mother-in-law and father-in-law

I am deeply indebted to Dr. Lawrence Ligon for answering my medical questions; to Shelby McDuff and Larry Wilhelm of *Quest* magazine, for sharing their library on India; and most of all, to the finest critique group in the world, Joyce Bell, Susan Wiggs, and Arnette Lamb.

FIRE ON THE WIND is an original publication of Avon Books. This work has never before appeared in book form. This work is a novel. Any similarity to actual persons or events is purely coincidental.

AVON BOOKS
A division of
The Hearst Corporation
1350 Avenue of the Americas
New York, New York 10019

Copyright © 1992 by Barbara Dawson Smith
Dance of Deception excerpt copyright © 1992 by Suzannah Davis
Inside cover author photograph by Ralph Smith
Published by arrangement with the author
Library of Congress Catalog Card Number: 91-93013
ISBN: 0-380-76274-9

First Avon Books Printing: March 1992

AVON TRADEMARK REG. U.S. PAT. OFF. AND IN OTHER COUNTRIES, MARCA REGISTRADA, HECHO EN U.S.A.

Printed in the U.S.A.

RA 10 9 8 7 6 5 4 3 2 1

Prologue

London—December 24, 1836

Tonight his mother would finally love him.

Damien Coleridge patted the gift in his pocket, the gift he'd spent hours perfecting. The rustle of the paper reassured him. Poking his small face between the scrolled posts of the balustrade, he peered down at the foyer. The chandelier threw diamonds of light over the white columns and checkerboard floor, over the green holly and red ribbons decorating the doorways. The case clock ticktocked over the tinkling of the pianoforte from the music room.

No one was in sight, not even a footman.

Damien ran a finger under his starched lace collar with its fussy bow. He hoped he'd knotted it correctly. His knee breeches itched and his leather half-boots pinched. He hated wearing girlish velvet. Such fancy clothing better suited Christopher. But tonight Damien wanted to please Mother.

Squeezing his eyes shut against the sudden sting of tears, Damien saw an image of his elder brother, asleep on his cot in the nursery, his bony hands ghostly pale against the blue counterpane, his fair hair tousled on the pillow. Christopher had had another spell today. The doctor had

1

shaken his head and murmured for a long time to Mother, then left a brown bottle of smelly tonic.

The medicine calmed Christopher and made him sleep. Maybe it would cure him. If not, Damien would burn in hell. Just as Mother said he would.

The scents of greenery and candle wax suddenly made him ill. He opened his eyes to the mass of scars on his palms and the puckered skin on his fingers. The hands of a devil.

Could Mother ever love him again?

She must. He'd worked so hard.

Damien swallowed a knot as rubbery as Mrs. Wadsworth's plum pudding. Tonight, Mother wouldn't ignore him. She wouldn't burn him with her flashing gold eyes. She wouldn't cut him with her sharp scoldings. Not in front of her guests.

He dashed away the last trace of babyish tears. Clutching the wrought-iron banister, he tiptoed down the grand staircase. His heels squeaked on the marble risers. Tonight she couldn't help but love him. Especially when she saw how clever he was, like one of the six soldiers of fortune in the Grimm Brothers' tale Miss Smaltrot had read to him before bedtime.

He was a storybook hero. He could shoot a fly two miles away. He sighted down the barrel of an imaginary rifle, aiming at the silver candelabrum on the newel-post.

''Bang!'' The candle flames wavered.

He could make a windmill go round from miles off. Sucking in a breath, he blew with all his might. A trio of tiny flames winked out.

He took the last two steps in a leap and landed on a black square of marble. Crouching low, he glanced cautiously around. Enemies lurked unseen behind pillars and around corners. The drawing room doors stood open to the gold-and-white furnishings. From down the hall, the pianoforte tune had given way to a sweetly lilting song. Harp music for angels.

His chest ached again. *He* might be a demon, but he could run faster than a bird could fly.

He dashed down the vast hall. Statues and paintings whizzed past in a blur of color. Like a soldier of fortune, he'd win the footrace. He'd earn a prize of gold and present Mother with the treasure. She'd hug him, call him her darling—

Rounding the corner, he thudded into someone emerging from the music room. Bromley's bushy brows lifted into a rare, startled look. "Lord Damien!" the butler said, steadying his silver tray.

Thrown off balance, Damien groped for the wall, but met the cold, carved stone of a pedestal. The figurine atop it teetered. The Chinese warrior toppled with a crash. Painted earthenware shards spewed across the floor.

The harp music ended in a jarring twang. Voices buzzed from within. Footsteps tapped and feminine skirts rustled.

"What is the meaning of this?"

The chilling tone prickled Damien's skin. He wanted to run. He wanted to hide. He almost gagged on a clot of panic. Slowly he lifted his eyes.

Blanche Coleridge, the Duchess of Lamborough, loomed in the doorway. Wearing a gown of shiny green, she brought to mind a dragon, golden eyes flashing, slim nostrils flaring. The disloyal thought rattled Damien. No, his mother was a fairy queen, with ropes of pearls circling her regal throat and a diamond crown glittering in her piled-up fair hair.

"I asked you a question," she said.

The words rang clear and cold as a church bell. Shamed, he looked at the shattered statue. "It . . . it fell," he stammered.

"It fell." With a sharp laugh, she glanced at the guests crowding behind her. "Imagine. My favorite T'ang figurine grew weary of its place and dashed itself upon the floor.''

The ladies tittered behind their fans; the men shifted in bored amusement. Feeling as small as a worm, Damien longed to crawl away.

"I . . . I'm sorry," he whispered.

His mother slapped a folded ivory fan against her palm. " 'Sorry' seems to be one of your favorite words of late. Why have you left the nursery at this hour? And for what purpose are you dressed?''

His mouth went dry. The urge to flee tugged at him, but he held still. She'd never love a coward. He reached into his velvet pocket and pulled out the precious roll of paper. "I wanted to give you this. My . . . my Christmas gift to you, Mother.''

Hesitantly he approached her. His shoes crunched bits of pottery. She looked taller and more mighty than ever. But she would praise him at last, smile at him in the same gentle way she smiled at Christopher. Damien proudly held up the gift.

Several of the ladies cooed. "What a darling lad.''

"How very sweet.''

"You never mentioned such a dear little boy, Blanche.''

His mother took no notice. "We're exchanging gifts in the morning.'' Frowning, she unrolled the paper.

"I know, Mother. But I couldn't wait any longer to show you. I . . . I thought it would please you.''

She stared at the drawing. Her eyes widened and her expression softened. Damien's heart thumped in agonizing hope. The fine lines of her face froze into a smile.

Whirling to her guests, she said, "Pray excuse us a moment.'' She took his arm and pulled. "Come along, Damien.''

His father ambled out of the throng. A ruddy hue tinted his cheeks, and his thinning black hair was slightly mussed. He waved a glass, the amber liquid sloshing. ''Here now, Blanche. 'Tis th' Eve o' Christmas. Don't be too hard on th' lad. He's only seven.''

She glared. ''I am not a hard woman, Ambrose. I merely want to thank dear Damien in private.''

Thank him? Damien's heart took wing. His plan was working.

Papa's blue eyes wavered. Leaning against a pillar, he took an unsteady gulp of brandy. ''If you say so, m'dear.''

Mother tugged hard on Damien's arm. Her fingers felt like claws. As she drew him down the hall, he had to scurry to keep pace. Yet she hadn't ridiculed his work. She held the picture tight against her gown, and her smile stayed as firmly fixed as a doll's. Joy hovered inside his chest.

She hauled him into the drawing room and let go so abruptly that he stumbled. Closing the double doors, she swung on him, her skirt swishing. She shook the paper in his face. ''How dare you?''

Bewildered, he glanced at the pencil sketch of her sitting on a garden bench, a loving smile on her face, he and Christopher at her feet. Damien had worked for hours, even when his scarred fingers hurt from holding the pencil.

''I . . . I wanted to give you something special. Mr. Emmott said it was my best picture ever—''

''How dare you try to place yourself in my affections? Your idealized drivel is pathetic.''

Hot tears blurred his eyes. ''But I . . . I only wanted—''

''Two years ago you lost your right to want anything. I rue the day I gave birth to you, Damien. You're a devil who deserves to burn in the flames of hell. You destroyed your own brother.''

Swift as an avenging angel, she swept to the

hearth, where a great Yule log burned. "Watch," she said. "Watch and remember the terror you put Christopher through." She flung the sketch into the blaze.

"No!" Sobbing, he raced to the hearth.

Yellow flames licked at his gift, curling the edges of the paper. Horror kept him from reaching into the fire. His fingers dug helplessly into the rigid scars on his palms. The blaze devoured his carefully drawn figures. The picture blackened, burning his dreams to ashes.

Memory hurled him down a nightmarish corridor where Christopher's frightened screams echoed.

Waves of sickness drowned Damien. Only half aware of his mother's hostile gaze, he retched again and again.

Then he turned and fled.

Chapter 1

Meerut, India—April 27, 1857

Today she'd be caught for certain.

Sarah Faulkner tiptoed out the front door of the bungalow. The veranda lay cool and shadowed, screened from the faint glow of dawn by bamboo trellises. Despite the early hour, the sounds of India invaded the dew-wet yard: a baby wailed somewhere, a crow cawed from the feathery foliage of a tamarind tree, a bullock clopped down the dirt road beyond the compound wall. The odor of burning dung drifted from the rear cookhouse, along with the *scritch-scratch* of Aziz wielding his twig broom over the pathways of the garden.

The familiar scene lulled her fear of discovery. She'd been awakened by the distant calling of the muezzins from the mosque in the native sector. Rather than lie abed like Aunt Violet, sipping tea and nibbling toast, Sarah savored the freshness before the scorching heat of the day. Risking disapproval, she often stole out to visit old tombs and temples, or to wander through rural villages. The excursions provided fodder for the essays she wrote secretly under a nom de plume for a Delhi newspaper.

Today a forbidden pleasure lured her. The

thought of exploring the native bazaar unescorted made her blood thrum with reckless anticipation. Decorum barred English ladies from the marketplace, where prostitutes and thieves roamed. Yet if she hurried, she could shop and return by breakfast, with her aunt none the wiser.

She settled a modestly ribboned topi helmet over her blond hair. The stiff brim shaded her fair features and blue eyes. Clutching the folds of her navy skirt, she descended the veranda steps. A man rounded the outside of the bungalow.

Her heart jolted. "Oh . . . Patel." Even after seven years in India, she was still unnerved by the silent approach of the native servants. "Good morning."

He bent into a deep salaam. The *abdur* wore dazzling white trousers and shirt, and a flat turban. His cummerbund was the forest green of her uncle's regiment. The new scarlet *tiki* mark on his forehead told of his recent ritual cleansing.

"A thousand pardons must I beg, missy-sahib," he said, his voice low. "My humble prayers to Shiva bring me late to our meeting time."

His merry dark eyes, etched by the wise lines of age, looked anything but humble. Sarah smiled. "You needn't accompany me this morning. Doubtless my aunt will keep you busy later with her plans for the dinner party tonight."

"Ah, but the memsahib, she sleep late." A mischievous grin lit his swarthy features. "The sahib, he share her bed last night. He wish to plant a son in her barren womb."

Heat washed Sarah's cheeks, but she kept a steady gaze. Patel meant no offense; he spoke with the Hindu nonchalance toward marital relations. "Nevertheless, you know how Aunt Violet will carry on if you're not here. I can go alone to the bazaar."

"Bazaar?" His cheery expression vanished. White rimmed his brown irises. "Bazaar very bad

place for English memsahibs. Much anger, much
hatred. You stay.''

''I shan't offend anyone. I must shop for the
party.''

He shook his head vigorously. His mouth
formed a tight line of disapproval. ''I go, then.
Weapon storehouse burned last night. The sahib,
he called to headquarters already.''

Shock held her still. ''Was anyone hurt?''

''No, but English not safe. Too many sepoys
angry over bullets. Very bad to touch. Make soldier lose caste and be reborn a snake.''

She frowned. Tension in the military stations
across northern India had been escalating for
months, ever since the British had issued new rifle cartridges with paper cylinders rumored to be
coated with animal grease. Beef fat was offensive
to the Hindu sepoys, as was pig fat to the Mohammedans. Handling the forbidden substance
would cause them to suffer banishment from
friends and family.

A few days earlier, eighty-five sowars, or native
cavalrymen, had refused to touch the bullets.
They now awaited sentencing. She'd attempted
to argue the injustice with Uncle John, but he'd
refused to listen to a mere woman.

''Nevertheless,'' she said, ''I'm going to the bazaar. I only mean to observe the people. I shan't
anger anyone.''

''Patel protect missy-sahib from wicked men.''
From the folds of his shirt he drew a brass-hilted
dagger. The slim blade gleamed in the pearly
light. ''No *badmash* dare to harm you.''

She shivered. Perhaps he was right; she
shouldn't venture out alone. ''Very well, then. But
we'll have to hurry.''

''Yes, missy.'' He tucked away the knife and
fell into step beside her. ''This way.''

They headed down the Mall and saw in the distance the parade ground, where troops were

mustering for early drills to the blaring call of a
bugle. Sabers flashed from the rows of dragoon
guards, and she tipped her head down, on the off
chance that someone might recognize her from
afar. A *palka-ghari* carriage rattled past, raising ed-
dies of dust on the hard-baked road. The muted
morning light warmed the thatch-roofed barracks
and, farther away, the steeple of the Anglican
church and the whitewashed walls of the hospital. Sarah wondered if Reginald was already on
his rounds.

She promptly forgot her suitor as the tidy
streets of the British quarter gave way to the
squalor of the native sector. The exotic sounds and
scents of the bazaar beckoned. For a brief time
she could escape the strict social mores and tire-
some etiquette that ruled her life. She could im-
merse herself in the pulsing life force of India.

A gabble of foreign tongues blended with the
cries of beggar children. Some of the chatter she
understood from her Hindi lessons with Patel;
other people spoke in unfamiliar dialects. The
stench of urine and rubbish from open ditches
underlay the fragrance of hot curries and frying
chupatties, the unleavened cakes that formed a
mainstay of the Indian diet. Flies swarmed the
goat carcasses hanging inside a butcher's stall,
buzzed the sores on the backs of bullocks, and lit
upon the brass trays of syrupy *jilibi* at the sweet-
seller's stand.

From within the tin-roofed temple came the
clashing of cymbals, the chanting of a priest, and
the sweetish perfume of incense. A half-naked
man draped the steps. Eyes closed, hands folded
at his waist, he lay as still as a corpse.

A ghastly feeling stirred in her stomach. "Patel," she said, pointing, "that poor man is dead.
Shouldn't we do something?"

"No, missy. He is yogi, disciple of Shiva. He

honors the god by slowing his breathing and disciplining his body.''

Fascination washed over Sarah. She made a mental note to mention the strange religious practice in one of her essays. The diversity of the people snatched at her imagination. The colorful saris of the Hindu ladies contrasted with black robes that veiled the Mohammedan women from head to foot, leaving only their dark eyes visible. Some men wore brilliant turbans, others skullcaps. A few sepoys sported the crimson shirt and dark trousers of the infantry.

She handed Patel the shopping list, and he led her through the crowded byways. Acrid blue smoke swirled around the Indian women who squatted before their cooking fires. Curiosity stirred in Sarah. What must it feel like to be a Hindu wife, watching her husband and sons eating their fill of rice and curry while she and her daughters humbly awaited the leavings? And what of the urchins, naked save for a strip of filthy cotton over their loins, their limbs often deliberately deformed for begging? And the leper who extended a hand crowned by stumps for fingers?

Along a narrow lane choked with sewage, a bleary-eyed woman with a baby suckling at her breast leaned against a doorpost. Red ribbons tied back her hair in English fashion. Around her garish gold sari peeped a lad of perhaps four years old. As Sarah passed, the woman thrust the boy toward her.

''Memsahib,'' he said, small hand outstretched, ''please, money.''

Sarah's heart melted. Dressed in rags, he wore the torn cap of an infantry private on his tousled black hair. A European look graced his features, a fairness of skin that contrasted with his big dark eyes. The boy was a half-caste, his mother one of the whores who haunted the bazaar. Sarah had heard whispers of such females . . . women frequented by the soldiers, women whom English ladies weren't supposed to even know existed.

Repressing the urge to stare at the whore, she slipped a half anna into the boy's hand. He salaamed in gratitude, then scuttled back to his mother.

Patel clucked his tongue. "You cannot feed every beggar in India, missy-sahib. Especially one born of that kind."

"Perhaps not." Impotence tugged at her. "Yet the money might keep at least one boy from starving today."

He shrugged. "The destiny of every man is in the hands of the gods. To starve is to ascend to a higher life so much the sooner."

The *abdur* started toward a butcher's stall. Sarah stood in a swirl of Indians, strange yet familiar people with friendly yet unfathomable faces. Despite her study of the Hindu culture, she often felt baffled by its fatalistic views.

A burst of raucous cries from around the corner drew her attention. While Patel bargained for a haunch of mutton, she wended her way toward the din and came upon a gathering near a spice vendor's shop.

In front of strings of dried garlic and red chili peppers stood a fakir. His bony body was clothed in a soiled saffron robe, his wild black eyes framed by long, tangled locks.

"It is thy destiny to drive the *feringhi* devils from the Raj," the holy man shouted in Hindi, using the derogatory term for the English. "They pollute thee with their vile ways! They mix the dust of cow bones in thy flour. They steal the land and wealth of thy princes and thy kings, men like Dhondu Pant and Bahadur Shah. They defile the caste of thy soldiers with their befouled bullets."

His arms flashed downward to a kneeling woman clad in an indigo sari. Her head was bent, her features veiled. Jerking her up like a puppet, so that her figure was profiled, the fakir said, "And see how the *feringhis* lure thy women into disgrace."

Sarah sucked in a breath. The woman was heavily pregnant, her rounded belly conspicuous beneath the fine silk.

Like a dust storm across the Rajasthan plains, angry mutters swept the crowd. A few *badmashes*, hard-eyed ruffians in tattered clothing, heckled the woman and laughed. A sepoy standing near Sarah turned to stare with a malice that shocked her.

The fakir yanked off the woman's *chuddur*, revealing lustrous black hair and an exquisite ivory-brown face. Her eyes as wide and frightened as a cornered doe's, she glanced at the throng. A ray of early sunlight gleamed on the tiny gold ring in her nose and glinted off the bangles adorning her arms.

"Look,' he said, sneering. "Look upon one who defiled herself with a foreign devil. Look upon the fruit of her shameful deed."

He ran a hand over her fertile form. She shrank from his touch, but his arm clamped tight, forcing her to endure his crude caress. Desperation haunted her fine-boned face.

"Cut out the *feringhi*'s bastard," a sepoy called.

Hoots and gibes echoed him. A *badmash* yanked a tulwar from his sash, the curved sword shining. "And when we're through, let us serve her up to Lord Canning himself."

Fear for the woman seared Sarah. Unthinking, she took a step forward, but someone caught her sleeve.

Patel stood beside her. "No, missy-sahib," the servant hissed. "Stay back. He is *sadhu*. Very holy man."

That Patel would break the strictures of caste by touching her emphasized his urgency. Yet

Sarah couldn't ignore the woman's plight. "Holy or not, he hasn't the right to abuse her."

"Stone the whore," someone yelled.

Rough voices took up the cry. People stooped to find rocks. Tears wetting her face, the woman cowered before the fakir.

"Quick, missy-sahib," said Patel, tugging again on her sleeve. Deep lines of worry etched his brow. "We must leave bazaar."

Glancing around, she saw few friendly faces. The assemblage was swiftly growing into a mob. Dear God, if anyone in the English community learned of her involvement in a native riot, she'd be shunned. She'd be the target of malicious gossip. Reginald might forsake her, and she'd lose the chance to be mistress of her own household. She might even become prey to the mob herself.

Yet she could not abandon the defenseless woman.

"Go if you must," she told Patel, "but I cannot."

Turning, she skirted the swarm of people. Resentful murmurs and pointed stares stung her, but no one blocked her passage. People stepped back, opening a path. Alarm twisting her stomach, Sarah held her head high and walked toward the fakir. The stink of unwashed bodies and unguarded hostility drenched her with the force of a monsoon.

As she drew close to the holy man and his quarry, a hush fell over the congregation. His ash-smeared skin showed the outline of his bones. His hair hung in greasy black clumps, and he reeked of sour sweat. With self-righteous satisfaction, he regarded his victim. The Hindu woman knelt submissively, her lovely eyes dazed with terror, her smooth cheeks streaked by tears.

"Excuse me, sir," Sarah said in Hindi.

The fakir raised his head and swung toward

her. A fanatic flame burned in his hell-black eyes. *"Feringhi* she-devil! Darest thou interfere?"

Each heartbeat thrummed like a hammer blow against her corset. She touched her trembling hand to her forehead in a respectful salaam. "The woman has committed no crime. Will you not release her?"

His nose as sharp as a vulture's beak, he hardened his expression. "Thou wouldst deign to speak our tongue. Yet thou meddlest in the rites of our religion."

Rumblings rose from the crowd. Several *badmashes* elbowed closer, hands gripping their tulwars. Gazing at the sea of suspicious faces, Sarah felt perspiration trickle between her breasts. The Indians she'd come to honor and trust now regarded her as a symbol of oppression.

Quickly she said, "I mean no disrespect, O holy man. This isn't a religious matter. I wish only to avoid an injustice. This woman has been granted no trial, no chance to speak in her own defense."

"Because she is guilty!" shouted the fakir. "Her crime is here for all to see. Thou needst no more proof than this."

He grasped a handful of silk covering the distended belly. The woman gave a gasp that was almost lost in the taunting calls of the mob, yet the tiny sound tore into Sarah's heart.

She stepped closer and lay a hand on one drooping shoulder. Shivers convulsed the woman. "You say she was lured into disgrace," Sarah said. "If she is weak, why hold her to blame? Why not seek instead the man responsible for her condition?"

The fakir bared his yellow teeth. "We must punish the whore. She forsook her caste to lie with a *feringhi*. Now she carries the English heathen's child."

"And if you kill her, you'll only bring English vengeance down on your heads." Sarah turned to the gathering. "On each and every one of you. Is that what you wish?"

The catcalls died to a restless muttering. Some people began to shake their heads; others whispered to one another. A baby bawled; its mother shushed it. Even the *badmashes* fell silent.

Taking advantage of the lull, Sarah seized the woman's hand and helped her stand. Slowly she began to back away, pulling the woman with her. The scents of garlic and chili peppers mingled with the delicate jasmine fragrance emanating from the Hindu woman, who stumbled as if confused. The slender fingers quivered inside Sarah's. Aware of the fakir's threatening presence, Sarah held tight, but trained her eyes on the crowd. Her only chance was to keep the tide turned in her favor. Surely there were enough peace-loving people here to overrule the violent.

"Bloodshed can solve nothing," she said, her voice steady despite the fear squeezing her throat. "We must work at finding ways to compromise. We can continue to live together in friendship, as we've done for over a hundred years. Harming this poor woman can bring nothing but misfortune to all of you."

While she spoke, she guided the woman toward the edge of the spice seller's stall. Here and there, people began to lay down their rocks. A few drifted away, back to their marketing or to their huts.

Fury contorted the fakir's expression. "The memsahib lies! Thee must not listen." He howled at the horde and waved his arms. "We outnumber the *feringhis*. We must drive the invaders from our land before they rob us of our religion. Before they pollute us further with their sinful ways."

A sepoy snatched off his white military cap and slammed it to the ground. "We must heed the holy man! The *feringhis* force us to taste the cow fat on their bullets."

"And jail any pious man who refuses," shouted another.

The outcries again built to a clamor. Swiftly Sarah steered the dazed woman down the length of the crumbling mud building. Beyond lay a fruit seller's shop, then the twisting byways of the bazaar. They might find help there.

The fakir pointed an accusing finger. "Stop them! We must satisfy Kali and mete out her justice."

Kali . . . the vengeful goddess who held a severed human head. Kali . . . who drank the human blood of sacrifices. What manner of justice could this frail woman expect from a monster-deity?

Sarah began to run, half dragging the pregnant woman. The dark faces of the Indians flashed by. A few seemed uncertain and moved to let her pass. But others jeered. Hands grasped at Sarah's sleeves, her skirts. The lace at her wrist ripped. The topi tumbled from her hair and rolled beneath the crush of people.

Heart thudding, she hugged the woman's awkward form and pressed her close to the wall. At the fruit seller's, they passed bamboo baskets piled high with watermelons and figs and coconuts.

"Be warned!" the fakir shrieked over the melee. "*Sub lal hogea hai!*"

Everything will become red. Like foul water in a gutter, the words slithered through Sarah. Blood. He meant a bloody uprising.

The prophecy slid away, banished by a more immediate nightmare. A man lunged into her path, a *badmash*. His unkempt mustache topped a leering grin. From the sleeves of his dirty red robe, his thick-knuckled hands stretched toward her.

She ducked beneath one of the long trays of fruit. Roaring, the ruffian barreled at her. His shoulder bumped a pole. The cotton awning tilted and collapsed. The man lost his balance and fell into a mound of green bananas, his arms and legs flailing. Tumbling baskets strewed their bright contents over the ground.

Dissension fell prey to greed. People snatched at the rolling fruit. The stout proprietor of the shop leaped up and down, alternately swearing and wailing.

Urging the Hindu woman onward, Sarah trod on a lemon. Her voluminous petticoats wrapped around her legs and she stumbled. Someone's hand clamped tight to her arm and held her upright.

She wrenched hard, but the fingers clung like the teeth of a mad dog. Panic misted her vision. She pivoted, fist swinging wildly.

"Ouch! Missy-sahib!"

Blinking, she recognized her captor. "Patel!" She'd never been more glad to see his genial, age-lined face.

"Come quickly," he said. "This way."

He drew them toward the corner of the building. Just as the mouth of an alleyway yawned ahead, a trio of ruffians broke from the agitated crowd. The one in the lead brandished a tulwar. The wicked-looking blade flashed in the sunlight.

"O Rama, save us," Patel moaned.

He yanked Sarah into the alley. Inside stood a cart piled high with musk melons. He squeezed behind the wooden vehicle and crouched. With her arm around the Hindu woman's waist, Sarah dropped to the rubbish-strewn ground beside him.

"We can't stop here," she gasped out. "For mercy's sake, at least draw your dagger."

"No, missy. Help me . . ." Grunting, he thrust his shoulder at the cart.

"Oh!" Grasping his purpose, she lent her own strength to the task. She held her breath and pushed. Pain splintered down her arm. The

Hindu woman cowered nearby, swaying back and forth, hands splayed protectively over her belly.

Loosing a barbarous screech, the *badmash* dived for the narrow space between the wall and the cart.

"Harder," Patel wheezed.

Sarah shoved with all her might. The wooden wheels groaned. The heavy vehicle shifted. The weight blessedly left her shoulder. A mountain of melons rolled downward and blocked the alley. The rogue and his cohorts fell, screaming curses.

"Now," Patel said, grinning as he hopped to his feet, "we go."

Elation brought an answering smile to Sarah's lips. She helped the woman up, and Patel hustled them along the dank passageway. The odors of refuse and sewage hung in the air, but Sarah inhaled deeply, for freedom had never smelled sweeter.

They emerged into the early sunshine where people went about their marketing, unaware of the commotion in the street beyond. The *abdur* hurried through the maze of shops and toward the fringes of the bazaar. Only then did Sarah realize they were heading back to the bungalow.

"Wait." Still supporting the Hindu woman, who sagged listlessly, Sarah paused in the shade of a leather worker's awning. Despite the bulk of her belly, the woman looked as fragile as a jasmine bloom wilting beneath the hot Indian sun. Wisps of thick black hair framed her dusky features. Her gaze was downcast, and her delicate cheekbones bore the tracks of tears.

Anger gripped Sarah. What Englishman had used this lovely woman, then callously left her to fend for herself? What Englishman would doom his child to a life of begging in the streets like that poor little half-caste boy?

She gently said in Hindi, "May we escort you to your home?"

The woman lifted her face, the haze clearing from her dark eyes, as if she were seeing Sarah for the first time. She gathered Sarah's hands, raised them, and kissed the backs.

"Memsahib, thank you," she murmured in softly accented English. "You have saved my life and the life of my unborn baby." She pressed Sarah's palms to the hard roundness of her abdomen. "Praise Sita, see how the child leaps for joy."

Against the silk-draped curve, Sarah felt the baby kick. Fierce yearning flooded her heart. More than anything, she wanted to feel new life growing inside her. More than anything, she wanted to marry and have children to love—

"Please, missy-sahib." Patel broke into her thoughts, jumping from one foot to the other as he glanced toward the milling shoppers. "You hurry. Or *badmashes* find us."

"Of course." Sarah turned to the woman. "But first I insist that we take you home."

The Hindu woman cast a fearful look over her shoulder, then touched her fingers to her brow, gold bracelets tinkling. "I would be most grateful. Come, please."

She led the way along twisting lanes and byways until the small party emerged at the edge of the bazaar. Near the mud-brick wall surrounding the military cantonment stood a curious boxy vehicle, painted a dusty white to ward off the heat of the sun. Two water cisterns sat atop the caravan.

The woman mounted the short steps leading to a door in the side. There, she paused and turned back. "Please, I would be honored for you to come in."

"You be safe here, missy," Patel told Sarah. "I will finish shopping, then hasten back for you."

She nodded, swayed as much by interest in the woman as by concern for her own safety. Aunt

Violet would be horrified should she learn that her niece was being entertained by a native woman. But Aunt Violet need never find out.

Sarah followed her hostess inside, where windows of yellow glass let in the sunlight. Amazed, she realized the vehicle was a miniature house on wheels, complete with a folded bed and cooking stove. Every inch of space was utilized, with bookshelves and cabinets, a collapsible desk and leather bench. A fine Persian rug covered the floor, and a brilliant red-and-gold curtain concealed one end of the dwelling. The stuffy air held the trace of a peculiar chemical aroma.

The woman waved Sarah onto the bench, then sat on a hassock. "I am Shivina." Apologetically she added, "I would offer tea, miss-sahib, but we've run out. That is why I foolishly ventured into the bazaar."

"Please, call me Sarah . . . Sarah Faulkner. And you needn't trouble yourself over me. You've had quite a fright."

Shivina stared down at her hands, folded over the mound of her belly. "The holy man, he held my arm and screamed at me. People gathered and stared. I could not move. I could not think of what to do." She shivered. "I do not know how he learned that my child has an English father."

Sarah suspected that more than terror had robbed Shivina of the ability to run; a Hindu woman's ingrained subordination to men caused her to endure the ravings of the fakir. Then anger invaded Sarah's compassion. "Where is . . . the child's father?"

"He goes to visit General Hewitt." A glow eased Shivina's expression. "My master is Damien Coleridge, a photographer. He seeks leave to go among the sepoys, to take pictures of the native soldiers at work."

Sarah blinked. "For what purpose?"

"He is making a book about India, about the

people here. We have traveled for months, stopping here and stopping there." A wistful sadness lit her dusky features. "In another month, our son will be born. But I fear . . ."

"Fear what?"

"I fear for my half-caste baby. People will condemn him, as they did today." Shivina's kohl-dark eyes went glossy, and she hugged her stomach. "I should not have gone out. But the air was so sweet and cool this morning. And I was restless after so many days of traveling." Tears began to spill down her cheeks again, and she pressed her face into her hands. "I wanted only to serve tea to Damien upon his return."

Sarah started to rise. How she'd love to offer comfort and friendship. How she'd love even more to speak her mind to one Damien Coleridge.

The scrape of a footfall yanked her attention to the door.

The towering figure of a man blocked the sunlight. Tanned dark, with black hair and brown eyes, he wore the white dhoti and tunic of a Hindu. At a glance he might pass for a native, save for his strong English features and exceptional height. A frown furrowed his brow as he stepped quickly to Shivina, hunkering down beside the weeping woman and sliding a possessive arm around her shoulders.

He aimed a hostile stare up at Sarah, a stare that chilled her despite the closeness of the air.

"Who the hell are you?" he demanded. "And what have you done to my woman?"

Chapter 2

Sarah burned with resentment. So this was the scoundrel who'd refused to wed his pregnant mistress and grant his child his name. Worse, he'd left her to the mercy of men like the fakir. Hidden in the folds of her skirt, Sarah's fingers curled into fists, but she was determined not to distress Shivina further by flinging recriminations.

"I'm Miss Sarah Faulkner. You must be Damien Coleridge."

His gaze raked her from blond hair to navy hem. She had the schoolgirlish urge to tidy her chignon. Crouched like a snow lion in a Himalayan cave, he dominated the caravan.

"I asked you a question, Miss Sarah Faulkner," he snapped, mimicking her starched tone. "What did you do to upset Shivina?"

Nestled within the cradle of his arm, Shivina lifted her tearstained face. "Oh, but you mustn't blame the miss-sahib—"

"Quiet. Rest yourself." His voice gentled, then grew hard again. "Let Miss Faulkner speak for herself."

Shivina lowered her head in unquestioning obedience. Incensed by his despotic manner, Sarah said with icy politeness, "May I sit, Mr. Coleridge? I wouldn't wish to speak down to you."

"You may hang your prim little arse out the window so long as you tell me what the hell I want to know."

Shock stung her cheeks. No man of her acquaintance ever spoke so coarsely to a lady. Her palm itched with the impulse to slap him. He'd probably slap her back. Choosing the safest path, she lowered herself to the bench and folded her hands in her lap. "What I've done is hardly deserving of your censure. I helped Shivina escape being stoned by a mob."

Damien Coleridge gave a start of surprise. His eyes widening, he swung toward Shivina, his broad back blocking her from Sarah's view. She wondered if he touched his mistress with tenderness or if he glared in anger. "Is this true?" he asked in a low voice.

"Yes," Shivina whispered. "The miss-sahib was most brave."

He remained still for another moment, then whipped his dark head back to Sarah. "Where?" he barked. "What happened?"

"It was in the bazaar, a short while ago. A Hindu holy man reviled her for being your mistress."

"*My* mistress?" he demanded sharply. "He spoke my name?"

"No. But he convinced some rabble-rousers to threaten her." She couldn't resist imbuing her voice with scorn. "It's fortunate that I happened by. Since *you* weren't there to protect her."

Damien Coleridge stared at her. His stern features and penetrating brown eyes offered no clue to his thoughts. If anything, he still looked suspicious, and she felt a deepening ripple of resentment. Of course, she hadn't expected—or even wanted—his gratitude. It was enough that Shivina and her unborn baby were safe.

Rising with hard-won self-possession, Sarah ignored the man squatting beside the hassock. She focused on his mistress's downcast face. "I'm sorry we met under unhappy circumstances, Shivina. I do hope we might see one another again."

Lifting her head, Shivina smiled, a timid quality lending her an ethereal beauty. "I would be honored, miss-sahib."

Sarah smiled warmly back. "The honor is mine. Please don't hesitate to call—or send a message and I'll be happy to come here. I live with my uncle, Colonel John Thorndyke."

Damien Coleridge shifted suddenly, whether from impatience or some ulterior emotion she couldn't tell. With the limber grace of a tiger, he got to his feet and regarded her.

The top of his head nearly brushed the caravan roof. Her eyes were on a level with his jaw, and her gaze met the black stubble peppering his sunbrowned skin. The loincloth draped his thighs, but bared his legs from the knees down, and the short-sleeved tunic left his muscled forearms exposed in a manner no proper Englishman would affect in mixed company. She felt an alien tightening deep inside her, a reaction no doubt arising from her aversion to this man, who, despite his strength and arrogance, had failed to safeguard his mistress.

"Does your uncle know you're here?" he said.

She swallowed hard at his calculating look. Would he tell Uncle John? "No. As I hardly expected to come here when I left this morning, how could I have told anyone?"

Damien Coleridge extended a hand. "Until we meet again."

The subtle mockery in his tone robbed the phrase of all civility. Despite his uncouth behavior, he certainly knew a gentleman should wait for the lady to offer her hand first. A retort leaped to her lips. She aimed a haughty glare at his hand, and a gasp emerged instead.

A webwork of scars marred the back of his hand

and covered his long fingers. The paleness formed an unnatural contrast to the tanned flesh of his wrist and arm. She glanced at his other hand; it bore similar markings. Burns?

"Is something wrong, Miss Faulkner?"

Coloring, she yanked her gaze up to his face. His eyes were narrowed, defensive somehow.

"Of course not." With deliberate graciousness, she grasped his outstretched hand. His scarred flesh lay smooth and firm against hers, and for an instant his physical warmth radiated into her. Strangely agitated, she drew away.

Shivina stirred on the hassock. "Damien's hands are blessed by the gods with the gift of an artist."

She pressed a gentle kiss onto his palm. As he gazed down at her, his expression softened, the harsh edges dissolving until he looked almost human . . .

Uncomfortable at intruding on a private moment, Sarah took a step toward the door. "I must go now," she told Shivina. "My aunt will be wondering what's become of me. Please inform Patel that I couldn't wait any longer."

"I will do as you ask," said Shivina. "Thank you again, my friend." She bent her head and humbly touched her brow.

Descending the short ladder, Sarah caught a last glimpse of Damien Coleridge staring after her. The stony look had returned to his face, a look that banished the brief impression of humanity. *Feringhi* devil.

The memory of the fakir's words made her shudder. Blinking against the bright sunlight, her feet stirring dust on the baked road, she walked past the deserted parade ground. Perhaps on that one count, the holy man was right; Damien Coleridge was a callous devil for using Shivina, for bringing a child into the world to suffer the stigma of bastardy and mixed blood. Regardless of the social strictures against an Englishman marrying a native, he should act honorably and legitimize his relationship with Shivina.

Unless he already had a wife back in England.

The heat of the sun dimmed beside the disgust and anxiety scorching Sarah's heart. What would become of Shivina should he return to England? Would he abandon her and the child? Did she have relations somewhere who might take her in? Living a nomadic life, she must have scant opportunity to make acquaintances. Sarah resolved to offer friendship to Shivina.

In the British sector, the officers' homes sat in military precision along the Mall. A feathery tamarind tree in the front yard marked the Thorndyke bungalow, a single-story dwelling built of whitewashed mud-bricks with a thatched roof and a wide veranda.

The *bhisti,* his leather bag slung over one shoulder, walked slowly through the rear garden, spraying water over the pathways to keep down the dust. It must be later than she'd thought, Sarah realized with a guilty start. Pray heaven Aunt Violet still lay abed.

But the older woman must have been peeping out an unshuttered window, for she bustled onto the veranda. Plump as a pomegranate, Violet Thorndyke wore a pink tea gown with a crinoline that added needless width to her figure. Her skin was sallow from lack of sunlight. Despite her thirty-nine years, she styled her plain brown hair in the sausage curls of a young girl.

"Oh, merciful heavens, you're safe," she said, hovering in the shade as Sarah mounted the veranda steps. "Wherever have you been? I could scarcely manage a bite of breakfast for worrying."

Sarah swallowed. There was no need to magnify her aunt's agitation by revealing the episode at the bazaar. Nor to risk losing Reginald's esteem by admitting to her visit to the forbidden place.

"Please forgive me, Aunt. I . . . went for a walk, and the lateness of the hour escaped me."

"A walk, you say?" Aunt Violet's fretful pacing jiggled her hair ribbons, and she twisted a lace handkerchief in her beringed fingers. "In this horrid heat? Oh, such a wicked girl you are to wander off without telling me! And just when I needed to consult you on the seating arrangements for dinner. I couldn't find that rascally Patel, either."

"He accompanied me." Sarah hesitated; she couldn't let her aunt think Patel was shirking his duties. She phrased an excuse that wasn't precisely a lie. "On our way back he . . . stopped at the bazaar to do the marketing for tonight."

"The bazaar? Thank heaven you at least had the good sense not to join him there." Aunt Violet dabbed at the perspiration dotting her brow. "Such a den of iniquity it is, or so the colonel tells me. Imagine, natives swarming everywhere, breeding like flies. I suppose it's fortunate they lack our more delicate sensibilities, else they couldn't bear to live in such filth."

Sarah struggled between anger and caution. "Perhaps they haven't any choice. So many Indians lack the means to buy adequate shelter or even food and clothing. But that doesn't make them any more immune to suffering than you or I."

"Oh, dear me, I believe I may swoon." Aunt Violet sat down, the wicker chair creaking. She languidly fanned her face with the handkerchief. "Fancy, my own niece defending heathens. Oh, what would Charlotte think? My dear sister entrusted you to my care, but I've failed her miserably."

Accustomed to such histrionics, Sarah smiled at her aunt. "Please don't fret so. Mother would be most grateful for the generosity you and Uncle John have shown me."

"Humph. Yet despite all my careful instructions, you left this morning without permission. And without even a hat! This dreadful Indian sun can scorch a lady's brain, you know."

"I'm perfectly fine. Really I am."

Her aunt heaved a sigh. "Well, I do hope no one of consequence saw you gadding about like a native. Else the burden of averting a scandal will fall upon my shoulders, as everything else here does. Mercy me, running this household is a chore."

Affectionate exasperation touched Sarah. *She* managed the household, while her aunt lolled in bed most days, indulging a variety of real and imagined illnesses. "Then allow me to help. I promise I shan't go out the rest of the day."

"I trust so," said Aunt Violet, an injured pout dragging at her mouth. "Don't forget, we've the packing for Simla ahead of us. You have a duty to your uncle and me. You mustn't forget the sacrifices we made for you and your dear departed mother."

Shame trickled through Sarah. She *did* owe much to her aunt and uncle. At the tender age of twelve, her father having died the previous year, she'd watched consumption alter her energetic mother into a sickly shadow of herself. Aunt Violet had taken them in and helped nurse her elder sister, Charlotte, during the months of lingering illness. And when Mama died, Aunt Violet had grieved alongside her orphaned niece.

Then, when Sarah was sixteen, Uncle John had accepted the military post in India. The hot climate that withered Aunt Violet's spirits made Sarah blossom. Here, she'd fallen into the role of housekeeper. And here, she'd fallen in love with her exotic new home.

Bending, she stroked her aunt's fleshy hands. "You've done so much for me," she murmured.

"I'm happy to do whatever I can to return your kindness."

"There, there, dear, you've been a daughter to me, the daughter Our Lord never saw fit to bless me with. He took all those babes from me . . ." Her sulky features easing into a mournful smile, Aunt Violet went on. "Which reminds me. The colonel has invited Dr. Pemberton-Sykes to our dinner tonight."

Reginald. A spark of interest glowed inside Sarah. For the past few months the gentlemanly doctor had courted her, twice asking her to marry him. Only duty and a nagging uncertainty about the depth of her feelings had kept Sarah from accepting. "He adores your parties, Aunt Violet. And he'll make a splendid addition—he cuts a dashing figure."

"Yet I do trust you'll continue to put him off, won't you, my dear? I simply don't know how I'd manage without you here to lighten my burdens."

"I'll try my best, Aunt."

"As you say." Puffing with effort, Aunt Violet levered herself from the chair. "Now, if you wouldn't mind seeing to the dinner preparations, I must go lie down. This heat gives me the most frightful headache."

As her aunt lumbered into the bungalow, Sarah sighed. How had Aunt Violet managed to make her feel guilty for wanting a suitor? She chided herself for being manipulated once again. Aunt Violet must realize that Sarah craved her own household, her own husband, her own family.

Yearning inundated her again, the same intense hunger she'd experienced upon feeling the kick of Shivina's baby. That moment had crystallized Sarah's restless dreams. With all her heart, she ached to feel the movements of her own child, to cuddle a newborn to her breast, to bask in the love of a husband.

Most women of twenty-three were already married, with a brood of children. Surely her years of toil had repaid the debt to her aunt and uncle. She ached for her aunt, who had suffered so many miscarriages, but it was time to make her own life. A life with Dr. Reginald Pemberton-Sykes.

She leaned against a mud-brick pillar and let the intensity of the sun burn away the last of her misgivings about accepting his suit. A hawk wheeled against a sky so blue it brought tears to her eyes. Anticipation curled warmly within her, and the future loomed as radiant as an Indian morning.

She thought fondly of Reginald's solid character, his attractive features, his polite bearing. Without warning, the image shimmered like a mirage and transformed into Damien Coleridge. She recalled his appraising stare, his blunt speech, his muscled form. The scanty garb that suited the Hindu men only served to dramatize the uncivilized nature of Damien Coleridge.

Renewed resentment simmered inside her. Would he cherish his baby? Or would he cast Shivina and the infant aside, and leave them to the mercy of fanatics like the fakir? Would his child be forced to beg on the streets like that poor half-caste boy?

Sarah gritted her teeth. Despite duty and the lack of a dowry, she possessed the respect of society and the right to decide the course of her life. Shivina deserved the same honor. Flagrant abuse of the native women must not continue.

Stepping purposefully along the veranda, Sarah headed to her bedroom. Dinner preparations could wait. I. M. Vexed had an editorial to write.

"By Jupiter, the author of this essay ought to be tossed out of the Raj," Uncle John told the guests assembled in the drawing room that evening. A stolid man of forty-six, clad in the dark green uniform of the Bengal Infantry, he rattled a copy of the latest *Delhi Gazette*. "The fellow writes for a British paper, yet he preaches against our military policies."

"Indeed so," said Major General Hewitt. Stuffed into an armchair, the jowly commander waved his glass of sherry, which glowed amber in the candlelight. "Any idiot can see the native troops are behaving steady and soldierlike."

"Being a lady, I would never dream of reading one of those horrid newspapers myself," said Mrs. Amelia Craven, the most outspoken of the officers' wives present. A willowy woman, she fluttered a fan at a mosquito buzzing around her gray-and-cherry striped bodice. "Whatever does the editorial say?"

"It proposes that we release the insubordinate sepoys," said Uncle John. "He's gone too far this time, the cheeky bastard."

Aunt Violet gave a little gasp. "My dear Colonel Thorndyke," she murmured, dabbing her brow with a lace handkerchief. "Pray remember the ladies present. Have a care for our delicate sensibilities."

"Begging your pardon." His walrus mustache twitched as he flung the newspaper onto a teak table. "I. M. Vexed, indeed. The fellow is free enough with his opinions, but he hasn't even the courage to sign his own name."

If only Uncle John knew why, thought Sarah, shifting uneasily on the rose chintz settee. Though it was unlikely that anyone would notice the faint ink smudges on her fingers, she kept her hands folded in the lap of her apple-green muslin gown. Her call for clemency in the rifle-cartridge incident was bold enough. What would people think of the scathing editorial she'd posted just hours ago? They'd be mortified if they knew they were debating the opinions of a woman.

Beside her on the settee, Reginald held his

broad-shouldered frame erect. "Perhaps courage isn't his problem at all," he said drolly. "Poor chap probably suffers from brain fever. I shall have to consult my colleagues at the military hospital in Delhi. Perhaps someone there has seen such a patient."

Uncle John snorted. "Any Britisher who sides with the Indians would have to be mad as a jackal."

"Well put," said Hewitt, lifting his empty tumbler. "The natives are rather like children, you know. We must rule them with a firm hand and guide them into civilization."

"As you say, sir," agreed Uncle John. He beckoned to the servant standing impassively by the door. "Zafar, another round of sherry."

Zafar bowed, then fetched the decanter from the sideboard. Watching the bearded *khidmutgar* with his hooded dark eyes, Sarah wondered if he resented serving people who regarded him as an inferior being. She felt a stab of shame at the frank comments eddying through the hot evening air, stirred by the punkah fan flapping overhead.

Aunt Violet leaned forward, her sausage curls wilting. The lemon-yellow gown made her plump face appear more sallow than usual. "Speaking of medical matters, Doctor, I should like to solicit your expert opinion. Is it true that a daily dose of Indian tonic water builds an immunity to cholera?"

"Alas, no." His handsome face came alert with professional concern. "I read so recently in a paper on cholera, published by the Royal Society of Physicians. Brought back fond memories of my days in academic research."

"A flannel cummerbund worn next to the skin prevents many ailments," Mrs. Craven declared. "My Archie swears it kept him healthy during last summer's campaign. Isn't that so, Archie?"

Lieutenant Craven shyly scratched his ginger

side-whiskers. " 'Twould appear so, m'dear. I defer to Dr. Pemberton-Sykes's judgment."

The ladies began to ply Reginald with questions on ailments from mental languor to blistered feet. Bored, Sarah watched a moth swoop through an unshuttered window and flutter around one of the oil lamps, the light picking up the delicate gold-and-silver tissue of its wings. The whir of cicadas came from the darkness outside, along with the distant beat of native drums.

An indefinable ache spread through her, the yearning to fly out of this stuffy room and soar into the black silken night. Usually she was content to guard her secret thoughts, to join in the discussions of the women, to behave in the decorous manner expected of a lady. So why did she feel so strangely restless?

Reginald turned and patted her hand. "You're terribly quiet tonight, darling," he murmured. "Is something troubling you?"

Out of habit, she shook her head. "It's just been rather a long day."

"If you're sure."

She considered his groomed fair hair, the starched collar and smart black suit, the genuine concern in his blue eyes. His familiar bay rum scent enfolded her like an old friend. In the past months he'd been an entertaining companion at dinners and dances, a man she could trust, a man who made her feel needed and admired. A measure of contentment flowed into her heart. Tonight she would settle their future.

"Perhaps I do have something on my mind," she whispered. "Meet me in the garden after dinner, and I'll tell you about it."

"Alone?" A solicitous frown furrowed his brow. "It that quite proper?"

Couldn't he ever act on impulse? She banished the disloyal thought. She should be grateful for a man who wished to protect her reputation. "We shan't be gone but a few moments—"

The scuff of slippers drew her gaze to the doorway. Patel slipped through the split cane curtain, his face unnaturally solemn under the flat white turban. His eyes sought out Sarah and widened, as if he were trying to convey a message. A problem in the cookhouse? She started to rise.

The curtain rattled again. A man stepped through. His formal evening suit and crisp white shirt lent him the civilized trappings of a gentleman. Yet he moved with the fluid grace of a panther. As he entered the circle of chairs, the lamplight cast his towering shadow over the whitewashed wall. His dark gaze swept the ladies and gentlemen, and stopped on Sarah.

She sank back onto the settee, her heart beating as fast as the wings of a moth. Damien Coleridge—here!

Had he come to expose her excursion to the bazaar?

Patel bowed. "Your guest, Colonel-sahib."

His mustache quirked, John Thorndyke put down his sherry glass and got to his feet. "Er, I don't believe we've met . . ."

"My fault, old chap." Hewitt pushed himself up from the armchair. "Slipped my mind, y'see, what with all the goings-on at headquarters. Hope it isn't an imposition, Thorndyke, that I took the liberty of inviting a guest to your dinner."

"Of course not, sir," said Uncle John.

"Then may I present Lord Damien Coleridge," Hewitt went on. "Recently arrived in Meerut, he did. Thought he'd enjoy hobnobbing with the best of our local society."

Stiff with awe, Uncle John bowed. "A most unexpected pleasure, your lordship."

"*Mr.* Coleridge, if you please," Damien stated. "I use no other title."

Shock and curiosity tumbled inside Sarah as she

leaned back against the chintz cushion. A lord! She would never have guessed this rude, unconventional man belonged to the aristocracy. How had he come to wander India in a caravan? Why did he live openly with a Hindu mistress? And why would he forswear the status awarded him by fortune of birth? The answer was obvious; he'd somehow disgraced himself.

Her eyes agog, Aunt Violet bobbed a curtsy, her crinoline puffing her skirt into an enormous yellow bubble. "Oh, dear me, your lordship . . . I mean, sir. If I'd known we would be entertaining nobility at our humble table—"

He cut her short with a slash of his hand. "I trust my unexpected appearance shan't cause a problem?"

She stared at his scars, then clutched the handkerchief to her throat. "It's no trouble to set another place, sir," she hastened to say. "No trouble at all. My niece will be happy to see to the arrangements. Won't you, Sarah?"

Pinned by her aunt's sharp frown, Sarah had no choice but to rise. "Yes, Aunt."

In the dining room, snow-white linen covered the long table, laden with cutlery and chinaware. Ropes of ivy snaked down the center of the cloth, and scattered about were small dishes piled with pralines, stuffed dates, and pickled ginger. Patel was lighting the incense bowls; the smoky perfume would keep the mosquitoes at bay.

He blew out the match and scurried toward her. "Praise Rama, you come here, missy. Where you seat Coleridge-sahib? He is higher than Hewitt-sahib?"

While he could rattle off without error the intricacies of Hindu caste, Patel was invariably confused by British social precedence. "Mr. Coleridge claims to be an ordinary gentleman," she said tartly, "and so we'll treat him as such. We shall place him between Mrs. Craven and my aunt."

"Ah, the cock perch between two squawking hens."

Sarah gave a small smile. "Perhaps they'll keep his attention occupied."

Bending nearer, Patel whispered, "Coleridge-sahib, he live with Shivina. He know you go to bazaar today."

"Yes, I know." Trembling inwardly, she considered the consequences should society learn of her role in a near riot. Now she'd be caught for certain, just as she'd feared. She would suffer censure. Worse, she might lose Reginald.

Burying her trepidation, she gave instructions to Zafar. By the time another place of Dresden china and gleaming silver had been set, and she'd asked the servant boy outside to begin pulling the fan rope, Patel was ushering the guests into their chairs.

Seated halfway down the table, Sarah had a disconcertingly clear view of Damien Coleridge. The flames atop the branched candlesticks danced in the breeze of the swaying punkah. The servants began ladling out a creamy almond soup.

"What brings you to Meerut, sir?" Uncle John boomed down the table to Damien.

"I'll be spending a fortnight here, photographing the sepoys for a book I'm compiling about India."

Aunt Violet leaned forward, her jet brooch clinking against her soup bowl. "Why, how very singular. I've always believed that the less one consorts with the natives, the better."

Picking up his spoon, he regarded her with a polite smile. "Ignorance is bliss?"

A dull flush crept over her sallow features. "Oh, sir, pray do not misunderstand me. I merely wish to shield myself from a race that worships idols. We are, after all, a Christian people."

"The Hindus attribute their illnesses to evil spirits," added Reginald. He shook his head in amused pity. "They seek to heal themselves with a dip in the filthy Ganges, or by making a pilgrimage to one of their shrines."

"They merely practice their own religious customs," Sarah felt compelled to point out. "Just as we pray to our God in times of need."

He smiled down the table at her. "But thank heaven we also have the sense to rely upon the medicines developed by modern science."

He spoke with affectionate benevolence, as if she were a child. Annoyance stirred in her, yet Aunt Violet was already frowning at her, and Sarah reluctantly withheld further comment.

"These Indians haven't the sense of a cavalry horse," said Hewitt. A drop of sweat trickled down his ruddy features. "This incident over the rifle cartridges is proof of their ignorance."

"If I may be so presumptuous as to disagree." Damien Coleridge glanced around at the guests. "The British military have long disregarded the sacred beliefs of both the Hindus and the Mohammedans. The natives will not continue to take abuse of their beliefs lightly."

"Abuse?" echoed Mrs. Craven, daintily patting her mouth with a linen napkin. "That would seem a rather harsh term for asking a sepoy to handle the same cartridges as all soldiers, English and native alike."

Cocking a dark eyebrow, he set down his spoon. "Perhaps you fail to grasp the problem, madam. A Hindu would starve before eating food that an Englishman's shadow had passed over. He would die of thirst before drinking from a vessel polluted by an Englishman's touch. He would risk imprisonment, even death, rather than ingest fat from a sacred cow. To do otherwise is to lose his caste."

"I must confess," said Aunt Violet, "I've never understood all this nonsense of castes and forbidden tasks. Why, just this morning I asked Patel to remove a dead lizard from my bath, but he refused. He had to call the sweeper for such a simple task.'' She glowered at the *abdur*, who stood sedately by the sideboard, watching Zafar clear the soup bowls.

Piqued by her aunt's insensitivity, Sarah abandoned caution. ''His caste is his reward for piety in a previous incarnation. A good Christian like yourself can hardly blame Patel for wishing to preserve the sanctity of his soul.''

Everyone turned to look at her, Damien Coleridge included. Their eyes caught and held. She saw surprise there, along with a cool appraisal that ignited a curious warmth inside her. She'd been wrong to judge him another intolerant Englishman, believing in the imperial right of the British to rule. Instead, he shared the views she'd dared to express only in her editorials.

Except in regard to Shivina. Lips pursed, Sarah lowered her gaze. He was a hypocrite, for his arguments on behalf of the natives failed to include honoring Hindu women.

''Reincarnation,'' snorted her uncle. ''I'm astonished, niece, that you're even familiar with pagan hocus-pocus, let alone condone it. And defending the natives, who breed like ants because of their unchaste practices.''

''Because they read that vile book,'' Mrs. Craven murmured.

''Are you referring to *The Kama Sutra?*'' asked Damien Coleridge.

Aunt Violet gasped. Mrs. Craven blushed. Sarah sat on the edge of her chair and studied his dark features. She'd heard whispers of the Indian guide to erotic love. Had he read the forbidden book? The thought sparked a strange tingle inside her.

''We do not mention such filth in mixed company,'' Uncle John snapped. ''Rather, we must concentrate on our duty to save the poor heathens from eternal damnation."

A reply jumped to Sarah's tongue, but she kept silent. As long as she lived in this household, she owed her aunt and uncle love and esteem. Better to save her rejoinder for another editorial by I. M. Vexed.

"Yet your niece is right," Damien Coleridge told her uncle. "The Hindus believe the English are condemning their souls. They've no wish to be converted to Christianity. India can never be at peace until all of us come to respect the religious beliefs of the natives."

"Rubbish," said Hewitt. "Surely you aren't giving credence to these rumors of an uprising? Such talk'll come to nothing, just like that ridiculous *chupatty* movement a few months back. Can't imagine how passing filthy cakes all over India could be construed as a signal to mutiny."

"By Jupiter," Uncle John said, thumping the table with his fist, "the natives lack our organization and leadership. They shan't revolt."

"Indeed?" Damien replied. "You might consider the riot in the bazaar this morning."

The ladies gasped. Blood buzzed in Sarah's ears. Lounging in his chair, his bronzed features gilded by candlelight, he stared straight at her. A faint gleam of challenge shone in his eyes.

Would he reveal her role in the episode?

"Riot?" Aunt Violet wheezed, waving a napkin at her flushed face. "In that sordid place? Oh, dear me, I may swoon."

"It was a minor disturbance," said Hewitt. "A few rabble-rousers tried to stir up the crowd. Nothing to bother yourself over."

"Like as not, the fire last night was set by the same few scoundrels," added Uncle John. "You mark my words, all of this unrest will die down in a few days."

"And in the meantime you needn't fret, Mrs.

Thorndyke," said Reginald. "Most natives prefer to live in peace. We mustn't fly into a panic at every rumor coming out of the bazaar."

Nods and murmurs of agreement circled the dining table. Aunt Violet sat back, a limp smile on her face. Damien Coleridge merely arched a black brow and studied his glass of white wine.

Freed from his piercing regard, Sarah felt a dizzying relief. She bent her head and pretended interest in dislodging a flake of whitewash that the punkah breeze had wafted onto her tinned salmon.

Yet the words of the fakir haunted her. *Everything will become red . . .*

Was Damien correct in his assessment? Had the Indians been pushed too far, their religious practices degraded to the breaking point, their dignity trampled upon until they would tolerate no more? She had seen for herself how easily the fakir had whipped up the angry mob.

No, she must have faith that a nonviolent solution could be found. That Reginald was right, and the majority of the Indians preferred to live in harmony. That her editorials might eventually help her fellow Britons learn to heed the local customs.

As Zafar silently served slices of mutton, she found her gaze straying again to Damien Coleridge. He enthralled the ladies with a lively discourse about his visit with the Maharaja of Kashmir, and Aunt Violet and Mrs. Craven vied for his attention. This charming side of him intrigued Sarah. How she envied him the liberty to express his views! Being a man—and a member of the ruling class—Damien Coleridge needn't protect his reputation.

With a twinge of bitterness, she recalled Uncle John's rebuke over her unguarded remarks. She detested subterfuge, yet what other choice had she? Except for the pittance paid by the newspaper, she had no source of income, and no prospects save marriage to Reginald.

With pride and hope in her heart, she looked at him as he smiled and talked with the ladies. She would find contentment as his wife, as the mother of his children.

Laying aside her discontent, she joined in the conversation. After the final course of mango cream and lemon tarts, the men remained at the dining table while the ladies withdrew to the drawing room.

No sooner were they settled in chairs than Mrs. Craven leaned forward. "What do you make of his lordship, Violet? Quite a deliciously handsome man."

"But entirely too eccentric for *my* tastes. Imagine, traveling all over this heathen land just to photograph the natives."

"Still," mused Mrs. Craven, "it's a shame he bears those dreadful scars on his hands."

Aunt Violet shivered, her huge yellow bosom quivering. "Simply appalling. Dear me, it was a trial to keep from staring."

Sarah's stomach twisted with sympathy. "But imagine the pain he must have suffered. The scars must be the result of terrible burns."

"Quite so." Her gray eyes alight, Mrs. Craven went on in a conspiratorial whisper. "Do you know, I recall a scandal surrounding his lordship."

"Scandal?" echoed Aunt Violet, vigorously fanning herself. "Why, Amelia, whatever do you mean?"

"Damien Coleridge is the second son of the dowager Duchess of Lamborough. I know, because my Archie's family comes from the neighboring district. The strife between Lord Damien and his mother had tongues wagging for years." Mrs. Craven clucked, shaking her elegant head.

"Poor woman, to have such a wicked son. A son who'd brought her so much tragedy."

Sarah couldn't resist asking, "What tragedy?"

"For one, when he was only a boy, he deliberately set a fire and nearly burned down the ancestral mansion. That's where he must have gotten those scars. The frightful incident turned his elder brother—the current duke—into a halfwit."

"Dear heavens!" said Aunt Violet.

"Then, just before I left England ten years ago, the old duke died in a fall from a balcony at their home in Kent. There were rumors that the death was no accident."

Aunt Violet gulped. "Do you mean . . . he took his own life?"

"Perhaps I shouldn't say any more," Mrs. Craven demurred, primping her cherry-stripped skirts. "After all, nothing was ever *proven*."

"Pray, don't stop now, Amelia." Aunt Violet patted a bead of perspiration from her upper lip. "What is it? What happened?"

Despite her loathing of gossip, Sarah sat stiff and alert, her fingers gripping the teak arms of the chair.

"Well . . . if you ladies insist upon knowing," Mrs. Craven said. "Lord Damien left home even before the funeral. Some say Her Grace forced him out." A self-important gleam in her eyes, she regarded her audience. "You see, people whispered that the duchess had accused him of murdering his own father."

Chapter 3

❦

S arah escaped into the rear garden, the tension
inside her dissolving under the spell of the
exotic night. Stars spangled the black velvet sky,
and a half-moon shimmered silvery light over the
pathways, leaving the perimeter of the compound
in dense shadow. The clove scent of the few remaining geraniums wafted to her, along with
fuchsia and bougainvillea, though the more
tender plants had already withered from the
scorching daytime heat. Lights winked inside the
row of huts where the servants lived. From the distant bazaar floated the nasal chanting and rhythmic drumming of the natives.

Her petticoats whispering, she walked slowly
along the path of beaten earth. A gecko lizard
chirruped somewhere nearby. Beyond the hedge
of plumbago marking the front yard, the gatekeeper's lantern glimmered like a fallen star. The
clink of glasses and the tinkle of laughter emanated from the yellow-lit windows of the bungalow, where the men had rejoined the women.

Sarah slapped at a whining mosquito as her
mind strayed to the after-dinner gossip. Could
Damien Coleridge truly be guilty of patricide?

The notion seemed monstrous. Yet she knew
so little about him. Despite the warmth of the
night, a chill iced her skin.

The sudden hollow scrape of footsteps descended from the veranda. She whirled. Moonlight gleamed over a man's fair hair, his regular features, his squared shoulders.

"Reginald," she breathed, and started toward him.

Meeting her halfway along the path, he gathered her hands in his. "Why, you're shivering. Come, my pet. Tell me what's disturbing you." He guided her onto a wrought-iron bench, then sat beside her.

Somehow she was loath to bring Damien Coleridge's name into the evening. "I was reflecting on our dinner discussion," she lied. "Do you really suppose there'll be an uprising?"

"Of course not. You heard the commander. Rumors of revolt have been circulating for years. It's just a lot of idle talk."

"But what if the new rifle cartridges push the sepoys to mutiny? The issue has certainly united the Hindus and Mohammedans in one cause. Look at the men who went to jail."

"And when they're sentenced, it'll act as a deterrent to further revolts." His mouth formed an indulgent grin. "I commend your sympathetic nature, dear Sarah, but you're entirely too lovely a lady to bother yourself with military matters."

His patronizing attitude irked her. "But it's unfair to ask a man to betray his religious—"

He touched a cool finger over her lips. "Please leave the problem of the natives to our commander. You've developed such a habit of fretting that perhaps I shall have to start calling you I. M. Vexed."

Her hands tensed around the soft muslin of her skirt. Her pulse surged in panic. Had Reginald guessed her secret identity?

In the moonlight the corners of his eyes were crinkled, and his features held a familiar teasing humor. The rigidity of her muscles ebbed. "If I

am vexed,'' she bantered back, ''you are impertinent.''

Laughing, he said, ''I don't mean to be, my
pet, not tonight.'' His voice lowered to a murmur
that was almost lost to the chirp of crickets. ''I'd
half hoped that what brought about this meeting
was your lamenting the few weeks we have left
before you and your aunt depart for Simla. It
seems a dreary prospect, these hot summer
months ahead, the ladies off in the mountains. I'll
miss you.''

Her heart softened. ''As I'll miss you, Reginald.''

''Then perhaps you'll accept a token to remember me by.'' Reaching into his coat pocket, he
drew forth something and placed it in her palm.

The cool weight of gold tickled her palm. ''A
locket?'' she said, tilting her head at him.

''Open it.''

She carefully unsnapped the clasp. In the silver
moonglow lay an oval miniature of Reginald, stiff-
shouldered and solemn-faced.

''Perhaps it's a bit impertinent of me,'' he said,
flashing her a sheepish smile, ''but I didn't want
you to go off and forget me.''

Touched by the gift, she said, ''I wouldn't have
forgotten you, Reginald. That's why I wanted to see
you alone.'' Hesitating, she bit her lip against an
unforeseen attack of cowardice. ''You see, I . . .''

''Yes?''

His blond eyebrows lifted in an endearing expression. Her fingers closed tightly around the
locket. In a rush, she said, ''I wondered if your
offer of marriage was still open.''

He grasped her hand. ''What of your aunt?
You've always been so devoted to her, especially
given her . . . ill health.'' He made a delicate reference to Aunt Violet's most recent miscarriage.

''You yourself said she's quite recovered,''

Sarah reminded him. "It's high time I got on with my own life."

"Of course, my pet. Every woman wants her own house, her own children. You've been an unpaid companion to your aunt long enough to repay any debt you owe her."

Relief filled her. "You've been so understanding."

"My dearest Sarah, nothing could make me happier than to have you as my wife." Lifting her hand, he brushed a warm kiss across the back. "Shall we set a date for the autumn?"

"Yes," she breathed. "Yes."

"I must wait for the right moment to approach your uncle, then, and ask for your hand. I know how much your aunt values you, so perhaps it's best you gently prepare her first."

Didn't he want to shout his elation to the heavens? The thought flustered Sarah. He was being considerate, she told herself. His loving concern washed away her doubts and submerged her in a weakening tide of tenderness. How she needed his affection, his regard! Overwhelmed by impulse, she swayed toward him, touching her lips to the smooth warmth of his mouth.

His arms moved around her, clasping her tight. For a moment he returned her kiss with all the tender fire of a man in love. Her heart beat faster as she rejoiced in a sensation of perfect security and reveled in the wonder of her first real kiss.

Abruptly he drew away, frowning. "You're ever a surprise, Sarah," he said, sounding half breathless, half chiding. "I shouldn't wish your aunt or uncle to discover us like this."

"But . . . don't you *want* to kiss me?"

Laughing, he patted her hand. "What a question for a pretty girl to ask a gentleman! Surely you know as well as I that we must restrain our . . . ah . . . urges for now." He stood and offered her his hand. "We'd best go back inside."

Somehow she couldn't face the airless bungalow, the idle chatter. She wanted to bask in the moment that promised to change her life, and savor the lingering warmth of his kiss. "You go on. I'll be along in a moment."

He nodded, then strode back into the house. From one of the neighboring yards came the soft strains of a sitar and the haunting melody of an Indian folk song. Only half listening, Sarah tried to sort through her mixed emotions. Why did she feel a nagging disappointment, a nebulous desire for something more, as if she'd gone to the stars but returned empty-handed? For mercy's sake, she ought to be riding the clouds!

But Reginald hadn't spoken of love, a voice inside her whispered. And he could so easily draw away from her . . .

She shook her head impatiently. She'd agreed to a worthy match, all a woman of her station could hope for. Sudden understanding lightened her spirits: surely the emotion darkening her heart was only a bride's nervousness over the private side of marriage, the side a lady must not dwell upon. But Reginald would treat her with consideration and respect.

Respect. A cold fist closed around her happiness. Respect and honesty went hand in hand. She should have told him of her nom de plume. A woman of honor wouldn't withhold a part of her life from her intended husband.

And if he forbade her to editorialize about injustice?

Drawing a deep breath of scented night air, she fastened the locket around her neck. She would ease him into understanding by cautiously expressing her views. She would bring him around to her way of thinking. Then, at a judicious time before the wedding, she would reveal the truth. He'd probably applaud her.

Feeling better, Sarah rose from the bench. Wistfully she thought of their kiss, and a soft sigh of longing escaped her. On their wedding night Reginald would sweep her off her feet—

A tiny hissing scratch emanated from beyond the veranda.

Startled, she sought the source. Alongside the shadowed bungalow, in the gloom beneath a peepul tree, she spied the glow of a match and the black outline of a tall man. The flame lifted, illuminating his harshly handsome face as he lit a cheroot.

Damien Coleridge!

Had he witnessed her meeting with Reginald?

Indignant heat scorched her cheeks. She marched across several yards of *doob* grass, the dry blades rustling beneath her slippers, and stopped in front of him. "Just how long have you been standing there?" she demanded.

Holding the match high, he studied her as the flame licked slowly down the stick to his scarred fingers. Only then did he casually shake out the match. Cigar smoke and a trace of sulfur scented the air. *Feringhi* devil . . .

Had he committed patricide?

She braced herself against another chill. "I asked you a question. You might have the decency to answer, sir. Or shall I say 'my lord'?"

"Damien will do." He paused, his expression obscured by darkness. "You might give me the benefit of the doubt, Miss Faulkner. Judging from the disapproving look on your face, you've already tried and found me guilty."

"You were listening to a private conversation."

"I wonder what my sentence will be. A dose of your priggish opinions? Ostracism from your drawing room? Or perhaps you won't let me dance at your wedding." He sounded amused, rather than apologetic. "Besides, my pet, I didn't intentionally eavesdrop."

His mocking use of Reginald's endearment

made her skin burn. "A gentleman would have made his presence known."

"Don't ever mistake me for a gentleman. I wouldn't have missed that touching scene for the world. I must say, you two make a handsome couple. May I be the first to congratulate you?"

"Thank you," she forced herself to reply.

Drawing on his cheroot, he leaned against the outside of the veranda. "It's a shame dear Reggie refuses to listen to your views on India."

"He's a very intelligent gentleman. He'll come around."

"Will he? The British sahibs are too caught up in their own superiority to imagine the lowly natives daring to rise against them. Nothing you say will give vision to their blindness."

"I have more faith in Dr. Pemberton-Sykes's judgment."

"Or perhaps you're just as blind as he is."

His cynicism raised her hackles, when she ought to be glad that he, at least, saw the Indians as people deserving of respect. What was it about Damien Coleridge that aroused this instinctive dislike, this turbulence inside her? It was more than his illicit relationship with Shivina. It must be the charge of murder.

"I wouldn't expect you to understand," she said stiffly. "You claim to value the Hindu people, yet you show little enough regard for Shivina. Where is she tonight?"

"She's safe. As she wouldn't have been here." He waved the cigar toward the bungalow. "Those old biddies in there would have roasted her alive. Even if *suttee* is illegal."

Sarah knew he was right, yet a devil's impulse pushed her on. "So you left her alone again. What if the fakir comes back?"

"He won't."

"How can you be so certain?"

"Because he's on the road to Cawnpore."

"You can't know that."

"I can, indeed."

The hard edge of his statement sliced her with surprise. Had he gone after the fakir and threatened him? She tried to read Damien's expression; the gloom hid all but the slash of strong cheekbones and the glow of his cigar.

"What did you do to him?" she asked.

"Do?" He chuckled. "I instigated a rumor about Nana Sahib calling a secret meeting of holy men. The fakir is on his way there now."

"How clever," she murmured.

"Thank you."

Dhondu Pant, better known as Nana Sahib, was the adopted son of a maharaja who had been dethroned by the British and granted a pension in exchange for his dominions. Upon his father's death the pension had ceased, and Nana Sahib vowed to regain the money. He was one of many Indian princes who carried a grudge against the English.

"What will happen when the fakir discovers the truth?" she asked. "What if he returns?"

"Let him. I'll be moving on before long."

"With or without Shivina?"

A cricket chirped over the dry rustle of peepul leaves. Damien blew a smoke ring. "You disappoint me, Miss Faulkner. Most Englishwomen are more devious at ferreting out information."

Anxiety for her newfound friend overrode Sarah's scruples. "I'd rather be candid than cautious. I don't wish to see Shivina left to beg for a living, like the women in the bazaar. She needs a husband to protect her."

"What makes you so certain I intend to abandon her?"

"Why else would you deprive an innocent baby of his father's name? Unless you're already married."

"No, I'm not."

A stab of grim pleasure caught her unawares. "Then perhaps you're ashamed for your noble family back in England to learn of your half-caste child."

He paused in the act of carrying the cigar to his mouth. Despite the shadows, she sensed a sudden violence of emotion in him, and knew uneasily that she'd ventured into forbidden terrain. Abruptly he ground out the cigar beneath his heel.

"I'll leave marriage to the romantic dreamers like yourself. What a dull place this world would be if we were all as civilized as you and your darling Reggie."

She bristled. "Reginald and I treat each other with respect and love."

"Respect? Domination is more the word. Love? He won't even allow you to express affection."

Stung by his derisive reference to the unfulfilled kiss, she snapped, "You undoubtedly would have taken everything you wanted without bothering with clergy. And without a care for ruining my reputation."

Damien Coleridge stepped into the moonlight and stopped mere inches away. He reached out and caressed her beneath the chin. The feel of his sleek scars sent a shiver over her skin. "Judging by your passionate display on that garden bench, you undoubtedly would have loved it, Miss Faulkner."

Fire swept over her, a fire sparked by fury and indignation, a fire that burned away her retort. The lush fragrance of jasmine perfumed the hot dark air. The evening was so still she could hear the soft melody of the neighbor's sitar, the quiet rasp of Damien's breathing, the beat of blood in her ears. She couldn't move from his warm fingers. She couldn't tear her gaze from him, from his moon-silvered black hair, his hard brown eyes and clean-shaven face. The blaze within her flared into a mind-drugging urge. The urge to draw his head down to hers, to slide her fingers into his hair, to taste the smoothness of his lips, to feel his body pressed against hers . . .

A burst of laughter from the bungalow pierced the spell. A cold wave of horror washed over Sarah, and she took an instinctive step backward. How could she feel drawn to Shivina's lover? How could she forget her own commitment to Reginald?

Her fingers closed around the locket at her throat. "If you're done with insults," she said in a voice steadier than her heartbeat, "I must ask you to leave."

Damien gave a humorless laugh. "Spoken like a true lady. Ah, well, my pet, we must all have our dark and secret desires." He started toward the front yard, then swung back, his head cocked in a watchful attitude. "By the way, I came out here to apologize. I leaped to the wrong conclusion this morning. Thank you for helping Shivina."

He turned and strode off into the night, and a moment later she heard the deep murmur of his voice and the indistinct reply of the gatekeeper.

Sarah slumped against the veranda rail. So Damien Coleridge was noble enough to admit a mistake, civilized enough to express gratitude. Yet one gentlemanly gesture couldn't justify her moment of scandalous longing.

Shame and bewilderment engulfed her in a murky tide. No respectable lady would think—even for an instant—of kissing a near stranger . . . a stranger she didn't even like. Only an immoral hussy would feel desire for an insolent rogue.

Shaken, she turned her flushed cheek to the cool rail and tried to fathom the depth of her response. *We must all have our dark and secret desires.* Yes, she had a hidden side, her identity as I. M. Vexed and her hunger for adventure. She didn't, as Damien implied, conceal a passion that any man could arouse, even a man who scorned her moral code. His abrasive manner must have shocked her into a false reaction, that was all. She loved Reginald—dear, kind, honorable Reginald.

Yet for a long time afterward she gazed into the shadows of the garden and wondered about the secret Damien Coleridge harbored.

"A visitor, missy-sahib."

Sarah finished recording a sum in the stores book, then looked up to see Patel hovering in the doorway of the small pantry. Sunshine outlined his slim, robed figure, and he glanced behind him, then looked beseechingly at her. From his aura of nervousness, she guessed this was no ordinary visitor.

"Who is it?" she asked.

"Come, you see." He motioned dismissingly to Hamil, the cook, who squatted before the open cupboard. "You finish later."

Hamil contorted his moon face into a scowl. "I will anger the memsahib," he said in melodic Hindi. "She will scold if the rice pudding is not ready for dinner."

"By Krishna's benevolence, how long does it take to boil rice?" Patel retorted. "If you would but work as many hours as you sleep upon your charpoy—"

"Please." Sarah rose from the cane stool and shot Patel an exasperated look. Turning to the cook, she said, "The pudding can be made this afternoon, and in the meantime, you've already measured the ingredients to bake rum cake for tea. You know how fond my aunt is of your wonderful cakes."

Hamil grumbled under his breath, but he looked mollified as he tipped the allotment of flour from the hand-held scale into an earthenware bowl. Then he got to his feet and plodded out of the room, heading across the garden to the cook-house.

"Quickly, missy," Patel urged again, gesturing toward the door. "While the memsahib still lies abed."

"A visitor Aunt Violet shouldn't find out about?"

Patel wagged his dark eyebrows. "Come. You see."

His mysterious manner intrigued Sarah. "One moment." Using the key tied to her waist by a ribbon, she locked the large cupboard containing the household supplies of sugar and salt, sherry and beer, scouring soap and shoe polish. Since Aunt Violet required a daily accounting of the items in the storeroom, Sarah pocketed the note-book, then removed the white cotton apron from her aquamarine gown and smoothed her upswept blond hair.

"Perhaps I should freshen up first," she said.

"No need." Patel flashed her an uneasy grin. "It is not your handsome doctor-sahib who awaits."

As he glided out, she touched the gold locket hidden beneath her bodice, and her cheeks grew warm. Did the *abdur* guess that three nights ago she and Reginald had pledged to marry? The na-tive grapevine of gossip worked with mysterious speed. But no one else, not even her aunt and uncle, had heard the thrilling news yet.

Except Damien Coleridge.

Her heart did a queer somersault. Banishing the memory of his darkly compelling face, she stepped into the brilliant sunshine. The heat of late morning enveloped her with the intensity of a furnace. In the garden the *mali* and his two boys tended the hedge of wilting fuchsia, and the snip of their clippers blended with the screech of a fork-tailed kite overhead. Mystified by Patel's reticence, Sarah followed him around the side of the bungalow and up the steps to the rear veranda.

He waved a brown hand to his left. "I will order refreshment for you and your guest." Bowing, he vanished into the house.

Sarah blinked against the dimness. The bamboo blinds had been let down, turning the veranda into a cool bower filled with potted plants and cane furniture. On the edge of a chaise longue sat a woman, a butter-yellow sari draping her heavily pregnant figure and a *chuddur* shrouding her inky hair.

"Shivina!"

As Sarah hastened forward, Shivina braced herself on the cushion and pushed awkwardly to her feet. "Miss-sahib," she murmured, bowing as she touched her ivory-brown forehead. "I do not mean to intrude."

"Of course you're not intruding," said Sarah. "How timely your visit is. I'd meant to call on you later today." Noticing the way Shivina's shoulders drooped, she added, "Please, sit."

Shivina's serene smile glowed against her lovely features as she sank onto the chaise longue. "Thank you. Damien's child grows heavy."

Her maternal contentment brought an ache of longing to Sarah's heart. "My aunt has kept me terribly busy packing these past few days," she said, sitting in a cane chair. Guiltily, she knew that a reluctance to encounter Damien Coleridge had kept her away. "We're to leave for Simla in a fortnight. But tell me, have you been feeling well?"

"Yes, Miss Sarah. Well enough to bring you a *dali*—a gift for helping me in the bazaar." She reached for a small bundle at her feet.

"That isn't necessary. I wanted to help you." Reluctant to offend, Sarah took the parcel and unwrapped the brown paper. "I certainly never expected—oh!"

Inside lay a shimmering bolt of lavender-blue silk, spangled with silver threads and fanciful embroidery. The cloth floated through her fingers like a length of twilight sky. How wonderful it would be to escape the bondage of stiff corset and skirts, and drape the soft fabric over her skin. Reginald would disapprove, but perhaps in the privacy of her bedroom . . . "It's lovely," she breathed. "Will you show me how to wear it as a sari?"

Shivina looked startled; then she gave a tinkling laugh. "How odd that you would say this. When I have come here to ask you . . ."

"Ask me what?"

Anxiety clouded her dark eyes. "I am glad to speak to you alone," Shivina said, resting her hands on the mound of her belly. "I do not wish anyone to overhear us."

Sarah stiffened. What had Damien Coleridge done now? Abused Shivina? Announced his intent to leave her? "You needn't be afraid of Mr. Coleridge. I won't let him harm you."

The Hindu woman shook her head, rippling the silk *chuddur* and revealing a cluster of button-sized marigolds tucked behind her ear. "Oh, but Damien would never harm me. It is only that he left early this morning for his photograph work. I did not wish him to return and guess what I am about."

"What is it, Shivina? What's wrong?"

"Nothing is wrong. I would seek a favor of you."

"Anything."

A shy earnestness stole over her face. "Will you teach me to dress as a lady? An English lady?"

Stunned, Sarah sat back, the cane chair hard against her spine. She fingered the silk in her lap and tried to imagine Shivina wearing a corseted gown. Absurd! She was the picture of exotic beauty, her slim nose pierced by a tiny gold ring, her smooth skin the hue of burnt ivory, her features as fragile as a jasmine bloom. The sari enhanced her natural grace of form and gave her the aura of Ganga, the heavenly river goddess. To bind her into the mold of a proper Englishwoman would be a sacrilege.

"Gowns are too hot, especially for a woman in your condition," Sarah argued. "You'll be far more comfortable as you are."

"It is not for now," said Shivina. "I wish gowns for after the child comes."

"But why would you truss yourself up in this stifling heat?" Sarah persisted, then fell silent.

Zafar glided onto the veranda, a salver balanced on the flat of his palm. His black eyes widened slightly, and he hesitated at the sight of her receiving a Hindu woman. Sarah motioned the Mohammedan forward. He presented each with a glass of soda and lime, then left a pitcher on a nearby table.

She leaned forward and murmured, "Why do you wish to change yourself, Shivina?" Anger stirred inside her. "Is Mr. Coleridge displeased with your appearance? Is he forcing you to do this?"

A wistful smile touched the woman's mouth, and she set aside the glass without drinking. "No, miss-sahib," she said. "It is my wish. I seek to honor him. To become the woman of his heart."

Resentment crowded Sarah's throat as she sipped the cool lime drink. Damien wasn't worthy of unflinching adoration. "You already honor him. You're the mother of his child."

"Yes, but even a son is not enough. I have not given Damien what he needs most."

"Nonsense," Sarah snapped. "The man is too callous to appreciate your devotion, your kindness, your sacrifice in choosing him over other men."

"But that is why he needs understanding. He cannot love like other men."

"Why do you say that?"

"The answer lies hidden in the shadows of his past. I think his childhood was most unpleasant."

"His childhood?"

"Yes. He will not discuss it. But sometimes he has terrible dreams. He cries out for help." Shivina's gaze drifted to one of the bamboo blinds, where filtered sunlight played over a potted fern. "My heart can hear the pain in his soul. It is a pain that makes him fear to show love."

Sarah remembered the story of the fire, the accusation of murder, the scars, the stuff of nightmares. Yet she couldn't help but think Shivina fancied depths to him that didn't exist. "You're a beautiful woman just as you are, Shivina. Don't change yourself for a scoundrel who neglects you."

"But I must change. I wish to look like you, Miss Sarah. And I wish to show my humble gratitude to Damien. You see, he saved me from death."

Frowning, Sarah set down her drink. "What do you mean?"

Shivina went as still as a statue of Parvati. Her dark eyes were wide and staring, as if gazing into faraway thoughts. The quiet *snip-snip* of clippers drifted from the garden, along with the distant clang of pots from the cookhouse.

The Hindu woman bowed her head and sighed. "I must not say. Damien has forbidden me to speak of what happened." Holding her abdomen, she looked up. "But you must believe me, miss-sahib. I live now for the child Damien has given me. You must see why I wish to become a lady, to honor him."

Bubbling with questions, Sarah gripped the lavender-blue cloth in her lap. She had no right to pry; she had to trust Shivina's word. "I'd like to help you, truly I would . . ."

"Please, I have the means to pay you." Shivina slid several rich gold bangles from her slim arm. "Take these."

Sarah's objections faded before the appeal in Shivina's eyes. Setting aside the silk, she reluctantly took the bracelets. "You'll look stunning in English garb, although I warn you, you'll be uncomfortable. I'll speak to my aunt's *dirzee* about sewing your gowns."

"May the gods bless you. You are so kind—" Rising, Shivina gasped. A gush of liquid pooled around her sandal-clad feet. "Sita help me," she gasped. "The birth waters . . ."

Sarah's heart rolled over. "The baby?"

Shivina drew in a breath. A weak smile curved her lips. "It is three weeks too early. But today I hope to hold Damien's son."

Alarmed, Sarah slipped an arm around the Hindu woman's frail shoulders. "Come inside. It's cooler there—"

"Gracious! Patel didn't mention hiring any new servants." The startled voice rang from the doorway. Aunt Violet stood wagging a handkerchief at her fleshy face.

"She isn't a servant, she's my guest," Sarah said. "If I might help her into the house—"

"Into *my* house?" Her aunt blinked at Shivina. "But, my dear Sarah . . . a native woman? It hardly seems suitable to entertain her here."

"I'm not speaking of a social call. Shivina needs to lie down." In blunt disregard for modesty, Sarah added, "Her water has broken."

Aunt Violet's gaze skittered away from the puddle. The handkerchief fluttered faster. "Oh, mercy. Oh, mercy me."

"Please," Shivina murmured. "It will be many hours before the baby comes. I will go home."

Aunt Violet blew a heavy sigh of relief. "A capital notion. I shall be happy to lend you the use of our *palka-ghari*.''

''No,'' Sarah said, recalling the hot, cramped quarters of the caravan. ''She'll be more comfortable here. I'll send for Reginald.''

''But, my dear girl—''

''It's best this way, Aunt.'' She played her trump card. ''Surely you wouldn't wish to offend Lord Damien Coleridge.''

''His lordship? But what has he to do . . .''

''I bear his son,'' Shivina said, pride glowing in her eyes as she cradled her belly.

A flush tinted Aunt Violet's pasty cheeks. She sagged against the doorframe. For once, she appeared in true danger of swooning. ''His . . . oh, merciful heavens.'' Twisting the handkerchief, she looked torn between the disgrace of harboring a fallen woman and the chance to win the favor of a nobleman. ''Oh, dear me. I suppose we mustn't turn the poor creature out.''

Chapter 4

The brassy sun dazzled Sarah's eyes as she hastened through the sector occupied by the native soldiers and their families. She'd gone first to the caravan, but Damien Coleridge wasn't there. She'd also checked at the garrison headquarters and the canteen; no one had seen him.

A heat rash prickled under her tight corset, and her brow felt stickily wet beneath the brim of a new topi. Dust clogged her throat and gritted her eyes. She longed for the shuttered coolness of the bungalow, then felt a spurt of shame.

Shivina suffered from the increasing pains of labor. She'd begged for Damien. The least Sarah could do was to find the scoundrel. It wasn't fair that he went blithely about his business while Shivina endured the agony of bringing his bastard into the world.

The encampment lay in drowsy silence. Mud huts crowded dirt streets that stank of dung and rubbish. She made a mental note to address the issue of better living quarters in a future editorial.

In the shade of an occasional tamarind or peepul tree, men napped or sat talking. The scorching midday hours after the morning parade were leisure time, and most of the native soldiers had discarded their heavy uniforms in favor of looser dress.

Their stares followed Sarah, and a few men whispered behind their hands. She wondered if they'd known the sowars who had refused the new bullets and now awaited sentencing in the Meerut gaol. A cold shiver crawled over her hot skin.

Sub lal hogea hai. Everything will become red.

Nonsense. She didn't feel malevolence; her imagination was fired by the memory of the fakir. Her anxiety over Shivina stoked the sensation. The soldiers likely commented on the curious sight of an Englishwoman hurrying through their domain, that was all.

Before one thatched hut, a barefooted woman in a turquoise sari bent over a cook fire. The pungent aroma of curried rice drifted from the pot. Nearby, several sepoys crouched on their heels and smoked a hookah. Cinching the white tunic of one man was a cummerbund the forest-green color of Uncle John's regiment.

Buoyed by the familiar sight, Sarah walked toward the soldier. He and the other men fell silent, watching. She was careful to keep her shadow off the cooking vessel, since most sepoys belonged to one of the two highest castes, Brahman and Kshatriya, and practiced strict religious views on pollution.

She salaamed and murmured, "Greetings. I am the niece of Colonel Thorndyke."

The man stroked the jagged scar bisecting his cheek. Then he drew on the hookah. Its watery rattle pierced the stillness as he looked her up and down. Was he surprised by her fluent Hindi or by her identity?

"What do you wish of me?" he asked.

"I seek only the answer to a question. Might you know where I can find the English photographer, Mr. Coleridge?"

The man shrugged and looked to his companions. She had the oddest impression that the other sepoys relaxed.

A sallow-skinned Hindu said, "I saw the *feringhi* at the temple at Shiva, near the bazaar." He gestured out of the encampment.

"Thank you," she said, then turned and walked away. The prickly sense of unease persisted, but she forced herself to resist glancing back.

The smells of dust and spices and sewage heralded the bazaar. A few brown-skinned children darted past, chattering and laughing. The shrine marked the entrance to the maze of shops. Sunlight glinted harshly off the pointed tin roof. Offerings of withered marigold garlands and grains of rice strewed the steps. In the shade of the arched doorway, an aging priest sat cross-legged, his thin body swathed in a saffron robe. His eyes were closed, and she couldn't tell if he was meditating or sleeping.

Before the temple stood a cumbersome camera on a tripod. Several urchins clustered around it, talking excitedly while peering at the strange black box.

"Is the Englishman here?" she asked in Hindi.

One of the boys pointed to a small tent erected in the shadow of an acacia tree. "There, memsahib. He pay us a rupee to guard his camera-machine." Dark eyes aglow, he held out a coin in his grubby palm and added in coarse bazaar dialect, "But he say not to bother him."

"Thank you, but this is a matter of urgency." She marched across the dusty ground and stopped before the closed canvas flap. A faint metallic aroma tugged at her memory. It was the same smell that permeated his caravan. "Mr. Coleridge? Are you in there?"

"For God's sake, don't open the flap," came his muffled reply. "I'll be out in ten minutes."

"It's Sarah Faulkner. I must speak to you immediately."

"I don't care if you're the Second Coming. You'll just have to wait."

Perspiration seeped down her neck. Annoyed by his sarcasm and worried about Shivina, Sarah flung back the flap. "Excuse me, but this can't wait."

He swung around, his broad form crouched within the dim interior. Foul fumes poured from the tent. In one hand he clutched a dripping square of metal.

"What the bloody hell!" he exploded. "You made me ruin another plate."

Equally angry and unwilling to indulge his unsavory language, she said, "I'm sorry about your photograph. But you see—"

"I doubt you see anything but your own narrow-minded interests." He dropped the flat square into a bucket of liquid, where it landed with a splash. Then he seized a rag to dry his hands. "Damned oven in here, anyway," he muttered. "Chemicals get too hot to develop the plates properly."

She held herself stiffly. "I hope you'll be interested in what I have to say. It's about Shivina."

He cocked an inquiring eyebrow, then ducked out of the tent. Beads of sweat rolled down his throat and dampened his white tunic. He tilted his head back and wiped his neck with the rag. In loose Indian clothing, his lower legs bare, he looked startlingly like a native. Sarah touched her locket. He was handsome, she conceded, in a hard and unrefined sort of way. For no discernible reason she recalled that night in the garden, the scent of jasmine swirling around them, her skin tingling from his touch and her heart thrumming madly with the urge to kiss him . . .

"Well?" he said rudely. "Speak up."

Sarah lifted her gaze from the dark hair furring

his calves. "Shivina came to visit me this morning. While she was there she . . . started her labor. She's resting now at my uncle's house."

Damien went still, the rag dangling from his hand. "You mean . . . the baby? But it's not supposed to come for a month."

"Fancy that. The little mite already has a mind of its own."

"Damn," he said, frowning. "I was planning on leaving here in a few days."

His tanned skin showed the stark outline of his cheekbones. He looked so stricken, she softened her tone. "I'm afraid not. You shan't be going anywhere for a while, Mr. Coleridge."

He continued to stare at her for another moment. Then he wheeled toward the beggar children. "Watch my equipment," he said in Hindi, and flipped a coin to their leader. Without a word to Sarah, he started at a jog down the dusty road, his dhoti outlining his powerful thighs.

She clutched her skirts and scurried after him. Sympathy formed a warm pool inside her. Could this hard-hearted man really care for Shivina?

Far ahead, he veered away from the row of officers' bungalows and headed toward the parade ground. The truth struck. He was going to his caravan!

She stopped and blew out an exclamation: "You . . . *devil!*" Yanking off her topi, she used her cuff to blot the perspiration from her brow. So the knave meant to run out on Shivina after all. No doubt he would bring the caravan around and collect his camera gear, then hightail it out of the garrison.

Fury and frustration raged inside Sarah. She wanted to race after him. She wanted to blister his ears with curses. She wanted to slap some honor into his cowardly soul.

Instead, she clamped the hat back on her head and paced toward the bungalow. Now was no time to lose her temper. Now more than ever, Shivina needed her.

She found the Hindu woman resting in the care of an ayah, and took the maid's place beside the bed. The closed shutters kept the room dim, and the hot air was stirred by the punkah. She concocted a tale about Damien going off to take photographs, and Shivina seemed resigned to his absence. Sarah dreaded the moment when she'd have to tell Shivina the truth. Assuming she survived the untimely birth . . .

As the afternoon wore on, her pains grew harder and closer. Sarah maintained a cheerful facade despite the worry biting at her. When Reginald arrived at last, she leaped up in relief. "Thank heaven you're here."

He drew her to the door. "My Hindi is quite rusty," he murmured. "Will I need an interpreter?"

Sarah shook her head. "Shivina speaks English. Reginald, you should know the baby is early. Her water broke, and she's been having pains about every ten minutes or so—"

"Shush, my pet." A ruddy blush crept upward from his starched collar. "You leave her to me. A lady needn't worry over such a delicate matter." He shooed her out and shut the door.

Annoyance rippled through her, but she squelched the feeling. Reginald would take fine care of Shivina.

Restless, Sarah wandered through the bungalow. Upraised voices enticed her to the drawing room. Peering through the split cane curtain, she saw Uncle John and Hector Harte, the stoop-shouldered minister. Another man faced them, his back to her. Even in the braided suit of a gentleman there was no mistaking his towering build or the thick black hair brushing his collar.

Damien Coleridge.

Her heart took flight. So he hadn't abandoned Shivina.

"This is highly irregular," the minister was saying.

"Shouldn't you think this over, sir?" added Uncle John. "What will people say?"

Damien shrugged. "Let them gossip. It's nothing new to me. I'm sorry to involve you, Colonel, but I haven't a choice."

Sarah stepped toward the men and formulated an excuse to satisfy her curiosity. "Pardon me. May I fetch you drinks?"

Uncle John swung on her. "By Jupiter, forget the blasted drinks, niece! Perhaps *you* can talk some sense into Mr. Coleridge."

"Don't bother," Damien said icily. "My mind is made up."

He stared at John Thorndyke until the colonel harrumphed and folded his arms across the front of his uniform. "Begging your pardon, sir. Didn't mean to offend."

"Will someone please tell me what's going on?" she asked.

Damien aimed his stony gaze at her. "I'm marrying Shivina. Now."

The announcement robbed Sarah of breath. She couldn't speak, could only stare at his resolute features. He truly meant to defy society and wed a Hindu woman.

Her swell of self-righteous smugness ebbed, leaving a peculiar flatness, heavy as the late afternoon heat blanketing the room.

"How is Shivina?" Damien said.

He might have been asking the price of a mango. "Doing well enough," Sarah said tartly. "Reginald is with her now."

"Then perhaps he'll consent to stand witness along with you." Turning to the minister, Damien took a paper from his pocket and held it out. "You'll want to see the special license."

Harte peered at the document. "It looks iron-clad to me. Signed by Lord Canning himself. No higher authority in the Raj."

"Yes. I met with the governor-general in Calcutta a few months back."

"But . . . did he know you intended to wed a native woman?"

Damien glanced at the minister. "I hardly think my choice of a wife is your concern. Shall we get on with it?"

Harte gulped visibly, but made no further protest.

Damien extended his arm to Sarah. Still astonished, she curled her fingers around his sleeve and felt the hard warmth of his muscled arm.

As they walked out, she couldn't resist murmuring, "You certainly waited long enough to use the special license."

"And you take an unmerited interest in my personal decisions."

"Nevertheless, I'm glad you heeded my advice about marriage."

"Sorry to deflate your self-satisfaction, Miss Faulkner, but I changed my mind because of something else."

She tilted a dubious look up at him. "What's that?"

"An editorial I read in yesterday's newspaper about the shabby way we English treat the native women." Damien flashed her a look that seemed to mock himself as much as her. "You see, I owe my change of heart to a fellow who calls himself I. M. Vexed."

"Your son, sahib."

Damien swung around. Illuminated by the light of a single lantern, a plump ayah stood inside the drawing room doorway. She cuddled a small, white-shrouded bundle.

Dumbfounded, he stared. How many hours

had passed since that hurried wedding ceremony? Since he'd pledged his life to a woman
whose need for love he could never fulfill? Since
he'd insisted on being left alone here with only
the prayer wheel of his thoughts for company?

*Forgive me, Shivina. Forgive me for snatching you
from one fiery torment only to plunge you into another.
Forgive me, for you deserve better than the paltry ashes
of my heart . . .*

As if seen through an unfocused camera lens,
the image of ayah and baby turned fuzzy. He had
always taken care not to scatter bastards wherever he roamed. This child was a mistake. The
mistake of a man who had gratified a casual desire. The mistake of a man who had indulged a
momentary craving for companionship.

His punishment was a son. *A son.*

He wanted to run. He wanted to hide. He almost gagged on a clot of panic.

Hand shaking, he set down his brandy glass.
How could he presume to raise a son? He knew
nothing of being a father! He knew even less of
tenderness and affection, for his mother had
taught him an early lesson, that love bred only
pain, that trust brought animosity and despair.
Better to stay aloof and keep his emotions intact.
Better not to let anyone strangle him with the ties
of sentiment.

Long ago he had vowed never to marry, never
to sire a son. Now, a moment's weakness had
bound him to a woman he didn't love and a child
he didn't need.

He should have let the Coleridge name die out,
he thought with sudden savagery. He should
have ensured that there were no future dukes of
Lamborough.

The baby squalled. Damien blinked, and the
ayah came back into focus. Despite the lateness
of the hour, she waited patiently. "Sahib? The

miss-sahib, she said you would wish to see your son.''

Miss Sarah Faulkner. Seeking a release valve, his explosive emotions vented steam. Miss Sarah-Holier-Than-Thou-Faulkner. She likely meant to flaunt his error. To make him do penance for the sin of fornication. A pinch-mouthed spinster like her didn't understand—would never under-stand—the pleasures of physical passion.

The servant stepped toward Damien and lay the squirming bundle in his arms. He started to thrust it back in a violent motion. *No,* he wanted to shriek. *Take it away!*

Then he looked down at the small form. Swad-dled in a bleached cotton blanket, the infant felt surprisingly compact and sturdy. The face, dusky in color and wrinkled from crying, resembled that of a baby monkey.

The boy ceased whimpering and went still. He stared up at his father. His dark irises rounded into a faintly quizzical expression. In the lamp-light, he had ivory-brown skin and the wide Lam-borough brow, high cheekbones and a rosebud mouth. He looked vulnerable, utterly trusting. Damien touched the child's hand. Soft and new, it grasped his scarred finger in a tiny fist.

His chest tightened with a yearning so fierce it hurt. Tears blurred his eyes. Quickly he turned his back on the ayah and tried to rein in his run-away emotions.

He couldn't possibly love the boy. It was only a baby, no different from thousands of others.

Yet something long buried broke free inside him. *His son.* The notion now brought waves of pride and awe and protectiveness. This child, Da-mien vowed, wouldn't suffer as he'd suffered.

''Christopher,'' he murmured. ''I'll call you Christopher.''

With the unqualified trust of the innocent, his

son continued to study him. As Damien's elder brother had once regarded him.

Oh, God, could the boy ever love him?

Panic and longing choked Damien. Or would he ruin his son's life, too?

Spinning around, he thrust the child into the hands of the startled ayah. Then he plunged through the split cane curtain and fled into the dark Indian night.

Quill in hand, Sarah sat at the teak desk in her bedroom. From outside came the cheep of a cricket and the far-off thump of drums. Distracted from her editorial about improved quarters for the sepoys, she gazed out the unshuttered window and watched the last brilliant rays of sunshine pierce the heavens. With a swiftness unique to India the sun plunged below the horizon, and dusk spread a silver-violet veil across the sky.

Little Christopher—dubbed Kit—was a week old today. And today, against Sarah's protests, Shivina had insisted that she and Kit rejoin Damien in the caravan. Already Sarah missed the sweet joy of cuddling the baby. Even Aunt Violet had been torn between relief and melancholy. Of course, Sarah intended to visit Shivina—tomorrow she would deliver the first of the gowns the *dirzee* had sewn for the Hindu woman.

Sarah hoped she wouldn't encounter Damien Coleridge.

Idly she twirled the raven feather of the pen. What an odd man he was! As cold and remote as a Himalayan peak. Hardly the image of a happy bridegroom. This past week he'd taken scant notice of his new wife and son, and Sarah ached for Shivina. Yet the Hindu woman either was content or hid her hurt well.

Guilt left a sour taste in Sarah's mouth. Most likely Damien regretted the hasty nuptials. Perhaps her zeal for justice had made her overlook his faults. Perhaps he would mistreat Shivina.

Perhaps he really *was* a murderer.

No, she mustn't entertain the frightful thought. Much as she disapproved of his moral character, in her heart she couldn't believe his nature was so twisted that he could cause Shivina or Kit physical harm.

By candlelight, she reread the editorial. Satisfied, she neatly penned *I. M. Vexed* at the bottom. She sanded the wet ink, folded the paper, and stuffed it into an envelope.

Damien might read this editorial, too. She allowed herself a moment of pleasure. Her private satisfaction would have to be enough. It was a shame she dared not tell him that he owed his change of mind to her.

A sudden knock made her tense. She slid the envelope beneath the leather desk pad and scurried to open the door. "Oh, Patel."

He tossed a furtive glance over his shoulder. "Missy-sahib," he hissed. "I must speak to you alone."

"Do come in." Sarah stepped back. "But you know I always bring my Delhi letters to you."

"I have not come for letters," he said, closing the door. "I have news, terrible news. I have come from the hut of my cousin."

"The sepoy in Captain Craigie's regiment? I do hope he isn't ill."

"Oh, no, missy." Patel sketched a quick salaam, his turban flashing ivory in the candlelight. "It is you who are in danger!"

She regarded his wrinkled face dubiously. "Me? In danger?"

"Brahma save you, yes. On my cousin's own doorstep I heard three sepoys speak of mutiny!"

Despite the heat, a chill shivered through her. "Surely you misunderstood."

"No, missy. The sons of snakes vow death to

all the *sahib-log*, men and women alike. Death even to the *baba-log*, the children. My cousin tried to shush the men. But the bhang they smoked made them bold.''

''When is this mutiny to take place?''

''In two days, as the prisoners are punished.'' He clasped his brown hands. ''Please, missy-sahib, you must leave, I beg you. Go to Simla tomorrow. You will be safe high in the hills.''

Disbelief throbbed inside her chest. Most Indians she knew were like Patel, peace-loving people who shared her abhorrence of bloodshed. Yet there were also fanatics like the fakir.

Everything will become red.

Suppressing a shudder, she paced past the bed with its mosquito netting of white gauze. She had seen the signs of unrest, witnessed the power of the mob, felt the uneasy impression of resentment from the sepoys. Could Indian soldiers engage in indiscriminate slaughter?

The ugly image was unthinkable. Yet Damien's warning in the garden echoed inside her. She must not let complacency blind her.

''I'll warn my uncle,'' she told Patel. ''He'll know what to do.''

''I'm glad you came to see me instead of your uncle. But I do wish you'd notified me that you were coming.'' Cheeks red, Reginald quickly knotted his neckcloth and donned his jacket.

Sarah had never before seen him in undress. Her uncle had gone to play billiards at the Meerut Club, so she'd taken the *palka-ghari* to Reginald's bungalow.

The lamplit study smelled of medicines and leather-bound books. Neat rows of bottles lined the shelves. Her fiancé stood behind a small desk that bore an empty soda-water bottle, an inkstand, and the Hindustani dictionary she had given him for his birthday. The breeze from the punkah gently stirred a stack of papers.

"Now, about this wild tale," he said. "I've been in India for nine years, and no matter where I've been stationed, I've heard rumors of imminent revolt come out of the bazaar."

Sarah felt oddly like an outsider invading his private domain. Too restless to sit, she paced to a glass-fronted cabinet. "You must believe me," she said. "This is no bazaar tale."

He smiled indulgently. "Where did you come by your information?"

"Patel heard so from his cousin—a sepoy."

"Stuff and nonsense. You heard Hewitt at the dinner party. Meerut is the last place a mutiny would occur. Why, ours is the only military station in the Raj where English soldiers aren't vastly outnumbered by the native troops."

"But the imprisoned sepoys are angry. Patel said—"

"Patel is just another wild-eyed Indian, afraid of his own shadow. I shall have a word with your uncle about his servants spreading idle chatter." Reginald came around the desk and took her hand. His grip was gentle and reassuring. "I must speak to him soon anyway, my pet. About us."

"Of course." She was ashamed to admit their betrothal had flown her mind of late. "With a baby in the house, I confess I haven't had a chance to soften Aunt Violet to your cause."

Reginald compressed his lips. "At least that Hindu woman is away from there at last. I must say, I felt uneasy standing witness to their wedding. I can't imagine why his lordship would make a half-caste his legal heir."

Sarah bristled. "Because he sired the baby. Surely you wouldn't want him to thrust Shivina and Kit into the streets?"

"Of course not, darling. You miss my point.

Lords don't go around marrying native women, that's all.''

''Perhaps not. But he did right by her, and for that I'm glad.''

Reginald smiled. ''Your integrity is one of the things I love about you, Sarah. I'm anxious to announce our engagement to the world.''

Disquiet stirred in her. She ought to tell him about I. M. Vexed. Yet something stopped her. ''I'm anxious, too,'' she said. ''But please, promise you won't cause trouble for Patel. He believes he spoke the truth.''

''If you wish, my pet.'' Reginald patted the back of her hand. ''I don't doubt he may have heard a few malcontents talking. But if our commander trusts the loyalty of his regiments, then so do I.''

His steady blue eyes made Sarah uncertain. *Was* she overreacting? Surely a few rebels couldn't incite a friendly majority to riot . . .

''Perhaps my aunt and I should leave early for Simla anyway.''

''Nonsense. You've time aplenty.'' He guided her to the door. ''Now, darling, you shouldn't be here alone after dark. I'll have Ali Khan escort you home. I'd do so myself, but I must prepare the hospital's supply lists for the mail packet to Calcutta tomorrow. Dashed boring task compared to your lovely company.''

His tender regard made her fears dwindle. It was only as she lay abed that night, listening to the drone of mosquitoes and the distant howl of jackals, that her misgivings came creeping back. The Indian people had suffered injustice at the hands of the British. Would the rifle-cartridge incident tip the scales toward revolt?

She stared into the darkness, watching the elongated shadow of the peepul tree dance on the bedroom wall.

Did she truly have time aplenty?

Chapter 5

Beneath a sky dark with clouds, a gust of wind swirled dust devils across the road. Sarah blinked her smarting eyes. She perched on the edge of the leather seat as Ram Lall, the Thorndykes' syce, guided the *palka-ghari* through the crush of conveyances. The hot morning air hung heavy and breathless, like the oppressive hours before the onset of the monsoon.

Amelia Craven arranged her skirt of topaz silk. "Do sit back, Sarah. You needn't perch like a caged canary."

Sarah slid back a fraction. "I'm just so terribly anxious."

"We all are. I wouldn't have missed this exhibition for a furlough to England."

"It isn't meant to be a spectacle," Sarah said sharply. "Imagine how those poor prisoners must feel, about to be sentenced like common criminals simply for displaying the courage of their convictions."

"They've been court-martialed for disobeying orders. My Archie witnessed the firing-drill during which they refused to touch the new cartridges."

"Because they believe the fat on the bullets violates their religious beliefs."

"Humbug. A jury of their own native officers

convicted them." Mrs. Craven wagged a kid-
glove finger. "You've a tart tongue, Sarah Faulkner. I'm chaperoning you today as a favor to
Violet. She and your uncle, the colonel, would be
scandalized to hear of your radical remarks."

Alarm stirred in Sarah. "Forgive me," she
murmured. "I meant no offense."

"It's quite all right." Mrs. Craven grimaced.
"This dreadful heat can get the best of one. Thank
heaven we'll be off to the hills next week. Why,
my Archie swears he saw the thermometer reach
one hundred and twenty-five degrees here last
summer."

As the woman droned on about the weather,
Sarah's thoughts veered to more troubling matters. The past two days had dragged. She'd related Patel's warning to her uncle, but he, too,
had scoffed. Half of her shared his faith in the
native soldiers; the other half brooded upon their
complaints. Her own danger she discounted. A
few Indians supported zealots like the fakir, but
the natives she knew and loved would never rise
against women and children. If mutiny did sweep
the ranks, she prayed it would mean only a reading of grievances, a bloodless attempt by the sepoys to convey their protests to the English
officers.

Ram Lall jockeyed for position at a choice spot
near the infantry parade ground, where red-
coated sepoys marched in under the keen eyes of
the English. The tramp of their booted feet lent
an air of solemnity that Amelia Craven must not
have noticed, for she immediately engaged in a
lively dialogue with the ladies in the neighboring
carriage. As if they'd come to watch snake charmers and sword swallowers, Sarah thought in distaste.

She leaned forward again. The entire garrison
assembled in the dusty heat to witness the punishment. Rows of men formed lines along three

sides of the square: cavalry, native infantry, dragoon guards, horse artillery, foot artillery. Apprehension jerked at her stomach; the English troops held rifles ready beside the unarmed sepoys.

At the open end of the square waited a group of soldiers on horseback. Straining to see past the throng, she recognized the robust form of Commander Hewitt, flanked by her uncle and Colonel Carmichael-Smythe, the officer whose cavalry regiment now faced sentencing.

Then she spied Damien Coleridge.

Stationed near the officers, he tinkered with a camera mounted on three long wooden legs. In deference to the sober occasion, he wore the white shirt and trousers of an Englishman, though without a coat or topi. A gust of wind ruffled his black hair.

An odd thought struck her. In his own way, Damien had the same purpose today as she—to chronicle the event.

Her hand strayed to the gold locket at her throat. A queer tumbling sensation assailed her insides. She couldn't abide the man, she told herself; it was a struggle to respect him even for doing right by Shivina. Despite his blue blood, he possessed few noble attributes. Yet she must approach him and take advantage of the chance to help Shivina and Kit.

Sarah turned to her companion. "If you'll excuse me a moment, Mrs. Craven. I must greet a friend."

"But, my dear, you mustn't wander off alone."

"I'll only be a moment." Careful of her navy skirt, Sarah stepped down from the carriage.

Ignoring the woman's prying gray eyes, Sarah slipped through the knot of spectators and lectured herself to behave with courtesy. When she reached Damien, he was bent behind the camera, his head shrouded beneath a black cloth.

"Mr. Coleridge? I should like a word with you."

He emerged from the cloth and straightened. His mouth pressed tight with annoyance, and his brows clashed in a scowl. His short sleeves revealed bare, tanned forearms, and unlike Reginald, he looked completely at ease with a lady seeing him in undress.

"You," he said. "I might have guessed I'd run into you here."

His cold hauteur made her feel like a swatted mosquito. "I'm happy to see you again, too."

"Don't hand me your sarcastic claptrap, Miss Faulkner. You never miss a chance to meddle, do you?"

"What is that supposed to mean?"

"It means you're a hypocrite. You spout sympathy for the poor downtrodden natives, then turn around and force them to fit into your own mold."

Despite her good intentions, she felt her temper flare. "I beg your pardon?"

"The goddamned gowns," he enunciated, as if she were hard of hearing. "The English gowns you talked my wife into wearing."

His attack raised her hackles. "Shivina came to *me* about the gowns. She asked for my help, on the very day she gave birth to your son."

He stared. "They were her idea?"

"Yes. *You* must have said something to make her feel inferior." The urge to lash out gripped Sarah. "You probably don't even realize how badly she wants to please you. Though why she would trouble herself over a ungrateful boor like you, I can hardly fathom."

"She didn't tell me," he said without expression.

Fleetingly Sarah wondered what they *did* talk about, since he knew so little of his wife's desires. "Then next time, give her the chance to speak."

Her anger collided with anxiety for Shivina. "And speaking of hypocrites, I should like to know if you intend to abandon her and Kit when you return to England."

For an instant his dark eyes focused beyond her, as if he were seeing not the regiments of stony-faced men, but a past shrouded by secrets. "I don't ever intend to return there."

Her gaze flashed to his scarred hands, and her heart did a strange little twist. "Why not?"

"You're too damned nosy, Miss Faulkner. Stay the hell out of my life. Meddlesome do-gooders aren't my cup of tea."

Turning away, he ducked beneath the cloth again. She stared at his broad back and strove to contain an upsurge of resentment. What an uncivil, odious man! No wonder he was the black sheep of his family.

"Mr. Coleridge."

He surfaced again. Impatience creased his brow. "Now what?"

"I came here to warn you." Glancing around to make sure no one could overhear, she murmured, "Patel, our *abdur*, heard a rumor that the sepoys plan to mutiny."

"A revolt? I don't doubt it." Damien looked toward the group of officers on horseback, who sat watching the proceedings, their eyes stern and their posture rigid. "Damned fool, Hewitt. He should have quietly sent the men off to prison. No need to humiliate them in front of their comrades."

"For once I agree with you, though I could have done without the profanity."

"So you can trust my ethics on this one issue."

"Yes." Without thinking, she touched his forearm. His hard-honed skin warmed her fingers. "It's to happen today."

As if stung, he jerked back. "Didn't your aunt teach you to keep your damned hands off men?"

Her cheeks heated. But she mustn't let embarrassment distract her. "Didn't you hear what I said? The sepoys intend to mutiny today."

He shook his head. "Not against the might of the entire garrison. They'll bide their time and catch the British off guard."

His decisiveness made Sarah shiver. "Listen to me. Take Shivina and Kit away. They're too near the native infantry lines. They might be hurt if any fighting breaks out."

He quirked an eyebrow. "Damn, maybe you do have something between your ears besides air."

"And I pray you have something in your chest besides ice."

"Touché, Miss Faulkner. For once, I'll heed your advice." His mouth formed a sober half-smile. "As Lord Canning himself so succinctly phrased it, there's a devil's wind blowing. Time for me to move on."

Damien swung toward his camera. Troubled, Sarah walked slowly back to the carriage. She wondered if she'd ever see him again. Aware of a poignant emptiness inside her, she resolved to visit Shivina one last time. Poor woman! Doomed to a nomad's life in a hot, airless caravan with Damien Coleridge for company. Praise God she had Kit to keep her happy. Yet for an instant, Sarah felt a sharp yearning to wander India, to see exotic sights and learn more about its fascinating peoples . . .

Dum-da-da-dum. Dum-da-da-dum.

The rhythmic sound of a drum drew her attention. She climbed back into the *palka-ghari* to see the eighty-five convicted men march into the center of the square. The shuffling of their feet accompanied the whisperings of the crowd. In full uniform they looked identical to the other soldiers, but for the dullness of defeat on their dark faces.

The drumroll ceased.

The onlookers hushed, with only an occasional cough or jangle of harness. A subaltern read out the sentence: imprisonment with hard labor for ten years.

A collective gasp swept the gathering. The drum resumed, a slow, somber tone like a death knell. Officers moved along the ranks, yanking the buttons from the prisoners' uniform coats and removing their boots, flinging them into small piles on the dusty ground. Most of the men submitted to the stripping with resigned expressions, but a few wept openly as they gave up medals won in battles fought for their English masters. One older sowar fell down and beat the earth with his fists.

"Poor fellow," said Amelia Craven, dabbing at her brow with a handkerchief. "Imagine, ten years! One almost feels sorry for them."

Too devastated to criticize the woman's belated sensitivity, Sarah murmured, "I've never seen a more wretched sight."

Gloom blanketed the crowd. The wind tossed needles of dust, and the dark clouds hung like a pall. Even the air bore the taint of melancholy, as dreary as dried sweat.

Armorers went from man to man, fastening heavy iron fetters to the ankles of each prisoner. The clang-clang of hammers echoed inside Sarah, stirring a mix of despair and anger. She wanted to rail at the officers, at Carmichael-Smythe and Hewitt and her uncle, who sat on horseback and piously regarded the proceedings.

Damien was right. However one might argue the justice of the court-martial, the prisoners should have been spared this shame.

When the last manacle had been secured, the convicted men were marched off the field while their comrades stood at attention. Clanking irons blended with high-pitched cries and wails. Some walked away with shoulders slumped in disgrace; bitter tears wet the faces of others.

A few shouted curses in Hindi and with man- acled hands hurled their boots at the officers, the distance causing the missiles to fall shy of their target. Many railed at the other native soldiers. "Remember us, brothers!" "*Bhainchutes!* Will you let the *feringhis* imprison us?" "Rise up, you cow- ards! Release us from bondage!"

An ominous muttering rippled from the native soldiers. The British stood in rigid silence; the dull daylight glinted off rifles held ready and sabers honed to deadly sharpness.

Sullen stares followed the parade of prisoners. Sepoy and sowar alike exchanged glances. Men shifted position. Dark eyes flashed. Fists clenched. Beneath a surface of military obedience, a cauldron of outrage simmered.

But no one broke rank.

Sarah laced her fingers to still their trembling. Even the usually cheerful Ram Lall glowered after the last convicts being herded toward the gaol. From beside her came the cadence of Amelia Craven's voice, but the meaning of the words eluded Sarah.

As the driver clucked to the horse and began the jolting ride home, she tried to calm the un- easiness roiling inside her. Had she been a super- stitious person, she might have called the feeling an omen.

An omen of disaster.

"This is a disaster!" Aunt Violet fretted on the church steps the next day. "Mercy me, I never expected *them* to come here, among good Chris- tian people."

Sarah turned to see what had thrown her aunt into a dither. Her gloved hands tightened on her prayer book. Alighting from a carriage beside the low stone fence of the churchyard were Damien and Shivina, who carried little Kit.

Sarah's eyes widened in admiration. The Hindu woman wore one of the new gowns, a soft primrose-pink that complemented her exotic features. Her lustrous black hair was drawn back in English fashion and crowned by a modestly feathered bonnet.

Other people arriving for the Sunday morning service stopped and stared, officers in their summer uniforms of frock coat and white trousers, women in their best laces and silks. Upraised eyebrows and taut mouths conveyed disapproval. Even the children sensed the tension and gawked from behind their mothers' skirts.

Shame stirred inside Sarah. The English preached Christian virtue, yet slammed the church door in the faces of the Indians. Though given to eccentricity, Damien Coleridge had an impeccable bloodline that had made him acceptable to society. Now that he'd wed a Hindu woman and acknowledged his half-caste child, he and his family were pariahs, no more welcome than the mangy *pi* dogs that prowled the alleys in search of scraps.

Looking at her aunt, Sarah said in a low voice, "You must speak to them. Shivina was a guest in our home."

"That unhappy circumstance couldn't be avoided." Aunt Violet's plump mouth sagged in distress. "But now . . . heavens, I should have to greet her as an equal."

What makes you think you're so much better than she is? Sarah stifled the question and said, "Would that be so very dreadful? She's a fine woman, and much kinder than most."

Reginald stepped forward, his hands clasped behind him, sunlight gilding his tidy fair hair. "Your benevolence is to be commended, Sarah.

Yet you must see the awkwardness of the situation."

She ached to make him understand. He could be so vexing. "But surely Our Lord would wish us to show compassion at His house of all places. We should invite them to sit with us."

"Oh, dear, here they come," whispered Aunt Violet. Twisting her handkerchief, she appealed to her husband, who stood behind her. "Please, Colonel, can't *you* make our niece see reason?"

"Sarah, the doctor is right," Uncle John said, shooting her a severe look from beneath bristly brows. "Fraternizing with the natives encourages insubordination—precisely what brought on yesterday's punishment parade."

"I understand your feelings," Sarah said in an undertone. "Yet we must be civil—"

"As you like. But there'll be none of this sharing of pews. So long as you live in my household, you will obey me."

His imperative vehemence silenced her. Then Damien and Shivina approached the white-washed Angelican church. In his formal black suit and stiff white shirt, he exuded power and refinement. His features harsh with aristocratic arrogance, he rested an arm around his wife's waist.

People stepped back to let them pass. Ladies whispered behind their fans. Cradling the baby, Shivina darted fearful glances from beneath her lashes. As if she expected to be stoned by an angry mob, Sarah thought in abashment.

The couple reached the wooden steps. Damien gave a nod of greeting to Uncle John and Reginald, then bowed to the women. "Gentlemen, ladies. How good to see all of you again." An ironic pitch deepened his voice.

The men murmured stiff hellos.

Aunt Violet's sallow cheeks went pink. Her mouth opened and closed like a trout's. "Indeed," she squeaked.

A moment of awkward silence ensued. Shivina kept her gaze downcast. The cynical tightness to Damien's mouth told Sarah he'd expected their cold reception.

Embarrassed, she stepped forward. "I'm glad you could come today. I trust you and the baby have been well, my lady?"

The title wrested a faint gasp from Aunt Violet. Sarah kept her eyes trained on Shivina, who shyly looked up. "Yes, Miss Sarah. Kit will someday be as strong as his father."

Her loving gaze dropped to the infant in her arms. He opened his velvet-dark eyes, sighed, and then settled back into slumber. A bolt of pure envy sizzled through Sarah. How she longed to hold her own child, to experience the joy of watching him grow and learn. Smiling at Reginald, she said, "Isn't Kit the most darling little boy?"

He cast a quick frown at the baby. "Quite so."

His indifferent response sapped the pleasure from her. Softly she said, "*I* think he's wonderful."

Damien gave her a cryptic stare. "Thank you. My wife and I share your sentiment." Turning, he let his gaze sweep the sunlit gathering. "As we're departing tomorrow morning, my wife wishes our son to be baptized today. Unless someone here objects to prolonging the service."

A charged silence blanketed the yard. People exchanged guarded glances. Silk and taffeta rustled faintly. A crow cawed from its perch on the roof.

From inside the church came the thumping melody of the pump organ. The signal broke the tension, and the congregation began to surge toward the opened doors.

People kept a polite distance from Damien and Shivina, as if they were lepers. Sunlight gleamed on the tiny gold ring in her nose and the ivory fronds of her feathered bonnet. No woman here could match her sloe-eyed beauty, Sarah thought, nor could they surpass Shivina's gentle bravery in tolerating so many hostile looks.

"Time to take our places," muttered Uncle John, putting a hand at his wife's plump waist.

Sarah hesitated, wondering if she dared disobey. Reginald caught her arm. "Shall we go in?" he said.

The words were more a rebuke than a question, and his firm hand held her in place. The faint scowl on his handsome face conveyed a warning: *Don't disgrace your aunt and uncle.* Her courage wavered in the face of duty. Reluctant to cause a scene, she let him escort her to the door.

She glanced back and caught Damien's eye. "Until we meet again, Miss Faulkner," he said.

She had the distinct impression that he preferred never to cross paths with her again. His pessimistic regard accused her of being a hypocrite, the same as all the other churchgoers.

Hurt and resentment flashed in her. What did he expect? That she make herself an outcast along with him? Didn't he see that no matter what her private feelings, to find happiness in this closed society she must obey its tedious rules?

Through the long-winded service, her anger slowly burned out. By the time Kit wailed from the waters of baptism, an ember of shame glowed in the ashes of her heart. As Damien and Shivina left with the baby, the feeling flared uncomfortably hotter.

She returned home with her aunt and uncle, and retreated to her bedroom. Perhaps Damien was right. Perhaps by failing to live her beliefs she *was* a fraud. Perhaps she, who prided herself on her enlightened opinions, might as well practice the same intolerance as the majority of the English.

Like a bitter pill, the possibility stuck in her

throat. Only the thought of her editorials kept her
from choking. At least she could rest easy with
the knowledge that she worked toward educating
her fellow Britons.

To exorcise her conscience, she spent the
drowsy afternoon hours writing a detailed ac-
count of the sentencing parade. Yet her sense of
uneasiness failed to lift. She firmly resolved to
make amends for her actions by stopping for her
last visit with Shivina and Kit after the evening
church service.

At six o'clock, Uncle John departed to review
his troops. Shortly thereafter, she joined Aunt Violet in the *palka-ghari*, and they left for their second ride to church.

The beauty of the hour pulled at Sarah's heart.
The sun was sinking in a blaze of blood-red heat
over the plains. Golden light poured over the officers' bungalows along the Mall. A dark-skinned
boy shooed a flock of goats past, their hooves pat-
tering on the hard-baked dirt. Black-and-white
starlings pecked at the small dry figs on a peepul
tree.

As the carriage neared the turnoff to the old
town and the bazaar, the scents of dust and spice
perfumed the air. Down the middle of the road
plodded a sacred humpbacked cow, unperturbed
by the closely following carriage.

"Oh, isn't it lovely?" Sarah said on impulse.

"What is?" Without awaiting a reply, Aunt Violet leaned forward, her bosom straining against
her gold bodice. "Oh, do hurry, Ram Lall. Go
around the beast, else we'll be late."

"Yes, memsahib."

The driver clucked to the horse. The carriage
veered to the side of the road, the wheels precar-
iously nearing the ditch as they passed the cow.
At the same moment Sarah heard a distant hum-
ming, like a hive of bees. The sound came from
the bazaar.

She looked past her aunt to the tiny mud-baked shops with their colorful awnings, the temple with its pointed brass roof glinting in the last rays of sunlight. The noise grew to a dull roar of voices. Out of a side street poured a mob of people. Their upraised arms brandished clubs and guns and swords.

A gasp froze in her throat. The screaming throng was pursuing a lone English soldier.

Chapter 6

Like a terrible tide, the horde surged toward them. Sarah's hands went cold with fright. The crowd was a conglomerate of *badmashes* and tradesmen, whores and sepoys, Hindus and Mohammedans. Their dark faces bore identical looks of animal rage: bared teeth and wild eyes.

The Indians swarmed after the soldier. His cap flew from a shock of reddish-brown hair. He stumbled to his knees, his hands slapping the dusty earth. Curses and jeers of victory rose from his pursuers.

"Merciful heavens!" shrieked Aunt Violet. "Have they gone mad? Someone stop them!"

The man glanced over his shoulder and scrambled up. Panic paled his youthful features. Legs pumping, he ran again.

Clutching the wicker half-hood for balance, Sarah hung over the side of the carriage and waved frantically. "Over here!"

She knew he couldn't hear her over the din. But he spied the *palka-ghari* and veered toward it, the mob hard on his heels.

The snap of gunfire split the air. Ram Lall dropped the reins and seized his chest. Blood blossomed on the back of his white shirt. He toppled from the seat.

Aunt Violet loosed another shrill scream.

The horse reared. Swallowing her horror, Sarah threw herself across the driver's vacant seat. She snatched the dangling reins and pulled hard. The *palka-ghari* tilted drunkenly as one wheel skittered into the ditch.

For the span of a heartbeat she feared they would crash. Then the carriage righted. The horse snorted and danced. She held tight to the leads and looked over the side.

Ram Lall lay unmoving in the ditch, his face in filthy water.

Her stomach lurched. Clenching her teeth against rising bile, she wriggled upright on the seat. Her unwieldy hoops snagged on the whip socket. The buzz of the rabble grew louder. She yanked hard and her gown tore free.

The soldier made a running leap for the carriage. The instant he clung to the outside, she turned the vehicle in a wide half circle, away from the maddened masses.

Get home, a refrain ran in her head. *Home to safety.*

The horde bellowed in frenzy. The leaders loomed scant yards away. People hurled rocks and daggers. Blunted thuds struck the hood.

"Merciful God . . ." squealed Aunt Violet.

A *badmash* pounded alongside the carriage. From the corner of her eye, Sarah saw the flash of his curved tulwar.

He grabbed for the seat handle. Gasping, she snatched the whip and slashed it across his face. A scarlet gash striped his bristly cheek. He fell back, howling.

She concentrated on controlling the frightened horse. A stone struck her shoulder. Pain splintered down her arm, but she snapped the reins.

Jolting and swaying, the carriage pulled away from the bazaar. The horse galloped down the open road. Sarah's heart thudded as fast as the animal's hooves. The clamor of the crowd began to fade.

Home, she thought in a daze. *Home to safety.*

The soldier half fell inside. "Friggin' beasts!" he panted. "Killed me mate, 'Arry. Chopped him to bits at the ginger-beer shop."

The words pierced her stupor. "Killed? But why?" she asked over her shoulder. She caught a glimpse of his tumbled auburn hair, his ashen, boyish face. "Why would they attack you?"

" 'Cause they're black beasts, that's why." He paused, wheezing. "Christ Almighty. Look what they done to *'er.*"

The shock in his voice made Sarah look around. Aunt Violet sat back, the hood supporting her sagging head. The wide-brimmed hat had slipped askew over her neat sausage curls. She held her prayer book against the bodice of her gown, the gold now dyed red with blood. From her plump breast protruded a knife hilt. Her eyes were glazed, staring in sightless dread.

Everything will become red.

"No . . ."

The dry wind whipped away Sarah's whisper. With her hands tight around the reins, she tried to grasp the truth. Aunt Violet . . . dead! Dear, complaining, frivolous Aunt Violet.

"Bloody bastards—beggin' yer pardon, ma'am, but them murderin' devils won't get away with this."

The soldier jabbered on, but Sarah's mind went numb. Her throat thick, she turned her eyes back to the avenue. The horse slowed to a trot and headed straight back to the bungalow.

Home. Home to safety.

All looked as before, the tamarind tree waving its feathery fronds, the veranda deep and cool with greenery, the black shutters opened to catch the evening breeze. The same golden twilight gilded the plumbago and bougainvillea bushes.

Unreality wreathed her. Had only a few minutes passed? It seemed more like hours.

Patel scampered down the front steps. His aging dark face wrinkled in concern, he hurried to the carriage.

"Missy-sahib! I have just heard—" His voice broke off and his gaze widened on Aunt Violet. He raised his hands to the heavens. "O Rama, save us. It is true, then. The sepoys have risen against the sahibs."

"It's mutiny," the soldier said. "I'll make them black devils pay for what they done!"

He jumped down, bobbed a farewell to Sarah, and dashed off toward the infantry lines.

"Quickly, Miss Sarah." Reaching up, Patel took her hand and tugged. "No English safe. All the servants have run off—Zafar, Aziz, even Hamil, may he die and be reborn a snake."

She let him help her descend from the carriage. "Ram Lall is dead, too." Shivering from shock, she glanced back inside and fought off an overwhelming grief. "We can't leave Aunt Violet here. We must bring her inside."

"Later," he said, drawing her around the outside of the house. "Now you hide in my hut."

A dull cracking noise in the distance iced her stomach. Gunfire. From the direction of the barracks.

Dear God. Shivina and Kit.

What if Damien had gone on one of his photographic jaunts? What if he wasn't there again to protect his wife and child?

Everything will become red.

Alarm swept away the cobwebs of sorrow. "I'm going to the caravan," she said. "I'll bring Shivina and the baby here."

"Coleridge-sahib, he will see to them! Please, missy-sahib, you must guard yourself."

Patel would stop her; she knew it in her heart.

Carefully, she said, "Go to your hut. I'll disguise myself in a sari and join you there."

Shaking off his hand, she rushed up the steps and into the bungalow. In her bedroom, she worked with trembling fingers at her laces and buttons until she stepped out of both gown and corset. Clad in cotton underdrawers and chemise, she pulled the length of lavender-blue silk from a japanned chest.

Threads of silver shimmered in the waning light. Sarah's heart wrenched as she remembered the day Shivina had given her the cloth. If only the baby hadn't come so soon, Damien would have taken Shivina away. She and Kit would have been safe.

They were safe, Sarah told herself. Yet the memory of those blood-crazed faces dug into her mind like talons.

She had to make absolutely certain.

Wrapping the cloth around her like a sari, Sarah clumsily draped one long end over her head and shoulder. Then she drew the *chuddur* low on her brow and tucked in a few loose strands of blond hair. Peering at herself in the mirror, she caught her breath. In the evening shadows she looked like a native woman. The blue eyes and fair features gave her away, but if luck was with her, no one would examine her closely.

A weapon. She might need to defend herself.

She hastened downstairs to her uncle's office. Her gaze went to the glass-fronted gun cabinet. No, she didn't know how to load, let alone fire a rifle. Digging frantically in a desk drawer, she found a brass-hilted dagger.

Holding the knife at her side, she went out onto the veranda. Patel, thank the Lord, was nowhere in sight. She descended the steps and started down the Mall at a trot.

She forced herself not to look back. Ahead, a pall of black smoke draped the cantonments. A

reddish glow like an unearthly sunset tinted the
dusk sky. Flames? The snap of musketry fire and
far-off shouts almost drowned the ordinary
sounds of chirping crickets and barking dogs.

The rioting seemed restricted to the bazaar and
the military sector. She prayed the rapid fall of
night would prevent the outbreak from spreading.

She touched her locket, a small lump beneath
the silk, the gold warmed by her flesh. Was Reginald safe? And Uncle John? Odd, she'd almost
forgotten them in her worry over Shivina and Kit.

Whispering a prayer for them, she held the
dagger at her side, half hidden in the folds of her
sari. Though the sky retained the purple vestiges
of daylight, gloom lay in the ditches, along fences,
and under trees. The din grew progressively
louder. Too loud, she thought, frowning. As she
rounded a bend in the road, near the edge of the
British sector, the flames of hell met her eyes.

The thatched roof of a bungalow leaped with
fire. The windows shone with orange light.
Smoke billowed up in great ebony puffs. The
Cravens' home, Sarah realized in shock.

Outside, bazaar ruffians yelled and laughed and
gyrated like dervishes, trampling the once-neat
bushes of roses and plumbagos. The howl of their
voices joined the hiss and crackle of flaming timbers. One of the men brandished a bloody tulwar;
in his other hand he held aloft a round object.

It was a severed head, a woman's head.

His fingers tangled in a froth of light-colored
hair. Firelight danced on features frozen into a
mask of horror.

Mrs. Craven.

Impossible, spoke a voice inside Sarah. *Impossible.*

She gripped the dagger. The enormity of the
crisis deluged her, weakening her knees and lap-
ping at her courage. Then a blinding jolt of fury

struck. Wanting to plunge the blade into the murderer's heart, she started forward.

A sound stopped her. Raucous voices, coming closer. Sarah shrank into the shadow of an enormous peepul tree.

Another band of mutineers surged down the road. Their torches cast yellow light over filthy turbans, over ragged robes spattered with blood. Alongside the *badmashes* marched sepoys in red tunics and white trousers. They carried guns and sabers, clubs and knives. Ivory teeth flashed in swarthy faces. She spied the man from her uncle's regiment, the man with the scar bisecting his cheek. Hindu and Mohammedan alike wore expressions of inhuman gaiety, as if they were on their way to a macabre party.

Creating a hullabaloo of obscenities and lewd songs, the gang hastened by without seeing her crouched form.

The sheer number of them snapped Sarah to her senses. Fear bruised her fortitude. What was one woman against the maddened throngs?

Already the men poured into neighboring yards. Feminine screams and pleas for mercy drifted into the night. She bit her lip so hard that the metallic taste of blood flooded her tongue.

She must not get herself killed for naught. She must save Shivina and the baby. Even Damien might die at the hands of the mob.

Choking down a sob, she forced herself to turn from the grisly scene. Keeping to the back streets, she skirted the edge of the bazaar. Mayhem reigned everywhere. The sharp report of firearms blended with the excited calls of the mutineers and the sizzle of numerous fires. She took care to hold the veil low over her forehead. Their bloodlust focused on the British, the hooligans paid no heed to a lone native woman slipping through the shadows.

Turning a corner, Sarah stumbled over a heap

in an alley. She blinked from the sting of smoke
and looked down. The corpse of a British infan-
tryman rested in a crimson puddle. His eyes were
wide and staring. A lock of auburn hair draped
his youthful brow. He had been hacked to death;
both his arms lay a short distance from his body.

He was the soldier who had climbed into her
carriage.

The sight overwhelmed Sarah. Bending, she
lost the contents of her stomach into the stinking
gutter. She leaned against a whitewashed wall
and took shallow breaths, her head tilted back.
The moon had not yet risen. Flames illuminated
the heavens so brightly she could see no stars.

Dear God. Dear God, this cannot be happen-
ing.

Her eyes were parched, her throat sour, her
heart dulled. Cold perspiration dotted her hot
skin. Only the pop of gunfire in the distance rallied her.

She walked past the huts of the native quarter,
down cramped streets where women huddled in
darkened doorways and beggar children cried in
fear. At last she neared the cantonments.

Hoping by some miracle to find the caravan already departed, she came upon the open area behind the bazaar.

Her prayers went unanswered. Ten yards away,
by the low mud-brick wall, the boxy vehicle rested
in its usual spot. The traces lay empty; nearby, a
pair of bullocks bellowed mournfully, pulling at
their tethers. In the doorway of the caravan, her
face a dusky oval in the fire glow, stood Shivina.

A weakening wash of relief brought Sarah to a
halt. The din of yells and gunshots kept her from
calling out a greeting. Clad in the emerald hooped
gown of an English lady, Shivina looked slim and
exotic and scared. She hugged the doorframe and
peered toward the cantonment wall, as if watching for someone.

For Damien Coleridge, no doubt.

Sarah pursed her lips. So she'd been right to come here. She'd been right to think he'd be off somewhere, leaving his wife and son alone in the midst of peril. Shivina might believe Damien had saved her life once, but the man was far from reliable.

At least Sarah had arrived in time to guide them to safety beyond the city walls.

"Kali! Kali!"

The demonic chant rose above the noise. Sarah swung sharply to the sound. From the bazaar streaked a saffron-robed man. His oily black locks flapped around a thin brown face. In his hand gleamed a tulwar.

Her limbs went numb. The fakir!

"*Sub lal hogea hai!*" he shouted. "Kali be praised."

Calling on his vengeful goddess, he dashed toward the caravan. Shivina turned. Her scream pierced the hot night air. She made a move to slam the door, but the fakir was too quick.

He reached up and yanked at the dress that marked her a traitor. She crumpled across the short steps, the crinoline billowing around her in a cloud of green silk. Like a butcher wielding a cleaver, he raised his tulwar. "Kali, Kali!"

A sob burst from Sarah. Her paralysis ended and she raced across the compound. Her legs seemed to churn in slow motion.

The curved sword sliced downward.

A mist of horror and rage enveloped her. She aimed her dagger at his gaunt yellow back.

"You guarantee this stuff will keep my family well?" Damien asked.

He lifted his gaze from the amber bottle in his hand to the man peering into the opened drug cabinet. Dr. Reginald Pemberton-Sykes straightened, squaring his shoulders. The last rays of

sunset streamed through the study window and
illuminated his classic features. He looked like an
artist's conception of male perfection, Damien
thought with a touch of acidity. Like one of the
statues the Duchess of Lamborough collected.

"There is no proven preventive for dysentery,"
the doctor said. "But I believe a teaspoon of castor oil taken once a day will help keep you and
your wife healthy. The boy, of course, won't need
any so long as he's drinking only his mother's
milk."

His coolness rankled Damien. Not for his own
sake; over the years he'd learned to let undercur-
rents of censure roll off his tough hide. But he'd
make bloody well certain that people treated his
wife and child with respect.

"You don't approve of me marrying a native
woman."

Reginald arched one fair eyebrow. "It isn't my
place to approve or disapprove, Mr. Coleridge."

"But you do disapprove. I've ignored the class
distinction between the races, between sahib and
slave."

The doctor made a show of locking the cabinet
and pocketing the key. Then he sat on the edge
of his desk and tilted his neatly groomed head in
a thoughtful pose. "Since you're being so frank,
yes, I suppose what you say is true. You speak in
favor of the Hindu cause. You garb yourself like
a native. It seems you respect the Indians more
than your own people."

Damien felt goaded into saying, "The Hindus
are my people, and they're yours, too, if only you
could see it. The Brits are wrong to set themselves
up as superior beings."

"Come, now." Smiling, Reginald shook his
head. "Someone must be the master. Someone
must make the rules, else we'd have chaos."

"Heaven forbid the English should suffer chaos
while invading another country."

"We bring civilization to the primitive peoples of the world."

Damien tightened his fingers around the medicine bottle. "The Indians have had a civilized culture since long before *our* ancestors were warring barbarians."

Reginald snorted as he got up to light a lamp against the encroaching dusk. "That depends on what you call civilized. *Suttee*—a widow who's expected to throw herself onto a burning funeral pyre? Thugees strangling innocent travelers to satisfy the bloodlust of Kali?" He blew out the match and tossed it into a brass dish. "Or how about the polygamists who take more than one wife? Surely even you cannot endorse such practices."

"Some of their customs might seem peculiar, even savage," Damien conceded. "Yet the Indians might view *us* as odd, too. We condemn our children to die in filthy workhouses. We force men to labor fourteen-hour shifts in the bowels of coal mines. And, of course, we profess to believe in only one God instead of a host of remarkable deities."

"Remarkable?" Folding his arms, Reginald sank back onto the edge of the desk. "I'm afraid I cannot share your views."

In his tropical white garb he looked like a complacent snow leopard. And a leopard can't change his spots, Damien reflected.

This was the man who would marry Sarah Faulkner.

Damien wondered why the thought disturbed him. She and Reginald were a matched pair, both blond and handsome, both with that typical British bearing of valor and self-righteousness. They differed only in that Sarah Faulkner professed empathy for the natives. A spark of anger smoldered inside Damien. Her open-mindedness was a sham; that must be why she bothered him so.

He burned with the memory of the moment at church yesterday when she'd turned her back on Shivina and Kit.

He couldn't abide a hypocrite.

"At least you're honest," Damien told the doctor. "I'll give you that much."

He stuck the bottle in his pocket and offered his hand. As Reginald rose to shake hands, he frowned.

"I say, if you'll excuse my professional interest, you've quite a lot of old scar tissue. You must have suffered terrible burns. A long time ago?"

The familiar wall reared inside Damien. He stepped back. "I was five."

"Such extensive burns can be crippling. Yet you appear to have regained full use of your hands."

A lightning bolt of memory struck Damien . . . the painful hours of opening and closing his fingers to stretch the puckered skin, the agony of grasping a pencil again, the torture of learning to draw. His determination to become whole again had been buoyed by the futile hope of winning his mother's forgiveness.

In a chilly voice that invited no more questions, he said, "I simply exercised my hands. It was successful, but I don't recommend it."

"I did my medical training at the Royal College of Physicians in London. Perhaps I knew your doctor."

"I doubt it. He retired nearly twenty years ago."

"A shame. I'd have enjoyed corresponding with him." A pensive look came over Reginald's face. "I wonder if other burned children might follow a similar therapy regimen. Perhaps you wouldn't mind describing in more detail how you—"

"I'm afraid that's impossible," Damien broke in. "I'm leaving Meerut before dawn tomorrow, and I've preparations to make yet."

"Of course. How stupid of me. I haven't the time now anyway, else I should be late for the evening service—" Reginald paused and cocked his head. "I say, what's that?"

The stamp of running feet sounded outside and then came closer, into the bungalow. A tall Hindu bearer, the tail of his green turban dangling down his back, burst into the room.

"Sahib-doctor," he said, panting, "you must come quickly. To the infantry lines."

"What is it?" asked Reginald, already reaching for his black medical bag.

"The native regiments have arisen. Much fighting, many wounded."

The news hit Damien like a nasty fall. He swore under his breath. "Get us mounts, and quickly," he told the servant, then sprang out the door.

Racing to the veranda rail, he peered toward the cantonments. Against the evening sky, clouds of smoke billowed from the blazing barracks. The distant crackle of musketry fire drifted from the infantry lines and the parade ground.

"My son." The words leaped from Damien.

Reginald joined him. "Good God,' he breathed. "Ali Khan must be mistaken. They can't have mutinied."

Damien glanced at the doctor's ashen face. "What do you think they're doing, having a barbecue?" he snapped. "I'm as much a bloody fool as you for not seeing this would happen so soon."

Reginald only pursed his lips and began pacing.

The bearer came running toward the veranda, holding the reins of a bay charger. A syce hastened after him, leading a black horse.

Damien dashed down the steps and flung himself onto the black. Reginald fastened his bag to the bay's saddle, mounted, and turned his horse toward the cantonments.

"If you'll excuse me, old chap—"

"Damn your English manners," Damien cut in savagely. "I'm going back to the caravan, so I may as well ride along with you."

"As you like."

The doctor took off at a gallop, dust flying. Following, Damien crouched low over the ebony mane. Fear sparked his fury, a fury aimed more at himself than anyone else. God! He should have obeyed the warning of his instincts. He should have left Meerut days ago. He shouldn't have softened to Shivina's plea to delay until after Kit's christening. But she asked him for so little.

Dread tortured his heart. If anything happened to either of them . . . All of his adult life he'd resisted entangling himself with other people. Commitment sucked a man into a quicksand of emotional dependence. A quicksand that smothered him in a slow, painful death.

Damn! If he got his family out of here alive, he'd never leave himself vulnerable again.

The fastest route back to the caravan lay through the cantonments, where tongues of flame licked at the thatched roofs of barracks. Throngs of infantrymen danced in wild jubilation. Men shot muskets into the air, weapons stolen from slain English officers whose mutilated bodies scattered the ground.

Beside Reginald, Damien reined to a halt in the shadows a short distance from the regimental magazine. More than a hundred sowars, sepoys, and *badmashes* milled around the stone building. The threat of violence hung as acrid as the smoke in the evening sky.

"God help us," muttered Damien, "if the riffraff of the bazaar get their hands on more guns."

"I must restore order."

He swung his gaze to the doctor. "Don't be a damned fool, Reggie. One man doesn't hold a prayer against so many. Besides, you're needed at the hospital."

"Fewer guns will mean fewer casualties."

Resolution hardened Reginald's face. Damien bleakly conceded the battle of dissuading the doctor. There was no arguing with an Englishman blinded by duty.

Reginald's bulldog valor plunged Damien into one hell of a dilemma. Unless he distanced himself fast.

"Curse your bloody heroics," he said. "I won't be dragged into this. I'm getting the hell out of here."

He wheeled the black around and galloped off.

Reginald watched horse and rider vanish into the night. Curiously, he felt a glimmer of understanding for Damien Coleridge. At least the odd fellow lived his beliefs to the letter. Might have guessed he'd desert rather than fight his precious Indians.

Which left Reginald in a frightful pickle.

He swallowed, tasting dust and gunpowder. Never had he felt more utterly alone. Madness inflamed the faces of the rebels. Teeth bared like tigers, they exhorted each other to break open the magazine. If ever he'd wondered what the devil looked like, now he knew.

Steeling his nerves, he rode toward the mob and stopped a few yards away. As one, the multitude swung toward him.

"Lay down your arms," he called out in English. "Disperse yourselves immediately."

Jeers and catcalls flew at him. "By whose order?" a turncoat sepoy shouted. "You are no longer our master, *feringhi!*"

A roar of agreement rose to the inferno-lit sky. Like the swell pushed ahead of a typhoon, the crowd surged toward Reginald.

Palms sweaty, he gripped the reins and kept his face calm. "In the name of the Queen, lay down your arms now and your punishment will be fair."

''As fair as the punishment you gave our brothers?'' yelled a cavalryman. ''You treated them like sons of snakes.''

''Remember our brothers!'' Enraged voices took up the chant, a chant Reginald understood despite his rusty Hindi. ''Our brothers, our brothers!''

Saber upraised, a bearded Mohammedan in a blood-splashed shirt pushed to the front of the mob. ''Kill the infidel!''

''*Maro!*'' someone else bellowed. ''Kill him!''

A musket ball whizzed past Reginald's ear. The frightened horse reared. Sawing at the reins, he fought to restrain the bay.

A knife-wielding sepoy charged. Iron-shod hooves slashed down onto the man. He fell backward, his arms wheeling, his mouth open in a scream.

''More guns,'' yelled a flat-nosed *badmash*. ''We must seize the *feringhi* guns!''

In a frenzied hubbub, half the crowd turned to storm the magazine. Within moments they battered down the door. Men grabbed the arms and ammunition.

''Stop, I say,'' Reginald cried out. ''You must cease this madness at once!''

His order was lost to the hullabaloo. Everywhere, sepoys and *badmashes* crouched to load their pilfered muskets. The men were beyond control. A bleak thought flashed in his mind: he should have left with Damien Coleridge.

Yet Reginald knew he could have followed no other course.

''*Maro! Maro!*''

Wild shots exploded all around. Eyes rolling, the bay danced and snorted. A mutineer toppled, felled by a stray bullet, a bloodied hole in his chest.

Knowing he hadn't a second to lose, Reginald jerked his horse around. Hands caught at the reins, his trouser legs. Someone ripped his medical bag from the saddle. With his fist, he knocked away a club and then chopped at grasping fingers.

A grinning ruffian lunged out of the confusion. Howling a curse, he slashed his tulwar downward. Even as Reginald snapped the reins free, numbness burned into his thigh.

The horse bolted. Warm wetness soaked Reginald's leg. Through the darkness he saw that his thigh was opened at a diagonal angle, neat as a surgeon's cut. Blood pumped sluggishly from the wound. Judging by the rate of the flow, he realized the sword slice must have nicked an artery.

His only hope was to head for the British infantry lines beyond the parade ground.

Gunfire cracked from behind. Angry howls chased him. He was nearing the cantonment wall when the bay squealed suddenly and stumbled. The reins jerked from his grasp and he flew from the saddle. Wind and firelight rushed past. He hit the earth with a bone-jarring thump.

Agony burst like flames down the length of his body. Each breath seared his throat. The pain crawled downward, settling its fiery claws in his thigh.

With clinical detachment he knew he would die within minutes—if not from blood loss, then at the hands of the insurgents.

Yet the will to live burned stronger than any pain.

Fighting for breath, Reginald spared a glance toward the magazine. Doubtless they'd seen him tumble. From his vantage point he couldn't spot the men, but already their inhuman screeches sounded nearer.

He dragged himself away from the fallen horse and into the shadow of the wall. There he wriggled upright. Removing one of his suspenders, he struggled to tie a tourniquet around his upper thigh. The bleeding slowed to a warm trickle.

Hands shaking, he leaned dizzily back against the cool wall.

Sarah, he thought in sudden anguish. *Are you safe? I'll never live to know . . .*

The chanting of the mob grew closer. Gunfire popped. Now he could see the glow of their flaming brands, could hear their crazed curses and the tramp of their footsteps. In a matter of moments, they would find him.

He knew his pockets were empty, yet he fumbled laboriously inside them anyway. Drat. If only he possessed a weapon.

But he was a healer, not a killer.

He closed his eyes and said a prayer. He tried to conjure an image of Sarah. Somehow her lovely features slipped away like the blood soaking into the dusty ground.

His mind drifted upward, leaving bodily torment behind, soaring like a kite upon a gust of wind.

I should have listened to you, Sarah. You were right about the natives. You and Damien Coleridge.

Something hard clamped onto his arm and yanked him back to earth. A voice buzzed like an angry hornet in his ear.

"Get up, damn you."

He felt himself being hauled to his feet. Pain seared his leg. Panting, he staggered back against the wall. A face swam before him. A man's face, swarthy as a native's but with the square-cut features of an Englishman.

Damien Coleridge.

Reginald blinked. His dazed mind must be playing tricks. "But . . . you came back—"

"Yes, and that makes me as much the bloody fool as you," Damien snapped. "Now, are you going to loll about here like an offering to Kali?"

"My leg—"

"Damn your leg. It's your throat you should worry about."

And mine, Damien wanted to add. Bracing an arm around the doctor's back, he helped the injured man hobble toward the black gelding tethered farther down along the wall. The mutineers were too damned close for comfort. Glancing over his shoulder, he could discern the frenzied faces of the leaders as they neared the fallen horse. If it weren't for the concealing shadows, he and Reginald already would be fodder for the vultures.

Reginald gasped, "Right good of you, old chap—"

"Just walk, for God's sake. Walk."

The throng milled around the bay. One of the ringleaders loosed a savage shriek and pointed at the two Englishmen. A crescendo rumbled from the rebels. Weapons raised, men darted toward them.

Damien growled, "Make that *run!*"

But Reginald slumped as if disoriented. Cursing under his breath, Damien half carried the doctor the remaining few yards. The horse waited in the gloom, straining at its tether. Its eyes rolled wildly at the scents of smoke and blood.

The whoops and hollers of the mob swept closer. Muscles straining, Damien flung Reginald over the pommel. He jerked the reins from beneath a rock and leaped into the saddle. Even as his feet hit the stirrups, he spurred the black to a gallop.

A volley of shots snapped past. He crouched low and kept a tight hold on the wounded man. Reginald lay limp, unconscious, Damien hoped. It'd be the devil's own luck if he'd risked his neck to rescue a dead man.

Slowly he pulled out of musket range, but tension still throbbed inside him. The horse blew hard under the exertion of its double load. He eased the animal into a trot along the back routes of Meerut, past flaming buildings and mangled

English bodies. As he forced himself past yet another fire, he felt cold sweat soak his tunic. The carnage sickened him. The city bore an uncanny resemblance to Hades, peopled by merciless demons.

For the first time in years he found himself whispering a fierce prayer: *Dear God, protect Shivina. Protect my son.*

Reaching the English infantry lines, he found mass confusion. Several officers called roll; others shouted orders. Soldiers ran in all directions, some men only half dressed. Dragoon guards sat mounted and waiting. Teams pulled out heavy artillery guns. In the midst of chaos, General Hewitt stood surrounded by subalterns and scratched his balding pate.

Why the hell hadn't he sent out troops immediately to quell the violence? Damien wondered.

But the elderly commander's incompetence was hardly his concern. All Damien wanted was to find his family and get the hell out of Meerut.

He dismounted near the hospital and signaled to a pair of bearers. As they loaded Reginald onto a canvas stretcher, he stirred and opened his eyes. "You're a noble chap after all," he muttered. "Forgive me for misjudging . . ." He slumped back into unconsciousness.

Damien shrugged and hurried away. From the severity of the wound, he doubted the doctor would live. If the loss of blood didn't kill him, gangrene or infection would.

So much for heroics.

He remounted and rode off into the night. Sporadic shooting sounded, and more than once he had to detour around a roving band of sepoys. As he neared the bazaar, smoke from burning buildings clogged the air and made him cough. A nauseating fear quaked inside him, a fear that drenched his palms in icy sweat. Oh, God, if Shivina and Kit were trapped in a fire . . .

· The blaze of memory licked at his courage.

He spurred his horse to a gallop. At last, through a grove of trees, he spied the caravan. Relief poured like opium through his veins. No flames consumed the vehicle.

But the sight he saw next sliced into his heart.

Chapter 7

Sarah rushed at the fakir. Like an avenging demon, he held his sword high. Beside the caravan steps, Shivina lay in a foam of green skirts. She feebly crossed her arms over the bloodied front of her gown.

The fakir meant to finish her off.

Outrage beat a savage song against Sarah's ribs. She clenched the dagger, poised to strike. A low cry escaped her.

The fakir pivoted. His eyes glowed like coals in his ash-smeared face. His teeth were yellow, the teeth of a scavenging jackal.

He swung the tulwar at Sarah. "Kali, Kali!"

She swerved. The toe of her sandal caught on the sari. She stumbled. The blade whooshed through the air half an inch from her ear. His fingers caught her wrist and yanked her upright.

He squeezed hard. Numbness weakened her hand. Horrified, she watched her fingers release the dagger. It hit the ground with a dull plop.

She lunged for the weapon. With a zealot's strength, the fakir slammed her against the caravan. Pain exploded over her shoulders and shimmered down her back. Her knees crumpled. As she started to slide downward, he thrust himself against her.

He stank of sweat and filth. Gagging, she tried

to wriggle away, but her arms were trapped against his chest. The veil slipped off her head. Blond hair spilled over her shoulders. Recognition rounded his eyes and flared his nostrils.

"So, again thou flyest to the aid of the whore." Sneering, he kicked the dagger beneath the caravan. "Thou shalt die, too, *feringhi* she-devil."

He pressed his arm like a taut wire against her throat. Stars wheeled before her eyes. Panic reared inside her as she struggled to draw a breath.

"Thou shalt not rob me of my gift to Kali again."

The holy man raised the tulwar. Blood dripped down the blade, flowed over the back of his hand, and stained his dirty yellow sleeve. Shivina's blood.

Fury and desperation drove strength into Sarah. She freed one arm and attacked his face. Her nails drew thin scarlet stripes through the gray ashes.

The fakir yowled and jumped back a step, allowing her space to duck beneath his arm. She ran toward the bazaar. Safety lay in the shadowed alleyways. But he caught the edge of her sari and she fell. The side of her head struck the hard earth. Dust clogged her mouth, and her ears rang. Coughing, she rolled to the side, fearing the cold steel bite of the sword.

I tried, Shivina. I really tried . . .

A grunt and the shuffle of feet sounded behind her. Dazed, she scraped the hair from her eyes and cautiously sat up. Silhouetted against the fire-lit sky, the fakir grappled with a tall man.

Damien Coleridge.

Mighty as an avenging angel, he wrested the tulwar from the holy man. She melted back onto the ground. She'd never been more glad to see him.

Her relief lasted a mere instant. "Shivina."

Sarah pushed herself upright and raced toward the caravan.

Alarm leaped inside her anew. Shivina lay on her side, one slender arm stretched toward the caravan steps. A sword cut scored her abdomen. Blood pumped from the wound and stained the emerald silk of her gown. Shallow breaths lifted her chest.

Sarah's mouth dried. Despite the slaughter she'd witnessed tonight, this wound brought home the savagery of every act of madness.

She scrambled inside the caravan. By the light of a low-burning lantern, she looked frantically around. The baby slumbered in his cradle. She snatched up some clean rags and dropped down beside Shivina.

The black lashes flickered. "Kit," she moaned. "*Baba.*"

"He's fine. Let me help you." Her hands shaking, Sarah pressed a wad of cloth against the hideous wound and kept up a soothing refrain. "Just rest, Shivina. You mustn't try to talk."

Shivina opened her dark almond eyes. She lifted a frail hand and rested it against Sarah's knee. Through the silk sari, her fingers felt cold. Deathly cold.

"My friend," she whispered. "Watch over Kit. Promise . . . when I am gone . . ."

"Don't be absurd," Sarah said, tamping down her rising dread. Blood soaked the rags at a frightening speed. "Damien will take you to the hospital. Reginald will fix you up."

"Please, my friend." Shivina coughed, a thin bubbly sound. "Love my son. Care for him."

"I will. Of course I will. But you'll raise your own son and have many more."

Shivina smiled sadly. "You will raise him, Miss Sarah. You and Damien."

She's ranting, Sarah thought. *How could Shivina believe Damien and I have a future?*

Shivina's hand slipped to the floor and her head slumped back. The strength flowed from her as swiftly as the blood that formed a crimson pool beneath her. The rise and fall of her bosom slowed and ceased.

Sarah added a fresh towel to the sodden mass. Tears flooded her eyes. "You aren't going to die! You can't! You can't."

A movement near the steps caught her attention. She looked up to see Damien Coleridge towering over her, his gaze focused on Shivina. How long had he been standing there? Had he heard?

Blood streaked his white tunic and dhoti. The unnatural light cast his features into sharp relief. No emotion softened the stark angles of his face. His expression was the cold, stony visage of a statue.

His lack of sorrow sparked a wild wrath in her. "Don't just stand there!" she shouted. "Do something!"

He never even glanced at her. He bent and pressed his thumb over Shivina's throat for a few moments. Then he straightened.

"There's nothing I *can* do," he said in a low flat tone. "Nothing at all."

Her eyes blurry, she turned away, her anger dwindling as swiftly as it had arisen. In the shadows at the edge of the clearing, a man sprawled lifelessly in the dust. His saffron robe was stained scarlet from a sword cut across the abdomen. Fleetingly she noted the similarity of his wound to Shivina's.

Seeing the fakir lying dead brought Sarah no satisfaction, only a dull emptiness.

A thin wail carried from inside the caravan. She rose and slowly walked to the cradle. Pinch-eyed and crying, Kit flailed his tiny arms. As if he sensed his mother's death.

Tears burned down Sarah's cheeks. She picked him up and hugged him close, pressing her face to him and drawing in his clean, milky scent. He whimpered once, then quieted, his breathing an irregular rasp in her ear. His warm life poured strength back into her soul. Sympathy for his plight ached in her. Sarah knew the loneliness of losing a mother.

"I'll take care of you, darling," she whispered. "I don't know how, but I will."

Cuddling him against her, she dashed the moisture from her eyes and looked out the doorway of the caravan. Beyond the cantonment wall, firelight painted the night sky in garish shades of orange and red. Gunshots and screams rent the air.

Damien still stood, his fists balled, gazing at his wife's body lying on the ground. Sarah wondered if she was wrong to think he felt no pain. Swallowing the tightness in her throat, she said, "We must take Kit away. He isn't safe here."

Damien lifted his eyes to the sky. "I can't leave her like this," he muttered.

She followed his gaze. Ominous black shapes wheeled against the fire glow. Her stomach churned. Vultures and kites. Birds of prey drawn by the scents of blood and death.

Damien crouched to gather Shivina against him. Her head lolled over his arm, her black hair spilling nearly to the steps, her body frail in the voluminous green silk.

Holding the slumbering baby, Sarah stepped down to let Damien pass. "What are you going to do?"

"The only thing I *can* do."

He ducked inside the caravan. Sarah paced, listening to the turbulence, anxiety climbing inside her. She heard the slam of windows closing and the clang of metal. What was taking Damien so long? A last he emerged alone, carrying the low-lit lantern.

Understanding knifed into her. There was no

time to bury Shivina. The caravan must be her funeral pyre.

He sprang down the steps and turned. The lamp at his side, he gazed at the darkened vehicle.

"Go ahead," Sarah urged. "We can't take the caravan anyway—it's too slow. We'd be caught for certain."

Still he hesitated, his face gray and pained. The clamor of fighting came from both the bazaar and the cantonments. The prospect of being trapped between two blood-crazed hordes made Sarah tighten her arm around the precious bundle of baby.

"Hurry, Damien. We haven't time to waste."

"I can't," he said through gritted teeth. "I can't do this."

Compassion gripped her chest. Then a sickening wave of suspicion rolled through her. Did he balk at burning Shivina—or at incinerating a year's worth of photographs?

Sarah snatched the lamp from him. Swinging it in a wide underhanded arc, she flung it through the doorway.

A crash accompanied the tinkle of shattered glass. Flames lapped at the walls and curtains, lighting the interior with an eerie glow. In the midst of the blaze, Shivina lay perfectly arranged on the floor, her arms folded over her bosom as if she were sleeping.

Pain trampled Sarah's heart. She had never had the chance to apologize for turning away at church. She'd make up for the snub by mothering Kit. Bowing her head, Sarah whispered a prayer of farewell. Then the baby mewed, snapping her back to the present.

The howling from the bazaar sounded closer.

She pivoted toward Damien. "We mustn't linger."

Like a cobra mesmerized by the snake charmer's flute, he stared at the inferno. His eyes were large and dark, his black brows quirked, his fists clenched. She had the impression he hadn't even heard her, that his mind was focused on thoughts far from this hub of madness and danger.

The crackle of the fire blended with the cater-wauling of the mob. Her stomach knotted. She should abandon him to his own devices. Instead she tugged hard at his sleeve.

"Come, Damien! Or will you let your son die, too?"

His gaze fell to the infant. A frown ridged his brow. He touched the boy's smooth cheek. "Christopher . . . ?"

The bafflement fled Damien's face. At the same instant a pack of *badmashes* streamed from the bazaar.

"Good God," he said. "Let's get out of here."

To her bewilderment, he dashed up the caravan steps and shut the door. Jumping down, he seized her arm and yanked her toward a clump of trees.

A roar rose from the throng. The men had spied them!

Holding Kit close, she scurried to keep pace with Damien's jogging strides. Something moved in the shadows of the trees. A big black horse pawed at the ground.

Hope flashed inside her. They had a chance after all.

Damien snatched up the reins and vaulted into the saddle. The horse danced sideways. He spared a moment to stroke the ebony mane until the horse stood quiet. Then he reached down, and his hands closed hard under Sarah's arms.

With a grunt of effort, he hauled her up and deposited her astride in front of him, tightly wedging her between the pommel and his chest. As he grasped the reins, his arms encircled her in a warm vise.

The gang loosed a collective bellow of fury. Only

one escape route lay open . . . back toward the cantonments. She felt tension harden Damien's muscles as he turned the horse toward the burning caravan. One end of the vehicle now leaped with flames.

Snorting, the animal trotted out of the shadows and shied from the fire. Damien held the horse still.

Alarm thumped through Sarah's veins. In the clearing, they sat like targets for the rabble.

"What are you doing?" she gasped. "We have to get out of here!"

"Just shut up and hang onto my son."

The marauders surged closer. Their jackal-like shrieks joined the snapping of the blaze. Waves of heat poured through the night air. Sarah curled herself protectively around Kit's tiny form. Scant yards away, she spied the violence in maddened eyes, the glint of firelight on butcher knives and curved swords.

The killing mob was almost upon them.

She coughed from the smoke. "For mercy's sake, Damien—"

He dug his heels into the horse's flanks. The mount took off like a shot, leaving the horde in its dust. Sarah swayed and lurched. Only Damien's enfolding arms kept her from falling out of the saddle. The *badmashes* howled and chased after them.

Boom!

An explosion rocked the night. Glancing back, she saw one end of the caravan disintegrate into flaming tinder. Men lay strewn like leaves after a windstorm. The survivors dived for cover.

The fog of shock in her mind cleared. The chemicals must have detonated. His photographic chemicals. He'd known and waited for the explosion.

The baby squawked and squirmed. She clung tightly to him, murmuring soothing nonsense, unaware of what she was saying. Damien slowed the horse to a trot as they traversed the crooked lanes of the bazaar. A band of excited natives mistook them in the dark for fellow rebels and let them pass.

The rhythm of riding soon lulled Kit back to sleep. Before long, a wide earthen avenue unrolled like a ribbon across the bright moonlit plain. They were outside the city, on the Grand Trunk Road, Sarah realized in hazy surprise.

She could scarcely believe that danger no longer crouched around every corner. The horrors of the night flitted through her mind. Aunt Violet. Mrs. Craven. The auburn-haired soldier. Shivina. God alone knew the fate of her uncle and Reginald.

Like a hare running from a merlin hawk, Sarah fled the hideous memories. She concentrated on the warm wind rushing across her face, the tiny parcel of life slumbering in her arms. Moonlight bleached the thorny bushes and scraggly trees, and coated the landscape with an unearthly silver beauty. The steady thudding of hooves tranquilized her. She leaned back, slumping into a heated cradle that felt irresistibly comfortable despite its hardness—

Starch firmed her spine. The cobwebs of exhaustion dropped away. Unhappy circumstance might have thrown her against Damien Coleridge, but she must maintain a suitable inch of distance.

"Don't play Miss Priss." His breath tickled her ear. "Go ahead and rest against me."

"No, thank you. I'd sooner cozy up with a cobra."

His shoulders brushed her in a shrug. "Please yourself, then."

Instead of relaxing her, his words jolted her with mortification. She'd never before sat so intimately close to any man. She could feel the rigidity of his arm muscles as he held the reins. His alien scent of sweat and cigars surrounded her. For the first time, she realized her unladylike dishabille.

Riding astride exposed her legs from the knees down. Her thighs were pressed to his. Her uncorseted breasts bobbled with each hoofbeat. Her bottom was braced firmly against his . . . his . . .

Embarrassment blistered her skin. She held herself stiffly upright and angled a glance back at him, catching a glimpse of his square-cut jaw and the austere outline of his face. He gazed over her head, his expression dispassionate, as if he'd already forgotten the inhumanity and destruction, even the horrible death of his wife.

"Why did you come to the caravan tonight?" he said suddenly. "To assuage your conscience after snubbing Shivina?"

"I wanted to make sure she and Kit were safe." Sarah's voice caught. "If only I'd gotten there a few moments earlier."

Damien said nothing. She wondered if he, too, felt the empty despair, the painful guilt. She pursed her lips and went on. "What were *you* doing, setting off that explosion? You nearly killed us."

"But I saved your hide instead."

His sarcasm irked her. "You knew the caravan would detonate."

"Yes."

"You shouldn't have kept volatile substances in your home. Your wife and son might have been killed by a dropped lantern."

"Hardly. Ether and alcohol are safe with proper ventilation. Vapor has to collect in an enclosed space before it'll blow. I opened the jugs and shut the windows and door."

"And what if you'd misjudged?"

"Would you rather I'd ridden straight through the mob? That would have meant certain death."

"We could have gone toward the cantonments."

Damien snorted in disgust. "That's where I'd come from. The damned place was crawling with mutineers. They would have spotted our English faces by the light of the fires. We wouldn't have survived twenty yards."

His logic robbed her of a reply. She seethed in silence for a moment. "May I ask where we're going?"

"To stay with the headman of a village—a friend of mine."

"A friend?"

"Yes, Miss Faulkner. Believe it or not, I do have a few friends."

His deep tone of irony grated on her nerves. It was no use trying to converse with such an uncivil man. As soon as possible, she would part company with him.

She gazed down at Kit. His baby features were as smooth and serene as an oasis in the Punjab desert. The knot inside her chest loosened, releasing a flow of tenderness and love.

She could never leave this little boy to the uncertain care of his father.

No doubt Damien would be thrilled at the discharge of paternal responsibility. Granted, he seemed protective of Kit, but hauling an unweaned baby on a vagabond's jaunt across India was a different matter. She would give Kit a secure home and raise him as her own son. She'd promised Shivina.

Of course, first she must persuade Reginald . . .

Her heart lurched. Closing her fingers around the locket at her throat, she breathed a deep-felt prayer for his safety. Surely with the dawn of a new day, the madness of mutiny would end. Soon she could return to Meerut and find her fiancé and Uncle John. They would bury their dead, mourn their losses, rebuild their lives. She would attain happiness as Kit's mother and Reginald's wife.

Soon all would be well again.

Her weary mind embraced the tidy solution. Her arms ached from holding the infant. She removed her *chuddur* and fashioned a sling to hold him at her waist. Then her gaze drifted over the boundless plains, over the silvery clumps of scrub and the groves of mango and tamarisk trees silhouetted against the moonlit sky. The peaceful scene held horror at bay.

Soon.

The rocking motion of the horse soothed her exhausted body. An overwhelming fatigue weighted her eyelids. The warm pressure of Damien's chest against her back suddenly seemed more appealing than appalling.

Soon.

She awoke to a piteous wail.

For an instant Sarah puzzled over why the bed swayed so, why her pillow felt so hard, why a baby was squalling. The events of the night gushed back. The mutiny. Shivina's death. The harrowing escape on horseback with Damien. Kit squirmed in his sling at her waist.

Sarah opened her eyes. She drooped against Damien in a shockingly intimate fashion. Her arm was tucked into his abdomen, her elbow riding the ridge of his hip. Her cheek was pressed to his ribs. Against the open neck of his tunic, her lips brushed the coarsely tickling hairs on his chest.

Flustered, she jerked upright.

"Easy," Damien muttered. "You'll spook the horse."

"If the baby hasn't done so," she snapped, "then I doubt I will."

Night lay thick around them. The moon had set, and only the dim sheen of starlight spangled the barren landscape.

She jiggled Kit, but he kept crying. He angled his face toward her breast and rooted against the silk of her sari. Biting her lip, she tipped a glance back at Damien. His features were indistinct in the gloom.

"He's hungry," she said, raising her voice above the din.

"That's apparent."

"What should I do?'

"Hell if I know. See if you can calm him."

Annoyed by Damien's nonchalance, she gave the baby the tip of her little finger. He sucked lustily for a few moments, then resumed squalling.

"Can we get milk where we're going?" she asked.

"I hope so."

"How much farther is it?"

"It's hard to tell in the dark. You'll have to hold him off."

She tried her fingertip again. The infant accepted the pacifier for only an instant before bawling louder. She hummed a lullaby, but to no avail. His distress jangled her nerves.

She said over her shoulder, "I don't think he wants to wait."

"He'll have to."

"He's got to have milk, Damien."

"Well, I don't happen to have any. Do you?"

His gibe snapped the frayed strand of her temper. "Your son could starve to death. Don't you even care? But of course not. You'd probably just as soon be rid of him."

The instant the words were out, she was shocked at herself. It was a vile sentiment to voice, even to a scoundrel. Damien Coleridge inspired the worst in her.

"Thanks for the lecture, Miss Faulkner. But it's you I'd as soon be rid of."

She clenched her teeth. Though she deserved

the rebuke, she wanted to lash back at him, to say she despised being close to him, too. But she was stuck for this miserable night in the circle of his arms.

Bowing her head, she focused on calming Kit. She took him out of the sling and rocked him back and forth in her arms. At last he managed to get his fist to his mouth. His indignant wail turned to loud smacking interspersed with an occasional whimper. Finally he lapsed into a restless sleep.

Poor mite, Sarah thought. Already he suffered from the loss of his mother. He'd never know Shivina. She vowed to tell him about his mother when he was old enough to understand.

Helplessness hammered at Sarah. If she couldn't get milk, he really *would* die.

Awake and tense, she peered into the murk for a sign of life. Her body ached from holding the baby and from the constant jostling of the horse. Her mouth tasted of dust. After a time, a pearly luminescence tinged their surroundings. Blinking to clear the grit from her eyes, she realized the sky was beginning to brighten to the right. They must be heading north.

The flat alluvial plain stretched in every direction, its surface broken by rocky hillocks. A thin fog snaked over garden plots lying fallow for the monsoon rains and the summer planting. Hope shot through her. They must be nearing a settlement. She wanted to ask Damien when they'd left the main road, but she was reluctant to risk awakening the baby.

Sounds wafted through the mist. A cock crowing. The singsong melody of voices. The bleating of goats.

Through the ghostly grayness a cluster of huts loomed into view. The hamlet sat beside a stream, likely a tributary of the Ganges, Sarah thought. In the early dawn, silver-bangled women fetched water, their clay pots balanced on their heads.

Others pummeled their wash on flat stones along the bank. Men in loose pajamalike clothing sat mending plows and harrows.

On the crooked path that divided the village, they passed an oxen cart creaking under a load of sugarcane. The boy perched atop the mound stared and then grinned, waving his long switch.

"*Burra* sahib!" He twisted around to gaze after them. "But where is your picture-box?"

"I'll bring it another time," Damien said.

As the cart and boy trundled out of earshot, Sarah couldn't resist murmuring, "Great master?"

"Feel free to address me so, if you like."

"If ever you're my master, I will." Her sarcastic tone implied the impossibility of such a circumstance.

A sacred cow, chewing its cud, lifted its head to fix them with a bovine stare. Chickens ran clucking across the dusty lane. Half-naked children stopped playing to study the newcomers, and the women who squatted upon doorsteps hastily covered their heads at the sight of a man and a strange woman.

A trio of barking dogs circled the horse. The baby squirmed and began to wail again. Though her arms and back hurt, Sarah tried to shush the infant. Outside the largest hut, several girls of stair-step ages sat plaiting each other's hair. From inside emerged a small wiry man in baggy trousers, his head crowned by a bright orange turban. He shook a bamboo pole at the dogs; they turned tail and scattered.

Damien swung out of the saddle. Sarah waited for him to help her down, but instead, he bowed to the middle-aged man. "Salaam, Jawahir."

"Your honor, it is I who salaam," Jawahir said in Hindi. Jabbing his pole into the dust, he bent low; then he looked Damien up and down. "What is this mark of blood upon your clothing? I pray you are not hurt.''

''I'm fine. I seek shelter for me and my son.''

''Your firstborn is a son, then. I was burdened with seven daughters before Madakka bore my heir.''

Jawahir shuffled closer and flashed a gamin grin at Sarah. She tugged at the bedraggled sari in an embarrassed attempt to cover her bare calves. But he was already squinting at the infant.

''Ahhh,'' he said in satisfaction, swinging back to Damien. ''The boy has a hearty cry for one so small. He bears the look of Shivina.'' The headman's brown-toothed smile vanished. ''But where is the boy's mother?''

''Dead,'' Damien said. His eyes were black and distant. ''She was killed during the fighting last night in Meerut.''

Jawahir went perfectly still. Then he passed a gnarled hand over his face. ''So. She moves on in the wheel of life. You must tell me how it happened.''

''It is a long story—''

''Excuse me, Damien,'' Sarah broke in loudly. ''I trust you haven't forgotten that your son needs to eat.''

His gaze whipped to her, then to the whimpering baby. To the headman, he said, ''May I ask your assistance in this matter?''

''Of course,'' said Jawahir. ''For you, *burra* sahib, I would give milk from my own wife.''

Hurrying to the house, he shooed away the girls and clapped his hands. Two women appeared in the doorway, one with a leathery face and beaky nose, the other smooth-skinned and fine-boned, her nubile form clad in a blue cotton sari. He motioned to the younger one. Her eyes lowered, she followed him to the horse.

''This is Madakka, my second wife,'' he said. ''She will share my son's milk with your son.''

Sarah gratefully handed down the infant to Madakka, who gave her a timid smile before scurrying inside.

"Lakshmi," the headman said to the matron standing on the doorstep, "take the woman of my friend inside."

Mortification stung Sarah. "I'm not his—"

"Run along, Sarah," Damien cut in. Turning to Jawahir, he said, "Now, my friend, I shall tell you of Meerut."

The men sank onto their heels, Indian fashion, and launched into a discussion of the mutiny. Exhausted and furious, Sarah dismounted. Her legs wobbled, and she leaned against the lathered horse to keep from falling. Her head throbbed from lack of sleep. Her whole body hurt, from the bruises caused by her tussle with the fakir to the sore muscles inflicted by a night in the saddle.

Resentment invigorated her. How dared Damien pass her off as his woman. How dared he dismiss her in his rude, arrogant way.

The tantalizing aroma of curry and rice wafted from the hut. Her stomach grumbled. Lakshmi waited, a patient Hindu wife, ready to offer food and drink, perhaps a comfortable place to rest. The prospect suddenly lured Sarah from the urge to confront Damien.

Walking toward the hut, she aimed one last glare at his broad back. Why bother arguing anyway?

She'd be rid of the rogue soon enough.

Chapter 8

S he didn't know it yet, but she was going with him.

Damien stood beside the charpoy and studied Sarah's slumbering form through the shadows of dusk. She lay curled on her side, one arm flung over her head, the other crooked around Kit. A borrowed sari in gold-banded olive silk wrapped her slim figure. The Indian garb looked incongruous beside the honey-hued hair fanned around her pale English features. Her gentle, dreamy expression lent her an aura of soft femininity.

An unwelcome warmth disturbed the deadness inside him. He entombed the feeling in the cold reaches of his soul.

He wasn't deceived by her innocent repose. Sarah Faulkner was a snooty do-gooder, a meddlesome female. But he needed her.

Instead of awakening her, as he'd come to do, he leaned against the mud wall inside the women's sleeping room. A wisp of evening breeze penetrated the window slit, stirring the sultry air and fluttering the saris strung like colorful ghosts from a rope stretched across the ceiling.

Sarah Faulkner baffled him. She had the manners of a shallow Englishwoman, concerned only with selfish vanities and sham righteousness. Yet she had risked her life in an attempt to rescue Kit and Shivina.

Shivina.

Shame and self-loathing clamped around his throat like a suffocating shackle. Damien tilted his head back against the cool wall. His breathing rasped through the quiet room. Once again he'd failed someone close to him.

Memory crucified him. He saw poor Shivina hacked to death. He smelled the copper scent of her blood. He felt her limp body, still warm and soft. Then came the unspeakable horror of watching the flames devour her like the maw of a nightmarish monster . . .

His fingers dug into the familiar mass of scar tissue, smooth and thick. The horny claws of a devil.

A devil with an angel for a son.

He looked down at the sleeping infant, and his savage emotions melted into unbearable tenderness. Wrapped in a thin cloth, Kit lay nestled against the pillow of Sarah's breasts. Even in the semidarkness, he was the picture of innocence. Wisps of black hair haloed his sweet face. Dark lashes set off his pure ivory-brown skin. His tiny fists were propped against plump baby cheeks.

He looked so fragile . . . so vulnerable . . . so dependent.

Sweat drenched Damien's tunic. Groping in the pocket of his jacket, he located the stub of a cigar and a match. God help him, he was unfit to be a parent. He didn't know the first damn thing about babies. He'd ruin his son's life.

That was why he needed Sarah Faulkner so badly.

He struck the match against the wall. His hands shaking, he carried the tiny flame to the cigar. A lungful of smoke calmed him. Odd, how she could appear so girlishly sweet in slumber when, awake, she irritated him like a heat rash that could drive a man insane. But she had one redeeming grace. She loved his son.

He watched the speck of fire burn nearly to his fingertips before crushing the match beneath his heel. Sarah would give Kit the proper care. She'd see to his feeding and comforting.

She'd make sure he didn't die.

Bending, Damien shook her shoulder. "Sarah. Wake up."

The voice reached Sarah down a long dark tunnel. Heaviness weighted her lashes. Her mind resisted leaving the warm sea of unremembered dreams.

"Sarah. I must speak to you. It's about Kit."

She opened her eyes. Damien's swarthy face loomed above her, so close she might reach up and touch the bristly unshaven shadow along his jaw. She started to lift her hand. In the same instant she came fully awake. Other than the baby asleep beside her, she and Damien were alone.

Alarm swept over her. She sat up. "The fakir—?"

"—is dead." Damien peered curiously at her. "You must have been dreaming."

Panic ebbed and she scooted away, careful not to awaken the baby. She scrubbed the sleep from her eyes, adjusted the wrinkled sari, and began repinning her hair. Surreptitiously she studied Damien. He'd exchanged his bloody clothes for an ill-fitting white tunic that strained across the breadth of his shoulders, and a short dhoti that revealed muscular calves.

"I need to talk to you about Kit, too," she said.

"We're leaving in the morning," Damien stated. "You're coming with us."

The news slapped her like a dash of ice water. She stopped pinning her hair and stared. "To where?"

"To safety in the hills. You'll watch over Kit."

"I'll gladly care for him. But I can't go to Simla

yet. As soon as the mutiny is over, I'll take him
with me back to Meerut—"

"No." Damien paused to draw on his cigar.
The tip glowed orange in the dimness. "It's too
damned dangerous. The Ganges plain is a powder keg of military stations ready to explode."

She wrinkled her nose at both the profanity and
the odor of his cigar. "You speak as if the entire
country is in revolt. You can't know for certain
that the violence will spread."

"A sepoy passed through the village while you
were asleep. He brought word that the rebels have
marched to Delhi. The city's already fallen."

"That's impossible!" But Sarah remembered
the frenzied faces of the mutineers, their insatia-
ble fury against the English for the unforgivable
violations of religious creed. A dismal shock reverberated inside her. She must have been
dreaming to think she could return home today.

"There's bound to be more bloodshed,"
Damien said. "And whatever you think to the
contrary, I won't put you or my son in danger."

The memory of her vindictive words came
hurtling back. She met his hard gaze. "I know
you won't," she murmured, rising to her feet and
clasping her hands. "Please forgive me for what
I said earlier. I . . . was overwrought."

He accepted the apology with a nod. "We'd
both been through hell."

He stared at the neat rolls of bedding along the
far wall. She wondered if he was recalling Shivina. How much grieving did he permit inside his
stoic soul? Sarah didn't know the answer; on the
matter of thoughts and emotions, he was as com-
municative as the mud-brick wall he lounged
against.

She looked down at Kit's tiny features and
knew with a heavy heart that she could not carry
him back into peril. "I'm sorry," she told Da-

mien, ''I can't go with you. Reginald will worry about me.''

Damien closed his lips in a taut line. With a peculiar intensity, his gaze bored into her. Abruptly he swung around and peered out the window. ''No, he won't worry. He's dead.''

The softly spoken statement slammed into her heart. She couldn't breathe, couldn't move, couldn't do anything but stand trapped in a void of shock. In sluggish motion her legs wilted, and she sank onto a low wooden chest.

''You're lying,'' she accused in a hoarse whisper. ''You can't know that. How can even you be so cruel?''

''It's the truth, Sarah. I saw Reginald fall myself, cut down by a *badmash* in the cantonments last night.''

He turned to look at her, and his somber gaze persuaded her of his candor. Bowing her head, she groped for her locket and held hard to the flesh-warmed gold. She recalled the night in the garden when Reginald had given it to her. He'd been so pleased at her acceptance of his proposal, so impatient to marry her, so . . . *alive.* Now her handsome, debonair fiancé was gone forever, the promising doctor who would have given her the family she craved.

Blinking back tears, she murmured, ''Tell me how it happened.''

''He tried to stop the mutineers from taking the magazine.'' Damien paused. ''Perhaps it's little consolation, but he died a hero.''

''You might have told me earlier.''

''There didn't seem a good moment. As you said, you were already overwrought.''

She swallowed past the thickness in her throat. Loneliness draped her like a heavy woolen blanket. She had lost everything, everyone, the last of her blood kin, even the future.

''My aunt was killed, too, did I tell you?''

"No . . . I'm sorry."

His regret sounded so genuine, fresh tears bathed her eyes. Years folded back, unveiling memories of a time when both her parents had been alive, when their London home had rung with laughter. Among all the holidays and special occasions, one episode shone with brilliant clarity.

"Do you know," she mused aloud, gazing down at her clasped hands, "when I was a little girl, Aunt Violet would come visit us from time to time. She always brought me sugarplums. Once I ate the entire tin at one sitting and got frightfully ill. She shooed away Mama and Papa, and sat with me the entire night. I still remember waking up in the morning and seeing her squashed into the nursery chair beside the bed, sound asleep and snoring, her curls gone limp and her ribbons sagging. Even though I was only five years old, I knew then how very much she loved me."

With a wistful sigh, Sarah brought her eyes up to Damien. Shoulders hunched, he met her gaze for only a moment before looking away. He tapped his foot and fiddled with his cigar.

"I didn't mean to bore you," she said. "Aunt Violet must have seemed shallow to you, but believe me, she was a good woman. Surely you had an aunt or grandmother like her."

"No." He ground the cigar stub beneath the heel of his sandal. "No one."

"Oh." Too late, she recalled Shivina's words: *His childhood was most unpleasant.* Curiosity burned in Sarah, but she suppressed the urge to question him. His past was his own affair. And she had things to hide, too. "At any rate, I owe it to my aunt's memory to return to Meerut. Uncle John will need me."

"He'll have his hands full subduing the riots.

He doesn't need a female to worry about. If he isn't dead already.''

The gruesome possibility made her shiver. ''I must believe he's alive. I *must*.''

''You'd be a damned fool to walk back into a bloodbath. You're safer staying with me.''

She sat up straight on the wooden chest. ''With you? You must be joking.''

''I never joke,'' he said brusquely. ''I'll pay you to be my son's nursemaid. Five hundred pounds—until the mutiny dies down and I can find a permanent nanny.''

Her mouth dropped open. He couldn't be serious. ''That's a ridiculously large sum.''

''Don't you think you're worth it?''

''You live like a pauper. How do I know you can afford to pay me so much?''

''Trust me, Miss Faulkner. My parents may have disowned me, but I have resources. I'll get you a bank draft the instant this madness is over.''

Hope sparked in the void of her grief. She'd lost Reginald and the security he offered. She could buy her independence. Yet why would Damien Coleridge do her any favors?

''You detest everything English,'' she said. ''Why would you employ me when you could engage a woman from the village—a woman like Madakka?''

''Madakka can't leave her husband. I need someone reliable to care for my son. For all your other irritating qualities''—his gaze raked her from head to toe—''I know you'd never desert Kit.''

She repressed the urge to tidy her wrinkled sari again. Annoyed, she snapped, ''Perhaps you should watch him yourself.''

''All I know about babies is that you feed one end and clean the other.''

''I hardly know much more.''

He shrugged. "You're a female. You have instinct on your side."

Pig, she wanted to say. He settled onto the charpoy, the ropes beneath the flimsy straw pallet squeaking under his weight. Propping his hands behind his head, he stretched out his long legs. Sarah gazed at him in fascinated distaste. With his mussed hair and the stubble of a beard shadowing his jaw, he looked every inch the disreputable knave.

Hardly pleasant company for the long trek to the hills. And definitely an unacceptable companion for a lady.

She bit her lip and remembered her vow to Shivina. "Why not hand Kit over to me?" she said. "I'll take him to safety. Then you can go on your merry way."

"Believe this, Sarah. I'll never give up my son."

Conviction lurked in his steady gaze. She hadn't thought him capable of that. Neither had she thought herself capable of even considering an offer like his. Yet what other choice did she have?

"Well?" Damien said. " Do we have an agreement?"

Glancing down at Kit's trusting face, Sarah felt the binding tug of affection. "I'd have to send a message to Patel. He and Uncle John will be frantic."

"I'll fetch you paper and pencil in the morning. When the danger dies down, one of the village boys can deliver your note."

"All right, then. I'll go."

There. She'd committed herself to spending the coming days—perhaps even weeks—in the company of a scoundrel.

"Excellent," Damien said. "We'll leave before the first light."

He crossed his legs and adjusted his position

on the bed. He looked disgustingly comfortable. Too comfortable.

Gloom gathered in the small room, creating an uneasy aura of intimacy. Sarah folded her arms over her bosom. "You'd better go now," she said. "The women will be coming to bed soon."

"Not here they won't."

"What do you mean?"

"I needed to speak to you in private, and I didn't know how long it would take to persuade you. So I told them you and I would be spending the night together."

She reared off the wooden chest. "You told them *what*?"

"Shush, or you'll wake the baby."

"Explain yourself," she said in a harsh whisper.

Damien shrugged. "What's to explain? They think you're my woman. It's expedient to let everyone go on believing so."

"That's another thing I've been meaning to talk to you about. How dare you let Jawahir believe that you and I—"

"Calm down, Miss Priss. I don't much like this charade, either. You aren't exactly my kind of woman."

"Thank heaven for *that*."

"There's a reason behind my madness. You see, Jawahir and a few of the villagers have agreed to travel with us. To avoid being murdered by any mutineers we meet on the road, we'll dress and act like Hindus. You'll be more protected as my wife."

Disbelief jolted her. "Your *wife!* This is getting worse by the moment."

"Come now, surely you can manage. When we see other travelers, keep your face and hair veiled. We'll pose as pilgrims on our way to Hardwar, in the foothills of the Himalayas."

Hardwar, revered as the origin of the Ganges,

and one of the seven sacred sites of the Hindus. Despite her antipathy, she was intrigued by the prospect of visiting the holy city and viewing the shrines and temples there.

"And what about you?" she asked. "People will surely guess you're English."

"I'm dark enough to pass as one of the lighter-skinned people from Kashmir. I'll grow a beard to obscure my features."

"But what if someone sees through our disguises? Someone might challenge us."

"Then he'll be damned sorry."

His cold, brutal tone crawled over her skin like a deadly serpent. She leaned against the wall and rubbed her arms through the thin silk. With absolute certainty, she knew Damien would kill to save his son. With stunning shock, she realized she would do the same.

In that, at least, they shared a common bond. Perhaps through protecting the infant, she and Damien could become friends. The thought chased away the chill inside her and left a mellow warmth.

"Go back to sleep, Sarah. You'll need a good night's rest so you don't hold everyone up tomorrow."

He rolled onto his side and presented his back to her.

She glared at the ghostly white of his clothing through the shadows. Hold everyone up, would she? Just when she felt a small softening toward him, he managed to vex her again.

The urge to kick him in the shins seized her. Let him explain to the villagers why his "wife" had thrown him out.

Releasing a breath, she controlled the wild impulse. Good sense resurrected itself. Despite the day of rest, her muscles still screamed for more. She lay down beside Kit and fit his small body against hers. Conscious of Damien's deep breathing from the adjoining charpoy, she stared into the darkness. She had never before slept in the same room with a man. Lying so near to him roused a peculiar fluttering in the bottom of her stomach.

A gentleman would have offered to sleep elsewhere. But Damien himself had admitted he was no gentleman.

She closed her eyes. Her virtue was safe, though, for no one in his right mind would believe they were man and wife.

Chapter 9

"What a handsome man," said Lakshmi. "He makes you a fine husband."

Pursing her lips to hold back a retort, Sarah followed the older woman's gaze to the small group of men a short distance ahead. Sunlight flashed off the distant, snakelike Ganges River, and she shaded her eyes with her hand. Jawahir and Damien led the band of villagers along the dirt track.

White native homespun draped his hard-honed form and left his legs bare from his knees to his rope sandals. He bore a remarkable similarity to the Indians, yet his height and his arrogant carriage hinted at his blue blood. With the heavy beard darkening his jaw, he resembled a *dacoit*, one of those robbers who haunted the back roads and preyed upon lone travelers.

He *was* handsome, Sarah supposed, if one favored scoundrels.

Madakka plodded behind the two men, holding a black umbrella over her husband's head. The other women trailed them, Lakshmi and Sarah bringing up the rear. The faint *chink* of the women's silver bangles mingled with the murmur of voices.

Dust coated Sarah's clothes and gritted her eyes. Kit wiggled in the makeshift sling at her hip, and she stroked his downy hair until he settled back into his nap. Her "fine husband" hadn't even offered to carry his son.

"I did not think," Lakshmi continued in her frank but friendly way, "that the English could take a second wife. How did the *burra* sahib do so?"

"It's rather complicated," Sarah hedged. "Perhaps you should ask him to explain."

"Oh, but I could never question a man."

"I suppose that's just as well. On second thought, Damien likely wouldn't speak of the matter, anyway."

Gracefully balancing a huge basket on her veiled head, Lakshmi turned a thoughtful glance at her companion. "Ah, you mean your people did not acknowledge his marriage to a Hindu."

"Something like that."

Sarah hated having to lie. She hated misleading this guileless woman. Most of all, she hated posing as Damien's wife.

Her stomach squeezed with dull pain. Seven days ago, she'd been a young woman happily anticipating marriage to a man who promised her security. Now she posed as wife to a despotic knave who roused only resentment in her heart.

Damien annoyed her at every turn. He alternately treated her like his personal slave and acted as if she didn't exist.

Broiling beneath the midday sun, she adjusted the bundle of sleeping mats atop her head. A week of walking hadn't accustomed her to the clumsy load. Her neck and shoulders ached perpetually. Her legs quivered from constant fatigue. Her bare feet bore painful blisters. Though Lakshmi and the other women toted the heavier cooking pots and sacks of food, her own burden felt as weighty as a granite statue of Brahma.

Like the other men, Damien strolled along, unhampered by any burden, oblivious to all but his own selfish needs. Perhaps what irked Sarah the

most was the way he fell so easily into the patri-
archal role of an Indian male.

Her submissive pose was all part of the charade, she reminded herself, the charade that made
her wear the silver bride bangles and anklets of a
Hindu wife. The charade that required her to
darken her fair skin with walnut juice and to dye
her blond hair black. The charade that would help
them reach safety in the Himalayan foothills.

Luckily, so far from the main roads, they'd met
few travelers. Yet she burned to see someone who
could give news of the mutiny.

At least now she could write from firsthand experience about the harsh lot of the Hindu women.
She felt guilty at the freedom and privilege she'd
enjoyed in English society, a life she'd chafed under.

Careful of her burden, she turned to study
Lakshmi's sharp features, the beaky nose and
squinty eyes. "We're grateful to you for allowing
us to travel with you on such short notice."

"Every day you tell me so," said Lakshmi.
"Every day I tell you there is no need for thanks.
My husband merely wishes to repay the *burra* sa-
hib."

"Repay Damien for what?"

"I do not think it is my place to say."

The statement roused Sarah's curiosity. "Tell
me, please."

Lakshmi hesitated. "For his kindness in rescu-
ing Jawahir's sister, Shivina."

Sarah nearly stumbled. Her weariness faded
before the startling news. "His sister? Shivina was
Jawahir's *sister*?"

"See? I should not have told you." Lakshmi
glanced ahead and grinned, displaying horsey
teeth against shoe-leather skin. "The second wife
does not always care to hear tales told of the first
wife."

"I have no such prejudices." Making sure the

others were out of earshot, Sarah hastened to keep up with Lakshmi on the rutted track. She stepped on a sharp rock and winced in pain. "Why doesn't Jawahir grieve for his sister?"

"He did not know Shivina well. You see, he was many years older than she. In truth, we were already married when she was born. She was wed as a child and went to live with her husband's family in Delhi."

Sarah blinked. "Shivina was married before?"

"Yes. Her husband was scribe in the court of Bahadur Shah."

"The King of Delhi?"

"Yes. Raman was not a kind man, unlike my Jawahir." She cast a fond smile at the headman, who walked with a boyish spring to his step. "Raman ruled his wife with a harsh hand. He beat her when she failed to bear him a son."

Sarah was incensed. "As if it were her fault! My Aunt Violet also never bore a child, but my uncle still respected and loved her."

"Ah, but Raman was a weakling. A strutting peacock who could not make Shivina's womb quicken." A grin wrinkled Lakshmi's cheeks. "But how swiftly she bore a son for Coleridge-sahib. His seed must be potent, indeed."

Her shrewd gaze swept over Sarah, as if she were checking for more evidence of his virility. A flush hotter than the sun scorched Sarah's cheeks. Hastily she said, "What happened to Raman?"

"By Sita's will, the cholera took his life more than a year ago. He held to the old Hindu rites, and left orders that his widow should join him on the funeral pyre."

Horror iced Sarah's skin. "*Suttee* has been banned. Bahadur Shah would never allow one of his people to flout British law . . ." Her words trailed off as she remembered how swiftly Delhi had fallen. The Moghul ruler must have thrown in his lot with the rebels.

Once, she had prided herself on her awareness of the political climate. How smug I. M. Vexed had been; how insignificant her editorials seemed now. Like a vulture flapping its great black wings, ghastly memories of the mutiny shadowed her. Aunt Violet with a knife in her breast. The soldier lying spread-eagled. Shivina gasping her last breath . . .

Sarah bit her lip hard. If only she'd had the courage to speak out, at the dinner party or at the punishment parade or at a score of other occasions, perhaps she might have done her small part to ward off the bloodshed.

"The King of Delhi makes his own law," Lakshmi went on. "He knew the wish of his loyal scribe, and promised to look the other way so long as the rites were held outside the city gates."

"Yet Shivina escaped. Do you know how? Were *you* there?"

"No, I heard the story from my husband's sister. The ceremony was to be held at dawn, the day after Raman's death." With the air of a seasoned gossip, Lakshmi dropped her voice to a dramatic whisper. "At the darkest hour of the night, the court ladies dressed Shivina in her wedding sari. A group of mourners—all friends of Raman—escorted her to a secret temple far down the Jumna River. A temple dedicated to the honor of Kali."

Sarah shuddered. In her mind she heard the echo of the fakir screeching the name of the blood-goddess, the Destroyer. "Shivina must have been terrified."

"She was too faithful a wife to disobey the command of her husband and his family. As the priest chanted mantras before the rising sun, she walked to the funeral pyre and knelt beside the body of Raman." Lakshmi paused, and the eerie whistle of a pariah kite carried from high in the brassy blue sky.

"Then what happened?" Sarah prodded.

"Then the priest held a torch to the tinder. The flames began to dance and smoke began to rise." The Hindu woman lifted her brown hands to the heavens. "My husband's sister smelled the stench of Raman's burning flesh. Slowly, slowly, the fire crept toward Shivina until the flames licked at the edge of her sari."

Her heart beating fast, Sarah imagined the inferno inching closer. "What did she do?"

"She prayed for deliverance. And suddenly out of the tall reeds along the riverbank, Coleridge-sahib appeared." As if conjuring up a magician, Lakshmi waved her arms, the bracelets chiming. "He pushed aside the friends of Raman. He ran to Shivina and snatched her from the flames of death."

Sarah released a breath. "Didn't the mourners stop him?"

"Pah! What could they do to one so bold? Like a thundering god, he said that his picture-box had captured their images and he had sent the picture back to Delhi with his bearer. He swore if they did not let Shivina go with him, everyone present would be imprisoned by the British for practicing *suttee*."

"He really did that?" Sarah said in disbelief.

"Indeed so. The friends of Raman grumbled and threatened, yet in the end they had no choice but to let the *burra* sahib carry Shivina to a new life. She became an outcast, but Jawahir was grateful nonetheless."

"I see."

Sarah suspected that with the Indian love for a good story, Lakshmi had embellished the tale. Yet sympathy burrowed through her mistrust and formed a tender nest inside her heart. Absently she touched Kit's silken cheek. No wonder Damien had balked at burning Shivina. No wonder he'd stared with strange fascination at the flames.

He must have been reflecting on the sad irony of saving her from *suttee* only to relinquish her body to the blaze.

He himself knew the horror of fire. His scarred hands were proof of that.

Sarah turned her gaze to him. Among the bright oranges and blues and greens worn by the pilgrims, Damien in his simple bleached garments commanded attention. The shimmering heat enveloped him in a mirage; pure white sunlight limned him with radiance. She pictured him charging from the underbrush like Krishna swooping down from the heavens.

Now she could almost see why Shivina had been blindly devoted to him. The poor woman had been bound to him by gratitude for his swashbuckling rescue. Like a pilgrim prostrating herself before a deity, she'd worshipped at his feet.

A disagreeable notion occurred to Sarah. Perhaps he expected homage from *her*. Because he'd rescued her from a bloody mutiny.

"Look," Lakshmi said, pointing to a grove of dark green mango trees near the winding river. "Jawahir has chosen the place for our afternoon rest."

A sigh slipped from Sarah. Needles of pain pricked her legs and back. Her head ached under the weight of the sleeping mats and the endless hours of gazing into blinding sunlight.

It seemed they'd been walking forever without getting anywhere. For days the foothills had remained a hazy shadow on the northern horizon.

Reaching the cluster of trees, she eased the bundle off her head. Monkeys chattered in the branches. Sunlight dappled the dusty earth and created a cool, refreshing bower. Sarah longed to rest her tired body, but Kit awakened and began squalling for his milk. She untied him from the

sling and he ceased crying, giving her the wide-
eyed look that touched her heart.

Lakshmi unpacked the cook pots and food. Her
youngest daughter, Reena, a girl of fourteen,
hefted a brass lota atop her head and went to fetch
water from the river. Blinking the travel grit from
her eyes, Sarah changed Kit's nappy, then left
him with Madakka and scoured the area for fallen
branches to use as fuel for the cook fire.

The men lounged a short distance away. Leaning on an elbow, Damien puffed on a *bidi*, tobacco
rolled in a dried leaf. Its pungent scent drifted
through the hot air. He gestured and talked to the
men, and their laughter wafted to her.

The dry boughs poked her ribs, and a sharp
twig scored the tip of her index finger. Glowering
at Damien, she sucked on the sore spot. The in-
equity of male and female roles nagged at her. He
and the other men lay about like rajahs while the
women labored like slaves.

She lugged the unwieldy bundle of tinder to
Lakshmi, who sat on her heels, her swift hands
rolling balls of millet and honey.

"I've been thinking about our talk this morning," Sarah said. "Would *you* ever burn yourself
for a man?"

"I will not have to. My husband abides by the
laws of the *sahib-log*."

"But if he didn't?"

With a fatalistic shrug, Lakshmi said, "If he
wished it of me, who am I to argue? It is a woman's sacred duty to obey her husband."

Sarah knelt and absently formed a ball of sticky
honey and kernels of grain. "And what of his
duty to honor you?"

"He honors me by keeping me in his house, as
his first wife."

"But he makes you share him with another
woman. What would he say if you wanted a second husband?"

Lakshmi laughed. "Pah! Whoever heard of a woman with two husbands? She would be forever with child."

"The number of husbands or wives isn't the point," Sarah persisted. "We women deserve respect, too. Why should we bow to men? Why should we work so much harder than they? Why must we speak to them only when spoken to? Why should we always walk in their dust?"

"Because that is the lot of women." Lakshmi clucked her tongue. "You English have strange notions."

Sarah blew out an exasperated breath. If only she could convince Lakshmi of her own worth. If only she could improve the life of the village women. But I. M. Vexed had lost the means to air her views on equality. Her fingers itched for pen and paper.

"Hsst." The Hindu woman drew her blue veil over her lower face. She dropped her gaze in the posture of a modest wife.

Sarah looked up to find Damien standing behind her. Days under the merciless rays of the sun had darkened his skin to a mahogany hue. The dashing wrap of his turban dramatized his stark male features, and the black, stubbly beard made him seem harsher, more wickedly attractive.

The devil himself couldn't have looked more unsavory.

"I'd like to wash," he said. "Fetch me water."

The brusque order nettled Sarah. Yet a slight softening endured within her. Just as she had confronted the fakir, Damien, too, had rescued Shivina from a mob. Perhaps a trace of integrity lurked within his unprincipled heart.

He turned to go. Sarah quickly said, "Walk with me down to the river."

His dark eyes narrowed. "Why?"

"Come, and you'll find out. Excuse us, Lakshmi."

Rising, Sarah wiped her sticky hands and picked up a clay pitcher. As she started down the path through the jungle of plumed grass, she heard the tramp of his feet behind her. She was conscious suddenly of the flimsiness of her garments, the sway of her hips and breasts. The sari gave her a sinful sensation of freedom, a sensation more deliciously lovely than the metal cage of a crinoline and the stiff whalebones of a corset. Glancing down at herself, at the nut-stained arms with the silver bangles, at the bare toes peeking from beneath the olive silk, Sarah marveled at her native appearance. Unfettered by the constraints of English society, she felt younger, almost giddy.

She wondered what Damien thought of her metamorphosis. He probably hadn't even noticed. *You aren't exactly my kind of woman.* Sourness sapped her frivolous feeling.

The high grass ended near the river. With the summer rains due within a month, the green-tinged water ran low through a labyrinth of channels. A massive banyan tree reached skyward, its bare roots anchored in the sand. The musical burble of the current over rocks blended with the screeching of monkeys and the squawking of birds.

Beyond the banyan, a small shrine caught Sarah's attention. Rounded columns supported a peaked roof. She walked to the steps and peered into the shadowy interior. To her surprise, Lakshmi's daughter Reena stood beside a simple stone sculpture.

The girl's wide brown eyes skipped to Damien and her white teeth flashed before she lowered her gaze. She sprinkled water on the stone object, then bent and tenderly pressed her lips to it. Lifting the brass lota atop her head, she pranced out of the temple and smiled demurely at Damien. He smiled back, watching her disappear into the plumed grass.

Sarah tugged the veil tighter over her black-dyed hair and fought off annoyance. If he wanted to act the lecher, let him. His proclivities were nothing to her.

She set down her jar and stepped into the shade of the temple. The cool floor soothed her sore feet. In the center of the room stood the waist-high statue. Rounded at the top, it was shaped like a thick sausage standing on end. A string of withered marigolds lay at the base, someone's now-dusty offering.

She walked to the sculpture and turned to see Damien standing in the doorway, the sunshine outlining his tall form. Moving her hand over the smooth curved top, she commented, "This is an odd piece. Do you know what it represents?"

"A *lingam*."

She frowned. "A what?"

One corner of his hard mouth quirked upward. "You speak Hindi so well, I'm surprised you've never heard the word."

His smirk annoyed her. "Just tell me what it means."

"A *lingam* is the male sex organ."

Her cheeks burned. She snatched her hand back. "You're only saying that to irk me."

He chuckled darkly. "Why would I bother? It really is a *lingam*. In honor of Shiva."

"Why Shiva?"

Damien leaned against a column. "I take it you haven't heard the story."

His knowing brown eyes bored into her. Aware of the beating of her heart, she told herself to walk away. Curiosity got the better of her. "What story?"

"Brahma and the other gods caught Shiva and his wife making love. Shiva was so engrossed in his pleasure, he kept on with it. When his passion was spent, he died of shame. But before he expired, he ordered mankind to worship him in the form of his finest part, his *lingam*.'' Damien waved a hand to encompass the small chamber. ''So the Hindus erected shrines like this all over India.''

Sarah wet her dry lips. The epitome of idle masculinity, he lounged against the stone pillar. Her gaze skittered away from him, then irresistibly crept back. ''Why did Reena sprinkle water on the . . .'' She couldn't bring herself to say the word.

That odd half-grin again touched Damien's mouth. He looked her up and down in a way that made her insides contract in a peculiarly pleasant sensation. ''It's a rite of worship,'' he said. ''To cool the organ's hot passion.''

''Oh.''

Flushed, she could no longer meet his penetrating gaze. She made a wide circle around him and picked up her pitcher. Desperate to collect her composure, she paused on the step and focused on the wide expanse of the Ganges.

Brilliant shafts of sunlight picked out sandbanks in the shallow water. Far downstream, a pair of fishermen drowsed in their boat. On the opposite shore a brown-skinned boy tramped behind a bullock.

She tensed as Damien walked up behind her. He stopped so close she fancied she could feel the warmth of his body.

Birds twittered into the silence and a monkey chattered. Her pulse fluttered. ''*Ganga Ma*,'' she murmured to break the awkwardness. ''The Hindus revere Mother Ganges as the most sacred river on earth.''

''You're blushing, Miss Priss,'' he said in a low-pitched voice threaded with humor. ''And you're changing the subject. Does it disturb you to think of women worshipping a man's—''

''Stop it!'' Willing away the hotness in her

cheeks, she swung to face him, the pitcher clenched like a shield to her breasts. "I didn't ask you here to listen to your lewd remarks."

"Then why did you ask me?"

She groped among her scattered thoughts. "Because I just found out Shivina was Jawahir's sister."

"I see you've been gossiping." He propped his hand against a pillar; sunlight whitened his scars. "I never did know two women who could get together without spreading rumors and causing havoc."

Determined to be civil, Sarah forced a smile. "Lakshmi told me about the *suttee* incident. It's unnatural to keep such a secret. She said you faced down a mob to save Shivina."

"I faced down a sorry collection of white-faced weaklings. A crusader like you could have done as well."

"Nevertheless, threatening them with that photograph was most effective."

"The photo was a bluff."

Nonplussed, she tilted her head. "It was?"

"Yes. I hadn't even silvered the plate yet."

"Damien, they might have killed you—"

"Don't make a damned romantic hero out of me."

Sunshine gleamed on the flecks of gold in his dark brown eyes. The scruffy black beard shadowed the bold angles of his jaw and cheeks. "I doubt anyone would mistake *you* for a romantic hero," she retorted. "Still, what you did was noble."

"I saw the chance to acquire a mistress. A mistress who was so indebted to me for saving her life that she'd serve my every lusty wish. Isn't that what you're waiting to hear?"

Disgust trampled Sarah's good intentions. "That's precisely the sort of crude behavior one would expect of you."

"You wanted the truth." He straightened.
"Now, if you're through with your damned complaining, I'm heading back to camp."

She held out the pitcher to him. "Then fetch your own water, *burra* sahib. Your slave just quit."

His expression infuriatingly cool, he regarded her. "You're no slave. I pay you a huge salary."

"I've yet to see a penny of my much-lauded salary. How do I know you'll keep your word?"

"You don't. And in case you've forgotten," he said with elaborate patience, "there's a reason behind our masquerade."

"Hah! You're using that as an excuse to treat me like your personal drudge."

"Shush," he said, casting a quick glance around. "God help us if the wrong person were to overhear you. You're supposed to behave like a Hindu woman."

"I'll lower my voice," Sarah murmured, "but don't expect me to meekly accept my role. We should be setting a good example for the others. We could show them how a husband and wife can work together. We might better the lives of the Hindu women."

"So you've found a new crusade. I might have known you couldn't leave well enough alone."

"The way these women work isn't 'well enough.' I'm merely trying to make the world more equitable to all people."

"Well, my philosophy is to respect the local customs. Now quit complaining and fetch me the damned water."

His constant profanities and arrogant attitude set her teeth on edge. "You might at least make an effort to be civil. Didn't your mother teach you to say please and thank you?"

He stood perfectly still, feet planted apart, hands on his hips. A puff of hot wind fluttered the tail of his turban. His dark features might have been carved from teak. Yet she had the impression of a tempest raging inside him.

"Is it help you want?" he said. "All right, then." He lunged at her and grabbed the jar. Stomping over the sand to the river, he bent and sloshed the pitcher into the muddy water. Then he returned and shoved the dripping container back into her arms. "Say thank you, Miss Priss."

The heavy vessel dampened the front of her sari, but Sarah clutched it as tightly as her temper. "Now you keep *your* voice down. I'm asking you for a little cooperation, that's all. Together we might ease the harsh lives of Lakshmi and Madakka and the other women."

"We? Just what the hell do you expect me to do?"

"Educate the men. Help me in front of them. Watch Kit while I collect firewood. Show the men that women aren't beasts of burden and inferior beings."

"No, thanks. I'll leave the reforming to do-gooders like you." His insulting gaze swept her, lingering for a moment on her bosom. "Hell, maybe some women *are* inferior."

He turned toward the camp. A great surge of rage broke inside her, drowning her judgment in a hot red mist.

"Mr. Coleridge."

He swung back. "Miss Faulkner?"

"You've forgotten your bath."

She hurled the contents of the pitcher at him. He leaped back, but water slapped him in the face and drenched his tunic and dhoti.

Shocked at her lapse of restraint, Sarah stood immobile. The shrill cawing of crows sounded over the quiet melody of the river. The soaked cotton adhered to his torso, outlining every sleek curve and hard muscle. The sight abruptly struck her as comical. A bubble of mirth rose within her.

Clasping the clay container, she swallowed hard, but a burst of merriment pushed past her lips.

"Damn you," he sputtered, shaking the sodden sleeves of his tunic. "What the hell are you laughing at?"

"You look ridiculous," she said between giggles. "Like a wet heron flapping its wings."

He glowered for a moment. Then his bad-tempered expression eased into something halfway between a scowl and a smile. He snatched up a piece of driftwood.

"You're bloody lucky I'm not a true Hindu husband, else I'd take this rod to your prim little arse."

Stick in hand, he strolled closer. Was that a twinkle in his eyes or a trick of the sunlight?

Her heart tripping, she left the temple step and backed away, the sand hot beneath her feet. "You can't be angry over that trifling amount of water."

"Oh?" He slapped the stick against the flat of his scarred palm. "If I were you, I wouldn't be quite so certain."

Her feet splashed into the warmth of the river. She barely noticed the sting of her blisters. Damien Coleridge had no sense of humor.

Or did he?

Daringly she taunted, "Ganges water is supposed to wash away sin. Are you feeling the least bit redeemed?"

"No."

"Then perhaps you should have been completely submerged."

"Go ahead and try," he said. "By God, I'll pull you in with me."

"You'll have to catch me first."

Holding the empty pitcher, she spun around and ran. Hot wind rushed past her cheeks. The sari whipped against her legs, the wet hem sticking to her skin. His footsteps pounded behind her. At some deep level, she was shocked at her rash behavior, but an inexplicable caprice drove her on.

Ripples of heat undulated over the slim strip of sand and the wide expanse of water. A vulture sailed overhead, black wings outstretched. A small flock of cranes scattered before her on the sand. Their squawking covered the tinkling of the tiny silver bells on her anklets.

Nearing a bend in the river, she veered to avoid a fallen tree trunk. A huge turtle rose to the surface of the water and blinked sleepily. A fin flashed as a *mahseer* glided through the river. Holding her veil in place, Sarah risked a glance backward.

Damien grasped her arm and brought her to a skidding halt. His rough-hewn features loomed over her. His warm palm cupped the softness of her breast through the thin sari. Gasping, she felt her belly twist with the same stunning urge she'd felt that night in the garden. The urge to feel him touch her naked skin, to press her body to his, to drown in the warmth of his lips . . .

But his hand dropped away. His hard brown eyes focused beyond her.

She turned to look.

Along the embankment, half hidden by the waving grass, two dark-skinned men squatted beside something lying in the sand. The blood-red coats and filthy white trousers marked them as sepoys, though they wore turbans instead of the regulation white caps.

The fatter man shifted position, and she saw the object of his interest.

A lightning bolt of horror struck her heart.

Chapter 10

Damien yanked the veil down over Sarah's face. In the same instant both sepoys spun around.

With the clarity of a photograph, the scene imprinted on his mind. One sepoy was rapier-thin, with a flattened nose and a low brow. A milky cataract colored one of his eyes, giving him the leering aspect of a Cyclops. The second man had the hulking build and broad face of a bullock. He gripped a bloodied knife.

Behind them, the Englishman lay spread-eagled on the sand. Flies swarmed around his bulging eyes and bushy brown side-whiskers. The uncongealed blood drenching his throat and neckcloth proved he'd been dead for mere minutes.

Sweat iced Damien's palms. The sun scorched his back. A family of monkeys squabbled in a nearby clump of trees. He inhaled Sarah's faint feminine fragrance, felt the rigidity in her slim body as she recoiled against his chest. For all her sharp claws, she didn't stand a chance against these two blood-crazed murderers.

Hellfire and damnation. If they'd spotted her blue eyes and English features, they'd come after her. Fierce protectiveness assailed him. He'd kill the bastards.

But the hunk of driftwood in his hand felt all too fragile.

Maybe he could bluff his way out. He stepped in front of her. "What is the trouble here?" he asked. "What has happened to this *feringhi*?"

"Who are you to ask questions?" retorted the smaller sepoy. His Cyclops eye twitching, he raised his fist. "Be still, stranger, before Keppu plies his blade on you, too."

The little bugger's scared, Damien thought. A frightened man might attack without the slightest provocation. He wasn't about to turn his back on them.

"Since when does Keppu take vengeance upon poor pilgrims?" Damien felt Sarah peering over his shoulder and prayed she'd keep silent. "I am Dharam. My wife and I are traveling with friends to worship at the shrines of Hardwar."

"Friends? Where are these people?"

"That way." Damien pointed the stick toward the mango grove. "They are resting from our long morning walk. Perhaps I should hail them." He opened his mouth as if to call out.

"No, no!" Cyclops waved hastily. "There is no need to summon anyone. We believe you."

"You, Lalji, would trust a Mohammedan," growled the big man called Keppu. "This one"— he pointed his gory dagger at Damien—"has an English look about him."

Steeling his nerves, Damien scowled back. "English, bah! Praise be to Shiva that my father is not alive to hear you insult our honored name. I was born in the vale of Kashmir."

He clenched the driftwood and took a step forward. Behind him, he heard Sarah's sharp intake of breath. Keppu made a rumble of rage and brandished his crimson dagger.

"Hush, both of you," Lalji chided. "Brothers need not spill each other's blood." Then he looked at Damien and a grin parted his lips, revealing teeth stained red from chewing betel nut. "So you, too, hate the *feringhis*."

Damien's tension eased a fraction. Thank God, they must not have overheard the argument he'd had with Sarah. He might yet talk his way out of this unholy muddle. If only he could count on Sarah to keep her mouth shut.

"I spit on the *feringhis*," he said. "But what is the trouble here?" He strolled closer and stared down at the Englishman's pasty features, the bloodied mess of his throat. Tasting bile, Damien forced a kindred expression toward the rebels. "Did this one threaten you?"

"No, the gods brought him here to meet his rightful fate," Lalji bragged. "We must all join together in the mutiny."

"Mutiny?"

"Have you not heard?"

"No. We pilgrims have traveled the back roads."

The sepoy thrust out his puny chest. Sweat and food droppings spotted his red coat. "Our people have arisen at last against the *sahib-log*. We will rid our land of every last foreign devil."

I'd like to rid India of you, Damien thought. Damn, how widespread had the revolt become? "Ah, we make a brave stand. But the *feringhis* have many weapons. They will slay us all."

Lalji spat on the sand. "Great gods! A big man like you cannot be a coward."

"Not a coward, but a cautious man."

"The time has come to throw caution aside. Our people are butchering the English snakes in every corner of India. Only one week ago, the mutiny began in Delhi and Meerut, and all the English there are dead already."

Sarah gasped. "You cannot mean—"

"Silence," Damien snapped, whipping toward her. At least she had remembered to use Hindi.

"When will you learn a wife speaks only when spoken to? Now sit."

Sarah stood unyielding. Her nut-stained fingers gripped the clay pitcher. Only the shadow of her features showed through the olive-hued veil, but undoubtedly she was steaming with outrage.

Damn, if her outspokenness made her forget the danger, she'd give away their identities. They both could die. His heartbeat stumbled over a queer, unfamiliar ache. Kit might grow up without ever knowing his father.

Damien knew what she'd say to that: *He'd be better off without you.* Maybe she was right.

The idea irritated the very devil out of him. He didn't know why; long ago, he'd learned to please only himself rather than solicit the approval of others, least of all a prissy do-gooder.

Beyond them, the river whispered over sand and rock. Wind soughed through the tall plumed grass. He felt the eyes of the sepoys burning into his back.

Slowly she sank to her heels. Yet the sulky set of her shoulders hinted that her obedience was temporary.

He released a breath. Swinging back toward the men, he said, "I am ashamed to have strangers witness Shivina's disobedience." He hated like hell giving her the name of a sweet-tempered woman.

"No wonder you were chasing her with a stick," observed Lalji. "Is that why your clothing is wet? Did the little woman push you into the river?" He slapped his thigh and sniggered as if he'd made a great joke.

Damien gritted his teeth against a defensive retort. "I fell. We are newly wed, and she thought to escape her duties."

Keppu crouched to wipe his bloody dagger, leaving brownish-red streaks on the sand. "You must be a poor master. Or an inept lover. My woman would never dare to run from me."

"Go ahead and flog her," said Lalji, eyeing the driftwood. "We will watch you reclaim your honor."

His gleeful expression disgusted Damien. Sarah's sullen posture tempted him. "I think not. She'll obey from now on. Won't you, Shivina?"

Sarah nodded, the veil fluttering. He was struck by her aura of gentle docility, by her meek womanly appearance. Only he knew the creature that lay beneath that veneer of fine silk: an acid-tongued viper poised to strike.

To distract the mutineers, Damien said, "From where do you two hail?"

"My friend and I are on leave from our regiment at Kurnaul." Lalji gestured at Keppu, who sat glowering. "We will rejoin our brothers and pursue our divine mission. This worthless snake is only the first of many English we will slay." He kicked the corpse in the ribs.

Damien controlled the urge to kick him back. "Did you know the foreigner?"

"He is Hugh MacMurtry, an agent of the British Raj. For many years he has been stealing food from the mouths of our children and calling it taxes. But we will reclaim at least part of what he has stolen."

Hunkering down, the short sepoy resumed rifling the dead man's pockets. He pulled out a gold watch and then a handful of silver rupees, which he dropped into a small leather sack.

Dacoit, Damien thought contemptuously. You and Keppu will keep the money instead of returning it to the natives.

The sepoy hurled something away. The forlorn scrap landed on a damp strip of sand at the edge of the water. Damien stepped closer and saw a daguerreotype, a cheap, grainy image of the wire-whiskered man standing stiffly beside a horse-faced woman and three homely children.

Poor devil.

He curled his fingers into his scarred palms and denied a spurt of maudlin emotion. The Raj had been too stubborn and bullish to respect the natives. Hugh MacMurtry likely was another dull English sod who had believed himself sahib over the natives, who had acted lord of his humble abode, who had spent Sunday afternoons snoring on the veranda instead of conversing with his wife and children.

Just as Damien's father had hibernated in a drunken stupor . . .

In a faint rustle of silk, Sarah glided past. Damien tensed. What in hell did she mean to do now?

He was about to chastise her when she reached down. Quick as the flash of a shutter, she whisked the small plate inside her sari.

Torn between fury and fear, he glanced at the sepoys. Lalji was counting the money and Keppu sat watching, as glum as a debutante with an empty dance card. Thank God they hadn't noticed her folly.

Of all the bloody stupid things to do. Trust Sarah Faulkner to jeopardize their safety for a worthless photograph.

She knelt by the water's edge and filled her jug. With her head bowed, she was the image of a modest wife. But he could well imagine her smug expression.

Just wait until he got her alone. He had a good mind to take Lalji's advice and apply his stick to her prim little bottom.

A shadow slid over the sand, then another.

"Our friends await their meal," said Lalji, grinning up at the circling vultures. He seized the sack of money, sprang to his feet, and stepped back.

"We must go so they may gorge on stinking white flesh."

Nausea twisted in Damien. He didn't dare suggest burying the body, for the Hindus cremated the dead.

"Put him in the river," Sarah murmured.

The three men turned toward her. She knelt beside her pitcher, her hands folded in her lap and her head tipped back to the great black birds.

"Your wife has yet to learn to keep still," said Keppu.

Damn and blast, Damien thought. She really *was* determined to get both their throats cut.

"Do not listen to her," he said hastily. "She is only a witless woman who hungers for a beating."

"Put the sahib in the river," she repeated in perfect Hindi, tilting her veiled face toward the two sepoys. "Else you will displease *Ganga Ma*."

A strong breeze rippled the silk against her body, outlining the shapeliness of her breasts and hips. Lust shone in Lalji's single good eye, and he absently rubbed his crotch.

"Eh?" he said. "What do you prattle about?"

The urge to throttle the skinny sepoy swooped over Damien, an urge so strong it wiped out his anger at Sarah. His feelings of protectiveness and jealousy startled him. Hell, he was only on edge. Maybe she had a good idea, to lay MacMurtry to rest in the only humane way possible.

"My wife is impertinent, but right. She fears to displease the goddess. You," Damien added, jerking his head at Keppu, "come and help me." He tossed down the driftwood and took hold of the dead man's hands. The flesh was as cool and clammy as rubber.

The huge sepoy remained hunkered on the sand. Shaggy eyebrows lowered, he snarled like an old tiger with a toothache. "I do not take orders from strangers."

Lalji spat on the ground. "We cannot pollute Mother Ganges with this unbeliever. Only the faithful may take their final rest in her sacred waters."

"She witnessed your deed," Sarah said, her voice soft and humble. "No doubt she would like everyone to view what happens to English dogs."

"Bah! The crocodiles will eat him first." To Damien, Lalji said, "I do not envy you putting up with a chattering female."

"The goddess will carry him safely away for all to see your brave achievement," Sarah persisted. "Do you dare to anger her?"

Lalji tugged at his earlobe. The prospect of displeasing the river goddess clearly disturbed him. He shrugged and turned to his comrade. "Keppu, help our brother."

"I do not heed the woman," Keppu growled. He stepped closer. "There is a foreign lilt to her voice. Let her draw back her veil so we might view her face."

Damien half straightened. The dead man's arms dragged at his hands like waterlogged Wellington boots. The chatter of monkeys filled the silence. Damn. Bloody double damn.

"You insult me again," he said hoarsely. "My wife's accent comes from her girlhood, when she spoke the Kashmiri tongue. And I cannot let you gaze upon her face." He cast about wildly for an excuse. "Beneath that veil, she's pockmarked from smallpox."

Keppu scowled. "Why would you wed an ugly woman?"

"For her large dowry. And she has the body of a goddess." Damien paused, schooling his features into hardness. "But heed how you describe her. I do not allow strangers to insult my wife."

Sarah knelt, rigid and still. Lalji watched her, crafty interest lighting his flattened features. "Are we strangers, then? Or brothers?"

"You are brothers," she murmured. "Let you not quarrel, lest you forget the greater cause of the mutiny. You must not destroy yourselves like the jackal who feeds from his own wounded body."

"Your woman is nimble with words," Lalji mused. Abruptly he addressed his comrade. "Save your suspicions for the English. Now get on with it, ere I toss you into the river, too."

The notion of the gaunt Lalji overpowering his massive companion was ludicrous. Yet with grumbling meekness, Keppu tucked the knife in his belt and lumbered over to take hold of MacMurtry's feet.

The fleshy Scotsman was even heavier than he looked. Dead weight, Damien reflected grimly. Muscles straining, he helped Keppu heft the man. They splashed into the river and heaved the body into the murky green waters. The current carried the bobbing corpse downstream and out of sight, thank God.

Mud squished between Damien's toes as he returned to shore. There he crouched a moment to wash his hands and arms in ritual cleansing. His sandals were probably ruined, another disaster he could blame on Miss Sarah-Outspoken-Faulkner. It had been a mistake to follow her to the river in the first place. It had been an even bigger mistake to let her suck him into another pointless argument, to lure him into chasing her.

He wondered at her unexpected playfulness. Perhaps she'd spent too many hours under the burning sun. He wondered even more why he'd joined in her frolicking mood. And when she'd gazed at him with those cerulean-blue eyes, a momentary madness had descended upon him, the madness of need and passion, the longing to lose himself in her warmth and closeness . . .

Ridiculous. As if a henpecking old maid could

heat a man's loins. He'd gone too long without coital release, that was all.

He surged to his feet. "Come, Shivina," he said, jerking his head at her. "I'm hungry." As she gracefully rose, he pivoted to the sepoys. "May Shiva guide you on your way."

"Wait." Lalji stepped into Damien's path. The sepoy picked up a twig and began to clean the dried blood from beneath his long fingernails. "Keppu and I leave at dawn for Kurnaul. In the meantime, we have no food and no woman to cook for us." The corners of his mouth slid downward into a hangdog expression.

Then eat dung, Damien thought. Again he cursed the devil's luck that had encumbered him with Sarah. He dared not arouse Lalji's suspicion by refusing hospitality. "Come back to our camp," he said grudgingly. "My wife will feed you."

Her arms sore from grinding millet for the evening meal, and her breast tight with restrained anger, Sarah sat in the midst of the women. A droplet of sweat rolled down her cheek. The thin veil over her face made the night seem even more stiflingly hot, and the scene before her took on the shimmery glow of a mirage. Keeping her eyes averted from Damien, who lounged beyond the low-lit campfire, she tried to concentrate on Jawahir.

In a high wailing voice, the headman sang verse after verse of a melancholy song about the past and the future, lamenting that life is forever the same, that all people are bound to the wheel of karma and cannot improve their lot, for the soul is punished for sins committed in a previous incarnation.

The flicker of the flames picked out the damp eyes and gloomy faces of his audience. Some swayed back and forth in an ecstasy of anguish.

Even the children listened with rapt interest and rare quietness.

Sarah pressed her fingers to the hard, dusty ground to keep from fidgeting. Under less volatile circumstances, she would have been intrigued by the ballad. But tonight her emotions were as taut as the strings on the headman's sitar.

Jawahir, she knew, was putting on a show to entertain their two guests and to keep the mutineers from asking too many questions. Pray God none of the villagers let the truth slip.

Her gaze moved over the small group of men. Damien sat on his heels beside Keppu and Lalji. Beneath her anxiety smoldered a self-righteous rage. Trust Damien Coleridge to flatter those barbarians. The three of them might have been old chums. He should have gotten rid of them by using his infernal cleverness. He must be completely uncaring to expose her and his son to the terrible risk of discovery.

Beside Sarah, Madakka cradled Kit. For tonight, the Hindu woman would treat the infant as if he were her own so that the sepoys wouldn't wonder why Damien's "wife" had already birthed a child.

Even so, Lalji seemed to stare straight at Sarah. His strange milky eye gave him a sinister aspect, and a shiver crawled over her skin. Praise heaven the sepoys would be departing at dawn. She couldn't look at them without seeing the ghastly corpse of poor Mr. MacMurtry.

She touched the photograph tucked at her waist. At least she'd rescued the keepsake from those villains.

Her stomach lurched. She had never expected the cause of native equality to take this appalling course. Too many sepoys had turned savage, spurning the notion of peacefully talking out their complaints in favor of killing every last English person.

How wrong she had been to hide her identity as I. M. Vexed. Perhaps Damien had been right to call her a hypocrite. She ought to have had the courage to speak out openly. She ought to have rallied her friends and neighbors. She ought to have opened their eyes to the gross injustices and done everything possible to avert the bloodshed.

Merciful God. Were it not for the mutiny, she would have been safely ensconced in Meerut, rather than living on the edge of peril. She would have been contemplating contentment with Reginald, rather than traveling with a callous knave like Damien.

The music melted away and the night chorus took over—the cry of jackals, the buzz of insects. Slowly the villagers began rising to their feet. Lakshmi shooed the children to their mats while Jawahir directed the two sepoys to a choice sleeping place near the low-burning fire. A place where they would be circled by the surreptitiously vigilant men.

Sarah rose to follow the other women. Madakka shyly drew Kit from beneath her sari, and Sarah couldn't resist pausing in the shadows to caress his velvety cheek. A sweet milky scent enveloped the drowsy infant. He blinked his long-lashed dark eyes, studying her with the solemn babyish look that wrenched her heart.

If he came to any harm . . .

"Wife," snapped Damien from behind. "Quit fawning over Madakka's baby."

The Hindu woman scurried away with Kit. Sarah whirled to find Damien towering over her. She could see through her veil that his chiseled features bore a look of impatience, his mouth taut and his eyes narrowed.

"Come," he said. "You'll sleep beside me tonight."

Gall rose in her throat. Not since the day after the mutiny had he slept at her side. She wanted to tell him precisely what she thought of his order. But the sepoys might be watching.

She placed her palms together and ducked her chin in the parody of a good wife. ''As you wish, O Great Master.''

His black eyebrows descended, but he merely turned on his heel. She dawdled over fetching their sleeping mats; then she spied Keppu stretched out by the fire. The gigantic man made no secret of watching her movements and leered knowingly.

Her heart tripping, she swung away and found Damien waiting in the gloom at the edge of the orchard. She was in dire straits indeed, Sarah thought, when she saw *him* as her refuge. She spread the mats a few feet apart. He bent and yanked them together.

''Lie down,'' he commanded.

He was probably enjoying the charade of exerting his power over her. Clenching her teeth, she sank onto her back, keeping her legs straight and her arms rigid. He settled down facing her. Sarah daringly drew the veil from her face and relished the refreshing breeze. The thin reed mat did little to cushion her from the hard earth. She yearned for a comfortable bed, a good book, a cup of tea. Instead, she had Damien.

She shifted position slightly, angling toward him. His musky male scent spanned the narrow gap between them. Her stomach cavorted in a strange little flutter. The memory of their light-hearted moment on the river came floating back. What had gotten into her to douse him with water and then flee? She was haunted by the sensation of him holding her breast in the warm cradle of his palm. She glared at his big dark shape and silently recounted all the reasons she was furious at him, all the grievances she burned to voice.

A short distance away, the rustling and murmuring of the villagers slowly died until only the sounds of the night remained, the far-off gurgling of the river, the lonely trumpet of a crane, the faint swish of mango leaves overhead. Insects buzzed and chirped loudly.

Sarah could keep silent no longer. "Why did you drag me over here?" she whispered. "I feel safer sleeping with the women."

"Believe me, I'd as soon make my bed with a viper," he hissed back. "But I had to get you away from my son. With all the attention you were paying him, Lalji and Keppu were about to get suspicious."

Her heart lurched sickeningly. *Had* she endangered the baby? "You're blowing an affectionate pat all out of proportion," she said. "All they'll think is that I love babies. You shouldn't have invited those two thugs into our camp in the first place."

"If you'd look past your own nose," he growled under his breath, "you'd see that it's better to keep the enemy out in the open rather than risk him skulking about in the bushes."

"That's the most foolish reasoning I ever—" She choked back the urge to raise her voice. "They're armed and dangerous. They could slaughter us all, your son included."

"Jawahir's watching them—he won't fail me. And speaking of fools, you almost got our throats cut at least three times. " 'Like the jackal who feeds from his own wounded body,' " Damien mimicked. "You can't even be original. You were quoting that columnist, I. M. Vexed."

She froze. Dear God, he was too astute. She'd have to watch herself. "I suppose you object to a woman reading the newspaper."

"You can read the bloody *Kama Sutra* for all I care. We're speaking of your stupid behavior. You couldn't obey an order if the Queen herself commanded you to keep silent."

"And you couldn't be civil if Prince Albert offered to knight you for it."

"The devil take your politeness," he said in a rude whisper. "What the hell did you want that daguerreotype for? Your scrapbook? Are you collecting souvenirs of the mutiny?"

She slapped at a gnat and wished it were Damien's sarcastic face. "I'm going to send the photograph to that poor man's family. It may be their last memento of him."

"So you risked our necks for a damned keepsake. It's not even a good photograph, for God's sake."

"Now who's being prissy? I wouldn't expect *you* to understand the great sentimental value of memorabilia." Swallowing hard, she clasped the locket beneath her sari and murmured, "I treasure my miniature of Reginald. It's all I have left of him. I'll keep it close to my heart forever."

Damien abruptly rolled onto his back and pillowed his head on his folded arms. He stared up at the canopy of leaves. "Lot of good that'll do you," he said, so low she had to strain to hear. "You'll still be wearing it when you're a gray-haired spinster."

"Better a spinster than an uncaring blackguard like you. You have no sense of loyalty, and even less appreciation of family values and devotion to loved ones."

"Thank God for that," he muttered. "At least I have my freedom."

"The freedom to do what? To be a vagabond for the rest of your days? What kind of life can you give Kit?"

"Better than a crusading do-gooder who meddles in the lives of everyone who has the misfortune to blunder into her path. I'm surprised you've resisted lecturing Keppu and Lalji on their ill-mannered behavior toward the British."

She kept a firm lid on her temper. "I don't lecture anyone," she whispered back. "I merely do whatever I can to secure justice for downtrodden people."

"What have you ever really done except complain?"

Sarah gritted her teeth. She dared not tell him about I. M. Vexed, or he'd proclaim her secret to everyone once she got back to English society.

"Obviously nothing," Damien went on, his tone subdued but smug. "Whenever you're at a loss for an answer, you turn into Miss Prissy Principles."

"Calling me names makes you feel superior," she murmured stiffly. "And you're changing the subject. We were speaking of the way you put your son and me in danger by inviting murderers into our camp."

"Then you'll be pleased to know that I'm escorting them away from here tomorrow."

She started to sit up, then caught herself. "*What?*" she said on a strident breath.

"I'm going with them. To make damned certain they go to Kurnaul instead of planning an ambush."

Fear churned away her anger. The thought of Damien leaving made her feel horribly alone. For all his boorish nature, he was familiar, her last link to the life she'd lost. "You can't abandon Kit and me. How do I know you'll come back?"

"Trust me, Sarah." Sarcasm deepened his low-pitched voice. "They're suspicious of us. I have to make certain they don't follow us. So I'll tell them I'm joining the glorious mutiny. Then I'll lose them in Kurnaul and rejoin you in a week."

She swallowed. His plan was far too risky, too foolhardy. She strained to discern his features through the darkness. "Suppose they discover who you are?" she said in a shaky undertone. "You could be hurt—even killed."

"Then you can celebrate my demise. You'll have Kit, just as you wanted."

His negligent attitude rankled Sarah. "Of course I'd care for him. I love him as my own son. But how am I to travel all the way to Bombay? How will I pay passage to England?"

Silence reigned for a heartbeat. "To England? What the hell are you talking about?"

"Your mother is the dowager Duchess of Lamborough. Surely she'd wish to meet her grandson and see to his welfare."

Damien's hand shot out and gripped her wrist. "You're never to take my son there," he said through gritted teeth. "Never."

His fierceness took her by surprise. "Why not?"

"None of your damned business. I have some rupees set aside that I'll give you in the morning. And a draft for my bank in Bombay. That'll do you."

His reticence intrigued her. "But if you die—"

"For God's sake, I'm not going to die." Letting her go, he blew out an exasperated breath. "You sound as if you'd miss me."

She stiffened. "I wouldn't wish anyone dead. Not even *you*."

"Your charitable nature overwhelms me," he drawled softly. "And here I thought you viewed me as an unfit father."

"Now that you mention it, I do have reservations," she couldn't resist murmuring. "You need to settle down. You can't drag Kit around a volatile country in another caravan."

"I suppose you and Reggie could have done better—a shrew and a bore."

Tears burned her eyes. She blinked hard, lest Damien spy the moisture through the shadows. It was absurd that the opinion of a rogue had the power to wound her. "Reginald was a fine, upstanding man. He would have made a wonderful father.''

"Too bad Sir Galahad wasn't there today to rescue you. No doubt he would have pulled out his shining sword and impaled those two *dacoits*.''

"Only you would mock his memory. You lack even an ounce of his honor.''

"Lot of good honor did him. What a damned shame your hero got killed in the mutiny. Now you're stuck with me.''

His bald assessment of her predicament slapped Sarah in the face. It was a test of her willpower to keep her voice hushed. ''Since you brought up the topic, I *am* growing weary of this charade. It's humiliating for me to come whenever you crook your little finger.''

"God spare me from humiliating you, Your Highness.''

"Lakshmi and Jawahir and Keppu and Lalji— they all saw me trot over here to join you, your devoted wife.''

"Ah,'' Damien murmured, ''at last we're getting to the heart of what's really bothering you. You're worried that everyone thinks we're over here making love.''

"I am not!''

"Shush.'' His scarred finger pressed against her lips. ''You're afraid they think I'm sliding my hands beneath your sari, touching your bare skin, caressing your naked breasts—''

She recoiled. ''No!''

"—lying on top of you and suckling your nipples until you're writhing with passion, stroking you between your legs until you beg me to put my *lingam* inside you—''

"Stop it, Damien!''

The dark, erotic images he painted brought a flush to her skin. Her breathing quickened at the notion of him exploring the places no man had

ever touched, at feeling his roughly tender hands
unveil the intimate secrets of her body, at tasting
the gentle pressure of his lips . . .

It was outrageous. Damien Coleridge could
never be tender. He could never be gentle.

"Do you truly want me to stop, Sarah?" His
velvet-soft question floated through the darkness.
Heat radiated from him, and he suddenly seemed
too, too close. "I wonder," he mused, "if there's
a warm-blooded woman beneath all your starch
and strait lacing. Maybe deep down you'd like me
to claim the privileges of a husband."

Fabric rustled faintly; then his hand slid up her
forearm, and she felt the smooth ridges of his
scarred palm, the callused pads of his fingers, the
warmth of his skin spreading over hers. She
couldn't speak; she couldn't move. Ever so slowly
his fingers glided upward, setting her whole body
to tingling. What did he mean, stroke her between the legs? In some unfathomable part of her,
she was conscious of a lush and throbbing heat,
the tantalizing ache to let him teach her . . .

His fingertips brushed her breast. The turmoil
inside her exploded. She scooted away, off the
mat. The gritty taste of dust entered her mouth.

"Now I understand why you're going off with
those murderers." The urge to lash out at him
possessed her. "A villain like you would feel right
at home with them. After all, you killed your own
father."

The instant the words were out, she froze in
shock. Merciful Lord, even Damien didn't deserve *that*. The rasp of his breathing blended with
the creaking of the crickets. She tried to see his
face, but the darkness obscured his expression.

His fingers bit hard into her arm. "Who's been
talking about my father?"

"M—Mrs. Craven. At the dinner party." That
naive time seemed ages ago, like a half-forgotten
dream. A web of remorse and doubt entangled

Sarah's heart. She didn't know if her accusation had hurt him or angered him. "Damien, I'm sorry. It was stupid gossip, that's all. I shouldn't have repeated it."

A gust of wind parted the mango leaves and let the faint starlight illuminate his face. His gaze glittered from stony features. She wanted to ask him to deny the rumor, but a belated sensitivity stopped her. Prying into his private affairs had brought her enough trouble already.

For a long moment Damien lay unmoving. Then he muttered, "Go to sleep, Sarah." His voice was flat, barren of emotion. He rolled onto his side, away from her.

His rejection left her feeling hollow inside. He had every right to be furious. She edged back onto her mat. As the night waned, she lay watching the play of leaves overhead and listening to his steady breathing. The memory of his touch lingered on her skin like a phantom caress. For some inexplicable reason, he possessed the power to plumb a hidden part of her, a part she wasn't certain she wanted to uncover. She thought of him departing at dawn, and an unbearable ache descended upon her.

So let him go, Sarah thought. She didn't need him. For all she cared, he could stay away forever. Resolutely she closed her eyes and went to sleep.

But in the morning, Lalji announced that he and Keppu had changed their minds. They were traveling to Hardwar, too.

Chapter 11

"**H**ow much for this *feringhi* weapon?"

"One hundred rupees," said the grizzled shopkeeper.

"That's robbery! My friend and I mean to join the holy uprising." Damien indicated Keppu, who stood nearby in sullen silence. "Surely you can give fellow patriots a fair offer."

"Bah. We have no English here in Hardwar. It is the sepoys far away on the plains who revolt against their masters. Still, I give the weapon to you for seventy-five rupees."

"You have the heart of a *dacoit*. Better I should kill a *feringhi* and steal his gun." Damien dropped the shiny revolver onto a pile of blankets and started to walk away.

"Wait, wait!" His dingy white robes flapping, the merchant stepped in front of Damien. "For a fighter of the great mutiny, I give a special price. Sixty rupees."

"For this poor piece? It isn't worth more than twenty."

"Fifty."

"Thirty, and I'll take a box of bullets besides."

The shopkeeper threw up his hands and groaned. "*Hi yi!* You snatch food from the mouths of my children." Yet he grinned as he wrapped the weapon and bullets in greasy brown paper.

Sarah watched from the rear of the tiny shop. The faint scent of gun oil underlaid the musty aroma of wool emanating from the mounds of handwoven blankets, the mainstay of the shop's trade.

Keppu seized the package. "I will hold this," he grunted. "And buy a rifle for myself, too."

"If you wish." Shrugging, Damien stepped back as the sepoy commenced haggling over another firearm. Sarah studied him, and her insides pulled taut. His broad form seemed larger in the low-ceilinged shop. Black-bearded and clad in turban and dhoti, he looked as dangerous and disreputable as a mutineer.

Damien's nonchalance, Sarah knew, was part of the nerve-racking charade they'd played for the past fortnight. Despite his repeated attempts to convince Keppu and Lalji to leave the villagers, the sepoys attached themselves to the group like leeches. With cool aplomb, Damien had fielded their many prying personal questions about him and Sarah. Battered by dust storms, hungry from food shortages, and limping on blistered feet, the small party of pilgrims had arrived the previous evening in the sacred town of Hardwar.

She tapped her fingers on a stack of scratchy blankets. At the rest house where they were staying, Damien had drawn her aside to whisper that he meant for them to slip away from the rebels soon. But he was infuriatingly closemouthed about the particulars of his plan.

Would he use the revolver to secure their escape? The old Sarah would have cringed at the thought. The Sarah she'd become knew the cold necessity of self-defense.

Keppu turned around to study her veiled form. Familiar tension gripped her belly. His piggy eyes and broad build gave him the appearance of a bad-tempered water buffalo.

Damien aimed a quick frown at Sarah. "Keppu,"

he said sharply, "I'd like to purchase a blanket. Do you need one, too?"

The sepoy shook his immense turbaned head. As Damien examined the blankets, Keppu turned back to pay for the guns, counting out a pile of silver rupees. Hugh MacMurtry's money.

Sarah slowly let out a breath. She mustn't forget her duty to the poor Scotsman. She still had the precious photograph of his family secured inside her sari.

This morning, Jawahir had taken Lalji to bathe at one of the sacred *ghats*. The others, Kit included, had stayed behind at the *dharmsala* while the women did the washing. Keppu had insisted that Sarah accompany him and her husband to the bazaar.

So he could watch both of them.

As swift as the snow-fed waters of the Ganges, the unbearable thirst for freedom swept over her. She had acted the obedient wife for too many days. She had endured the unsettling experience of sleeping beside Damien for too many nights.

Besides, she needed to discharge her duty to MacMurtry.

She edged around a pile of coarse blankets. Ducking past the cloth hung crookedly over the doorway, she stepped into the bustling bazaar. The silk of her veil muted the bright sunlight and gave the marketplace a gauzy green aspect. She inhaled the mingled scents of spices, incense, and excrement. The babble of shoppers blended with the harsh calls of hawkers.

Casting a single backward glance at the blanket shop, she slipped into the crowd. People thronged the many stalls containing heaps of foodstuffs, rice and sugar and lentils. Everywhere, shops sold the earthenware jars used to collect the Ganges water, considered holiest here at the Gate of Vishnu, where the sacred river left its Himalayan birthplace to enter the vast plains.

Pilgrims journeyed hundreds of miles to fill pots and carry them home for drinking at weddings and death ceremonies.

A man selling woven hats caught her eye. On his cart lay a tiny red cap that would keep Kit warm in the mountains. Quickly she struck a bargain with the man, then tucked the cap into the gathered material at her waist.

She bought paper and pen at another stall. She composed a brief note, wrapped it around the photograph, and securely tied the small bundle with string. She addressed it to the Government House in Calcutta. Someone there would know how to get in touch with MacMurtry's widow.

Debating how to mail the letter, she left the maze of the bazaar and reached a platform overlooking the Ganges. Through a gap in the hills, the river rushed relentlessly downward, foaming over boulders and gurgling an endless song. Beyond the green foothills loomed the hazy, white-peaked Himalayas.

The waterfront abounded with pilgrims. *Sadhus* in orange robes sat cross-legged. Some of the holy men had smeared their skin with sacred cow dung. Others had styled their hair into stiff cones of mud and wore the three-pronged stripes of Shiva on their brows. They blew conch shells and struck gongs until the high-pitched noises made Sarah's ears ring. The scent of burning incense from their coal-lit braziers stung her nose.

The filth and poverty tempered her fascination with sadness. A legless beggar slowly pulled himself across the cobblestones. Emaciated old men perched on the embankment, marking time until they died beside the holy Ganges. Children in rags took turns using an animal bone to bat at a pottery shard.

Near the *ghat*, Sarah saw a young lad staring hungrily at a pilgrim munching a *chupatty*. On impulse, she approached the boy.

"Would you like to earn some money?" she asked in Hindi.

He eyed her suspiciously. His somber dark eyes bore a poignant resemblance to Kit's. "How?"

"I must mail this to Calcutta." She held out the packet. "Can you get it there?"

"The mail packet leaves from Kurnaul." His dirt-smeared face alight with eagerness, he looked her up and down. "Please, I will take it there for twelve rupees."

"I have but ten."

"That is enough."

She took out the money, the last of the small stash Damien had given her, and placed the silver coins in the boy's grubby palm. Gripping the money and the parcel to his heart, he salaamed. "*Dhanyavad*, great lady. Thank you." Turning, he darted into the throng.

Her stomach squeezed tight. At least she had helped one urchin earn enough to feed him for a fortnight. Now that she'd fulfilled her duty, she could return to the blanket shop.

Sarah hesitated. What did a few more minutes matter? Damien must already be furious with her. Keppu, too.

An irresistible sense of discovery lured her onward, and she followed the riverbank. Tall *dharmsalas*, rest houses for pilgrims, crammed the byway alongside shrines and *ghats*. She spied the great bathing place where the headman had taken Lalji. Controlling a shiver, she made a wide detour around the place.

A prickly sensation made her look over her shoulder. She saw no familiar faces in the crowd, only the *sadhus* and old men and pilgrims with shaved heads.

Thankfully, the veil hid her face. Hardwar might not be one of the volatile military stations, but no doubt there were travelers here who hated the English.

Ahead, sunlight glinted off the triangular brass roof of a temple. Sarah carefully descended the few short stairs to the water's edge, where the flagstones were slick with moss. The shrine sat beside a small crook in the river, a quiet oasis amid the clamor of the city.

She rang the tiny string of bells at the entrance of the temple, then went inside the dim interior. A few pilgrims squatted beside pots of acrid incense. She stopped before a stone carving of the many-armed Shiva. On impulse, Sarah bowed her head to pray.

Please, God, help me keep Kit safe. Help Damien and me to escape our foes.

When she turned around, Lalji stood before her.

She staggered back. Her gasp echoed against the stone walls. His unnatural milky eye gave him an evil aspect. A smear of yellow marked the center of his forehead, and his turban was gone, his head shaved.

"Does my appearance alarm you . . . Shivina?"

Too frightened to speak, Sarah shook her head.

"Come outside with me," he said.

He beckoned and she saw no way to escape, no other exit from the shrine. Biting her lip beneath the veil, she followed him into the sunshine.

"I slipped away from Jawahir when I saw you pass the *ghat*," he said. "You are so seldom apart from your husband."

She edged toward the staircase. "What do you want from me?"

"A few words, nothing more." Lalji stepped in front of her. "One would think you are afraid of me."

"My husband will beat me if I talk to other men."

"What is this you have here?" He snatched the

red cap and turned it around and around in his long-nailed hands.

"A gift for Madakka's baby."

He handed the cap back. "You take great interest in a child who does not belong to you."

Sarah stiffened. Dear God, did he suspect? Willing her hands not to shake, she tucked the cap into her sash. "It is natural for women to like babies."

"Ah, you wish for one from your husband? The two of you enjoy sexual congress often enough."

Her cheeks stung with humiliating heat. So many nights she'd lain beside Damien to foster the illusion of man and wife. "That is none of your concern."

"For two weeks you have been avoiding me." Like a whiny child, Lalji turned the corners of his mouth downward. "Lakshmi and Maddaka answer my questions and treat me with respect. They show their faces to me. Why won't you?"

"I am ugly." Again she started past him, and again he blocked her path.

"Even ugly women need companionship. I had hoped to take you up the river and show you the footprint of Vishnu."

"You honor me, but I cannot go."

"You will not view the ancient mark of the god?" he said. "It is a sight all true pilgrims yearn to see."

He put a faint but unmistakable emphasis on *true*. Shakily, Sarah said, "My husband will take me to worship properly."

Lalji shrugged. "I would not wish to displease a man so big and strong as your Dharam. But you must at least allow me to buy you an offering." He flipped a coin to a passing urchin bearing a basket of trinkets.

"I do not think—"

"Bah. Everyone must make an offering to *Ganga*, men and women alike." He paused, peering at her with his strange eye. "Else why have you come to Hardwar?"

Fear paralyzed her limbs. Did he guess her identity? No, he could not be sure, or he would waste no time slitting her throat.

As he stepped closer to press the object into her hand, she caught the stench of curry on his breath. Looking down, she saw a tiny boat made of plaited green leaves and filled with marigolds and rose petals.

Lalji bought one for himself as well. Afraid to provoke his suspicions, she followed him to the embankment. He put his vessel into the rushing water. She bent and placed her own a few feet downstream. The current whirled the miniature boats in a dance that gained speed as they moved away from shore. The one dropped by Lalji shot after hers.

"See how my offering chases yours," he said.

His boat bumped hers and overturned it. The contents strewed the river and swirled swiftly away. His vessel bobbed onward until it vanished into the white, foaming water.

"Ahh." He sighed in satisfaction and turned to gaze at her. "So *Ganga Ma* lets me catch you. Perhaps it is a sign from her. Perhaps she means to reveal you to me at last."

He lunged at Sarah, caught her arm, and yanked at her *chuddur*. She grabbed desperately for the enveloping veil, but it slipped off her head and fell into the water. Her pulse beat madly in her throat. His dark face loomed into sharp focus. His body smelled of heavy incense.

"Aha! Eyes the color of the morning sky." He tugged at her hair; it tumbled in a black mass around her shoulders. "Keppu was right. You have dyed your hair and skin, but you are a *feringhi*."

"No," she said in desperation. "I am from

the hills. Some of my people have light-colored
eyes—''

''Bah.'' He spat on the ground. ''You have English features. And no pockmarks to mar your
beauty. I am sick of your lies. You have made a
fool of me for too long.'' He scraped his long fore-
nail over her jugular vein. ''Was it Delhi you fled?
Or Meerut?''

Terror struck her heart. Merciful God, she had
to distract him. A yellow-orange flash behind him
caught her eye. A *sadhu* emerged from the temple. The lanky man started down toward the river.

She raised her chin. ''Release me, and I will
reveal all you wish to know.''

Lalji regarded her with contempt. ''And let you
run from me? No, you will go with me to a private
place I know. There I will conduct your punishment.''

He tugged her in the direction of the stairs. Her
stomach clenching, she hung back. A short way
down the riverbank, the *sadhu* struck his gong and
chanted a prayer.

''If I am English,'' Sarah said, ''then you soil
yourself by touching me. You forfeit your caste
for the sake of revenge.''

His grip eased. ''For an Englishwoman, you
know much of our Hindu ways—''

She threw herself out of his grasp. Too far away
to risk the steps, she leaped toward the holy man.
His odor of cow dung nipped at her. ''Help me!''
She caught his arm, and his gong splashed into
the water. ''Save me from death!''

Glazed brown eyes peered at her from beneath
hair shaped with mud into a beehive. His mouth
formed a startled O. He swayed in a trance.

Lalji sprang after her. ''Do not listen! She is a
feringhi—''

She darted behind the *sadhu* and gave him a
mighty shove. He collapsed against the sepoy.

They clutched at each other like a macabre couple, teetering on the embankment.

Both men tumbled into the river. Lalji thrashed and howled. The water abruptly swallowed his curses.

Sarah spun around and ran for the stairs. Her trail-hardened feet sped over the mossy stone steps. She paused at the top and spared a glance back.

His dark yellow robes floating around him and his beehive sagging, the *sadhu* calmly swam toward the bank. Farther out, Lalji flailed with the panic of a nonswimmer. Already the swift current swept him downstream. His shaved head bobbed on the water like a huge billiard ball.

In a panic, Sarah hastened through the crowd. She tried to keep her gaze downcast so that no one would notice her blue eyes. She felt naked and vulnerable without the veil. Everyone seemed to be watching her.

Dear God, she shouldn't have slipped away from Damien. Touring Hardwar seemed frivolous now. Frivolous and dangerous. She felt no elation at besting Lalji, only the shaky comfort of a reprieve. He might yet reach the shore. With cold certainty, she knew that if he found her, he would kill her. And Damien.

Perhaps even Kit.

Spurred by fear, she half ran past a blur of holy men and pilgrims. The bazaar. She must get to the bazaar and warn Damien. He'd know what to do.

She reached the narrow streets of the marketplace. A hawker of clay pots snatched at her arm, but she shook him off. She pushed her way past the shoppers until the blanket shop came into view. Sidestepping the door flap, she entered the musty interior.

She scanned the small room with its heaps of

blankets and filthy clay walls. Dear Lord, Damien had gone.

At the back of the store, the grizzled proprietor was haggling with a customer. A man with a shaved head. Sarah gasped.

Then the man turned, so she could see his mild, bearded face. Her heart resumed beating. How foolish of her—he wasn't Lalji.

"Please," she breathed, stepping toward them, "have you seen my husband? He was here purchasing a gun a short time ago."

"So you are the wife who ran away," said the shopkeeper. He shook his finger at her. "He was very, very angry. He and his great bullock of a friend."

"Do you know where my husband went?"

"He said if you returned to send you to the *dharmsala*, to wait with the other women." Coming closer, the shopkeeper peered at her in open astonishment. "But what is this? You have the eyes of an Englishwoman."

"*Dhanyavad*, sir. Thank you for your help."

Sarah whirled and dashed out. She couldn't afford to wait with the other women. She had to find Damien and tell him of the peril they faced.

Where in heaven was he?

Where in hell was she?

One hand shading his eyes, Damien scanned the crowded waterfront. A breeze whipped down from the forested foothills, wafting the aromas of cedar and incense along with the stink of rubbish. The *ghats* by the river buzzed with life. His flute lilting, a man charmed a green snake from a brass spittoon. Astrologers beseeched business from shaven-headed pilgrims and yellow-robed *sadhus* reciting their private *pujas*. Beneath the spreading branches of a nearby shisham tree, a young penitent slept off the effects of the hookah cradled in the crook of his arm.

A sacred cow lumbered past Damien and paused to excrete a pile of dung. As the hump-backed animal ambled on, a *sadhu* bent and scooped the steaming heap into a clay jar, which he bore reverently away.

Damien focused on the scores of women pilgrims. There were saris in reds and pinks and whites and blues. He spotted none in a distinctive olive-green hue trimmed with gold, encasing a body that unaccountably drove him mad.

Damn you, Miss Sarah-Hardhead-Faulkner, he thought. *Bloody double damn you.*

He despised the fear that soured his stomach. The fear that he wouldn't find her in this swarm of people. The fear that when he finally did track her down in some dark back-street alley, she would be lying in a crumpled heap, her blue eyes wide and sightless, her slim throat ripped open in a bloodied gash.

He banished the grisly image from his mind. His imagination was running rampant not because he cared for her, but because he didn't want the trouble of finding another nanny for his son. Where else would he find someone who could cope half as well as Sarah? With Lalji guarded by Jawahir, the only real threat to her stood beside Damien.

"So," snarled Keppu, "where is your errant wife?"

Damien swung toward his bull-faced companion. "She's around here somewhere. You must remember she is only a country girl. She was probably swept up by all the strange new sights here."

"My woman would never dare to leave against my command."

The sepoy's cruel expression and flat voice disgusted Damien. "We probably missed her in the bazaar. She must have strayed off to examine some trinket or to have her fortune told."

"If you lie to me, I'll kill you and the other pilgrims."

"Why would I mislead you?" Damien said in an injured voice. "Have we not been brothers these past weeks? Am I not prepared to stand at your side and slay the *feringhis*? Once we have all cleansed ourselves in the holy waters, we will be ready to join the great mutiny."

Keppu grunted an indistinct sound that might have been an apology or a jeer.

"Let us return to the market," Damien added. "Perhaps she's gone back to the shop where we bought the gun."

"Perhaps, perhaps," Keppu grumbled as he fell into step beside Damien. "I grow weary of chasing a foolish woman."

Damien swallowed a retort. His fingers itched for the revolver or the rifle. He'd like nothing better than to plant a slug of lead in that oversized belly. But like a beggar clutching his alms, the sepoy jealously guarded both parcels against his watermelon stomach. Sunlight glinted off the dagger stuck in his belt, and his red uniform coat bore a brown splotch of dried English blood like a badge of dishonor.

Control yourself, Damien thought. *Just stick to the plan and you'll be rid of this scum. Don't let your fury at Sarah make you do something rash.*

He adjusted the bundle of scratchy blankets under his arm as he continued to scrutinize the throng. Just wait until he got his hands on that tart-tongued spinster. He wouldn't let her out of his sight again. And he really *would* blister her shapely little bottom.

The density of the crowd in the bazaar slowed their progress. People jostled him, shoppers hurrying from stall to stall and vendors vying for customers. The air held the heavy scent of frying *chupatties*, the piquant aroma of curry, the acrid smoke of dung-fires. A mangy cur lunged at a plucked chicken hanging in a butcher's stall; the proprietor swatted futilely with a stick as the dog dashed off with its prize. The scene was earthy and alive, yet anxiety darkened Damien's vision. Keppu scowled at every veiled woman they passed, and his murderous expression struck Damien like a killing frost.

A merchant with a pencil-thin mustache elbowed in front of him. The man swept back his dirty sleeve and shook an armload of clinking bracelets.

"O honorable pilgrim, will you not buy a bangle to take home to your wife? I have gold and silver and brass—"

"*Chale jao*," Damien snapped, thrusting the man aside. "Go away." Ahead lay the crooked door flap of the blanket stall.

If Sarah wasn't waiting there, he thought feverishly, he'd go to the *dharmsala*. And if she hadn't joined the women, either? Blast her to hell for leaving him to explain her behavior.

Another vendor tugged at his sleeve. He tried to yank himself free, but this one clung with the tenacity of a leech. Turning his head sharply, he growled, "Let loose, you son of a snake—"

He found himself looking down at Sarah's thick-lashed blue eyes and nut-stained face.

Relief and panic tangled his heart. He dropped his bundle of blankets and swung fully toward her, blocking her from Keppu.

He clamped his hands onto her shoulders. A keen awareness of her fine bones and warm skin pulsed through him. "Where in *hell* is your veil?" he hissed in her ear.

"I lost it," she said in a breathless voice barely audible in the din of the crowd. "Oh, Damien, Lalji tried to—"

He clapped his hand over her mouth and glanced back. Keppu was a few steps ahead, his

soiled turban rotating back and forth as he
scanned the stalls to the left.

"Are you mad?" Damien muttered to her.
"Don't call me that."

Sarah wriggled away from his hand. "Stop interrupting and listen," she whispered. "Lalji
knows about us."

The news jolted him. "Damn! What the hell
did you do?"

"Me? I had to push him into the river—"

She stopped abruptly and tilted her face to the
ground. Her dyed hair hung around her slim body
like an unbound ebony curtain, half shielding her
features from view.

"Why have you stopped here?" asked Keppu
from behind them.

Damien's stomach sank like a rock. "Praise
Vishnu, I've found the wayward wench. I am taking her back to the *dharmsala* immediately." He
quickly stooped to snatch up the blankets, then
grasped her hand and angled her away.

"But where has she been?" the sepoy said,
pushing forward. "And where is her *chuddur*?"

"She lost it. She said a beggar snatched it right
off her head. It was the finest silk from Benares,
too." Damien spoke over his shoulder as he propelled her toward the perimeter of the bazaar.
"She's earned herself a sound whipping this
time."

Like a bear stalking its quarry, Keppu followed.
"I wish to know where she has been."

"Wandering the shops, just as I'd guessed,"
Damien replied. "She was slavering like a child
over sweets and pretty bangles."

"Your words reek of trickery," Keppu growled.
"Halt where you stand. I will read the truth in
her face."

Damien stiffened and stopped. *Hellfire and damnation.*

Racking his brain for a plan, he turned slowly

toward the sepoy. People pushed by, some casting curious glances at the trio. Sweat prickled his brow. Clasped within his scar-thickened palm, Sarah's fingers felt as small and fragile as a nosegay of marigolds. Her head was bowed in the subservient manner of a Hindu woman. Yet beneath the olive silk, her shoulders were squared with the starched pride of an Englishwoman.

Damn her spirit. Damn her for ruining his escape plan. Damn her for plunging both of them into terrible trouble.

Damien knew only one way to get out alive.

He thrust her toward the waterfront. ''Run like hell!''

Her head shot up. Her eyes widened, a flash of blue against her brown skin. For one horrid instant he feared she meant to protest. Then she spun around and darted into the crowd.

Keppu loosed a bellow of rage and grabbed for his dagger. ''Lying *feringhi* dogs—*oomph.*''

His words ended as Damien thrust his bundle into the sepoy's belly. He shoved hard. Both parcels slipped from Keppu's hand. Like a giant fir toppling, he fell backward into a stall stacked high with earthenware pots.

Jars crashed. Pottery shattered. People screamed.

Keppu landed on his rear, his legs splayed. He shook the shards from his hulking shoulders. The rifle disappeared beneath a mountain of debris. Damien didn't stop to watch. He scooped up the package holding the revolver. Then he bolted into the multitude of shoppers.

He strained to see over the many bobbing turbans and shaved heads. At the edge of the bazaar, the throng parted momentarily. A few yards ahead, he spied Sarah's slim back. She turned around, shading her eyes to search the crowd. But she must not have noticed him, for she whirled and resumed her fast pace.

Damn! She was heading straight for the *dharm-sala*. Ice gripped his heart. Keppu didn't know Kit belonged to Damien. If she led the sepoy there, he'd put the baby to the knife along with the two of them.

"Sarah!"

Her name was drowned in the earsplitting blast of a conch shell, blown by a priest in a jeweled howdah atop a plodding elephant. A tight-packed band of *sadhus* paraded slowly by, ringing bells and chanting mantras. Damien glanced back. Keppu barreled after him like a maddened water buffalo.

Damien ducked into the group of holy men. Crouching to hide himself, he worked a path through the mass of orange-yellow robes. It was like wading through treacle. Entranced faces gazed dully ahead; the smell of incense stung his nose.

At last he broke free and ran after Sarah. He caught her near the entrance to a *ghat.* "Not that way, for God's sake," he growled in her ear. "Use your brain for once."

"We have to warn the others," she whispered. "Kit—"

"My son is safe with Madakka." Having lost sight of Keppu, Damien half dragged her inside the huge arched entryway. He hoped to God they blended with the pilgrims filing in and out of the sacred bathing place.

"But, Damien—"

"Don't argue." He hauled her toward a deserted corner, away from the custodians collecting the bathers' sandals. Behind a stone pillar, he released her and ripped at the greasy brown parcel. In low-pitched English he went on. "Keppu's out there somewhere. The game is up. I have to finish him off."

Her eyes rounded. "Finish him . . . you mean *kill* him?"

He flung down the paper. "I sure as hell don't mean to serve him cucumber sandwiches and tea."

"I'll help you. I can lure him over here—"

"Like hell you will." Damien's head jerked up in surprise. Sarah would help him draw a man to his death? God, he must be corrupting her. "You stay put for once. I won't be worrying about you getting into mor ouble."

She returned his fierce stare with quiet dignity. "What would you like me to do?"

"Nothing but wait here for five minutes and then head back to the women. I'll come fetch you there."

He drew out the gun and gripped the curved stock. A five-shot Adams revolver, rather new— likely stolen from an English officer. He opened the box of bullets and began to load the chambers.

"Damien, there's something you should know. Lalji may have guessed that Kit is your son."

His hands tensed. *"What?"*

"I'm not certain, but he questioned my relationship to Kit."

"Damn. Bloody double *damn!*"

She touched his sleeve. "I'm sorry. This is all my fault. I shouldn't have been so careless. I shouldn't have wandered off."

The misery shining in her eyes clutched at his chest. She bit her lower lip, and he found himself studying its fullness and wondering what her mouth tasted like. He tore his gaze back to hers and said gruffly, "Never mind. You told me you pushed Lalji into the river. Did you see him get out?"

"No, and he didn't seem to know how to swim. The river swept him downstream."

"Well, thank Mother Ganges for small miracles." Damien stood, tucking the revolver into his sash, where his tunic half concealed the weapon.

"Still, we can't be sure, so I'm changing plans. We'll head to the *dharmsala* and fetch Kit. If Lalji managed to pull his carcass out, he might well go after the boy."

"Surely he wouldn't hurt an innocent baby." She looked as if she were trying to convince herself.

"My son is half English," Damien said flatly. "You saw what the mutineers did in Meerut. Those murderers need no other excuse to kill him."

The possibility iced his soul. Wrestling down rage and panic, he drew Sarah toward the crowded entrance of the *ghat.*

"How will we hide Kit?" she asked.

"We'll take him into the mountains."

"But they could follow us. The villagers—"

He stopped short. "Oh, hell."

His fingers dug into Sarah's upper arm and yanked her to a halt.

"What is it?" she asked.

He pointed to the entryway. The sunlight pouring through the fretwork cast a lacy pattern over Keppu's bulky form. His big head swung from side to side as he searched the throng of pilgrims. The knife glinted in his hand.

Chapter 12

❧

Sarah's stomach did a sickening flip. She lifted her gaze to Damien's harsh, bearded features, the feral glint in his eyes. He looked tough and indomitable, ready to do battle. "Merciful Lord," she breathed. "We can't get out without him spotting us."

"Then we'll go this way."

He jerked her toward the wide bank of steps leading down to the river. She scurried to keep pace with his long strides. Glancing over her shoulder, she saw Keppu turn his head toward them. He lunged in pursuit.

"Damien, he's seen us!"

"Then run, dammit."

His arm slid around her back. He propelled her headlong down the steep stone stairs, elbowing past people who called out irate protests.

She and Damien reached the wide flagstone *ghat* bordering the river. Sunlight drenched the scene in brilliance. Custodians in booths guarded the clothing of the penitents. Barbers ensconced beneath black umbrellas shaved the heads and nostrils of their customers in the ritual manner. Hundreds of half-naked men waded in the shallow water near the embankment.

Sarah averted her eyes from the spectacle. The worshippers descending the stairs went around her and Damien. She spotted Keppu thundering down toward them.

She gasped out, "Hurry, Damien!"

"This way."

They plunged through the multitude and surged toward a building on the riverbank. Splashing noises and giggly conversation emanated from within the cedar-shingled structure. A pudgy attendant with his nose in a newspaper squatted in the doorway.

"Move," Damien snapped.

The attendant looked up. "Your woman may enter, but not you, *huzoor*. This is the ladies' bathing house. No men allowed."

Damien stepped over the servant. Hampered by her long sari, Sarah squeezed past the man's bulk.

"Stop! You must stop!" The attendant lumbered to his feet. He waved his newspaper like a prissy matron fluttering a fan. "Women only here. Women only."

Damien pulled Sarah into the dim interior. To the right lay a row of changing alcoves. Ahead and to the left stretched a great sunken pool crowded with unclothed women. Small statues of Hindu gods and goddesses gazed benevolently from niches in the walls. From the incense pots wafted the aromatic scent of burning joss sticks.

"There's another exit," Damien said, pointing to a door on the other side of the pool. He hustled Sarah toward it.

Shrieks and squeals pierced the air. Ladies covered their bare breasts with their hands. Others crouched chin deep in the shallow water, their black hair floating like banners.

"Women only!" The image of a wrathful Buddha, the attendant continued to shout and gesture. "Women only!"

Disregarding the uproar, Damien strode swiftly around the tiled lip of the pool. Sarah trotted after him. They'd gone only halfway when Keppu burst into the bathing house.

"Halt, *feringhi*!"

Damien thrust her in front of him. "Get the hell out!"

Sarah began to run. Realizing he wasn't following, she stopped and looked back. As dark and ominous as a thundercloud, he stalked toward Keppu. Dear God, he meant to confront the huge sepoy.

She stood cold and still. Keppu brandished his dagger. The dagger that already had been christened with English blood.

Surely Damien would draw his revolver. But he didn't. With dawning dread, she realized there were too many women about for him to risk a shot.

Fists clenched, he stopped a few feet from Keppu. The men circled slowly, warily.

The attendant waddled between them. "You must leave now, both of you. Women only here! Women on—"

Keppu whipped his meaty fist across the man's face. Several ladies screamed. The attendant went sprawling against a potted fern. The plant smashed on the tiles. He lay blubbering amid green leaves and scattered dirt.

In the second that the sepoy shifted his gaze away, Damien's arm flashed out. He landed a wicked blow to Keppu's jaw. The sepoy staggered back a step, shaking his bull-like head. With the quickness of a cat, he recovered and attacked. His dagger arced toward Damien's abdomen.

Sarah gasped. She anticipated the slice of steel, the spurt of blood. But he caught the sepoy's forearm and forced it back down. They struggled chest to chest, arms locked. Keppu backed Damien to the edge of the pool. Women screeched and splashed away. The sepoy's mighty hand inched upward until the blade neared Damien's throat.

Something fierce and wild rose in Sarah. Without giving herself time to think, she snatched a statue of Parvati from one of the niches.

She ran at the men. Damien grunted in an effort to throw off his opponent, but the sepoy outweighed him. She stepped behind Keppu. With all her might, she swung the heavy stone goddess at his skull.

A dull crack resounded. His back arched. A snarling groan parted his lips. Then his arms went slack and his dagger clattered to the tiles. Damien vaulted nimbly backward as the sepoy tumbled into the pool.

A tidal wave of water sloshed over the floor and drenched the hem of her sari. Keppu lay on his back, his arms and legs splayed, his face submerged. A haze of bubbles rose to the surface and obscured his features.

Nausea rolled in Sarah's stomach. Unable to tear her gaze from the fallen man, she stood panting, her heart squeezing. He was dead. The knowledge struck her deeply, for Lalji at least had been swept down the river alive.

Dimly she heard the exclamations of the Hindu ladies. Mere weeks ago, ensconced in the pampered security of her uncle's house, she could never have imagined the sick sensation of killing a man. Even if he was a murderer who had intended to murder again.

Someone unpeeled her fingers from the statue and took its weight away. She looked up. Damien's bearded face swam into focus. Faint astonishment shone in his brown eyes, and his hand glided with unexpected gentleness over her cheek.

"Well done, Sarah," he said. "At least now we can leave by the front entrance."

Settling his arm around her waist, he guided

her away. She leaned into him, needing to feel his warm strength and grateful that he didn't fuss as Reginald would have done. She wanted only the closeness of a friend, the bond of an ally.

At the door, she glanced back. One by one, the chattering naked women sidled toward the corpse. The attendant crouched by the edge of the pool and attempted to haul out the body by its feet.

"Only women," he muttered mournfully. "Only women allowed in bath."

Outside, the bright sunshine made Sarah blink. The *ghat* looked as before, with pilgrims swarming as thick as ants and penitents splashing away their sins in the Ganges. She pressed her nails into her palms. If only she could submerge herself in the river and rinse away the stain of guilt. If peril befell Kit, she would never forgive herself.

As they hurried up the steps, she glanced at Damien. Her own fear was reflected in his demon-dark features. Softness dawned inside her. He truly did care about his son.

In the crooked street outside the *dharmsala*, Jawahir paced with his bamboo walking stick. His movements were agitated, his orange turban and white robe vivid against the mossy-green wall.

He rushed forward. "*Burra* sahib! By Vishnu's benevolence, you and your woman are safe. I must tell you that Lalji slipped past me—"

"I know," Damien cut in. "He isn't here, is he?"

"I have not seen him in more than an hour. But how can you know?" Jawahir glanced beyond them. "And where is Keppu?"

"Gone to his next incarnation." Damien's fingers closed reflexively on the handle of his revolver. "Lalji might still be on the loose, though Sarah did her best to incapacitate him."

"He attacked you?" Jawahir asked, his brown

eyes widening at Sarah. "And where is your veil?"

"We'll talk inside," Damien said. "It's safer there."

He hustled them into the rest house, past a courtyard overflowing with weeds and children at play. People strolled by on their way to the shrines or baths. Sparsely furnished cells lined the corridor. Inside the sunlit chamber at the end of the hall, Lakshmi was cutting vegetables into a pot. Several young girls, daughters of Jawahir, took turns rolling a ball to his toddling son. Sitting on a charpoy in the corner, Madakka suckled the baby. When she saw Damien, she modestly drew the infant from beneath her sari.

"Kit," Sarah breathed.

She rushed to gather him close, and her fingers sought his smooth cheek, his wispy black hair, to reassure herself that he was unharmed. He squirmed, and she nestled him against her shoulder. Joy flowed through her as rich as the milk he'd just consumed.

Damien came up beside her. A distracted frown shadowed his eyes and lent starkness to his cheekbones. With endearing awkwardness, he patted the baby's back. His scarred hand looked large and dark against the infant's small form. Kit let loose a lusty belch.

Damien blinked. "Thank God he's eaten. That'll save us a few minutes. Gather our belongings, Sarah. We'll need food, too."

He turned away and joined Jawahir in the doorway. The men squatted on their heels and commenced a whispered conference. All the while Damien focused his gaze down the outside corridor. Watching for Lalji.

Handing the baby back to Madakka, Sarah wondered at their air of secrecy. What could they be saying? But urgency set her scurrying about the task of packing spare clothing and nappies for

Kit. Lakshmi's brown hands moved swiftly, too, wrapping parcels of rice and dried beans and spices.

She was replaiting Sarah's hair when Damien strode up. "Get the baby," he said tersely. "We need to hurry."

"But Lakshmi and Madakka haven't yet packed their things."

"Because they're staying with their husband. We'll travel faster alone."

Shock jolted Sarah. She glanced at the two Hindu women, now crouched at Jawahir's feet. The headman wore a bland expression; his wives looked as incredulous as she. "But Madakka has to go with us. How else will your son eat?"

"I have that problem taken care of."

"How? Did you find another ayah?"

"I'll tell you later." Damien snatched up the sack and paced to the door. "Right now we need to go."

The notion of setting out on a long trek with only him and the baby roused her resistance. She followed him to the corridor and whispered, "I never agreed to travel alone with you."

He rocked on the balls of his feet. "Oh, for God's sake. I'm paying you to watch my son. I'm hardly interested in stealing your cherished virginity."

Their earlier sense of camaraderie withered. "That isn't what I object to. You should have consulted me when you concocted your plan—"

"Look, Miss Priss, if it sets your old maid's heart at ease, Jawahir and the women will join us in a few days, once we're safely away in the mountains."

His hard brown eyes swung away to scan the corridor. How typical that she'd had to drag the truth out of him. Satisfied, she said primly, "Thank you."

She quickly fastened Kit in a sling at her waist.

Lakshmi draped another veil over Sarah's head and then embraced her. Madakka leaned down and tearfully kissed the baby. The girls gathered around, eyes wide and wistful in dusky faces. Jawahir said solemnly, "May Vishnu guide you."

As Sarah and Damien slipped out a back door, an intense feeling of sorrow caught at her. How swiftly she'd grown to love these warmhearted people who had put their own lives in jeopardy in order to offer aid. Though her resources were few, she vowed to find some way to repay them—perhaps by teaching them to read and write.

The thought cheered her. She would have their companionship until the mutiny died down. Certainly she could tolerate Damien's company for a few short days.

They hastened through the back streets of Hardwar. Damien kept one hand on the revolver hidden inside his tunic. Jittery fear stalked Sarah. Her arms wrapped protectively around Kit, she glanced over her shoulder and half expected to see Lalji's bloodthirsty face, odd-matched eyes, and shaved head.

But only pilgrims and sacred cows thronged the byways.

On the road out of town, she and Damien joined the stream of *sadhus* and penitents trudging northward along the bank of the Ganges. The broad and beautiful river churned and swirled its way down from the mountains. Islands thick with trees parted the swift-flowing water.

"This is the way to Rishikesh," she murmured. "Is that where we're going? Surely Lalji could follow us."

"Calm your nerves. We're heading another way."

Casting a look around, Damien took a firm hold of her elbow and steered her to the left, onto a dirt path that ascended toward forests of pine and cedar. He walked ahead, tall and surefooted, alert

204 BARBARA DAWSON SMITH

and watchful. She looked down and saw that the baby was asleep, lulled by the rhythm of her steps. Damien's vigilance eased her own wariness. He would protect her and Kit. Odd, how in that one respect she could have faith in him.

They passed an occasional *sadhu* deep in meditation, but after an hour they saw no one. The farther they ventured from the Ganges, the more desolate the landscape grew. Monkeys chattered from the high branches of *sal* trees. In the dry season before the monsoon, few wildflowers dotted the steep hillsides.

In the absence of people, Sarah drew back her veil. The balmy afternoon breeze felt delicious after the baking heat of their journey across the plains. The air dried the dampness of her hem. Through a break in the thick undergrowth she caught a panoramic view of a lush valley. They passed groves of mangoes, detoured around huge mossy boulders, and climbed on a steadily rising slope.

The path dwindled to an indistinct goat track. Despite the weeks on the road, the exertion of the upward trek made her pant. Her legs ached. How long had they been traveling? She tried to guess by the angle of the sun. Two hours perhaps. The baby might be waking soon. She watched vainly for a village, but saw only a hare bounding through the shrubbery, a yellow-throated martin winging across the blue sky, a mongoose sunning its long brown body on a flat rock.

Damien slowed his steps and let her catch up. Walking beside her, he said, "I've been wondering how you managed to run into Lalji. What did you do, go to the *ghat* looking for trouble?"

His critical tone pricked her. "Of course not. I left the shop because I needed to find a messenger to deliver a letter and the photograph to Mrs. MacMurtry—"

"To deliver *what?*"

Sarah met his furious gaze with regal dignity. "You heard me, Damien. The poor woman deserves to know her husband's fate."

"So you risked your life—mine and Kit's as well. For God's sake, Sarah, use sense instead of sentiment. Your messenger might have been a sepoy sympathizer."

"He was only a destitute boy. He looked quite trustworthy, I assure you. I gave him ten rupees, and he vowed to deliver the letter himself onto the mail packet at Kurnaul."

"Christ Almighty! Of all the bloody fool—" Damien bit off the curse. "Your messenger likely pocketed the money and tossed the letter into the nearest gutter."

She wrestled with the uneasy possibility, then drew a deep breath. "Perhaps *you* have little trust in anyone, Damien, but I prefer to have faith in people. I had to make the effort."

"Spare me the noble sermon," he muttered. "Tell me how you met up with Lalji."

"After I finished the letter, I thought I'd take a short walk around Hardwar—"

"Typical. You didn't give a damn that you'd left me to explain your outrageous behavior to Keppu."

She cast down her gaze and studied her bare toes against the mossy trail. For once, he was right to chastise her. Yet she ached to make him understand. "It was the freedom, the chance to do something on my own after acting the meek Hindu wife for weeks. I didn't see that a few more minutes mattered, so I walked to one of the temples on the river. I had no idea Lalji was following me."

Suppressing a shudder, she described the confrontation, the horrid moment when he'd pulled off her veil, her desperate effort to escape, and Lalji's tumble into the river.

The slap-slap of Damien's sandals and the far-off screech of a kite broke the silence. She risked a look at him. To her astonishment, a grin turned up the corners of his mouth, making him appear more youthful, less intimidating.

"What's so amusing?" she asked.

"I was picturing you pushing that *sadhu* into the Ganges," he said. "Good God, Sarah, that was quick. I wish I'd been there to cheer you on."

A warm glow unfolded within her, but only for a moment. Memory chilled her. "Do you really think Lalji's still alive?"

Damien shrugged. "It's a possibility. The current's strong. But if he could keep his head above water, he might survive. Somebody might have pulled him out. Even so, with any luck at all he was swept too far downstream to catch up to us."

She looked away. Her chest felt so tight it hurt. The thought of Lalji alive frightened her. But somehow the thought of him dead at her hand troubled her as well. And she remembered the awful smack of the statue against Keppu's skull . . .

"Sarah." Damien's low-pitched voice intruded, and his hand on her wrist drew her to a halt. "Don't brood. It was them or us. Quite frankly, I vote in favor of us."

Their eyes met and married in a breathless moment. The dreamy mood washed through her again, stronger this time. His gaze was a steady, tender brown beneath burnished lashes. Heat spread in her belly, unrolling its delicate fronds throughout her body. She was conscious suddenly of how isolated they were, alone for the first time in weeks, with the breeze drifting against her cheeks and the sun filtering through the canopy of leaves.

Kit stirred and squawked. Distracted, Sarah unfastened him from the sling and gently rocked him in her arms. He turned his head, his open mouth seeking her breast. His crying crescendoed; he waved his arms and kicked his legs. She moved him to her shoulder. He looked around and quieted, but sucked noisily on his fist.

Panicky alarm swept over her. Madakka had tended to his care and nourishment. Never had Sarah been more aware of her limited experience with infants.

"Damien, he's hungry. How are we going to feed him?"

"Goat's milk."

"Goat's milk?" Surprised dismay curled her lips, and she rubbed the flat of her palm over Kit's small back. "You're going to let your son drink goat's milk?"

Damien cocked his head at her. "Is there something wrong with that? You don't think it will upset his stomach, do you?"

He looked so anxious, she said, "I most certainly hope not. But still—"

"Good. It was Jawahir's idea. He said he knew of motherless infants who thrived on goat's milk."

"But, Damien, I thought you'd hired an ayah."

"I never said that." He started back along the upward trail. "You drew your own conclusion. A habit, you know."

Their truce vanished like a wisp of smoke. Sarah wanted to scream at him in frustration. Silently counting to ten, she tramped after him. "But how will Kit drink the milk? Do you have a bottle? And . . . something for him to suck on?" She couldn't bring herself to say *nipple*.

"Yes, everything is right here." Damien patted the sack slung over his shoulder. "Jawahir took care of that problem in the bazaar early this morning, before he escorted Lalji to the *ghat*."

She jiggled Kit to keep his whimpers from escalating. Her gaze swept the hilly ridges, the stands of tall, arrow-straight *sal* trees. "I don't see any goats."

"They're here." He strode up the ill-defined path. "Trust me."

She'd sooner trust a fakir who worshipped Kali, Sarah thought darkly. She derived meager satisfaction from scowling at Damien's broad back. She must have been wrong about him caring for Kit. The blackguard was all too casual about his son's well-being.

At the apex of a hill, they came upon a large mossy stone sprouting from a tangle of shrubs and thrusting toward the sky. It was a *lingam*, a phallic symbol. A blush heated her cheeks. She lowered her gaze to the withered marigolds scattering the ridged base. An unearthly melody drifted from beyond the slope.

"You see?" Damien said as he led her over the hill.

"I've seen quite enough," she muttered.

He chuckled. "Get your mind out of the gutter, Miss Priss. I wasn't referring to the *lingam*. Look."

Her gaze followed his pointing finger. Halfway down the grassy incline, a small herd of goats grazed. Their bleating accompanied the lilt of the music.

Like Pan in a book of myths, a wizened man squatted in their midst, playing a bamboo flute. Damien shouted a greeting. The haunting music ended abruptly. As the man leaped nimbly up, Sarah half expected to see cloven hooves instead of bare human feet.

"*Burra* sahib!" he shouted, waving. "Welcome back."

Damien strode down the slope to greet him. Curious about his acquaintance with a goatherd and anxious to feed the baby, she hastened after him. The man saluted Damien with a deep salaam.

"So many months I have not seen you, sahib. I wondered if you would be returning this year."

"I've brought my wife and son. Sarah, this is Vijay."

As she greeted him, the goatherd preened a beard as bristly as a billy goat's. "You will accept my humble hospitality, sahib?"

"We need to press on," Damien said. "But we'd like to buy milk, and a she-goat to take with us."

"I bring you my best nanny."

He dashed over to a shaggy-coated female with full udders. As he milked the creature, Sarah tried to soothe Kit, who now howled from hunger. She changed his wet nappy and sang him a lullaby. Rocking him in her arms, she watched Damien get out the bottle. It was an odd-looking contraption, a glass jar with a rubber teat fitted over the top.

He filled the jar with the warm milk Vijay brought in a leather bucket. Sitting on the grass, Sarah gently touched the teat to Kit's mouth. He spat out the nipple. She tried again. This time he sucked and choked, then turned his head away and screamed louder, his little face red with frustration.

"What's wrong?" Damien said over the din. "Can't you get him to eat?"

"It isn't what he's used to." Her nerves on edge, she added, "You should have thought of that when you dismissed Madakka."

Damien merely cocked an eyebrow. He studied her and the baby. "Maybe you can coax him into drinking. He's used to nursing. Angle him to your breast."

Before she could react, he reached down and turned the baby's body. His scarred fingers brushed the globes of her breasts, but there was no time to protest his familiarity. Kit rooted eagerly and she stuck the nipple into his mouth. He latched on, gulping and sputtering. After a few clumsy tries, he settled into a steady sucking rhythm.

Awash with relief and embarrassment, she looked up at Damien, who stood outlined against the blue sky. "Praise God you found Vijay. How did you know of him?"

"I've been through here before."

"So I gathered." Questions about his life crowded her throat. She looked over at Vijay, who had resumed playing his flute. How had Damien come to gain the esteem of so many people? "Did you photograph this place for your book about India?"

He shrugged. "This and a hundred other areas."

"Did the pictures you took here burn in the caravan?"

His gaze sharpened on her, then his black lashes lowered as he looked at the baby. "Some of them. Everything I'd accomplished for the past eight months was destroyed. I can never replace the photographs I took in Meerut. The sepoys, the punishment parade, things that should be chronicled for all the world to see."

A keen sympathy unfurled in her; she knew the pain of losing something precious. "I'm so sorry, Damien," she said softly. "About your photographs . . . and Shivina. Nothing can ever replace what you lost that night."

"I'll manage."

His jaw set in a rigid line, he turned on his heel and walked off to join Vijay. Sarah yearned to ask if he missed Shivina, if he ever ached for his wife in the darkness of night, if he ever felt so lonely that he wept for the closeness of another human being. How absurd, she thought with a shake of her head. Damien likely hadn't wept since he was a baby.

She looked down at Kit. His sucking had diminished, and the tiny fringe of his lashes lay against his cheeks. Gently she drew the bottle away and kissed his brow. If only she could nurture him forever. But he was Damien's son, and someday she'd have to leave him. The prospect carved a painful hollow inside her chest. She sighed and absently fiddled with her locket. Someday she'd find another man as kind and honorable as Reginald. Someday she'd have a child of her own to fill her heart. Someday she'd have a real home and a family to love.

Damien returned, leading the long-haired goat on a halter fashioned from a length of twine. They said their good-byes to Vijay and started along the trail again. The nanny bleated a protest, then ambled after Damien.

Sarah asked him more questions about the area, but his monosyllabic replies discouraged her. He reverted to his usual aloof self. Annoyance seeped into her somber mood. The uncivil cretin. She hadn't probed very far into his personal life. What had she done but inquire about his lost photographs?

She trod on a sharp object. "Ouch!"

"What's wrong?" said Damien, swinging back, his hand flashing to the revolver.

"I stepped on a stone." Taking care not to awaken Kit, she sank onto a flat rock carpeted with moss and rubbed her heel. "I'll be all right in a minute."

His breath hissed out between his teeth. "Let me look."

He left the goat to graze, then knelt beside Sarah. Grasping her ankle, he angled her foot onto his knee. The gentleness of his fingers made her insides quiver and soften even while her limbs stiffened at his unfamiliar touch. Her gaze riveted on the austere male beauty of his face, the beard that disguised his jaw and cheeks. His mouth was compressed, his black brows lowered, rousing in her the urge to smooth away the lines of tension.

Sarah forced a swallow past her madly beating heart. Lowering her eyes, she realized her hem had slid up to her knees and his thick brown forearm rested against her slim, bare calf. Did he feel as suddenly warm as she? The sole of her foot was as filthy and callused as a farmer's. No, he must be repulsed. Tangled in a web of embarrassed confusion, she twisted away.

"I'm fine now, really I am," she said. "I only wish I had a pair of sandals."

He straightened. Sunlight glinted off the tiny gold flecks in his irises, making his eyes shimmer in his bronzed face. "If your feet are sore, it's your own damned fault," he said. "Because of you, we had to flee before I'd purchased all the supplies. Now get off your arse and walk."

She bristled. "Is it quite necessary to use foul language?"

"Pardon me, your ladyship," he said, sweeping into a formal court bow that looked absurd from a man in a turban and dhoti. "It's going to be dark soon. Would you *please* get off your arse and walk?"

The temptation to defy him curled her fingers into fists. Instantly she reined in the impulse. She *was* guilty, and they did need to press on. Yet his rudeness nettled her.

Rising, she fell into step beside him. "I offered my apologies once," she said stiffly, "and I'll do so again. I made a dreadful mistake in slipping away alone this morning."

"A mistake? You make it sound like a faux pas at tea." He lifted a black brow. "I had the perfect escape plan worked out. Jawahir and I were going to slit their throats during the night. Instead, Lalji could be tracking us."

"Or they could be tracking the villagers."

Damien shook his head. "We're the English. They'd come after us."

With a shiver, Sarah glanced over her shoulder

and lightly stroked the sleeping baby's back. "It's not entirely my fault," she couldn't resist pointing out. "Don't forget, *you* invited those two murderers to travel with us in the first place."

"Forget? How could I?" Damien gave a dark chuckle. "You've managed to find some way to remind me so at least once a day for the past fortnight."

"Because *I* had to endure their lecherous stares." It was a relief to shed the charade, to uncork grievances kept bottled up for weeks. "If Lalji had leered at me one more time, I was going to slap his vile face."

"That would have been interesting."

"You never said one word to stop him from ogling me."

"You were veiled, for God's sake. Your arms were all he could see of your hallowed virginal body. Or were you worried that he might get a rise out of glimpsing your bewitching naked toes?"

Avoiding a thorny bush alongside the trail, Sarah bent her head to hide her chagrin. How naive of her to imagine *he* might be thinking lascivious thoughts while touching her bare foot. "What Lalji could or couldn't see is hardly the point. You were supposed to be my husband. A gentleman would have had the grace to ask him to treat me with respect."

A look of sham horror crossed Damien's face. "God spare me from being mistaken for a gentleman. Besides, you were doing a superior job of speaking up for yourself. I trust you'll do as well taking care of Kit."

"I had to speak up. You were busy inventing lewd tales about me to pique their interest."

Damien stopped so abruptly she almost collided with him. The nanny goat bleated and settled to nibbling a few blades of grass. "Lewd tales?" he said. "About *you*?"

"Yes. About all those nights the mutineers thought we were really . . . you know." Sarah started to dip her head, then willed herself to look straight at Damien.

Unexpected humor softened the strict line of his mouth. "No," he said blandly, "I don't know."

Ignoring the rapid beating of her heart, she clung to anger. "Lalji said you told him some interesting tales of . . . of my talents."

"I see. Go ahead, refresh my memory and relate one of those tales."

"He didn't say any more than just that. And I most certainly didn't ask him to elaborate."

Her huffy manner made Damien choke back a chuckle. For an old maid, Sarah Faulkner could look remarkably appealing with her clear blue eyes framed by dyed black hair, the hint of roses beneath the duskiness of her cheeks. Her unique blend of girlish innocence and womanly spirit made his imagination run wild with speculation. He wondered if she'd stained the skin beneath her clothing. He wondered whether her breasts were heavy enough to fill his palms. Most of all, he wondered if he could stroke away her inhibitions until she opened herself to him in sweetly provocative invitation.

He cursed the swell of life in his groin. Their sparring at least kept her at a safe distance. Turning his gaze downward, over her shapely figure, he looked at Kit's small, slumbering form angled against her hip. His son rested near the cradle of her pelvis, where Damien ached to put his mouth.

Gritting his teeth, he snatched the tether and tugged the goat up the trail. "Come on," he muttered to Sarah.

For too many nights he'd lain awake, sweating with the need to touch the woman sleeping beside him. Deep down, he knew why his body betrayed him. He knew why he could lust so hotly when only a month ago he'd watched his wife's body burn.

He had the black soul of a devil.

The old shame escaped its bonds and ravaged his chest. With the swiftness of practice, he clamped down on his emotions. Christ, it was just that he hadn't had a woman in too, too long. Once he'd learned of Shivina's pregnancy, he'd avoided her bed to salve his guilt. She was a fine woman, a woman he didn't deserve—shy and kind, the sort of female who fades into the background yet brings peace to a man's life.

Not a shrew who nagged so much he couldn't think straight.

Yet when he looked back to see Sarah valiantly struggling to match his long strides, he slowed his pace and admitted, "Lalji lied to you. I never told him any tales about your expertise in bed."

"You didn't?"

"No. I swear on my honor as a rogue."

Sarah found herself believing him. Especially the part about being a rogue. Despite his aggravating, uncommunicative nature, sincerity gleamed in his eyes. "That's a relief," she murmured. "I couldn't bear to think of you discussing me . . . in that manner."

"I never said we didn't discuss you. As a matter of fact, they wanted to know if a woman with a bold tongue was just as bold when lying with her husband."

Her eyes snapped to his. "What did you say to them?"

He studied Sarah, as if gauging her worth and finding her wanting. "I told them you were a rotten lover. That you just lay there like a dried-up gourd."

She almost stumbled on an exposed root. Damien caught her arm and held her upright. "You all right?" he asked.

"Yes." She pulled away, irked for reasons she

couldn't fathom. "How could you talk about your wife that way?"

"My wife? Thank God you're not that."

"Damien, answer me."

"Well, my description of your lovemaking is a hell of a lot closer to the truth than Lalji's version. Think about that when you assume I didn't try to protect your precious purity." He swung back up the trail.

Sarah pursed her lips and marched after him. She shouldn't be incensed, she should be grateful he'd made her sound unappealing to the sepoys. Then again, he shouldn't have looked so infuriatingly smug. As if he'd told a vulgar joke. A joke that somehow escaped her comprehension.

"I'll tell you what I think," she said as loftily as she could when addressing his broad back. "I'm glad the charade is finally over. I'm glad we needn't sleep together any longer."

Only hours later, she dearly regretted her statement.

Chapter 13

~~~⟡~~~

They camped that evening in a tiny ruined temple beside a clear stream. The burble of water over rocks filled the void left by their sparse conversation. Sarah made a silent vow to be civil for the few days until they rejoined the villagers.

She managed to swallow her opinion when Damien struggled to milk the reluctant goat. She was proud of her restraint in offering advice while he cooked dinner and she fed the baby. She permitted herself only a gracious compliment when she tasted his excellent curried rice and *dal*. She even managed not to inquire where he'd learned to cook so well.

Let him be secretive about his shadowy past, she thought as she cuddled Kit against the evening chill. Damien Coleridge was her employer. Their association began and ended with that.

Wanting to cover Kit's head, she reached for the cap, but it wasn't tucked into her sari. She frowned at Damien, who crouched and washed the dishes in the stream. "Have you seen the red hat I purchased in the bazaar?"

He shook his head. "Keep track of your own damned belongings."

As he returned his attention to his work, she stuck her tongue out at his back. The boar. Let him be rude, too.

The sky deepened through a succession of gold, red, and purple. With the swiftness of a blink, the colors vanished, leaving velvet blackness and a smattering of stars which Sarah could see through the fallen roof of the shrine. She settled Kit near the small fire on the dirt floor and lay down beside him.

A distant scream prickled over her skin. She shivered, as much from the eerie sound as from the coolness of the evening. She looked at Damien, who lounged against a vine-wrapped pillar. He drew on his *bidi*, and the tip glowed orange.

"What was that sound?" she asked.

"Panther."

She sat up straight, the blanket falling back. "Panther?"

"Don't worry, it was far away. I doubt it'll roam close enough to bother us."

"You *doubt*? How reassuring."

"There may be leopards and tigers out there, too, though I didn't see any pug marks. The big predators usually keep to the lowlands and valleys."

"Usually." She focused on the one word.

"We'll be safe enough inside here." He jabbed the cigarette toward the gun on the ground. "I'll keep the revolver beside me."

Somewhat relieved, she forced herself to lie back down, covering herself to her chin with the scratchy blanket. The stream gushed its endless melody. An owl hooted overhead. The goat bleated from its tether in the shadows. A faint snuffling noise came from the darkness outside.

She pushed herself up on an elbow. "Damien? Did you hear that?"

"It was probably a *chital*."

"A *chital*?"

"A type of deer. Go to sleep, Sarah."

She curled herself close to Kit's slumbering form. He stirred and sighed, then stuck his thumb in this mouth. The night seemed alive with sounds—the buzzing of insects, the rustling of leaves, the howling of jackals. And too many other noises she couldn't identify—an indistinct grunt, a muted thump.

She and Aunt Violet had stayed every summer in the hill station of Simla, but they'd resided in a snug bungalow, rather than camping out in the wilderness. Sarah resolutely closed her eyes and tried not to speculate on the savage beasts roaming the gloom. The crackle of the fire lulled her. Exhaustion weighted her limbs. Suddenly a loud shuffling noise came from nearby.

With a gasp, she shot up. "What was that?"

"That was me, Sarah," came Damien's laconic voice. He paused. "Look, do you want me to sleep beside you?"

Pride was an inadequate protector. "Would you?" she asked in her meekest tone.

She braced herself for a sarcastic remark, but he merely tossed his *bidi* into the fire and then stretched out beside her on the hard floor, drawing the blanket over them. Heat and comfort radiated into her. His strength and solidity soothed her tense muscles. Within moments, she was sound asleep.

After two more long days of traveling, Sarah awoke on the third morning to find Damien gone. Scrubbing the sleep from her eyes, she rolled onto her side and reached for Kit. Her hand found empty space. Alarm gripped her. The baby was gone, too.

The pink glow of dawn washed the densely forested area in pearly light. They'd reached the high area at dusk, too late to make the precarious trip across a nearby *jhula*, a narrow rope bridge spanning a rocky gorge. One misstep would send the clumsy traveler plunging to the river far below.

She sat up and peered frantically around.

They'd slept in the lee of a gigantic boulder, where a natural depression provided shelter. Pine needles carpeted the ground. Across the clearing and beyond the small campfire, the nanny goat was grazing in a patch of long grass. The tang of cedar and woodsmoke hung in the air.

Merciful God, where were they?

Then she spied Damien. Several yards away, he sat half hidden by a tall deodar tree, his back propped against the trunk, his long legs stretched out and crossed at the ankles. In the nest of his arm, Kit lay sucking contentedly on a bottle.

She leaned weakly against the boulder. How ridiculous to be frightened. If Lalji hadn't tracked them down already, he wouldn't now.

In the absence of fear, wonderment curled around her heart. She had never before seen Damien pay more than fleeting attention to his son. The baby looked tiny cuddled against his father's massive chest. They were angled slightly away from her, yet she could see in Damien's profile a tenderness alien to his rough-hewn features, and all the more touching for its rarity.

He'd left off his turban, and his thick black hair embellished his swarthy handsomeness. She was struck by the likeness between father and son, the same wide brow and high cheekbones, the same dusky skin. How remarkable that the sepoys had never seen the English resemblance.

He set down the bottle, pushed up his knees, and nestled Kit against the bracket of his thighs. The baby gazed wide-eyed at his father. Damien tickled him under the chin and then let his tiny fist enfold one scarred finger.

"Drank all your milk," he murmured. "What a clever lad you are. And gallant to behave so well. You've only complained when you were hungry. Can't blame a boy for that, can we?"

His gentle tone astounded Sarah. A knot of emotion unraveled deep within her, threaded past barriers of pride and propriety, and unfurled in a tender smile. *My heart can hear the pain in his soul. It is a pain that makes him fear to show love.*

Many weeks ago, Shivina had spoken the words Sarah had scorned. Yet now, in a bolt of revelation, she knew how very wrong she'd been about Damien, how very quick to judge him. The sensitivity beneath his gruff exterior shone as clear as his love for Kit.

She burned to know what had happened in his past to make him so reticent about showing emotion. Had the tragedy of the fire scarred more than his hands? Mrs. Craven had gossiped that he set the fire as a prank and turned his brother into a half-wit . . .

"You'll see birds and squirrels today," he told the baby. "I promise we'll be home by the afternoon. What do you say to that, son? Are you curious to see where we're going, you and me and Sarah, hmmm?"

The infant cooed, batting at the air.

Drawn irresistibly, Sarah rose and walked to them. Damien cocked his head up at her. The grin died a slow death on his hard mouth. He appeared oddly guilty, like a child caught filching a sweet. He lowered his gaze to his son.

"He smiled," Damien said, as if to explain his lapse in guard. "Kit smiled at me."

"Did he?" Surprised and pleased, she knelt beside him and watched the infant. Brown eyes regarded her from a sweetly chubby face wreathed in a happy smile. "That means he likes you."

Damien looked dubious. "How could he? He hardly knows me."

"Then show him the shining example of a father," she said tartly. "Take care of him more often. But even though you haven't spent much time with him, he can sense that you love him."

"Oh." Her words seemed to fluster Damien.

Without meeting her eyes, he shoved the baby into her arms. "I'll boil his bottle and pack up."

Holding Kit against her shoulder, she followed Damien to the fire. "What did you mean just now when you said we'll reach home by afternoon?"

He glanced at her, then pitched the bottle and nipple into the small pot of bubbling water by the fire. "Exactly what I said."

"But . . . home?" she asked in bewilderment. "Just where are we going? I've asked you that before, and you evaded the question."

"I'll show you." Crouching, he picked up a stick and sketched a precise map of India in the dirt, marking the major towns. "This is Meerut. And here's Delhi to the west. Sepoys have mutinied to the east of us in Bareilly, Budaun, and Fatehgarh. So it's a damned good thing we headed north." He drew a line upward from Meerut, then jabbed a dot to the northwest. "Here's Simla. Back in Hardwar, I heard a rumor of a battalion of Gurkhas revolting there. We'll stay in the mountains to the east, right here." He made an X on the ground.

"Is that Mussoorie?" she asked, naming a closer hill station.

"No. English settlements are too damned dangerous. Filled with the likes of Keppu and Lalji."

She tilted her head and shifted Kit into the cradle of her arm. "But, Damien, I still don't understand. We haven't seen anything in these hills except a few goats. Where exactly are we going?"

"To a hut where we'll be safe."

He brushed dirt over the map. By the way he avoided her eyes, she had the distinct impression he was holding something back. "Is that where we'll meet Jawahir and his family?"

Damien broke the stick and dropped the pieces. Sitting on his haunches, he looked up at her. His stone-brown eyes glinted in his handsome face. "We aren't meeting them, Sarah."

"What?"

"You heard me. They had to return to their village before the monsoon begins. So they can prepare for the summer planting."

Comprehension burst through her confusion, obliterating her tender mood. Her arm flexed around the baby's small form. "You tricked me," she whispered in disbelief.

He lifted his shoulders in a casual admission of guilt. "I had to. You were putting up a fuss about traveling alone with me. I told you what you wanted to hear because it was the quickest way to get you moving."

He'd let her blithely believe a lie. He'd played her for a fool. Hurt slashed her like a knife. "Get me moving? You know I wouldn't have endangered Kit."

"Then you shouldn't have argued. You should have come without a protest."

"And you should have told me the truth. All along you meant for us to spend weeks—possibly months—alone in the wilderness. And you've waited three days to tell me about it. Why?"

"We've been traveling hard. There never seemed to be a good time."

His nonchalance filled Sarah with trembling anger. "And what if Lalji goes after the villagers? He could kill Madakka, Lakshmi, the children."

"They'll be fine. Jawahir had a friend in Hardwar he intended to stay with for a few days."

"Oh, really," Sarah snapped. "I wonder if I can believe anything you say. How many other lies have you told me?"

His gaze shifted away. "Let's not waste time on another argument." He jumped up and went to the fire, using a stick to pluck the bottle from the boiling water. "We need to press on."

She marched after him. "Oh, no, Damien Coleridge. You're not going to weasel your way out of this one. Tell me, was my exalted salary a lie, too?''

''You'll get your money. Believe me, I'd do anything, say anything, to make you quit pestering me.''

''I'll pester you until I know the truth. Now I asked you a question. Answer me. What else have you lied to me about?''

He flung the bottle into the sack and pivoted to face her, his hands on his hips. ''You work for me. I don't owe you any explanations.''

''Then I quit.'' She held out the baby. ''You can take care of Kit yourself.''

Damien blew out a breath. ''All right, Miss Priss. The answer is one.''

She clasped the infant close. ''One?''

''I lied to you about one other fact.''

''What fact?''

He plowed his fingers through his hair. ''If you're so damned clever,'' he muttered, ''I'm sure you can figure it out for yourself.''

Her mind flashed over everything he'd ever told her, but she came up blank. Then she saw his gaze flit to her bosom. To her locket.

A ghastly possibility struck her heart. With cold fingers, she groped for the locket at her throat.

''Reginald,'' she whispered in dawning horror. ''You lied about Reginald's death. Didn't you?''

''No,'' he said, too quickly.

''Yes. For once in your life, tell the truth.''

Damien hunched his shoulders and moodily met her accusing gaze. ''All right, then. I'm sorry, but you gave me no choice. I needed a nanny for Kit. You wouldn't have come with me otherwise.''

Dear God in heaven. Reginald was alive.

Even as the miraculous thought leaped within her, icy rage throttled her. ''You manipulated me. All these weeks you let me grieve for a man who's still alive.''

"His leg was cut open by a *badmash*. He might not have lasted the night."

The news appalled her. "I could have gone back and tended to him. Damien, he needed me."

"Kit needed you more."

"That doesn't give you the right to play God with my life."

He shrugged without apology. "It's only temporary."

The callous lack of shame on his face blinded her judgment. She whipped out her hand. The flat of her palm met his cheek in a stinging crack.

"You *devil*!"

Spinning around, Sarah stalked away. Tears blurred her vision. Her stomach churned, her throat hurt. She felt betrayed, abused, cut so deep she couldn't form a logical thought.

Clinging tight to Kit, she half ran down the narrow trail. Stones scored her bare feet. The wind fluttered a wisp of hair across her cheek. As she rounded a boulder, a thorny bush caught her sari. She glanced down to yank the silk free.

When she looked up, a man sprang from the undergrowth.

She cried out and recoiled. Her arms clenched protectively around the baby. Dawn light gleamed on the man's shaven pate and glinted off the knife in his hand. His eyes of odd-matched brown and filmy white snared her with horror.

Then Lalji charged.

Chapter 14

⟨⟨❦⟩⟩

Her scream tore into Damien.

He sped out of camp and pounded down the track. Oh, God, he should have gone after her the instant she'd fled. But he'd simply stood there, his cheek smarting from the slap, his chest heavy with guilt, his mind devastated by her words. *You devil.*

He yanked the revolver from his sash. Ghastly images leaped through his mind. A panther had attacked Sarah and Kit. Or they'd tumbled down the rocky slope. Or—

He half skidded around a clump of rhododendrons. His worst nightmare stopped him cold.

Lalji held Sarah from behind. His knife blade caressed her throat. His grimy hand gripped her long black braid as if it were a thick rope. Her head was bent back to avoid the razor edge. She stood helpless, Kit wailing and squirming in her arms, her blue eyes achingly beautiful and terribly scared.

The sepoy curled his lips in a grin. "I have your wife, Dharam. Or do you have a *feringhi* name?"

"Never mind my name." Tasting bitter fear, Damien advanced slowly, the gun heavy in his hand. "Let the woman go," he said, his voice sounding hoarse and unnatural to his ears. "Your quarrel is with me."

"Bah. She threw me in the *Ganga*." He yanked her braid, and her head jerked farther back. "I will have my revenge."

"Harm her and I'll bury your worthless carcass in dog dung."

Lalji scowled, his red-stained teeth bared. "Do not mock me. I will kill both of them, and then you."

Desperate to buy time, Damien said, "How did you find us?"

"You dropped the baby's red cap. That told me which trail you took."

Damn! He should have paid more attention when Sarah mentioned the hat. "Put the baby down. He's innocent of any wrongdoing."

"I always thought the boy had the look of a half-caste. Is he yours or hers, I wonder?" Lalji spat on the ground. "It is no matter. The jackals will make short work of him once you and the woman are dead."

A killing rage gripped Damien. The pitiful sound of Kit's wail wrapped around his heart. He steeled his emotions and racked his brains for a plan. In despair, he could think of no way to guarantee the safety of Sarah and his son. He had no choice but to play this game with a losing hand of cards.

"You can't murder all three of us," he said, forcing a reasonable tone. "If you harm either of them, I'll put a bullet in your heart." He aimed the revolver at Lalji.

"Bah! Keppu was approaching your camp from the north side. He must have heard your woman scream. He will come at any moment."

It was a ploy, Damien thought. A ploy to make him turn and look. A ploy he might use to stack his own deck. He kept his eyes fixed on the sepoy. "Keppu is dead. I might have known you'd be fool enough to come after us alone." He cocked the hammer with a loud click.

Sweat popped out on Lalji's brow. "You won't risk killing the woman and child."

"Better I should take that chance than let you cut her throat."

A crafty gleam in his good eye, Lalji said, "Enough, enough. Do not act in haste. Give me your gun and I will let her go."

"Don't do it, Damien," Sarah gasped. "He's lying—"

"Silence, *feringhi* whore."

The mutineer tightened his arm. The blade depressed the tender skin of her throat. Her sharp intake of breath sliced into Damien. Kit continued to squall.

"Throw down the gun," Lalji warned again. "Far away from you, ere I spill her blood and the child's this instant."

Damien eased the hammer down. What did his life matter if Kit died here? He let the revolver slip from his fingers and clatter to the ground. He kicked it off the path, a few feet from him.

Bloody hell, he thought bleakly. So much for bluffing. He too might very well die on this desolate slope. For himself he couldn't mourn; he was never any good to begin with. But Sarah and Kit . . .

Maybe he could gamble on one last desperate move.

Lalji sidled toward the gun, dragging Sarah and the baby with him. "I always thought you a most prudent man, Dharam. How satisfying to see I was not wrong."

Damien kept his expression arranged in helpless defeat, an arduous task when he chafed to hurl the swine into the gorge.

The sepoy stopped beside the gun. Keeping his eyes trained on Damien, Lalji leaned cautiously down. As his arm strained toward the ground, the knife shifted a scant inch away from Sarah's throat.

Damien pointed down the hill. "Oh, my God, it's Keppu!"

Lalji jerked his head around. Damien dived for the knife. He clamped onto Lalji's arm and pulled it away from Sarah. He twisted the limb with punishing force. The dull snap of a bone resounded. Lalji screamed, a high-pitched animal noise.

The knife clanged to the rocky ground. The sepoy staggered back a step, his arm hanging at an unnatural angle. Moaning, he collapsed.

Sarah half stumbled, Kit whimpering against her breasts. Damien hauled her up and shoved her toward the camp.

"Get out of here," he gasped.

"But what about you?"

"For Christ's sake, this is no time to argue. Save Kit."

Glancing over her shoulder, she scurried up the path.

His face snarled with pain, Lalji closed his uninjured hand around the revolver. He started to raise the gun. Damien stomped on the sepoy's wrist. Lalji howled and fell backward. The weapon went flying.

Damien snatched up the dagger. He dropped to one knee beside the sepoy. In a single agile stroke, he carved the blade across the sepoy's dark throat. Lalji's cry ended in a muted gurgle. Warm blood spurted over his soiled red coat. He twitched once and went still, his mismatched eyes staring at the sky.

The savage buzz faded from Damien's ears. Revulsion rolled in his stomach. He flung away the gory knife and let his forehead fall to his knee. His hand felt befouled with blood. His soul felt dark with the deed he'd done. Sucking in deep breaths, he fought off a wave of dizzy relief.

Sarah. He had to reassure himself that she and his son were unharmed.

Surging to his feet, he left the corpse lying on the ground. Let the vultures and jackals feast today, he thought in contempt.

He found the revolver beneath a bush. After wiping his fingers on a patch of grass, he tucked the weapon into his sash and then sprinted up the path.

At the edge of the clearing, Sarah paced with the baby. Kit had ceased crying and was sucking his thumb. Damien clenched his sticky hand into a fist to keep from touching her. Fierce glory pulsed through his loins. Any other English-woman would have had hysterics, but not Sarah Faulkner. He'd done her wrong. She might look as delicate as a jasmine blossom, yet the will beneath her feminine fragility was like fine-tempered steel. He permitted his gaze to caress the petal-soft skin of her throat.

"Are you all right?" he said gruffly.

"I'm fine." She looked past him, down the path. "Damien, is he—?"

"Dead. There can be no doubt about that anymore."

Relief coursed through Sarah, as powerful as her joy at seeing Damien hale and alive. The brilliance in his brown eyes held her riveted. He looked so savage and intense that her thoughts scattered like leaves on the wind. Her belly ached with the same unnamed yearning she'd felt long weeks ago in the garden of her uncle's bungalow. The yearning to absorb Damien's sweat-dampened scent, to know the clasp of his arms, to feel this thick black hair sifting through her fingers.

"You saved my life," she murmured shakily.

His gaze fell to her parted lips. He inhaled a gulp of air and stepped back. "That makes us even, then. Gather your things, Sarah. We have to get over that bridge and deeper into the mountains."

He walked away. She felt frustrated, unexplored, chaste. Her churning emotions shocked her. How absurd. As if virtue were a sin to lament. *He* was the sinner—Damien Coleridge, who could fabricate a falsehood as glibly as a *sadhu* could recite a mantra.

She looked down. Kit had fallen asleep. Gently she fastened him in the sling at her side. While Damien knelt to wash his hands in a thin stream of water from the canteen, she untied the goat, then tugged the animal toward the bridge spanning the gorge. The nanny blinked its thickly lashed eyes and bleated a protest. The liquid rush of water echoed from far below.

She looked back and saw Damien shouldering the knapsack. Their earlier clash played through her memory. How peculiar to think of Reginald alive when she'd resigned herself to his death. Of course, if he'd been injured as badly as Damien said . . . She brushed off her fear and let herself imagine her fiancé waiting impatiently in Meerut. But would he want her now that Damien had ruined her reputation by hauling her off to the foothills?

Anger stirred in her again; she tightly controlled the emotion. She should have known better than to expect honesty from Damien Coleridge. Her palm still stung from the slap. She flushed. His uncouth nature must be rubbing off on her.

A sharp report split the air. She ducked instinctively. Something thunked into the dirt beside her.

"What the hell—" Damien bit out. "Run, Sarah! For God's sake, run!"

The urgency in his voice made her heart trip with alarm. She spun around to obey, then blinked in disbelief. At the rim of the clearing, a giant clambered over a mass of boulders. A giant in a soiled turban, red coat, and dirty white trou-

sers. Sunlight glared off the rifle in his oversized
hand.

"Merciful God, Damien! It's Keppu—"

The mutineer thundered toward them. Revolver drawn, Damien took aim. A shot cracked.
Keppu dodged and faltered, blood pouring from
his shoulder. With a mighty growl, he plunged
onward.

Dropping the knapsack, Damien thrust her toward the bridge. "This time do as you're damned
well told!"

Horrified, Sarah dropped the goat's tether and
dashed toward the *jhula*. Dear heaven, she had to
protect Kit. Clasping the side ropes, she stepped
onto the bridge. Bamboo strips formed a precarious walkway less than a foot wide. Far below, at
the bottom of the steep canyon, a great torrent of
water raged over a rock-littered channel.

The bamboo was smooth and slick beneath her
bare feet. The bridge swayed in a gust of wind.
Giddiness turned in her stomach. Her fingers
clamped in a death grip around the rough vine
ropes. Resolutely she kept her gaze pinned to the
opposite cliff as she inched her way out into the
middle of the gorge. She prayed she'd tied the
sling securely enough. She couldn't let herself
think of Kit falling to the ribbon of angry water
below.

Over the rumble of the river another shot
sounded. Holding tight to the bridge, she looked
back. The two men struggled. Damien knocked
the gun out of Keppu's hand and tried to turn his
own revolver. But Keppu kept his big fist
wrapped around Damien's forearm. With the
vigor of a bullock, the wounded sepoy slowly
backed Damien toward the abyss.

A scream clogged her throat as the men neared
the bridge. Keppu drove Damien toward the
gorge. At the last possible instant, Damien jerked

to the side. Instead of tumbling over the precipice, he slammed onto the *jhula*, Keppu diving atop him.

The ropes rocked violently. Sarah teetered and held tight. Her blood ran raw as ice. Yanking out a dagger, the sepoy struck at Damien. He rolled in the narrow space. His hand burst up to hit the knife away. The weapon fell like a glittering gem to the surging waters below.

The breath left Sarah in a whoosh. The bridge shook and quaked with the force of their fight. Dear God, she had never felt so helpless. She couldn't stand by and watch Damien die. She turned cautiously, desperate to give aid yet afraid to plunge to a rocky death.

A shot exploded. Both men went still.

Sarah froze in the grip of a hideous suspense. If the sepoy had wrested the gun away—

Abruptly Damien surged upward, heaving Keppu off him. The sepoy collapsed onto the side rope and hung there like a huge toy bear. A spreading crimson patch stained his chest. Then he slipped off the bridge, plummeting the long distance to the rocks.

As fast as she dared move over the slippery bamboo, Sarah rushed to Damien. He staggered off the *jhula* and stood swaying, his head bowed, his breath emerging in pants. Blood spattered the front of his white tunic.

Alarm battered her heart. In search of a wound, she hurried her shaking hands over the sweat-slick muscles of his arms, the steel-hewn contour of his chest. "Merciful heaven," she gasped. "Damien, are you hurt?"

He threw back his head. His eyes glittered with savage victory. "Sarah," he muttered hoarsely.

He hauled her against him, angling her sideways to avoid the sleeping baby at her hip. His mouth crushed down over hers in a kiss that was the antithesis of her romantic dreams and yet the perfect answer to every nameless question swirling inside her. Their bodies melded, and the solidity of him swept away all memory of terror and ignited in its wake the fire of desire. His mouth stroked hers with ravenous hunger, his tongue dipping inside to taste the nectar within. She fell headlong into a new world, a world of golden light and heightened senses, a world where her head swam and her soul soared and her body came to vivid life. Liquid warmth descended from her heart, shimmering through her limbs and settling like a deep pulsebeat in her loins.

His hands moved in caressing circles over the soft flesh of her bottom. Tasting desperation in him, she swayed and he steadied her, lifting her to him with insistent pressure. Trembling, she let her own hands roam on an upward journey over the unfamiliar terrain of his body. Her fingers found the masculine breadth of his torso, the strong column of his neck, the unexpected silken feel of his hair. His aroma of sweat and blood should have repelled her; instead, the scent tingled through her with the exultation of life.

His lips tracked across her cheek and nuzzled her ear. The smoothness of his palm slipped inside her sari to gently cup her breast, his thumb plying the tip. A tide of sensation washed her, powered by the beguiling feel of his hands and mouth, fueled by the fierce emotions burning in her chest.

"Damien," she whispered. "Oh, Damien."

Her breathless voice drifted to him through a mist of erotic urgency. The sound tugged at Damien, drew him from the mindless pleasure of lust unleashed. The woman in his arms was a stranger, all soft, yielding womanhood, a sweet seductive siren who lured him from the iron bonds of self-discipline. Yet on a deep level he recognized her throaty voice and unique essence.

The fog cleared under a gust of cold sanity.

God! What in hell was he doing? The woman in his arms was Sarah Faulkner.

He yanked his hand from the curve of her bare breast and jerked up his head. The double murder must have shaken him beyond reason. Her lashes lifted. Her eyes were a dreamy blue, her lips reddened and moist. Against his will, he felt the powerful pull of passion in his loins, a passion he rejected. Sarah Faulkner was a sourmouthed spinster, a crusading do-gooder, a meddlesome English lady who would dig and dig at a man until his secrets lay naked for all the world to ridicule.

He'd be damned if he'd let her wriggle her shapely way into *his* private self. He knew exactly how to keep her distant.

"Well, well, Miss Priss," he drawled. "For an old maid, you certainly know all the right moves. I wonder if Reggie is man enough to handle you."

His words hit Sarah like a needling blow. The gold flecks in his eyes flashed with mockery. Heat snapped to her cheeks, and the ardor inside her chilled. "Reginald is an honorable man," she said, reaching for the locket. "He knows how to treat a lady. An aspect of refinement clearly neglected in *your* upbringing."

"How very suited you both are—two perfect angels. What a pity you're stuck with a devil like me." Damien turned on his heel and walked away.

Watching him, she could still taste him on her tongue and feel his warm hand cradling her breast. The sensations both thrilled and appalled her. She had behaved as no lady should; she had melted into the embrace of an unprincipled rogue. With the news of Reginald fresh in her heart, she shouldn't have found pleasure in kissing another man.

Sarah shook off the sticky threads of shame. It was only the close escape from death that had made her react so immodestly. The altered circumstances of her life had submerged her inbred decorum. But she wouldn't lose control again.

A devil like me. She looked across the clearing, where Damien bent to pick up the knapsack he'd dropped. She had the impression his words mocked himself rather than her. It was almost as if he believed the worst of himself and strove to fit the wicked image of a demon.

Her gaze fell to Kit, sleeping peacefully in the sling at her hip. The baby had napped through both the frightful skirmish and the shattering kiss. A splotch of scarlet on her sari caught her attention. Startled, she saw blood smeared on her abdomen.

Her gaze darted to Damien. He was walking toward her, tugging the goat after him. A bloodied slit scored the left side of his tunic.

"You *are* hurt," she said.

"It's only a scratch. Besides, what do you care?"

She moved toward him. "I care because you owe me a salary," she said tartly. "Let me look."

He reared back. "Leave it, Sarah."

"And let you bleed to death out of bravado?" Mulishness coupled with fear made her reach for the folds of his tunic and lift the cotton fabric. At the indentation of his waist, blood seeped from a long slick gash. She touched the skin beside it and he winced, the iron muscles of his stomach sucking inward. Shuddering, she lifted her gaze to his. "If Keppu had struck a few inches over, you might have been killed."

"You might have been, too. Bird-witted female! I told you to run, but you just stood there like a damned sacred cow."

His ill-mannered speech tested the limits of her patience. "I am going to dress your wound," she stated. "Not because I care for you personally, but because I won't let you die and leave me alone in the wilds with Kit."

"God forbid I should inconvenience you," he muttered.

But he sank onto a flat stone and suffered her ministrations. She pressed a clean nappy against the injury. "I should wash this," she said. "The good Lord only knows where that knife has been. I wish I had some antiseptic."

"Quit fussing and get on with it. You're worse than a mother hen."

"And you're as cocky as a rooster in a hen-house."

With strips tied from another nappy, she bound the bandage in place. The work required her to press her cheek to his chest in order to pass the binding around his broad form. His male scent, his firm flesh, made her pulse leap. Gritting her teeth, she willed her body to recall how incompatible she and this man were.

To distract herself, she said, "I find it hard to believe Keppu survived that awful blow I dealt him back at the *ghat*."

"Look at it this way—at least you can sleep with a clear conscience tonight. Two more deaths on my black soul won't make much difference."

His self-scourging tone struck her as odd. Rising, she eyed him curiously. "Damien, why do you always disparage yourself?"

His gaze faltered; then he cocked an eyebrow up at her. "What a question to ask of a liar, a scoundrel, and a murderer."

"No one is completely wicked. Not even you."

"What about Lalji and Keppu? And the fakir?"

"They're men who fought back when their religious beliefs were trampled by the Raj. Perhaps our suppression of the natives brought out the worst in them."

"As you bring out the worst in me?"

She pursed her lips. "There you go again, resorting to sarcasm when I'm trying to hold a reasonable discussion.''

"Reasonable?'' Damien stood, yanking his tunic over the bandage. ''You're trying to turn me into your current crusade. Well, forget it. Contrary to what you believe, I haven't been languishing my whole life, just waiting for you to come along and mend my flaws.''

Frustrated, she said, "Perhaps I'm struggling to find some good in the man who's forced me to spend weeks with him. At least I can be assured you love Kit.''

''He's my son. It's not as if I have a choice.'' Damien's testy gaze dropped to the sleeping baby and softened, then snapped back to her. ''I hired you to take care of him, so spare me your prying observations.'' Wheeling, he picked up the tether and drew the goat toward the *jhula.*

Sarah followed slowly. The trek over the flimsy bridge held less terror for her this time. She glanced down only once and saw Keppu's lifeless body, tiny so far below, pinned between two boulders. It could have been Damien down there.

A gust of wind made the *jhula* sway. The sickening pitch in her stomach brought her gaze back up. Holding tight to the side ropes, she kept her eyes focused on Damien's back.

When her feet touched solid ground, she breathed a sigh of relief. With the bridge and the murderers behind them, she and Damien climbed a path barely visible on the steep hillside, where primulas and gentians flourished in the rocky soil. Clusters of pines towered to the achingly blue sky, and at the top of every hill, the great snow-clad mountains loomed on the northern horizon like a stairway to heaven.

Exhibiting no handicap from his injury, Damien moved effortlessly over the rough terrain, his thigh muscles bunching, his legs long and brown and sturdy. Her gaze wandered over the breadth of his shoulders, the leanness of his waist, the bronze sheen of his skin. Now she knew the silky texture of his hair, the power inherent in his male flesh.

And the infuriating quality of his character, Sarah reminded herself. With each step, she cited his failings. He was impossible to talk to. He was hopeless to befriend. He thought women were beasts of burden. I. M. Vexed could teach him a thing or two. Yet he was her solitary adult companion for Lord only knew how long. She envisioned silent meals, lonely nights. She envisioned him kissing her again, fondling her naked breasts—

She stilled a voluptuous tremor. He had her thinking like a hussy, acknowledging her own sensual nature. She must never sink to his level of jaded immorality. Her reputation might be in shreds, but she would behave with the dignity and honor expected of Reginald's fiancée. A stolen moment of lust wasn't worth the cost of her entire future. Besides, Damien had made it quite clear that he found her less than appealing.

You aren't exactly my kind of woman. His words nagged at Sarah like a sore tooth. She was conscious suddenly that her hair felt greasy from the black dye, her skin was a dreary brown instead of creamy rose, her sari hung limp and bedraggled after so many days of travel. He liked his women silent and subservient, dainty and doting, unsoiled and soft. She glowered at his back. The lout wanted to be worshipped like a rajah.

They made two brief stops to feed the baby. As expected, Damien reverted to his taciturn self. With typical discourtesy, he rejected her attempts to make polite conversation about Kit or the scenery. In the early afternoon, she was startled when he volunteered, "There. We're home."

Her gaze followed his pointing finger to a hut nestled in a clump of cedars on a slope so sheer that several of the trees grew at an angle. Built of logs, the house perched on a shelf of rock overlooking a green valley. Cedar shingles formed a steep roof shaped like a huge triangular hat, the brim curling outward in Tibetan style, shading a wide wraparound porch.

She fancied the home beckoning a warm welcome. The weight of the baby dragging at her, she trailed Damien over a swiftly flowing stream. The water chilled her toes. Without speaking, he turned and lent her a hand as she carefully negotiated the pattern of mossy rocks. Then they climbed the hill to the hut.

Damien ushered her into the dim interior. A musty, unused smell pervaded the air, along with the aromatic scent of cedar. He flung open the wooden shutters. Sunlight poured over a cozy parlor, sparsely furnished with a wooden settee and chairs topped by handwoven cushions. A simple desk stood beneath a row of bookshelves. Before the stone fireplace lay a tiger-skin rug.

Framed photographs decorated the log walls. Moving closer, she scanned a picture of a flat-faced mountain woman toting a basket of rice on her head. "These are your photographs."

"How astute," he drawled.

"Then this house belongs to you. Why didn't you tell me?"

"I called it home, for God's sake."

"I thought that was just a manner of speaking."

He sent her a look of black humor. "You should know by now that I haven't any manners."

He dropped the knapsack on a table in the corner kitchen. Then he rummaged in a wooden cupboard.

How incongruous to think of a duke's son living in a hut. She burned to ask more, how long he'd owned the place, if Shivina had lived here as his concubine. But his reserve stood between them like a granite wall. Sarah moved toward the nearest of two closed doors.

"Where are you going?" Damien said sharply.

"To lay Kit down."

"Well, don't go in there."

"Why not?"

"Because the bedroom's through there." He jabbed a finger toward the other door.

It was on the tip of her tongue to ask what hallowed secrets the other room held. But he probably wouldn't tell her. She was weary of prying information from Damien Coleridge.

In the tiny bedchamber, she found a charpoy and an ancient rattan dressing table. Carefully, to avoid awakening the baby, she untied the sling and settled him onto the low bedstead.

Two photographs hung on either side of the door. One portrayed a beggar boy in grubby clothes who stared with huge liquid eyes at a fruit stand piled high with mangoes and bananas. The other depicted an elderly Mohammedan kneeling beside his dead wife, his gold-capped teeth visible in a bushy white beard and his withered hands raised in prayer.

The powerful images unsettled Sarah. How could an insensitive man capture these sensitive portraits? The question magnified her curiosity and gave her yet another tantalizing hint of hidden facets beneath a rough-diamond exterior. Perhaps she could use his talent to break the ice.

Returning to the main room, she said, "Your photographs are poignant. They illuminate the heart of India. Will you use them all in your book?"

"How the hell do I know? I haven't even written the text yet. Do you remember where the stream is?"

"Yes, but—"

"Good." He shoved a clay jar at her. "Then go fetch some water. I'll milk the goat."

She held back a retort. Reforming his rude nature was a hopeless cause. "Will you please listen for Kit while I'm out?"

Unloading the knapsack, he grunted in reply. She marched out, her hips swaying with annoyance. The glorious view lulled her inner turmoil. The mountains stretched along the horizon as far as the eye could see, and the cedar freshness of the deodars perfumed the air. Beyond the craggy slope, green forest unrolled into a great valley. Thrushes twittered in the tall pines.

It was like a place in a fairy tale . . . and everything but Damien fit in. Unless he was the beast.

Walking over pine needles as soft as a thick-piled carpet, Sarah approached the stream and knelt on the grass. For long minutes she soaked up the dappled sunshine and the peaceful gurgle of the water. Ferns and wild violets grew thickly along the bank. She plucked a single purple bloom and anchored it behind her ear. Cupping her hands, she scooped up the water. It slid down her throat like chilling nectar, a delicious contrast to the warmth of the sun. With great reluctance, she filled her pitcher and started back.

Kit's high-pitched wail met her halfway up the slope. Dear Lord, what was Damien doing to the poor mite? She hastened her steps and went inside to find him holding a pail of milk in one hand and the baby in the crook of his other arm. He was jiggling Kit so hard that milk sloshed over the sides of the leather pail.

A merry laugh burst from her. "You might try putting down the milk," she said.

His forehead puckered into a peevish frown. "What the hell took you so long?"

"Pardon me, your lordship. I didn't realize I was on a strict schedule."

"You're neglecting my son. He needs a fresh nappy."

Setting the water jar on the table, she coolly

arched an eyebrow. "You're an educated man and a parent now. Are you incapable of changing a baby?"

He thrust Kit at her. "I don't do the smelly ones. At least not while I'm paying you a wage."

She cuddled the infant close; an odorous aroma wrinkled her nose. Toting him into the bedroom, she muttered, "Yes, O Great Master."

Damien chose to ignore her breathy comment. He positioned the glass bottle on the table and poured warm milk from the bucket. Maybe he shouldn't have spoken so sharply. But seeing the violet behind her ear startled him into wondering if Sarah Faulkner had whimsical depths beneath her tartness. Hosting her on his territory unsettled him. For five summers, he'd lived alone here. He'd found peace working by himself and cataloging his prints. Yet this time he felt crowded, restless with the urge to escape.

She wasn't the sort of woman who could keep her mouth shut and her legs open in the bedroom. Like a prickly nettle, she continually worked her way under his skin. He'd encountered billy goats that were less cantankerous.

Of course, he himself could hardly claim to be the ideal companion. A painful tightening gripped deep within him. He wasn't fit to dwell in close quarters with civilized people. His mother had spent years drumming that fact into his head.

He fastened the teat on the bottle and walked to the bedroom. Sarah's soft voice stopped him in the doorway. She was bent over the charpoy, her back to him. Kit lay before her, cooing and kicking while she pinned on a clean nappy.

"I do wish you could talk, darling," she said. The pressure eased inside Damien, giving way to yearning, like a rhododendron bud opening to the sun. God, she had the sweetest voice when she spoke to his son. "Yes, indeed," she went on. "Then I'd have someone pleasant to converse with, someone who didn't always snap at me like a testy old bear. And maybe you could even intervene for me. You could tell your father I'm weary of being treated like his slave.''

The mellowness inside Damien withered. Now she was even complaining to his son, for God's sake. He pushed away from the doorframe and entered the room. ''And while you're at it, son, you can tell Sarah I'm leaving.''

She spun to face him. Her eyes rounded, twin mirrors of the purple-blue violet tucked behind her ear. ''What?''

''You heard me. The larder is bare. So is the knapsack. I need to buy food if we're going to eat tomorrow.''

''Buy? Are there people nearby?''

''There's a village of Pahari—hill people—down in the valley.'' He spoke with exaggerated patience.

She snatched up the baby. ''We'll go with you.''

''No. It's getting late. I'll have to hurry. I can travel faster alone.''

''And if you don't return? What if you meet up with more sepoys?''

Her anxious expression made Damien think she truly cared whether he lived or died. He shook off the foolish thought. Her only interest in him was as a protector, someone to chase the wolves away during the night. ''There aren't any mutineers around here because we're far from any military station. Except for Keppu and Lalji, they're all down on the plains.''

''You could still die. You could fall down the mountainside.''

''Then feel free to claim this palace for your very own,'' he said. ''Now, is there anything you need? A ball and chain, perhaps? Or maybe a whip? Just so I can make you properly feel like my slave.''

She gave him a look that could have shriveled the violet in her hair. "Some warm clothing for Kit will do. He's growing so fast, many of his things don't fit anymore." Holding Kit in the nest of her arm, she ticked off each item on her slim fingers. "And for myself, I'd like paper and a pen, a cake of soap, and some pins for my hair. Oh, and something new for me to wear, too."

He couldn't resist looking her up and down, letting his gaze linger on the shadowed curve of her breasts. "My, my. Have you been growing, too? Or shrinking?"

A becoming pink washed her cheeks. She drew herself up and regarded him with the hauteur of a princess acknowledging a lowly subject. Someday he'd capture that look in a photograph, he thought. "I'll thank you to keep such indecent comments to yourself," she said, and grasped the locket at her throat as if it were a lifeline. "I realize it's difficult for your diabolical mind to manage, but if we're to survive the coming weeks, you must make an effort to comport yourself as a gentleman."

Annoyance slashed at Damien, along with self-flagellation. He'd given her ample cause to dislike him. He entombed the lonely feeling and reached for anger. Damnation. He was sick to death of her belittling lectures. He was sick to death of the oblique comparisons to her darling Reggie. Most of all, he was sick to death of seeing her fondle that locket as if it were a rare icon.

"Give me your locket," he said testily.

"Pardon?"

"Give me the damned locket so I can trade it for the things on your list."

"No!" Sarah curled her fingers in a protective embrace around the gold. "You may deduct the cost of the articles from my salary."

"Sorry, I don't keep much money lying about," he lied. He had to get that locket off her. It was driving him mad. "Not with this place unoccupied for half the year."

"Aha." Self-righteous disdain firmed her dainty jaw, and she shook her finger at him. "I knew you never intended to pay me."

"You can cash in your bank draft when I can safely get our arses to civilization. Now, if you don't hand over the locket, you'll have to forgo your new things."

She lovingly stroked the piece. "How unfeeling you are," she accused. "You lack the heart to understand what this memento means to me."

Damien felt his insides turn to warm slush. He froze the weakness. How could he soften toward a woman who considered him ill-fit to lick her beloved's boots? Why not act the callous bastard? She expected no better of him.

"It's only a lump of gold," he snapped. "Besides, isn't there a photograph inside for you to keep? Nail it to the bedroom wall and make a holy shrine of it, for all I care. Or put it under your pillow. Then you can moon over him all night."

"I do not moon over Reginald."

"There you go again, defending him."

Sarah hesitated. Decisively she reached her free hand to the clasp at her nape. Seeing her awkwardness while holding Kit, Damien found himself saying, "I'll unfasten it."

He set down the bottle on the rattan table. Moving to her in two swift steps, he lifted aside her rope of black hair and reached for the catch. She bent her chin to her chest, exposing the delicate column of her neck. The submissive pose struck him with a keen awareness of her femininity. His fingers brushed satin-soft skin, scattered by wisps of hair as fine as the fronds of a feather. She smelled faintly of womanly musk, a scent that curled deep inside him, touching off a slow, sensual pulsebeat in his groin.

Damn. He had to find a woman soon before he

did something rash—like seduce a busybody spinster with the body of a goddess.

The clasp let loose. The butter-slick chain slipped from his fingers; Sarah caught it to her breasts. Wordlessly she lifted her head and let him take the piece from her. He snapped open the locket and pried out the miniature of a stiff-shouldered Reginald. The honorable doctor looked like a man with a clear conscience who enjoyed the love of a woman, the man Damien would never be.

He slapped the picture into Sarah's palm. "Here's your hero, Miss Priss."

"Thank you," she murmured. "By the way, I'd also appreciate a comb, if you can bother yourself to find one."

His fingers clenched around the gold, still warm from her flesh. He felt like Judas accepting thirty pieces of silver. Yet he also felt a guilty satisfaction that he wouldn't have to look at the damned locket anymore.

"I'll do what I can." He fetched the bottle and thrust it into her hand. "Here, feed my son. And by the way, there's paper and pen in the desk out there. Just don't go writing any more incriminating letters."

Chapter 15

∿

5 June 1857, High in the Himalayan Foothills.

Himalaya is a Sanskrit word, hima meaning "snow" and alaya meaning "abode." Here in the Abode of the Snow, so far from the military stations of the Ganges Plain, one might never guess a mutiny rages over the face of India. The revolt is an abomination of blood and destruction, and yet a struggle for liberty, for the basic human right to freedom of religion.

A Hindu proverb says that truth is like a diamond with many facets; no viewpoint can reveal its entirety. So does the revolt of the sepoys have many sides . . .

Sarah lay down her pen. It was almost too dark to see. She rose from the desk and went out onto the veranda. From several earlier trips, she knew it took precisely twenty-one paces to walk from one end to the other.

Dusk spread a deep purple veil over the hillside. She rubbed her arms; the air had grown cooler. The cedar leaves whispered, and an owl hooted in the shadows. How peculiar it felt to be apart from Damien after so many weeks. The desolate setting gave her the eerie sensation of being the only person alive in the cosmos.

She peered through the gloom for his tall form. What if he'd taken a tumble into a gorge? What if he'd fallen down a rocky slope and broken his leg? Dear God, what if he really didn't come back?

Nonsense. If anyone could take care of himself, he was Damien Coleridge. He was too mulish a man to die.

She reached absently to her throat; then her hand dropped. A hollow ache yawned within her. The locket was gone. She struggled to summon a clear picture of Reginald and saw only the vague image of a handsome blond-haired man. Damien, however, loomed in her mind like a vivid, unforgettable photograph. She contrasted the two men: pallid and proper versus dark and dangerous.

She banished the disloyal comparison. Society would consider her dishonored because of her sojourn with Damien. Would her fiancé concur? Would he believe her unchaste? She expected a vast dismay, but felt instead only an indeterminate curiosity. Odd, how the opinion of others no longer seemed so vital.

Then again, perhaps there were no English left in India to censure her.

Sarah stepped back into the hut and lit a lantern. Too troubled to continue writing, she gathered up her papers and went into the bedroom. Quietly, so as not to awaken Kit, she secreted her work in a drawer of the rattan dressing table. God help her if Damien read the unfinished essay and realized she was I. M. Vexed. She'd never hear the end of his sarcastic remarks about her unworthy occupation. Heaven knew she endured enough of his ridicule already.

To distract herself while she waited, she perused the bookshelves above the desk. *The Arabian Nights. Fairy Tales* by the brothers Grimm. Pope's *Iliad* and *Odyssey*, translated into English from the Greek. A fanciful collection for a rogue like Damien. Her vision went hazy as she realized anew that he had depths he kept hidden from her.

An intricately carved box serving as a bookend caught her attention. She reached out, then drew back. She wouldn't sink to Damien's level by prying. Her gaze drifted like a magnet to the closed door of the unknown room. Nor would she peek inside the room. Let him keep his precious mysteries; she had private matters of her own to conceal.

She forced her eyes back to the books. A rare edition of Hammer's *Shakespeare*. Several tomes on ancient and medieval art. *The Kama Sutra of Vatsyayana*.

Her gaze riveted to the slim leather-bound volume. It was a classic treatise of Indian literature which Patel had once mentioned to her, a guide to erotic love she'd heard the English ladies whisper and speculate about.

She lifted a hand to the text, hesitated, then grasped it firmly.

Opening to a random page, she scanned the words: . . . *the man should rub the yoni of the woman with his hand and fingers (as the elephant rubs anything with his trunk) before engaging in congress, until it is softened, and after that is done he should proceed to put his lingam into her* . . .

Heat washed through Sarah, setting off a tremor deep within her belly. Was that what Damien had meant when he'd spoken of stroking her between the legs? And what exactly was a *yoni*? Where a man put his *lingam* into a woman?

Lurid curiosity glued her eyes to the page; guilty shame stopped her from reading on. Feeling strangely warm and weak, she clapped the book shut and shoved it back on the shelf. Merciful heaven. Aunt Violet would have been horrified to find her niece perusing the forbidden volume. She probably would have swooned—

''I'm back.''

Sarah gasped and whirled around. Her hands gripped the edge of the desk behind her. Framed

by the darkness beyond the doorway, Damien
loomed like a demon from hell. The lamplight
threw his handsome features into sharp contrast.
Blatant masculinity radiated from him, singeing
her with the intensity of a flame.

Had he witnessed her reading *The Kama Sutra*?
Mortification immobilized her. She couldn't think
of what to say, what to do; she could only gape
stupidly at him.

"Sarah?" Frowning, he strode into the room
and dropped the knapsack on the table. "Is something wrong?"

He hadn't seen. With the force of a monsoon,
relief blew away her paralysis. She walked jerkily
away from the desk and clasped her hands tightly
before her. "No . . . no, nothing's wrong. You
startled me, that's all."

"I see. Is Kit asleep?"

"Yes. He drank his bottle and . . . and we
talked for a while. I mean, *I* talked and he listened. He's really beginning to take an interest in
what I say. I rather doubt he understands me, but
he certainly smiles a lot."

Damien cocked an eyebrow at her. "Something
is wrong. You're babbling like a Sikh on hash-
ish."

Taking a breath, she collected her senses. "If
you must know, I was angry that you took so
long. It would be just like you to run off and leave
me alone with Kit all night. While he screamed
for his bottle, I'd have to milk the goat—"

"Do me a favor, Sarah. Leave off the nagging
for once. I'm tired. My feet are sore. And I'm
hungry."

Damien sank into a chair and propped his san-
daled feet on a brass stool. Leaning back, he laced
his fingers behind his head. Weariness bracketed
his eyes and mouth. He looked tousled and disreputable, a man hovering on the brink of ex-

haustion. Chagrined, she recalled his knife
wound.

"I'm so sorry," she said honestly. "Will you
be all right?"

"I'll survive. Your things are in the sack over
there." He angled his head toward the table.

She moved toward him. "I must check your
bandage. You may have broken open the wound
by overexerting yourself—"

"Don't come near me," Damien snapped. "I
knew you couldn't last a minute without pestering me."

She clamped her lips and veered toward the
table. "Go ahead and bleed, then," she muttered.

From atop the stores of food in the knapsack
she drew out a carved wooden comb, an assort-
ment of bright hair ribbons, and an eclectic set of
women's garb made of colorful, homespun *put-
too*. The fresh woolen scent imbued her with
delight.

"You've brought me wonderful clothes," she
said in surprise. "I can hardly wait to take a bath
and change—" She bit off her words. A lady never
discussed intimate matters in the presence of a
man.

"A pity I couldn't locate a corset," Damien
said. "I know how anxious you must be to truss
yourself up again."

She bristled. "Can't you accept a simple thank-
you?"

Turning away, she carried the precious garb
into the bedroom. In the morning she would haul
water from the stream, enough to have a lovely,
all-over wash. She would even scrub the disgusting dye from her hair and skin. She would feel
normal again after the long, dusty weeks on the
road.

When she came back to the doorway, Damien
lay stretched out on the settee, his eyes closed,

his crossed legs half hanging over the arm. A sinking sensation oddly like disappointment pulled at her stomach. So he wouldn't offer to sleep beside her tonight.

A sound jolted Sarah awake. Groggy from feeding Kit in the wee hours, she lay in the pre-dawn darkness and tried to orient herself. Her hand stole out to find the baby's small form. He slept the peaceful slumber of the innocent.

What had she heard?

Then it came again—a hoarse cry from the outer room. Mutineers? Leaping up, she cracked open the door and peered into the gloom. The faint starlight through the windows revealed the vague outline of Damien's large frame on the settee. He thrashed like a madman, then went still, muttering something unintelligible.

Her fear faded to concern. She pushed the door wide. "Damien?"

He didn't answer; he only tossed his head back and forth on the pillow.

With shaking fingers, she struck a match and lit a lamp. Then she pressed her hand to his brow. Her breast squeezed tight. His skin burned with fever. Dear God, his wound must be infected.

Suddenly he reared up, the blanket falling from his bandage-wrapped chest. His glazed eyes met hers, but she had the odd impression he didn't see her. "Save Christopher," he said in an ago-nized voice. "Save him, please save him."

What did he imagine was wrong with the baby? "Kit is fine," she said soothingly. "He's asleep. Damien, we've got to get your fever down."

She started to draw back, but his hand latched onto her arm, his fingers digging painfully into her flesh. "You have to save Christopher. He's locked inside there. He's burning up. Don't hate me, Mother. I can't reach him. I tried to put the fire out. Oh, God, I tried—"

Wrenching sobs choked off his words. Tears rolled down his cheeks. Sarah's mouth dropped open. The great Damien Coleridge, weeping? Surely she was seeing a sight no one had ever witnessed. His grip slackened and he fell back, his face buried in his scarred hands, his breath gusting harsh and hard.

His anguish cleaved her heart. Christopher must be Damien's older brother, the one Mrs. Craven said had been turned witless from a fire Damien set as a prank.

"It's all right, Damien. It's all right."

Quickly Sarah fetched the jar of water and several clean cloths. Dipping one, she wrung it out and draped it across his brow. Its coolness heated within moments, and she replaced it with another. His eyes closed, he muttered and squirmed as if suffering from intolerable pain, a pain as much of the soul as of the body. She wished she knew what Reginald would have done, but he hadn't shared his medical knowledge with her. In despair, she knew of no cure for the fever but to keep changing the wet clothes.

Her mind worked as fast as her hands. Dear God. Damien could die. She had known people who were alive and hale one day, then dead the next from cholera or a host of other tropical illnesses. Keppu's knife might have harbored any sort of deadly disease. The thought coiled in her stomach like a serpent waiting to strike.

After a time, Damien's brow felt cooler, and he fell into a fitful slumber. Sarah rejoiced in the small victory, yet her emotions were tainted by the remnants of fear and the heaviness of exhaustion. Cautiously she untied his bandage. The skin around the gash was reddened and crusty. Gently she cleansed the wound and applied a fresh bandage.

She sat back on her heels. Her shoulders drooped; her back hurt from neck to waist. She watched the rise and fall of his bare chest, let her gaze drift over the coarse mat of black hairs, over his lean waist and hips. Damien looked so very vulnerable stretched out asleep. Odd, it seemed perfectly natural to view him half clothed. The prim lady she'd been in Meerut would have been appalled. For a moment she teetered on the brink of a great discovery about herself, but her tired mind failed to catch the thought before it slipped away.

She closed her eyes. *Please, God, let him live. Let him live.*

Dawn spread a haze of light over the room. She blinked and straightened. Damien lay asleep, his arm thrown over his head, his face younger in repose, looking startingly like his son.

Kit would awaken soon. She hadn't ever milked a goat, but if Damien could, so could she.

Outside, she shivered from the dew-wet chill. The goat was tethered in a lean-to behind the hut. The animal bleated and sidled into the shadows. "Come here, sweet nanny."

Sarah moved close enough to grasp the halter. Pail in hand, she drew the reluctant goat out into the light and struggled to drive the stake into the rocky hillside.

Kit's whimpering cry came from inside the hut. Dear God, he'd awaken Damien. The goat watched her through thick lashes. Just as she reached beneath the silken hair and brushed the full udder, the nanny bleated a protest and leaped sideways.

Sarah grimly followed. "Come, darling. Baby needs your lovely milk. Please be a dear and co-operate."

Its bell tinkling, the goat trotted to the end of its tether and circled the stake, keeping several steps ahead of her. The look in its eyes was almost intelligent, as if this were a game.

She tried to recall how Damien approached the

goat. Distract the beast. She crossed to a clump of tall grass and yanked out a big handful, which she lay on the ground near her feet. The goat came over and began to munch.

Sarah placed the pail beneath the goat and tentatively squeezed the warm rubbery teats. Nothing. She compressed them again, to no avail.

"Bloody double—" She caught herself and pursed her lips. Lord help her, now she was cursing like Damien.

The baby's bawling ceased with a startling suddenness. She straightened her aching back. Merciful heaven, had Damien picked up his son? In his weakened condition, he might drop Kit.

Sarah hastened around the front of the hut. And froze.

On the veranda squatted a woman in a red vest and baggy trousers similar to the garb Damien had bought. A boy of about two played with sticks at her feet. A silver nose ring gleamed above her mouth, and scarlet beads adorned her brown throat. Her khaki shirt lay open, baring twin globes of maternal plumpness, where Kit sucked contentedly.

Baffled and wary, Sarah approached. "Who are you?" she demanded in Hindi. "Where did you come from?"

The woman's broad, flat features bloomed into a smile. She jabbered in a foreign dialect, and waved a hand toward the hut. The only words Sarah understood were *burra sahib*.

Realization hit her. Damien had arranged for a wet-nurse from the village. Relief gilded Sarah's spirits; annoyance tarnished the feeling. The least he could have done was tell her.

This was the last straw. She'd suffered enough of his reticence. The time had come for him to share some basic facts with her. The moment he opened his eyes, she would get the answers she wanted.

A sense of purpose simmered inside her throughout the day. He awoke twice and swallowed a bowlful of rice broth, then sank back into sleep. The longer his brow remained cool, the stronger her resolve grew.

The hill woman was called Batan. Despite the language barrier, Sarah enjoyed her companionship. A placid person with a ready smile, Batan helped with the most taxing chores, hauling water, fetching firewood, and cooking a stack of *chupatties*.

Sarah escaped into the bedchamber for her long-awaited bath in a cedar half-barrel. But the cake of harsh soap lightened her skin only a shade, and despite her scrubbing, she achieved only muddy brown hair rather than its normal blond. She dressed in her new clothes: a sky-blue shirt and a baggy tunic, cinched at the waist with a brown sash, and khaki Moghul trousers with perky blue dots. She felt cleaner and brighter, girded for battle.

Batan fed the baby from her breast one last time, milked the goat, and then departed at dusk, explaining by gesture that she would return in the morning. With Kit asleep inside, Sarah stood on the veranda and watched the Pahari woman step down the path, the boy toddling in her wake like a gosling after a goose.

When she turned, Damien was leaning against the doorframe.

Her heart jumped. His clothing was rumpled, his face lean and hollow-cheeked. "You shouldn't be up," she said.

"It was either answer a call of nature or ask you to mop up a puddle in my pants. Which do you prefer?"

She flushed. "You must be feeling better since you're back to your usual crude self."

"Crude? Keep criticizing your employer and you'll be seeking a new post."

"I never sought this one."

"Oh, yes. You were seeking a post as Reggie's wife."

He walked past her, heading toward the bushes. She fled into the hut and set a pot to boil by the fire crackling merrily in the stone hearth. Finding a brick of tea among the cache of supplies, she crumbled a handful of leaves into the bubbling water.

He walked back inside, his steps slow and his face ashen. Sinking onto the settee, he propped up his feet. "I'm hungry. Get me something to eat."

His weakened condition roused a twinge of sympathy in her. "As you wish."

"I don't want any more of that damned broth. Surely Batan cooked something with more substance."

Her compassion vanished. "It's so pleasant to hear 'please' and 'thank you,' " she muttered.

From the kitchen she brought two warm *chupatties* smeared with goat cheese. While he ate, she said, "Speaking of Batan, I must say, her sudden appearance shocked me."

"Everything shocks you."

Sarah held tight to her temper. "You should have told me about her."

He shrugged. "She's a widow. She's weaning her son, so she has plenty of milk for Kit."

"Why didn't you ask her to live here?"

"Her father-in-law expects her home to help in the evenings."

"I see." When he offered no more information, she said, "Would you care for a cup of tea?"

Damien grunted an assent which discouraged conversation. If he thought she would sit in docile silence, he'd soon discover otherwise. From the cupboard she fetched two cups of fine Chinese porcelain.

Her skin prickled; she looked over to find him

watching her, his expression dour. In a flash of self-consciousness, she wondered how he perceived her new clothes. He probably thought the trousers too mannish. Well, *he* was the one who'd selected them.

Disgruntled, she poured the tea and handed him a cup. Their fingers brushed and her thoughts scattered. She sank into a cross-legged position on the tiger-skin rug and gathered her resolve. Waiting until after Damien took a sip, she said, "Since you're feeling better, I should like to end your secrecy."

He swung his head up, wariness glinting in the devil-dark depths of his eyes. "My secrecy? About what?"

"About your past. You named Kit after your elder brother, didn't you?"

Her knowledgeable words hit Damien like a blow to the solar plexis. Damn. Bloody double damn. He had a hazy memory of Sarah's cool hand on his burning brow, of garbled nightmares alive with the flames of memory. God help him, he must have babbled in the throes of the fever. What had he said?

Tasting bitter fear, he decided to bluff. "Maybe I named him after Christopher Columbus."

"Don't prevaricate. Last night you spoke of saving your brother, Christopher."

"So? It's common to call a baby after a family member."

"But why the brother who was involved in the fire you set at your parents' estate?"

His blood ran cold. Only the cup of tea kept his palms warm. In his most lordly voice, he said, "More of your stupid gossip? You work for me, Sarah. You've no right to pry into my private past."

As slim and lovely as a Himalayan princess, she met his gaze with unflinching valor. The soft, loose garb somehow suited her English features, and the firelight glinted off gold strands in her hair. "On the contrary," she said, "I have every right to pry. You're ill. Last night you might have died. What if something like this happens again?"

"It won't. I told you, there aren't any sepoys around here to kill me."

"Regardless, I have to plan for possible calamity. If you were to die, what would I do with Kit?"

Damien's heart squeezed. "You'd care for him and raise him as your own."

"How? I can't provide for him. You never got around to giving me the bank draft."

"I admit I've been remiss in seeing to the transfer of funds. I'll write you a letter to take to my bank in Bombay. The village headman can witness the document."

"And what if Bombay has fallen to the rebels? There might not be an English bank in operation. Even so, I'd feel honor-bound to take Kit on to England to meet his family."

A gale of fear blasted Damien. Trying to conquer the emotion, he gritted his teeth and said, "I already gave you explicit orders to the contrary. But nothing's going to happen to me. So leave off the bloody nagging."

Sarah leaned forward, the deep V of her shirt revealing the shadowy cleft of her breasts. "Kit's grandmother is the dowager Duchess of Lamborough. His uncle is the duke. Your son deserves all the advantages of his noble blood."

"Noble blood be damned." Damien slammed his cup onto the brass footstool, so hard the porcelain cracked. Hot tea sloshed over his hand. "You're never to take Kit within half a continent of my mother. She would—" He broke off, sweating, his skin clammy and his limbs weak.

"Your mother would what?" Sarah asked.

She would hate him because he's my son.

Agony burned like a rope enclosing his neck. The blaze on the hearth lured his eyes. From the dark passageways of memory he heard his mother's icy voice. He tried to block it out, but her words devoured his soul as fire devours tinder: *I rue the day I gave birth to you, Damien. You're a devil who deserves to burn in the flames of hell. You destroyed your own brother* . . .

"Damien?"

His vision swam. He blinked, and found himself gazing at Sarah's earnest face, at the sun-kissed hue of her skin and the zealous blue of her eyes. As fresh and untainted as a lotus blossom, she sat gazing at him, her teacup cradled in her hands. The urge to seek refuge in her warm arms washed over him, an urge as abhorrent as this conversation.

"Damien, answer me. What would your mother do?"

He should get up and leave. But he felt too infirm to move. Besides, she'd still be here when he came back, waiting for answers, a tenacious crusader with her mind fixed on a cause.

Casting about desperately for a plausible explanation, he said, "My mother would despise Kit for his mixed blood. He'd be ostracized by her and by society."

Sarah shook her head. "It's more than that. She's his grandmother. It would be unnatural for her to hate him."

"You don't understand."

"Then make me understand. I won't abide by your order until you tell me the truth. You'll have to convince me that it's to Kit's advantage to stay away from your family."

The noose tightened. Damn her persistence. Yet another voice inside him whispered, *Bless her for wanting the best for your son.*

His choices had dwindled to one. He had to trust Sarah. Even if it meant giving her the most deadly ammunition to fire at him. Although he felt certain of his recovery, he dared take no risk of exposing Kit to the torture and loneliness of growing up unloved, without Sarah's care and affection.

"Tell me about the fire," she urged. "And about your brother."

"I hope to God you'll shut up about it then." He searched the swamp of his emotions for the right words. "Christopher and I are very different. As different as two brothers can be . . ."

"How so?"

"He has a delicate constitution and a docile temperament. I was the wild, hot-tempered one. I was always getting into trouble."

"What sort of trouble?"

He shrugged. "Putting a toad in the housemaid's bed, hiding Nanny's spectacles, leaping out and scaring the butler. God knows the number of times Mother had to send me to bed without supper. It was no wonder she favored Christopher's gentler nature."

"So you were high-spirited," Sarah said. "That's hardly an unusual trait for a boy."

"You haven't heard the worst." Feeling like a sinner on the verge of a hideous confession, he said, "One day when I was five years old and Christopher was six, Mother gave him an entire set of tin soldiers, cannons and cavalrymen, the whole works. She told me I wasn't to play with them, that I'd lose half of them and chip the paint on the other half."

"Why did he get a gift and not you? Was it his birthday?"

"No." Damien shifted his gaze from her inquisitive eyes. "He was the elder, the heir, so he had privileges that I didn't."

"Nonsense. That's favoritism. Children ought to be treated alike."

Her oblique attack on his mother raised Damien's hackles. "I didn't ask for your damned opinion,'' he snapped. "I'm trying to tell you what happened.''

Sarah ignored his anger. She tilted her head and quietly said, "Go on, then.''

"I'm trying to.'' He cleared his throat and gazed into the flames on the hearth. "Lord help me, I lusted after those tin soldiers. And for once Christopher wouldn't share his new toys, either. When I grabbed a dragoon, he cried for Nanny and she shooed me away.''

Damien paused, his throat tight. From the shadows of the past came the clear image of his fair-haired brother, his frail body bent over the troop of shiny soldiers.

"Did you ever get to play with the soldiers?'' Sarah murmured.

"Yes.'' The words gushed from Damien like water from an opened floodgate. "I waited until almost bedtime, when Nanny left to fetch Christopher his special cup of hot chocolate. He was sitting on the rug by the hearth, lining up his tin battalion. I asked him again if I could play, and he told me no. I . . . got so angry I shoved him into the cupboard where we kept our toys, and turned the key. He was crying, banging on the door, but I callously sat down and played with his soldiers.'' The pitiful memory of his brother's muffled sobs wrenched at Damien.

Sarah sat with her hands folded in her lap, like a governess poised to pass judgment. At any moment he expected disgust to curl her lips. "How did the fire start?'' she asked.

"I heard Nanny outside in the hall, scolding the footman about something or another. I knew I'd be in bad trouble this time, and I thought if I let Christopher out quickly I could accuse him of telling tales.'' Damien's voice faltered.

"And did you do that?'' Sarah prompted.

He moistened his dry lips and forced himself to go on. "I meant to. When I scrambled up to release him, I knocked over a side table. An oil lamp fell to the floor and shattered. The flames caught the window curtains and raced toward the cupboard where Christopher was locked.''

Damien stopped, clamped in the irons of his private hell. He inhaled the choking smoke. He felt the intolerable heat. He relived the horrible, helpless experience of hearing his brother's shrieks over the crackle of the inferno.

Sarah's eyes were wide, her face pale. ''What happened then?''

''For a moment I just stood there. I was too terrified to move. Then I grabbed Nanny's shawl and tried to beat at the flames. It was a stupid thing to do. I should have let Christopher out, or at least gone for help.''

Her gaze narrowed on his hands. ''Is that when you burned yourself?''

''Yes.'' Ashamed, Damien stared down at his scars. He clenched his fingers into a tight ball, but he could still see the ugly marks. The hands of a demon. ''I hit at the fire for an eternity before Nanny heard the commotion. She and the footman came running, and he rescued Christopher. But it was too late for my brother. The damage had been done.''

''Do you mean he was burned?'' An undertone of shock quivered in her voice.

Damien shook his head. ''Physically, he escaped unscathed. But his mind . . .'' His voice scratchy with emotion, he added, ''The trauma stole his wits. It turned Christopher into a simpleton. My mother called in doctor after doctor, but no one could ever cure him.''

The hearth fire snapped in the silence. A log popped and settled. He felt strangely better for the confession, as if he'd shed a portion of the dark and suffocating burden. Bracing himself, he slowly raised his eyes to Sarah. Only thoughtful interest lit her flame-gilded features.

His heart tripped, but he extinguished a flare of hope. She was hiding her revulsion, that was all.

"What is your brother like now?" she asked.

"Still a child in a man's body—at least he was the last time I saw him, about ten years ago." Despondency tugged at Damien's chest. He ached to see Christopher again. But it was an ache he could never assuage. "He's handsome and looks outwardly normal. He's also sweet and loving, though prone to an occasional tantrum."

"Then perhaps he'd like to meet his nephew. I still fail to see why you would forbid me to take Kit to England."

Fear strangled Damien. Knotting his fingers, he struggled to draw a breath. "Because he's my son. Don't you see? Mother never forgave me and never will. Not a day went by that she didn't remind me of the awful deed I'd done." Pain choked his voice. Unable to look at Sarah, he stared at the floor. "She said she wished I'd died in that fire."

Sarah heard the words through a veil of disbelief. The teacup lay cold against her fingers. From the twisting of his hands, the tremor in his voice, she knew he felt a soul-deep anguish. It was an anguish that reached out and wrapped around her heart. "Your mother surely spoke in the heat of anger. She couldn't possibly have meant such a dreadful thing."

"Yes, she could. What I did to Christopher was terrible, unspeakable. I destroyed him. And my mother."

Gazing at his averted face, Sarah glimpsed a raw wound laid bare. "It was an accident, Damien."

"Locking him in the cupboard wasn't. I did it on purpose. I hated him for being Mother's favorite."

"Of course you did. You wanted her love, too."

"But I didn't deserve it."

"Oh, for pity's sake. You were only five years old. You can't be held responsible for the impulsive act of a child."

He abruptly stood and went to the doorway, his gaze focused on the darkness outside. "The fact remains that, child or not, I caused my brother's deplorable mental state. My mother did her best to hide his tragic flaw. She kept Christopher at home instead of sending him to a private sanitarium. Whenever he suffered spells of illness, she nursed him and nurtured him with all of her devotion and love."

And left nothing for you, Sarah thought. Her heart beat in her throat. How ironic that she, who had grown up in genteel poverty, envying the aristocrats who could afford carriages and fine clothing, had been far richer in love than Damien. The advantages of birth had brought him only pain, a pain that had dogged him for nearly thirty years and thousands of miles. Now she understood his fascination with fire, why he had saved Shivina from *suttee* and why he'd balked at burning her body. He was haunted by the ghost of a childish prank gone horribly awry.

He loomed in the doorway, his shoulders slumped. Firelight glowed over his unhappy, handsome profile. She knew now why he scorned society, and why he rebuffed her attempts at friendship. An enormous burden of shame crushed his tender emotions. Within him dwelt the lonely boy who had been spurned by his own mother, and the man who feared to lay himself open to rejection again.

"Damien, don't you think you've suffered long enough? Your mother had no right to persecute her child."

He swung on her. Surprise and torment glittered in his eyes. "You still don't understand," he said fiercely. "She suffered far more than me.

She watched Christopher grow up an imbecile. I can't blame her for wanting to punish me.''

"Your own guilt has been punishment enough."

He slashed his hand downward as if to erase her words. "I stole Christopher's mind. I ended any chance he had at leading a normal life. His title made it easy enough for Mother to find him a wife, but . . ."

"But?"

"He hasn't been able to father any children."

Sarah set down her empty cup. "Merciful heaven, Damien. Surely you can't shoulder *that* blame, too."

"Yes, I can. It's my fault that he can't perform as a man."

She despaired of making him see logic. He wore his guilt with the same blind devotion as a *sadhu* who praised the gods by holding one arm up to the heavens for so long that the limb withered.

"You're heir to the dukedom," she pointed out. "And Kit will inherit after you someday. You'll both have to go to England eventually."

"No. Title or not, I'll never return. Neither will my son go."

The finality of his voice disturbed her. She tried another line of reasoning. "Where was your father while you were growing up? Didn't he defend you against your mother's hostility?"

Damien shrugged. "He spent day and night at his London club. He couldn't bear to face his half-witted heir. Or the devil he'd sired for a second son."

"Don't belittle yourself."

"Why not?" He aimed his hard, bitter gaze at her. "Am I encroaching on your territory?"

Sarah flushed. All these weeks she had been feeding his shabby view of himself. In confusion, she latched onto the gossip of the murder. "Tell me what happened to your father."

"Enough prying. I told you why my mother would hate Kit, and that's all you need to know. I want your word that you'll never take him anywhere near her."

"I'll think about it."

"You'll do more than think, by God. You'll honor my wishes."

"Do you realize what you're asking of me?" She tried one last time. "Kit might someday become the duke, yet you're saying I should deny him his birthright."

"Yes. His future isn't yours to decide. You're only the hired nanny."

His hardened expression closed off further discussion. Sarah blew out an exasperated sigh. "All right," she said. "I shan't take Kit to England without your permission."

But silently she vowed to work on changing his mind.

Chapter 16

◦───◦

1 *July 1857, High in the Himalayan Foothills.*
    Praylaya is Sanskrit for Potential. Water is a substance without shape, and therefore the perfect source of eternal potential. That is why the Hindus believe water has the power to cleanse away sin and purify the soul.
    From my window I watch the monsoon drenching the hillside. But even the life-giving water cannot wash away the horrors of the mutiny. Just as the rains bring a bounty of wildflowers to the mountains, so the mutiny makes the summer-parched plains blossom with the crimson of English blood—

The sharp nub of Sarah's quill pen scratched a hole in the damp paper. She stopped writing and ruefully regarded the damage. The humidity made everything soggy.

Water plop-plopped from the eaves, the sound almost drowned by the drumming of rain on the cedar shingles. Idly she watched a green lizard scamper across the windowsill and disappear outside. The deluge wrapped her in dreary isolation. Batan was feeding Kit in the bedroom. As always, Damien was ensconced alone in the spare room.

In the three weeks since his confession, she had seen little of him. He emerged only for meals, a few hours' sleep, and an occasional visit with Kit. He refused to say what he did in there, beyond

269

that it involved his photography and that he wished to remain undisturbed.

She had exercised staunch control over her natural curiosity. The wound on his side as well as the wound to his soul required time to heal. He needed the chance to adjust to another person knowing his painful secret.

What a viper he had for a mother! Sarah shuddered. Damien, who saw so much, so clearly, was blind where the dowager was concerned. He defended her; amazingly, he saw her as an angel of mercy. She had so twisted his young mind that even as a man he couldn't find his way out of the labyrinth of guilt. The injustice made Sarah steam with outrage. A woman had no right to wreak destruction on the emotions of her defenseless child.

Of course, Damien was no saint. The lies he'd told her, especially the one about Reginald, still rankled. Yet now Sarah suspected why Damien had been so desperate to employ her. He doubted his abilities as a father because he'd lacked a good example for parents.

Frowning at the closed door, she wondered if she'd been wrong to leave him alone. He might be brooding instead, sinking deeper into a quagmire of self-condemnation.

The prospect disturbed her. The dowager Duchess of Lamborough had dealt her second son a wicked, undeserved blow. The problem lay in convincing Damien of that fact. If only, Sarah thought, she could delve beneath the layers of his guilt and prove that, just like anyone, he possessed strengths as well as weaknesses, light as well as darkness. If only she knew more about his past . . .

She pushed back her chair and marched to the door. Her knuckles struck the wood.

''What is it?'' came Damien's muffled voice.

She opened the door. "Excuse me. I'd like to speak with you."

Two lanterns cast yellow light over the windowless room. The rank odor of chemicals came from a row of gallon-sized, cork-stoppered bottles. A stack of glass plates in the corner reached nearly to the ceiling timbers. Glass-backed photographs were propped against every available space.

Arms bare and tanned, Damien sat before a black, boxy camera perched on a littered table. Her heart constricted. She yearned to smooth away the harsh marks scoring his forehead, the ravages of inner pain. With the hair curling over his ears and his beard shaved, he looked younger, more vulnerable.

"State your business," he said. "Is something wrong with my son?"

"No. I . . . just wondered what you've been doing for so many days. Why did you forbid me to come in here?"

"Because I happen to like peace and quiet."

Ignoring his sarcasm, she ventured a few steps into the room. "Is this where you develop your photographs?"

"Yes." Using a small wrench, he tightened a bolt on the camera. "It's my darkroom."

"I'm glad to see you have a camera to replace the one you lost in the fire."

"I'm building it with some spare parts I kept for repairs. Now, if that's all you came in here for—"

"No, it isn't." She cast about for an excuse to linger and said, "I was wondering if you'd heard any report of the mutiny. From Batan's people."

"There hasn't been a scrap of news. Yesterday I sent one of the village boys down the mountainside to see what he could find out."

"Did you? That's a relief."

He gave her a pointed stare, his black brows

knit with impatience. "As soon as I hear something I'll let you know." His tone indicated dismissal.

"Thank you." Her gaze fell on a pair of long-handled scissors lying on the table. She moved forward and snatched them up. "Your hair has grown quite a lot. Would you like me to trim it?"

His wary eyes shifted from her face to the scissors. "Later."

"I'll be busy with Kit later. Better I should do it now, while Batan is still here to watch him."

She slipped behind his chair and let the ends of his hair curl over her fingers. The dense black strands felt as soft and vibrant as raw silk.

His back stiffened. "For God's sake," he muttered, "can't you leave me alone?"

"Oh, but you'll feel better when this hair is off your neck." Taking a breath redolent of his male scent, she lopped off an inch of hair. When he didn't move, her spirits took courage. "Have you been a photographer these ten years?" she asked, cutting carefully. "Since you left England, I mean."

Damien felt her nearness like a burning brand against his back. She stood so close he fancied he could feel her breasts brush against him. The slow snip-snip of the shears, along with the steady tattoo of rain on the roof, lulled his protests.

What was it she had asked him?

"I . . . always wanted to be an artist," he admitted. "I studied drawing in Paris for a few years. By chance, I read in an English journal about a new photographic process using collodion on glass—" He paused, uneasy with his babbling. He'd already revealed far too much of himself to Sarah Faulkner. "You can't really be interested in the boring details."

"Oh, but I am." She bent nearer, the fragrant warmth of her body enveloping him like a loving embrace. "What made you decide to do a picture book about India?"

"It was back in fifty-two." The raw pain of that time hurtled over him. He'd lived alone in a garret. He'd fought the deadly impulse to cross the Channel and tell his mother the truth about his father's death. Damn Sarah for resurrecting memories best left buried. Lamely he said, "The book seemed like a worthwhile project to occupy my time."

"Perhaps you needed to show your mother you're worthy of her respect."

He jerked his head away from her. Oh, God. Here it came. For three weeks he'd waited in suspense for Sarah to harass him about his fatal secret. "I don't care what she thinks of me," he snapped. "I don't give a damn what anyone thinks. I work only to please myself."

"Keep still." Sarah took gentle hold of his head and guided it back into position. "Else you might end up as bald as Lalji."

Her mild response nonplussed Damien. She moved around to his right side. Snip-snip. Another hank of hair drifted to the floor. As she worked, he felt the rhythmic gust of her breath against his ear. The sensation prickled over his scalp and descended hotly to his groin.

"I've been wondering," she murmured. "You must still keep in touch with someone back in England."

He tensed. "Why the hell would you think that?"

"If I had a brother who was infirm, I'd like to know how he was getting on. Besides, you seemed so certain that he hasn't fathered any children."

She was too damned astute. Reluctantly Damien admitted, "I exchange an occasional letter with the butler."

She tilted her head, her eyes wide, the shears dangling from her slim fingers. "The butler?"

"Yes. Bromley has been with the Lamboroughs since before I was born."

"Ah." She resumed clipping. "And what news has he reported recently?"

"Just the usual chitchat about Christopher." Damien trained his gaze on the round lens of the camera. It was somehow easier to talk while not looking her in the face. "He was ill during the winter, but he's better now. And Anne is back from nursing her aunt in Sussex."

"Who is Anne?"

"My sister-in-law. Christopher's wife."

"Oh. What is she like?"

"Plain but sweet, rather shy. And as devoted to him as Mother." Pincers of guilt closed around Damien's chest. "I thank God he has two people to watch over him."

"Mmm."

Sarah straightened and studied his hair. Her eyes were the clear blue of a Kashmiri lake. He shifted in the chair and tried to ease the rock-hard pressure inside his dhoti. God, he wished she'd back up and give him space to think.

"Hurry up," he growled. "I can't waste all afternoon on a damned haircut."

She curved her supple body toward him again. Her faint musky aroma eddied over him. "I'm going slowly on purpose," she said. "I've never trimmed a man's hair before, and I don't want to make any mistakes."

"Now you tell me," he muttered, raking his fingers over his head. "After you've hacked off half my hair."

She laughed, a sweet tinkling sound that warmed his insides. Hell, his insides were already hot. His loins were a furnace of raging lust.

"You needn't fret," she said. "I promise not to

ruin your image. You'll still look like a disreputable rogue.''

"Thank God for that.''

But Damien didn't feel like a rogue. A rogue would dispense with the chatter and pull her into his lap, rip her clothes off and fondle her nakedness, take his carnal pleasure in her tight virginal depths.

She leaned close to clip a strand over his brow. Oh, hell. Now he could see clear inside her blouse. Like an offering to Krishna, her unbound breasts rose and fell in a lush display that dried his throat and weakened his limbs.

"Did you ever stop to think,'' she said, "what you would do if your mother died?''

His muscles went rigid. His head shot up to meet her gaze. "Why do you say that?''

She shrugged. "You could go back to England then. She *is* the only reason you stay away, isn't she?''

Bitter confusion tormented him. "Mother won't die, not so long as Christopher is alive. She lives for him.''

"Ah. At least in one respect you take after her.''

He blinked. He must be too caught up in lechery to focus his thoughts. "What in hell is that supposed to mean?''

"It means you're both stubborn, headstrong people.'' She stepped around to his left side and snipped a lock behind his ear. "You must have inherited the trait from her.''

The comparison flabbergasted him. "You don't understand. I'm not at all like her.''

"Then tell me what she *is* like.''

Agitation stirred in him. "She's refined, noble, caring—''

"Your mother sounds like a paragon. So why did she drive her own son to the opposite side of the world?''

"She didn't," he ground out. "I chose to leave England of my own accord."

"Oh?" Sarah brushed a few strands of black hair from his shoulder. "I heard she accused you of murdering your father."

His pulse throbbed so loudly in his ears Damien felt dizzy. He surged to his feet, the chair legs scraping the floor, bits of hair scattering. "I've had enough of your questions, Miss Busybody Faulkner. My family is none of your bloody business."

Sarah coolly regarded him. "As long as Kit is my business, so is your family. Why are you afraid to tell me why you left home?"

"Oh, for God's sake, will you let up?" he shouted. "I left because I'm not fit to live with other people. You've implied that yourself damned often enough."

"Oh, Damien." Her teeth worried her lower lip, and in spite of his fury, he couldn't stop his eyes from focusing on the kissable curve of her mouth. "I *have* been a shrew," she admitted. "But only because I didn't know about your dreadful upbringing—"

"Spare me your pity," he broke in coldly.

"It's not pity. It's compassion and understanding." Astoundingly, she smiled at him, a warm, pensive smile that washed her features in gentle beauty. Her tender expression made his body swell with yearning. "I despise what your mother did to you, Damien. You've spent your entire life living up to the image she created. You want people to believe you're wicked to prove your mother was right."

He weighed the bizarre notion and rejected it. "That is the most asinine theory I've ever heard."

"Is it?" Sarah tapped the closed shears against her palm. "Can you offer a better explanation for your unsociable behavior?"

"Yes." Desperate to evade her discomfiting

questions, desperate to resist her tempting body, he said, "I dislike people. Especially plain-faced spinsters who pry into my past because they lack a life of their own."

The animation left her features and her skin turned deathly pale. Tears sheened the gentian-blue of her eyes. Regret flayed him like a lash. Oh, God. Despite all he'd done to her, Sarah had set aside her wretched opinion of him and leaped to his defense. Of course, her zealous nature motivated her. But that didn't excuse his cruel lie.

His insult was even worse than taking her locket. He had hurt her in the most mean-spirited way possible. All to spare his own miserable hide.

She lay down the scissors on the table. "I'm finished. You may add another guinea to my wage to pay for the haircut."

With graceful dignity, she pivoted and walked out, closing the door quietly. Damien stood paralyzed, aware of his heart beating in the hollowness of his chest. No wonder she loved an honorable doctor like Reginald Pemberton-Sykes instead of a wicked devil like Damien Coleridge.

Yet he ached to call her back. He ached to kiss away the brutal wound he'd dealt to her pride. Most of all, he ached to bask again in her warmth and tenderness.

Man is divided into three classes: the hare man, the bull man, and the horse man, according to the size of his lingam.

Sarah's eyes widened. In the privacy of her bedchamber, she blushed at the book propped in her lap. Was Damien a hare, a bull, or a horse? A horse, definitely. He was *so* masculine.

Heat seared to the depths of her belly. She slapped the book shut. Mercy! She was reading *The Kama Sutra* for its value as a classic of ancient Hindu dogma and custom. Not so that her imagination could use the text for unseemly conjecture.

Her cheeks felt pink and her heart beat fast. It was the height of indecency to speculate on the hidden parts of a man. Especially a man who had made it clear he had no interest in a plain-faced spinster.

Although more than a week had passed since his blistering condemnation, she still stung from the pain. Sometimes her spirits dragged with the conviction that the derogatory portrayal was true. At other times she perked herself up with the belief that she was a fine woman and he had been driven by the need to isolate himself.

He wanted her to think the worst of him.

Then again, perhaps he didn't care what she thought.

Buffeted by her vacillating emotions, Sarah let her gaze return to the leather-bound book. She must not apply every sentence to Damien. He had gone out this morning, and she so seldom had the chance to steal away and read. Curiosity thrummed hotly inside her. Unable to stop herself, she cracked the book open and flipped through the vellum pages.

By union with men the lust, desire, or passion of women is satisfied, and the pleasure derived is called their satisfaction—

A knock sounded. She jumped. "Sarah?" his voice boomed. "Are you in there?"

She fumbled with the book. "Yes, Damien," she squeaked.

"I need to talk to you."

"Just a moment."

Sarah sprang up and tucked the volume beneath the thin mattress of the charpoy. Oh, dear Lord. Perhaps he'd noticed the book was missing.

Hastening to the door, she started to smooth her clothes and hair. She forced her trembling hands to her sides. How ridiculous. She was acting like a schoolgirl caught reading . . . *The Kama Sutra*. Well, she was a grown woman with a scholarly curiosity. She had the right to read anything she wished.

Taking a deep breath, she opened the door and stepped into the main room. Damien had moved over to the hearth, near Batan. The Pahari woman squatted on the floor, one of her long knitting needles tucked beneath her plump arm in the Tibetan manner as she clacked away at the pattern for a red cape. Propped on the settee, Kit watched the swift motion of the needles and the gamboling play of Batan's young son.

Sarah's gaze shifted to the bookshelf. Apprehension coursed through her. She should have moved the books to hide the slender gap.

But to her relief, Damien wasn't looking at her; he was speaking at Batan. He wore a tunic and trousers today, and the homespun garb that hung baggy on other men fit him like a well-tailored glove. The sunlight slanting through the open window illuminated his sculptured features.

His serious tone and solemn expression piqued Sarah's interest. Over the past weeks, she had learned a little of the Pahari tongue, but today he spoke too fast for her to catch more than a few words. Something about Nana Sahib and Cawnpore. Batan's jolly face drooped with distress.

Sarah hastened forward. The instant he paused, she broke in. "Have you heard news of the mutiny?"

His deep brown eyes bored into her. "Yes."

He motioned her onto the veranda. The monsoon rains had subsided for the moment, and the sun sparkled from an achingly blue sky. The aroma of damp cedar tinged the air.

"Something happened in Cawnpore." Fists clenched at her sides, Sarah stepped closer. "Damien, tell me."

He lounged against the hut, one leg crooked,

his foot braced behind him on the wall. Scratching a match on a log, he lit a *bidi*. "Wheeler's garrison fell under siege last month." He stopped and studied her, as if debating how much to tell her.

She stared him down. "I want to hear every detail."

"The English entrenched themselves in the barracks," he said emotionlessly. "Women and children numbering in the hundreds were crammed in with the soldiers, enduring constant bombardment by the mutineers. The English held out for almost three weeks, until their food and water dwindled. People began to die of starvation and thirst. Then Nana Sahib made them an offer." His expression somber, Damien puffed on the *bidi*. The pungent perfume of smoke drifted to Sarah.

Suspense gripped her. "What sort of offer?"

"He said he'd let them go free if they would surrender their weapons. He offered to provide them with boats."

"Did Wheeler accept?"

"Of course. It meant certain death if they remained in the garrison. The entire British party—what was left of it—filed out of the entrenchments and down to the Ganges. Soldiers, women, children, the whole lot. They were escorted by a company of mutineers." He paused. "As soon as the English got into the boats, the sepoys opened fire."

Sarah touched icy hands to her cheeks. "No," she whispered.

"Yes," he said, his tone gritty with disgust. "It was a massacre. Nana Sahib left nothing to chance. He'd secreted smoldering charcoal in the thatched roof of every boat. The boats began to burn. People leaped overboard and tried to swim to the opposite shore. The sepoys shot them dead. Others drowned or burned. Except for a small group of women and children, every last one was butchered.''

''What happened to the survivors?'' Sarah asked in a faint voice.

''Rumor has it they're being held captive in a *bibighur*, the local house of ill-repute.'' Damien savagely crushed the half-smoked *bidi* beneath the heel of his sandal. ''Henry Havelock's supposed to be coming to their aid. But frankly, I don't give them an angel's chance in hell.''

The tinkle of the goat's bell drifted through the summer air. From inside the hut came Kit's whimper, and then Batan's voice crooning a soft lullaby.

Sarah viewed Damien through a veil of tears. On his harshly handsome features she saw a mirror of her own shock, her disbelief, her torment. Vile images marched through her mind. Soldiers like Uncle John, women like Aunt Violet and Mrs. Craven, babies like Kit, all mown down. She heard their shrieks, felt their agonized fear, saw the water run crimson with blood . . .

Her stomach lurched. Unexpectedly, Damien pulled her tight against him. ''I'm sorry,'' he said. ''I shouldn't have told you. You aren't going to be sick, are you?''

She shook her head. She ought to draw back, yet his arms eased the horror inside her. His chest rose and fell against her cheek, and she heard the steady thrum of his heartbeat. As if he, too, drew comfort from the embrace, he rested his chin on the crown of her head, his breath feathering her hair. His male aroma, part spice and part smoke, was as tranquilizing as incense. Warmth seeped into her cold body; his vitality was a salve to her grieving spirits.

His hand drifted over the nape of her neck; the other gently caressed her wet cheek. On impulse, she turned her lips to the smooth skin of his throat. He sucked in a breath, then grasped her shoulders and held her at arm's length. Shadows guarded his eyes, eyes that were dark with angry pain.

"The English have been bloody fools. Six years ago, they denied Nana Sahib his rightful place as Maharaja of Bithur simply because he was adopted rather than trueborn. They took away his title and his pension. The man seized his chance at revenge."

"But to kill so many." She shook her head in sickened awe. "Those poor, poor people. Thinking they were about to escape the horror of starving."

"Wheeler ought to have laid in more supplies." Frustration grated in Damien's voice; his hands dropped to his sides. "He was a damned fool, same as Hewitt was in Meerut. All the signs of dissension were there, but the English refused to believe their sepoys would dare to revolt."

Sarah thought bleakly of her own arrogance. At one time she believed she could ride the fence of her conscience by expressing her political opinions under the guise of I. M. Vexed while living as a demure English lady.

"I ought to have worked harder to make people understand," she said. "I ought to have insisted, instead of making idle commentary—" She broke off, afraid to speak the truth and shatter their truce.

He smiled sadly. "There was nothing you could have done."

"I wish I could believe that." Suddenly she ached to unburden herself, to share her secret with Damien, even if it meant suffering more of his sarcasm. He had confessed his darkest deed to her; she could do the same. "Wait here. I have something to show you."

Before she could succumb to cowardice she hastened to the bedroom and pulled open the drawer to the rattan dressing table. Hidden beneath silken folds of clothing lay a thin pile of paper, her editorial about the Meerut mutiny. Fingers trembling, she picked up the essay, marched back out onto the veranda, and handed the pages to Damien.

"What's this?" he asked.

"I've been keeping secrets, too."

Anxiously she waited until he scanned the neat script. His features assumed a succession of expressions: perplexity, interest, and contemplation. When he lifted his head, he regarded her with keen surprise.

"You're I. M. Vexed?"

"Yes."

His frown swept over her, as if he were taking her apart and putting her back together again, finding some missing pieces in the process. Sarah held her breath and refused to lower her eyes. Like any man, he preferred his women subservient and opinionless, and she girded herself for a derisive comment.

"I married Shivina," he said slowly, "because I'd read your essay on the shabby way Englishmen treat the native women."

"Yes. You admitted so. That was when I first suspected you had a conscience after all."

"You even stood as witness to the wedding."

"Yes."

To her great astonishment, he threw back his head and let out a hoot of laughter. "How in hell did you manage to restrain your sharp tongue? You must have been dying to claim responsibility for caging the wild beast."

"Well . . ." A tentative smile flirted at the corners of her mouth. "I admit I wanted to rub your nose in it. But I was afraid you might tell someone who I was, just to make me suffer the condemnation of society."

"Sarah," he chided. Unexpectedly he ran a finger over her cheek, with the same gentleness he might use to caress a rose petal. ''You don't know me very well, do you.'' It was a statement rather than a question.

Seduced by his soft touch, she shook her head. ''Perhaps not. I only see what little you've let me see.''

''Then know this: I would have cheered you on.'' He rolled her essay into a tube, which he tapped against his scarred palm. ''Because, despite our differences, we do share the same views on justice for the Indian people.''

''Then you can understand how awful I feel. I valued my position in society far more than doing the right thing.'' She let her gaze wander down the lush green hillside. ''I knew General Hewitt, yet I was afraid to approach him and rally support for the native cause. I . . . I was even afraid Reginald might refuse to marry me if he found out about my secret identity.''

Damien snorted. ''If he can't accept your writing, he can't love you very much.''

She frowned, trying to sort through her confused thoughts. ''He's simply misguided, like most Englishmen. If only I'd had more courage, perhaps I could have changed his mind. Perhaps in some small way I might have helped avert the bloodshed.''

Damien arched a black eyebrow. ''I doubt that. To put it bluntly, the military wouldn't have heeded the word of a woman. At least your nom de plume made men read your column and debate your opinions. Some men must have taken them to heart.''

''I suppose so.'' She wanted to believe him. Yet the load of regrets weighed heavily. Closing her eyes, she pressed her hands to her temples. ''But I can't stop thinking about all the people who might still be alive today if only I'd done something. Aunt Violet, Mrs. Craven, so many soldiers. And dear God, the innocent children, the babies—''

''Don't.'' Damien grasped her forearms and drew her hands down. ''Sarah, don't torment yourself. You had a hell of a bigger impact on public opinion than I ever did.''

She opened her eyes. His handsome features loomed over her. Fleetingly she wondered why he would try to comfort her. ''But you're writing a book about India. Photographs as poignant as yours are certain to make the English realize the Hindus are people, with the same rights as we have.''

''I'm too late to stop the bloodshed. So, you see, I have more cause to flay myself than you do.''

He held her arms in a warm bond. She looked down at the rolled essay, lying between his hand and her arm. He was touching her with the ease of a friend, and the thought stirred an absurd thrill in her heart. The oppressiveness within her began to lift. ''Perhaps we can share the burden of guilt.''

''I'm hereby declaring a moratorium on guilt.'' He released her and stepped back. ''You're a fine writer, by damn. You must have been sent to me by Saraswati herself.''

''Saraswati?'' she said, tilting her head in puzzlement. ''The river goddess?''

Grinning, he shook the cylinder of papers at her. ''For shame, Sarah Faulkner. You should know your Hindu namesake better. Saraswati is also the goddess of scholarship and the arts, including pen and ink. You're the perfect person to write the text to my book.''

As soon as the words were out, Damien could have kicked himself. He'd only meant to cheer her gloomy spirits. But the impulsive offer meant spending more time with her. A lot more time.

He worked best alone, certainly not with an out-spoken female who held the allure of a goddess.

"I've never written a book before," she said doubtfully. "Do you really think I could?"

Tell her no. "Yes," he heard himself saying. He was still shaken by the idea of the very proper Sarah Faulkner secretly composing radical essays. What other surprises did she hide? "Your writing is filled with insight and perception. Mine is dry and detestably dull. My sentences come out sounding as if they were written by the school dunce."

A smile sparkled like a sunbeam over her delicate features. "If I say yes, O Great Master, how many guineas will you add to my wage?"

Her teasing touched a chord of response deep within him, a chord which appalled him. He ruthlessly squelched the softening. He'd already softened too much. "So the five hundred pounds has failed to satisfy you. Your greed is showing, Miss Faulkner."

Her face sobered, her eyes as blue as the enameled sky beyond the veranda. "I shan't be working for you and Kit forever," she said. "I have no other money of my own. If both my uncle and Reginald are dead, I must consider how I'll provide for myself, if and when the mutiny ends."

Chagrin trickled through Damien. Even after ten years of living like a commoner, he sometimes still thought with the blind arrogance of the aristocracy. "I'll add on fifty pounds. And share any profits equally."

"My name must be on the cover."

He smiled. "I. M. Vexed? Or Sarah Faulkner?"

"My real name." Solemnly, she put out her hand. "We're partners, then. I hope we can become friends, too."

He grasped her hand. Her fingers felt feminine and fragile, and the softness of her skin blazed through him to smolder like a hot, hard coal in his loins. With the clarity of a photograph, he pictured her lying naked beneath him, her face aglow with passionate adoration and her thighs opening in sweet acceptance of his caresses—

He scoured the image from his mind. God! She was getting too close to him, proposing friendship, stealing into his very fantasies. He'd tried by turns ignoring her and insulting her; he'd even opened his black soul and let her see the ugliness within. Yet he hadn't driven her away. How was he to survive the coming weeks if a mere handshake aroused him to vivid lust?

Inspiration struck. He knew the perfect way to convince Miss Sarah-Prissy-Faulkner to keep her distance. If the *lingam* shrine had made her blush, what he had in mind would shock her to her prim little toes. He would force her to acknowledge the insurmountable differences between them and impress upon her what an uncaring rogue he really was.

"We'll start tomorrow," he said, releasing her hand. "I took some photographs last summer at a place in the hills nearby. We'll go there, and you can make notes for our text."

"What sort of place is it?" she asked.

"You'll see." And then run from me in horror, he thought.

"May I look at the pictures?"

"No." Smiling, more to himself than at her, Damien took her fingers and curled them around the rolled essay. "I wouldn't wish to spoil the spontaneity."

Chapter 17

11 July 1857, High in the Himalayan Foothills.
Karma is the Sanskrit word for "action." The
Hindus believe that how a person acts in life deter-
mines his next incarnation. The Untouchable deserves
his low status in society, for in his past life he might
have been a dacoit. In the same vein, the Brahman
must have acted in a saintly manner. Thus, if a person
has poor karma, he has no one but himself to blame.

Tramping beside Damien over a hillside bright
with poppies, Sarah reflected upon the journal
entry she'd made only a few hours ago. She'd
awakened before dawn, too exhilarated to sleep
any longer, too anxious to start a day radiant with
possibilities.

Even the fine weather harmonized with her
dreams. A golden oriole sang from the branches
of a walnut tree. Tilting her head back, she absorbed its liquid trill, two long notes and two
short ones. Happiness hugged her, as fresh and
fragrant as the summer air, as brilliant and beautiful as the rolling meadows and wooded slopes.
She must have good karma, she mused, for at last
Damien had extended the hand of friendship. The
notion of writing a book with him challenged her.

Surreptitiously she studied his long brown legs
beneath the white dhoti, the sun-burnished skin
of his arms, the polished perfection of his black

hair against the paleness of his shirt. Over his shoulder he toted the knapsack containing their goat cheese and *chupatties*.

Like him, she was sensibly shod in a pair of *chapplis*, the Kashmiri sandal with an inner-laced boot of soft chamois. Her Moghul trousers and tunic were far more comfortable than the snug corsets and wide crinolines required of English ladies. Today she felt freer, more natural, as if she had shed the last clinging cobwebs of strict society.

In Meerut, she would never have dreamed of striking off alone with a notorious scoundrel like Damien. Everyone would assume they had stolen away to engage in illicit lovemaking. In a delicious flight of fancy, she imagined herself clasped in his arms, his lips tasting hers, his hands caressing her breasts . . .

Warm and agitated, she reflected on her bodily yearnings. Aunt Violet had never mentioned desire, only the duty of a wife to her husband. But the liquid heat Sarah felt while gazing at Damien must be what *The Kama Sutra* meant by the passion of women.

Apparently the body could ignore the mind, for she desired a man who had lied to her, a man who had insulted her. A man who had scars on his heart as well as on his hands.

Damien certainly had his faults, but he was also a sensitive, complex person who could weep and hurt, laugh and tease. His compassion for the victims of Cawnpore sobered her for a moment. Yet today the horrors of the mutiny seemed only a distant shadow on the horizon.

Again her gaze focused on him. Over the past weeks, her feelings for him had undergone a subtle blooming, like jasmine unfurling its petals to the sunlight. Now she felt on the brink of a great adventure, as if they were turning over a new leaf in their relationship. It struck her that their destination mattered little. What did matter was the thrill of being together, truly alone for the first time, the baby left behind in the care of Batan. Perhaps she and Damien could put their differences behind them and start anew.

At the crest of a hill, he stopped. "Look," he said. "That's where we're heading."

He pointed down the slope. Nestled in a grove of deodars at the base of the hill sprawled a great ruined structure, the carved stone pillars twisted with vines, the domes and arches gilded by slanting sunbeams.

"How lovely," Sarah breathed. "It looks like a maharaja's palace."

"It's an abandoned temple." He gave her a strange look, keen and calculating. "No one comes here anymore."

Did he doubt her ability to describe the shrine? Perhaps this excursion was a test of her talents. Sarah made a private vow to prove herself to him, for otherwise he might yet withdraw his request for her to help with the book. The possibility dismayed her.

As they entered the copse of trees surrounding the edifice, she said, "This place reminds me of a cathedral—the branches interwoven into a roof. There's even a reverent hush in the air."

He cocked an eyebrow at her fanciful depiction. "Deodars are considered holy," he said. "The Hindus believe that spirits live in them."

"What sort of spirits?"

He shrugged. "Perhaps those lucky souls that have reached nirvana, the heavenly end to the cycle of life."

Beside the elegantly proportioned entrance to the temple lay a stone face sheared from a long-vanished statue, the great eyes perpetually staring up at the network of damp vegetation. The chitter of a few monkeys came from the turrets and high copings. The air held the earthy scents of greenery and crumbling mortar.

Damien motioned her through a cool shaded archway built of rock-hewn bricks. Hazy sunshine streamed through the fallen roof to light the vast room within, where thick grasses and colorful wildflowers carpeted the floor. Statues lined the nooks and crannies of the huge, circular chamber.

"It's like stepping back in time into a private paradise," Sarah marveled. "Is this temple dedicated to a certain god?"

"To Shiva," Damien said. "Take a look around."

The walls held panel upon panel of carved, life-sized figures. Curious, she moved past a pile of rubble and stopped before one of the sculptures. Her blood surged. Her eyes widened. She was gazing at a naked, copulating couple.

The erotic stone figures seemed to pulse with life. The woman straddled the man, her thighs spread and her feet hooked around his calves. Her face bore an absorbed look of inner ecstasy.

Sarah's cheeks burned. Chaos blistered her belly. She was acutely conscious of Damien setting down the knapsack and then walking to her. Words fled her mind, as if she were straining desperately to decipher a page of unfamiliar script. It was one thing to read *The Kama Sutra* in the privacy of her bedchamber, and quite another to view the amorous display with Damien watching her.

She moved her eyes to the neighboring panel. Another man and woman engaged in sexual congress, flanked by two bare-busted courtesans who caressed the couple's genitals.

Damien strolled to the sculpture and propped his scarred hand on the stone. "Fascinating, isn't it?" he said. "I thought you might be interested

to see how the Hindus revere the physical union
of male and female.''

He casually touched the courtesan's grapefruit
breasts. Rising from the hidden depths of Sarah's
memory came the searing pleasure of his hand on
her own breast. Shaken, she flicked her gaze away
and focused on a jasmine-wrapped pillar. ''You
took photographs of this place?''

''Come now, Sarah,'' he said, ''surely you're
not offended by these statues. Sensuality is a part
of India. If you're to work with me on my book,
you must set aside your virginal decorum.''

His voice was too smooth, too condescending.
But why? Suspicion brought her chin sharply up.
Studying Damien's face, a face as powerful and
compelling as the statues, she detected a tension
about him, a sense of waiting. It *was* a test.

He wanted her to be mortified. He wanted her
to shrink from him in disgust. Hurt stabbed into
the high happiness that had carried her through
the morning. He was waiting to laugh at the plain-
faced spinster who shied from the lecherous
rogue.

''Perhaps,'' he went on, ''you're shocked to see
a man enjoying more than one woman at once.
Are you, Sarah? No doubt you envisioned having
sex with Reggie in the dark, under the covers with
your nightgown pushed up to your waist.'' Damien paused. ''Or perhaps you're too prudish to
envision lovemaking at all.''

Like bullets hitting their mark, his words made
her heart bleed. Haughtiness hardened his features. Leaning against the wall, his arms crossed,
he looked lordly and aloof.

''So you planned this not to be a friendly out-
ing,'' she said. ''You brought me here to mock
my morals.''

''Let's just say I thought it was high time you
learned the kind of man I am.''

She tasted the sting of tears, the bitterness of

crushed hopes. Then fury blazed into the aching void of her chest. "So you think you're superior, do you?"

"In some things, I am more experienced."

"Oh?" Her gaze swept the wall and alighted on a sculpture. Marching toward it, she snapped, "Come over here. Unless you're too embarrassed to see one woman enjoying three men at once."

Frowning, he followed her. "Of course I'm not embarrassed—"

"Good, because neither am I." Moving to the next panel, Sarah spied a woman on her hands and knees, her lover mounting her from behind. "In case you didn't know," she said, sweeping her hand toward the carving, "this position is called 'congress of the horse.' "

His frown darkened. "Where did you hear that?"

She strode to another panel. "And this one, I believe, is known as 'the lotus position.' "

He afforded the naked, entwined couple a furious glance. "Sarah, answer me."

She advanced to the adjacent carving and craned her head to view the upside-down woman. "Oh, gracious, look here. This method requires lots of practice. It's called—"

"Stop it!" He caught her arm and yanked her around to him. "I asked you a question, by God. Where did you come by your knowledge?"

She tossed back her head and confronted his thunderous glare. "Perhaps," she said, imitating his lofty tone, "your plan to humiliate me failed. Perhaps you're mistaken about my innocence. Perhaps Reginald and I have been lovers."

Damien went still. He gave her a searching, scorching look. "You're lying."

"Am I? You don't know everything about me, Damien Coleridge."

Scowling, he perused her face. His fingers compressed the flesh of her arm. She heard the faint rasp of his breathing, the pulse of blood in her ears, the hum of a bee exploring a nearby jasmine vine.

Abruptly the violence smoothed out of his expression. A rare smile flitted over his hard mouth. "You've never let Reggie touch your hallowed body," he said with the satisfaction of solving a complex puzzle. "You've been reading my copy of *The Kama Sutra.*"

She tried to jerk free, but he easily held her tight against his firm body. "Unhand me," she said in her iciest tone.

Humor danced in his eyes, brown eyes flecked with gold in the dust-moted sunlight. "Admit it, Sarah. You sneaked the book from my shelf. I'll wager it's hidden somewhere in your room. It's probably beneath your mattress at this very moment."

Her skin blazed. Not for a maharaja's jewels would she admit he was right. To her utter mortification, tears altered his image into the visage of a darkly shimmering idol. She ducked her head and glowered at his shirt. "Don't you dare laugh at me," she said between gritted teeth. "I may be a plain-faced spinster, but at least *I* have principles. I don't bolster my pride at the expense of others."

Her words snuffed the glow of gratification in Damien. He gazed numbly at the crown of her head. Her hair draped her back in a thick braid of rich dark gold.

The thought of Sarah studying *The Kama Sutra* staggered him. The thought of her unplumbed erotic depths plunged him into a sea of torrid lust. Not that lechery did him a damned bit of good. He'd made her weep. He lacked even an ounce of honor. She'd never desire a miserable sod like him.

His forefinger nudged her delicate jaw. "Look at me."

"Since you seem intent on educating me," she said coldly, "I'd sooner look at the rest of the panels. Then I should like to return home."

"Wait." His thumbs tilted her unwilling chin upward. Her tear-wet eyes stirred a vortex of emotions inside him. "Sarah, I . . ." He burned in a maelstrom of regret. Catching a warm tear, he absently smoothed it over her cheekbone. Finally he managed to mutter, "I'm sorry for deriding your morals. And for calling you a plain-faced spinster. It was cruel and unforgivable."

"You needn't apologize for stating your true opinion," she said stiffly. "I far prefer honest dislike to insincere friendship."

"But that's just it. I lied." He was seized by the overpowering need to coax forth the wonder of her smile and the balm of her forgiveness. "You're anything but plain, Sarah. Shall I tell you what I see in you?"

"Not if you're going to tell me more lies."

It was hardly an auspicious beginning. He cleared his throat. "Well, I won't." Aware of a soul-deep desire to make amends, he let his gaze travel over her, the purity of skin dusted by roses, the steadiness of her blue eyes moist with the remnants of tears, the shimmering gold hair that seemed to have a life of its own. More than her physical beauty, he admired the way she stood straight and unafraid, ready to parry his thrusts as an equal, even if it meant enduring another blow to her feminine pride.

"I see a woman who's clever and brave," he said slowly. "A woman with the spirit and tenacity to survive a mutiny and a flight through enemy territory. A woman who would run to the rescue of a man she has every reason to despise. A woman who can listen to the sins he committed and not pass judgment."

She tilted her chin up. The bitterness still lurked like misty pain in her eyes. "You make me sound more like the warrior goddess Kali than a woman who would invite the interest of a man."

"Then let me correct that notion." His voice lowered to a husky murmur. "I see a woman as lovely as Saraswati riding the heavens on her peacock."

Wistful suspicion lifted the fine arch of her brows. She swung away and walked the few steps to the wall, her arms crossed and her head bent. "You must be teasing, Damien. It isn't like you to shower me with glib compliments."

He stalked after her. "I know it isn't like me," he said, irritated with his inept eloquence. "For God's sake, I hardly make a habit of baring my soul to women."

She shook her head, stirring the wisps of hair around her profile. "If you truly believed I was the female paragon you say I am, you would . . ." She glanced over her shoulder at him, her teeth nibbling her lower lip.

He watched her mouth with all the desperation of a drowning man glimpsing the shore. "I would what?"

"Oh, nothing."

"Tell me . . . please."

"You would feel drawn to me." Her voice was so low he bent closer to hear. "You would want to hold me close and kiss me."

Longing clenched his groin in a hot fist. His throat felt parched, his palms damp. The damnable thing was, he hadn't the faintest notion of what had motivated her admission. He pulled her around to face him. "Is that an invitation?"

Her clear blue eyes met his. "Damien, I—"

He so feared her denial that his lips came down on hers and stole the rest of her words. Their bodies surged together in an embrace that crushed her pliant breasts against him and enticed his hands downward to curve over her bottom and press her thighs to the part of him that burned for her. The honeyed elixir of her mouth sapped his willpower and bathed him in carnal desire.

He was consumed by the impulse to make long, sweet love to her. It was wrong. It was wicked. It was dangerous.

She'd hate him for seducing her. He couldn't live with that. He'd never before cared what anyone thought of him.

Yet he drew her down onto the sun-warmed grass and covered her slim body with his own. Their mouths blended in a slow, torrid kiss, his tongue tracing the shape of her lips and tasting the silken softness within. Madness beat in his blood, his loins, his heart. It was madness to hold Sarah's supple form, madness to inhale her intoxicating aroma, madness to lure her to this place where sensuality saturated the very air.

His lips coursed over her velvet cheek, then downward to the tender curve of her throat. "Sarah, sweet Sarah," he murmured against her fragrant skin. "I didn't bring you here for this. I swear to God I didn't."

Her fingers threaded gently through his hair, and he looked up to find her gazing at him, her eyes dreamy and drowsy. "I believe you, Damien. But I wanted you to kiss me. Part of me has wanted it for a long, long time."

Her naive declaration roused his dormant morality. She belonged with a man of integrity, a man who could give her security and love, a man who could promise her devotion and happiness for a lifetime. A man like the noble Dr. Reginald Pemberton-Sykes.

The thought so filled Damien with livid jealousy that he choked on the yearning to seduce her with empty vows. He could not lie to her, not here, with the sunshine illuminating her vulnerable, trusting face. He could offer her only fleeting ecstasy.

She would despise him afterward. When she

came to her senses, Sarah would condemn him forever as the devil who'd sullied her high morals and cheated her of the chance to bestow the wedding-night gift of her purity upon her husband.

He had only to stand up and walk away. But he couldn't bring himself to leave her scented warmth and the comfort she offered his shattered soul. "I'm speaking of more than mere kisses. If you don't stop me, Sarah, I'm going to make love to you."

Instead of the disgust he expected, a smile transformed her features into heart-stopping beauty. Her gaze flitted to the wall of erotic carvings. "*The Kama Sutra* describes so many positions," she said. "Which way will you do it?"

A chuckle of astonished delight swelled his throat. Damn the consequences. The world had turned upside down, and life was short. He opened the knot of her sash. A lacy pattern of sunlight draped the voluptuous glory of her breasts.

"My way," he said.

He settled his mouth over her breast and suckled the blush-hued peak. Leaving the nipple wet, he kissed a path to the other, and her muted sighs of pleasure seared him like fire on the wind. Her spine bowed as she offered herself to him; he devoured the sensual feast of her skin, a feast that made his blood flow with the hot sap of lust. Her arms enveloped him in a bond as soft as satin ribbons and yet stronger than iron chains. He could scarcely believe this was Sarah responding like a wanton miracle beneath him, starched and straitlaced Sarah who aroused him to hard, explosive need.

His fingers curled into her hair and worked the strands free of confinement until she lay beneath him, like an angel haloed in luminous gold. He submerged himself in the mysteries of her mouth, and she opened her lips to accept his ravenous kiss. She made him feel whole and good, unfettered by past mistakes, rich with hopes and yearnings too new to name.

Her lovely hands smoothed over his chest on a journey of discovery. He had never thought of sex as anything more than an act meant to appease bodily urges. Now he wanted so badly to please her that he hurt with the mere thought of it.

"You're shaped like a goddess," he said, tracing the tip of one breast. "A goddess molded of flesh and blood and fantasy."

For all her womanly attributes, she looked at him with the wistfulness of a girl wishing upon the stars. "Do you truly think so?"

"Truly. I'm through lying to you." Kissing her brow, he felt humbled and taut with the fear that he might fail her. It struck him that he'd never taken a virgin before; all of his women had known how to please a man and how to reach their own release. Fever seized him, the fever to be the first man to entice Sarah to the peak of womanhood. "By God, you're beautiful," he whispered. "For so many weeks I've wanted to lie with you like this."

He kissed her again, a deep and patient kiss that strained the bounds of his willpower. It was all he could do to keep from driving into her, from snatching the release he had craved for too, too long. He trailed more kisses over her face and throat and breasts, imbibing the taste of her skin until he felt dizzy and half drunk.

"I want to touch you, Sarah. All of you."

Her smile held a hesitant, ladylike quality. "Yes . . . I want that, too."

With unsteady hands, he divested her of clothing until she lay before him as pure as the morning dew, her bare legs gleaming in the sunshine, her perfectly formed breasts rising and falling. He propped himself on an elbow, his fingertips trailing up her legs, his eyes drinking in the intoxicating grace of her. The satin smoothness of her thighs lay closed, hiding her feminine secrets.

Seeking to woo her, he murmured, "Your skin feels like silk and cream. I've dreamed about this, Sarah. I've dreamed of holding you naked in my arms. I've dreamed of you opening yourself to me." He was surprised at himself. She managed to coax poetry from the devil himself.

He cupped his palm over the apex of her legs. Her eyes rounded and she drew a breath. "Damien, no one has ever touched me there before."

"Don't be afraid. It won't hurt. I promise it'll be the best feeling you've ever had." Bedazzled by the fear that she might yet refuse him, he distracted her by kissing her breast as he slipped his finger into the silky bush and found the sleek petals of a rosebud within, damp with the dew of desire.

"Ohhh." A sigh fraught with enchantment gusted from her. She clutched his shoulders, her long lashes lifting, then closing. "Oh, that feels . . ."

"How?" he demanded, greedy to hear her response. "How do you feel?"

"Strange . . . and wicked . . . and wonderful."

Her words enslaved him and pulled him deeper into her guileless web of witchery. Yet he sensed the tension gripping her limbs, a latent resistance that skirmished with her natural passion. Desperate to take her to the heights of glory, he murmured, "It's all right to give in to me, Sarah. All my meanness has been an act. I was fighting the need to love you like this, to touch you."

She whimpered in surrender. Her legs parted and she pressed deeper into his hand, accepting his feathery massage. She was ripe for him, ripe and ready. "Let it come," he crooned. "Relax and let it come."

Her brow wrinkled in rapt confusion. "Let what come?"

He bent and kissed her nose. "Shush . . . be patient and you'll see."

She hid her face in the hollow of his shoulder. Her hips eased into a rich flowing rhythm that kept pace with his seductive stroking. Her slick essence, her inarticulate sounds of pleasure, sharpened his own arousal to a violent pitch. Hunger savaged his groin, but he forced himself to go slowly, to let the bud of her passion swell and bloom until he coaxed her chaste body into full flowering.

"Give yourself to me," he murmured. "Trust me, Sarah . . . trust me."

Her breath quickened, hot against his shoulder. She arched in his arms, holding tightly to him as tremor upon tremor coursed through her. "Damien!"

Her head fell back, the wealth of sunbeam hair cascading over his arm and onto the grass. Eyes closed, lips parted, she was the embodiment of *ananda*, the state of perfect bliss. The swiftness of her response, the exultation on her delicate features, washed him in primal joy.

"Oh . . . oh, mercy." Lifting herself, she gazed at him with the fascination of a grand discovery. "I never thought . . . *The Kama Sutra* told of pleasure, but I never imagined you could show me such splendor."

The glow of her eyes lit the blackness of his soul. He felt as if it were his first time, too, and the queer thought wrenched his heart. Oh, God. If only he were worthy of her; if only he could bask in her adoration forever. Suddenly he craved the oblivion of his own release, and his insistent need burned away the foolish sentiment.

"The splendor is far from over," he said, yanking at the strings of his sandals.

Still weak from the spasms of rapture, Sarah

realized the act had yet to be consummated, a thought that heated her belly with renewed anticipation. Whatever lay ahead no longer frightened her. The stunning ecstasy left her forever transformed, as if Damien had reincarnated her into a new realm of womanhood.

She was conscious of her own nudity, of the tickling silk of her hair curling over her breasts and belly, of a hedonistic sense of contentment. The smells of crushed grass and earth blended with the faint musky aroma of his sweat on her body. A blackbird sang somewhere high in the luxuriant vines draping the temple. She could scarcely believe she was here with Damien, sharing the ultimate intimacy and feeling no embarrassment, only a deep emotional ardor.

Sitting up, she propped her hands on the ground and watched him undress. He peeled off his tunic to reveal the breadth of his chest and the pelt of black hair narrowing to a stem at his flat belly, leading downward into his dhoti. She was enchanted by the play of sunshine and shade over the male magnificence of his body. The thin white scar down his side made her shudder inside.

Then he unknotted the white loincloth and let it drop onto the pile of clothing. Her gaze traveled up his long lean legs and transfixed on his engorged member.

She drew a stunned breath. "You really are . . ."

He positioned himself lithely on his haunches. His intense brown gaze scrutinized her face. "I'm what?"

Heat pulsed in her stomach; suddenly shy, she studied a green lizard scuttling between a pair of entwined lovers in a stone carving. "Never mind . . . I was reminded of something I read in *The Kama Sutra*."

Touching her cheek, he turned her toward him. A grin stole over his face, imbuing him with heart-

catching handsomeness. "Now let me see," he
mused. "You were looking at my *lingam*. What
were you thinking?"

How could she say it? "Men are divided into
three classes according to the size of their . . ."
She faltered to a stop.

"Ah. And which group do I fit into?"

His teasing observation emboldened her, and
without thinking, she brushed her fingertips over
the smooth, fevered length of him. "The horse
man."

His grin died and his breath came out in a harsh
gasp. "And you're full of surprises," he said.
"I'm going to have to find a new name for you.
Miss Priss simply doesn't suit anymore."

How about Mrs. Damien Coleridge?

Banishing the startling thought, Sarah melted
beneath him onto the grass. She wanted him to
fulfill her physical fantasies and nothing more. He
stretched out on his side, his *lingam* burning into
the softness of her thigh. He lowered his head to
kiss her throat, his hand gliding over her arm, her
waist, her hip. The smooth ridges of his ravaged
palms sent tremors over her skin. The sun beat
warmly on her face and bathed her in the clear
light of exhilaration. They might be Adam and
Eve, entwined in a lush paradise, about to savor
the forbidden fruit and commit the first sin . . .

Sarah shied away from the thought. Nothing so
good could be wrong. The exalted emotions lifting her heart proved the rightness of this moment. She wove her fingers into his hair, caressed
his ear, traced his cheekbone and strong jaw.

His mouth grazed her breast and his tongue
curled wetly over the nipple, his lips tugging at
her. At the same time he slid his hand down her
belly and lower still, to caress her inner essence,
applying gentle pressure. The hot, honeyed sensations began to build in her again, and this time
Sarah knew what she yearned for; the golden

rapture only he could give her. She moved restively against him. "Damien . . . I need you."

"Patience, Saraswati," he murmured against her breast. "I want you to be ready when I make you mine."

"I am ready." She brought his hand to her lips and kissed the network of scars on his palm, wishing she could so easily soothe the scars to his soul. "Oh, Damien, I've waited for you all my life."

His flat belly sucked in. He lifted his head to stare at her. "God, Sarah." His voice was tortured; his dark eyes blazed with fire. "Don't say things like that. Please don't."

"Why not? It's the truth."

"I wish I could believe you . . . I wish we could be together forever . . ."

He shifted, crushing her to the grass, his leg nudging hers apart. Dazzled by the flood tide of sensations rushing through her, she willingly opened her thighs and enveloped him in a loving embrace. She let her hands roam over his hard muscle and heated flesh.

"I'll try not to hurt you," he muttered.

His words mystified her. "You aren't—"

A white-hot spear entered her body and probed her delicate membranes; then a sharp pain stabbed her. She flinched and cried out, and Damien went still, his brow tilted against hers, his chest moving in uneven tension against her breasts, his arms trembling around her.

"Forgive me," he whispered. "Forgive me for being rough. But oh, God, you feel so damned good."

He lay hard and deep within her, joining their bodies and souls, giving her a feeling of completeness she had never imagined in all her speculation on the act of lovemaking. The miraculous bond rinsed away her pain and left in its wake a throat-catching urgency. She cradled his face in her hands; the bronze of his skin was enhanced by the blue sky beyond the vine-twisted ruins of the temple.

"Show me how good, Damien."

She rolled her hips, the better to feel him. He hissed in air and squeezed his eyes shut, his brown throat arched back, his hard features gone soft with need. The knowledge of her power over him filled Sarah with feminine delight and sensual awe. Twining her arms around his neck, she hooked her feet around his calves.

"Sarah . . . Sarah . . . Sarah."

The chant rained from his lips as he thrust into her in a rhythm that matched the tempo of her blood. The purity of her emotions washed her in wonder. She felt herself ascending toward light, reaching for radiance. With her eyes closed, her other senses played to the magical harmony of Damien's body, a harmony that built to a crescendo and a soul-shattering peak. The darkness behind her eyelids fled with the suddenness of the sun rising over the horizon, pulsing through her body in great waves of brilliance. Damien shuddered and went still, her name pouring from him in a low sob of ecstasy.

His body settled over her like a comforting blanket. He nuzzled her hair as their heartbeats slowed in unison and her senses grew aware of the outer world. Leaves whispered overhead, and a monkey chattered somewhere beyond the temple wall, then fell silent. The feel of Damien holding her, needing her, suffused her in a tenderness far keener and brighter than the wild sensations of physical love.

Emotion crowded her throat and stung her eyes with tears of joy. All her hopes and fears and dreams of the past weeks merged into one vast, shimmering revelation, a revelation she could no more contain than she could stop the sun from shining. She turned her head and pressed her lips to his smooth-shaven cheek.

"Damien . . . oh, Damien, I love you."

Her voice filtered to him through a fog of perfect serenity. He wanted to lie there forever, secure in the sinless circle of her arms, sated by the sumptuous banquet of her love.

Love. His chest constricted with a yearning so strong he went stiff with fright. The temptation to believe her declaration battered him with the strength of storm waves pounding upon the shore of his heart.

He opened his eyes to the softness and certainty of her smile. Her sweetly reddened lips and tousled blond hair bespoke a woman who had been thoroughly pleasured. Her vulnerable expression bespoke a girl whose heart deceived her.

God. Oh, God!

He should have foreseen this. He should have known that Sarah of all women, Sarah with her open and honest heart, Sarah with her hunger for affection and security, would fall prey to the ultimate delusion.

No one could ever love a devil like Damien Coleridge.

He sprang to his feet and snatched up her tunic. "Get dressed," he muttered.

He tossed the garment to her; she caught it against her belly. Without covering herself, she sat up and blinked in bewilderment. "What's the matter?" Her voice lowered to a throaty murmur. "I said I love you, Damien."

"I heard you."

Hurt bruised the adoration in her eyes. "And all you have to say is 'Get dressed?' "

Against the backdrop of erotic art, she looked like a pagan fertility goddess, the nimbus of hair streaming around her naked body, her breasts thrusting proudly through the spun-gold strands. The powerful need to keep her forever coursed through him, pooling like liquid fire in his loins. Before she could see him harden with renewed desire, he turned away and reached for the length of white cloth, draping it around his hips.

"You're in love with what we did just now, that's all." With a savage jerk, he knotted the dhoti before swinging back to her. The stricken look on her face made him lower his tone. "You're a lady, Sarah. You could never be intimate with a man until you'd convinced yourself you were in love with him. I'll forget you ever said you were. I won't hold you to a promise made in passion's throes."

"How thoughtful of you." Her fingers clenched the blue fabric in her lap. "So you're saying my morality has misled my sentiments."

"In a word, yes."

"Don't presume to tell me how I feel, Damien Coleridge. I know my own heart and mind."

"I'm not presuming—I just know you'll come to your senses," he snapped, half from the need to convince her, half from the desperation to quell his own dangerous yearnings. He slid a glance down at her. "I can't deny that what we shared was wonderful . . . the best I've ever known. But there's a difference between being lovers and being in love."

"And you're an expert on both." She tilted her head, a contemplative light sweeping over her face. "Perhaps you're the one deluding yourself. Perhaps you're striking out at me because you're afraid."

"Afraid of what?"

"Why, of love." She scrambled to her feet, the shirt dangling from her hand. "You're afraid to love because it might mean getting hurt. You're afraid because of the brutal way your own mother rejected you. Well, you're a fool for letting her convince you that you're unworthy of affection."

His chest squeezed in a suffocating clash of

confusion and fury. Sarah was wrong. *Wrong.* Yet the walls of the temple seemed to close in, and he fought the urge to run from the cloying atmosphere of seduction, from the wise expression on her face. Unable to bear her scrutiny, he lowered his gaze to her bosom, where the sun-gilded nipples peeked from the drapery of her hair.

"The only thing I'm afraid of," he observed silkily, "is seeing you cover up those lovely breasts."

A flush tinted her cheeks, and she yanked the shirt over herself. "Don't change the subject. We were speaking of your mother."

He gave a dark chuckle and shoved his arms into his sleeves. "Now there's a damned peculiar postcoital topic. I wonder if Reggie will want to talk about his mother after you two share a bed." The very thought of the virtuous doctor touching Sarah made Damien want to run his fist through a wall. He settled for hurling a rock against a carving of idealized love, and reaped a juvenile satisfaction out of hearing stone strike stone.

"We were speaking of your ability to love," Sarah said. "Please leave Reginald out of this discussion."

"Like hell I will. He's your bloody fiancé."

She compressed her lips. "I'll decide that later. We're talking about you and me, and the feelings we have for one another."

"Feelings?" Damien scoffed. "Let's accept what happened for what it really was: a few moments of intense, physical passion."

"It was more than that—"

"Yes," he said bluntly. "It was a mistake. A mistake I have no intention of ever repeating."

The spirited light left her face, and she bit her kiss-bruised lower lip. "So, just like that, you can walk away from me. You can act as if nothing ever happened between us."

"Sarah," he said, his voice rusty with restrained desperation, "listen to me." He paused, aware of a heartfelt regret over hurting her, yet gripped by an even deeper dread that lurked like a fearful demon inside his chest. "What we did may have started a baby inside you. Believe me, the last thing in the world I need to complicate my life is another child."

A hush seemed to fall over the shrine. She stood perfectly still, staring at him. Oh, God. She'd hate him now for ruining her life, for turning her dreams of love into a sordid nightmare.

Her eyes drifted out of focus, and a strange look came over her fine features, a look he couldn't read. "Merciful Lord," she whispered. "I hadn't even considered . . ." As if imagining herself saddled with his bastard, she flattened her hand over her belly, drawing his eyes downward to the flecks of blood on the inside of her thighs.

Remorse flayed him anew. He strode to the knapsack, which lay atop a pile of rubble. Rummaging inside, he pulled out a cork-stoppered bottle of water and the cloth that had wrapped their *chupatties*. He wet the napkin and turned around to find the dazed frown lingering on her face.

"Lie down," he said.

She focused on the cloth. "Why?"

"Oh, for God's sake. Must you question everything?"

She sank to the grass. "As you wish, O Great Master."

Her face frozen, she gazed beyond him. God, she must be stricken with horror, he thought dismally. He deserved to be tortured for exposing her to unconscionable risk. She didn't flinch as he gently cleansed away the traces of their lovemaking, the blood that was the damning testament to her loss of innocence. He steadfastly avoided thinking about the place where he'd found the sweetest ecstasy he'd ever known.

After a moment, she said, "You must think me intolerably naive for not considering what we did as an act of procreation."

"I think you're a remarkably responsive woman," he said gruffly. "You were swept away by passion, that's all."

She was silent. Too silent. He looked up and nearly drowned in the warm blue pools of her eyes. "Think what you like, Damien. But I was swept away by love for you."

Her quiet assertion grabbed him by the throat. That she could still cling to her delusion made his heart hammer with impossible dreams and unbearable panic. He surged to his feet. "I've told you before, Sarah, don't turn me into your latest crusade. Let me make one thing perfectly clear. I can never love you. No matter what happens, I won't do the honorable act. I will never, ever marry you."

She sat up straight. Her mouth firming, she looked him up and down. "What makes you think I'd ever consider you as my husband? I'd never marry a man who couldn't give me a stable home, a devil who doesn't even want me to mother his children."

Her words stabbed deeper than the slash of a knife. Against his will, he saw the fantasy of her body beautifully rounded with his baby. "We're in agreement, then." He forced the words out. "Though, of course, if you discover you're pregnant, I'll provide for you and the child."

"I wouldn't dream of depending on you. I can manage on my wage and the money from the book. You've no other obligations toward me."

She rose lithely and began to dress. Sick with regret and a perverse longing, he watched her slip into her clothes and then plait her hair into a thick, golden rope.

A shadow moved over her and crept onward, enveloping him. He lifted his gaze past the ruined roof and saw charcoal clouds blotting out the blue sky, the signal of an approaching monsoon shower. A fitting end to a disastrous day.

Sarah looked at him. ''Since we obviously didn't come here for the book, we may as well go back.'' Turning, she walked toward the foliage-wrapped archway of the temple, a small but determined woman intent on salving her pride and saving her heart.

Damien clenched his fingers around the damp rag. He'd hurt her. Deeply, dastardly, deplorably. She'd never forgive him now. He ought to feel relieved to be shed of her.

He felt as if he'd lost his soul.

Chapter 18

26 *July 1857, High in the Himalayan Foothills. Like Hindu weddings throughout India, a Pahari ceremony is steeped in ancient ritual, followed by feasting and festivity. An astrologer sets the propitious hour and minute for the rite, and the couple sits before a fire which burns brightly from the ghee poured upon it. After they repeat the long Vedic verses, the priest ties a sacred thread to their wrists and symbolically binds them together. To seal the marriage contract, the bride and groom walk the Seven Steps around the nuptial fire. And then the voices of the guests lift to the heavens in joyous prayer for a lifetime of happiness—*

Her heart aching, Sarah looked up from the sheaf of paper in her lap and gazed at the wedding celebration going on in the apricot orchard bordering the village. She sat with her back to a cool stone hut, but in her emotions she felt farther than a few yards from the merry gathering. Afternoon light slanted through green leaves still dewy from the latest rainfall and illuminated the laughing, dancing villagers who commemorated the marriage of Batan's youngest sister to a local sheepherder. The throb of drums and flutes created a haunting melody that steeped Sarah in wistful melancholy.

As she had a hundred times already, she peered through the throng at Damien. In the midst of the revelers, tall and dark in crisp white cotton, he bent over the tripod-mounted camera and prepared to photograph the newlyweds. They posed cross-legged on a richly patterned rug, a banquet spread out before them, their broad Mongolian faces aglow with happiness.

Absently Sarah stroked the feather of the quill pen against her cheek. A liquid shiver slid over her skin and puddled deep in her belly, a bittersweet echo of Damien's caresses and empty compliments.

Stricken, she dropped the pen. Now she understood why lovemaking was a closely guarded secret, and why girls were chaperoned so strictly. Were they to discover the passions of the flesh, they would crave it again and again. As she did.

In the fortnight since their tryst in the temple, Damien had all but ignored her. He spent his days closed off in his darkroom. She spent her days caring for Kit and working at Damien's desk, rewriting the disorderly notes he had collected over the past five years.

Hardly the romantic scenario of her maidenly dreams.

But she was a maiden no longer. Damien had guided her, body and soul, into the sublime realm of a woman. He had given her a glimpse of heaven . . . and then abandoned her in the hell of unrequited love. He wouldn't marry her. He wouldn't even offer her the dubious position of mistress. Not that she wanted either post, for she could not cleave herself from English society forever. Or from Reginald.

The thought threw her into a muddle of confusion. Damien offered her nothing. Reginald offered her a golden chance to have her own home, a family, a husband who loved her. She prayed he could forgive her one lapse from grace.

Would lovemaking be as wonderful with him?

She tried to imagine him touching her intimately. But her thoughts veered back to Damien.

It was a mistake. A mistake I have no intention of ever repeating.

His beastly words still smarted inside her. He had pulled her from paradise and sent her crashing back to earth. Even now pain and anger tangled within her. He had used her. He wasn't a lonely, tormented man searching for love; he was a lusty, self-serving scoundrel who had wanted a woman . . . any woman.

Or perhaps he was both.

All my meanness has been an act. I was fighting the need to love you like this . . . I wish we could be together forever.

More of his lies? Or had the truth slipped past his defenses during a moment of great emotion?

He was certainly capable of intense feelings. He'd agonized over the tragic accident to his brother. He'd anguished over failing his mother. Beneath the hard hostile shell, Damien hid an inner core of gentleness and sensitivity. She longed for the tender man who had introduced her to ecstasy, for the perceptive artist who produced poignant photographs, for the affectionate father who cared deeply for his son.

She couldn't deny the love that ached in her heart. Yet she wanted nothing to do with the man who could hurt and insult her.

She burned to complete their India book, to view her name on the cover. That meant ending their estrangement and working together. Surely they could at least be partners.

She gazed across the crowd and saw him showing off Kit to the bride and groom. The pride in his smile confirmed her decision. She was adult enough to set aside their differences. As he handed the baby back to Batan, Sarah brushed a speck of dirt from her best lavender-blue sari and straightened her veil. She gathered pen, inkwell,

and paper, then wended her way through the
wedding guests to his side.

"Hello, Damien."

He shot her a churlish frown and glanced at the
slant of the sun. "It isn't time to leave yet."

"I know." Her mind went blank of all but the
marvelous sight of him, his dark, princely features and his strong, solid body. She wanted to
feel his arms sheltering her, to kiss softness into
his rigid mouth, to bask in the heat of his caresses. But that would be a terrible mistake. "I'd
hoped you could answer some questions."

He quirked a wary brow. "Questions?"

"About the wedding. I want to make our book
as accurate as possible."

"I see." He heaved a breath and rested his elbow on the camera. "So what do you need to
know?"

She turned her gaze to the newlyweds. Clad in
a brilliant scarlet dress, the darkly pretty bride was
looking at her new husband. The male guests
joked and laughed as he tasted a bowl of strange
gray food. "What is he eating?" Sarah asked.

"The testicles of a panther." Damien gave her
an oddly probing look. "It's supposed to make a
man's seed more potent when he takes his wife
to bed."

A tremor started deep in her core. She denied
the sensation and regarded him coolly. "I hope it
works for them. The Pahari people value children
and family." *Unlike you*, she wanted to add.

"Sarah, there's something I've been meaning
to ask you." He snared her wrist and drew her
out of the noisy throng and into the private, dappled shade of an apricot tree. He stared down at
her. A snake charmer's flute couldn't have mesmerized Sarah more than Damien's intense brown
eyes. He radiated a tension that wrapped her in
absurd longing.

In a low-pitched voice, he said, "Have you started your monthly courses yet?"

Heat stained her cheeks. She hugged the sheaf of paper like a shield against her breasts. She wanted to look away, but his gaze imprisoned her as tightly as his fingers. "Yes," she murmured. "Last week."

"Thank God."

His heartfelt response roused her to unreasoning anger. "My sentiments exactly. Though I'm sorry you think our child would have been a burden."

He frowned. "For God's sake, I'm thinking of you, Sarah. You'd be cast out of English society if you bore a baby out of wedlock."

"You should have thought of that *before* you seduced me. And before you lied in order to get me to spend the summer here in the hills with you."

His stern gaze lowered to his hand on hers. He loosed her wrist and stepped back. "You're right," he said tonelessly. "I shouldn't have been so selfish."

His admission stole the steam from her fury. There was no point in continuing the painful argument.

He looked at the wedding revelry and motioned to her. "Come," he said curtly, "you'll need to write a piece on the dancers. I took some photographs of them earlier."

Aware of a sharp disappointment, Sarah followed him. Her first attempt to restore their friendship had ended in a crashing failure. But at least he hadn't walked away from her.

They found an open place and sat down amidst the rapt villagers surrounding the small troupe of men and women. Clad in brilliant costumes of scarlet and blue, the dancers leaped and pirouetted, their bare feet slapping the hard-packed earth. Their savage rhythm and barbarous grace embodied the uninhibited behavior of children.

Sarah set down her paper and pen. "Where are the dancers from?" she murmured.

"Several belong to this village. A few are guests from the other end of the valley."

One female dancer seemed taken with Damien. With her almond eyes and sultry smile focused on him, she whirled to the melody of flutes and drums, her gold-embroidered red skirt swirling around slim legs. Thin, silver rings studded her ears and nose, and her unbound black hair eddied like a thick silken veil. Breasts thrust high and bangles clashing, she circled him like a moon revolving around a heavenly body.

His clasped hands tucked beneath his chin, Damien eyed the dancer, his gaze sliding up and down her nubile form. Stiffness invaded Sarah's limbs. The dancer reminded her of the whores she had seen in the bazaar. She was seized by the sudden burning need to divert Damien's attention. "What will you do when you finish this book?"

He shrugged, glancing at her. "I'll start work on another. I'm considering one on China."

The news sank like a stone in her chest. She shouldn't be surprised, Sarah told herself. Damien was a vagabond, a restless man who could never plant roots and thrive in one place. He'd spend his life on the road, forever searching for the affection he never received from his mother. It only went to prove how ill-suited they were. "So you and Kit will move there."

"Yes."

His gaze returned to the girl. Situating herself blatantly before Damien, she danced in wild abandon, gyrating her hips and rotating her hands with sinuous grace. Despite the other men present, she focused her carnal smile on him as she curved forward, her hips undulating in a rhythm Sarah knew, her bodice drooping to expose voluptuous, unbound breasts.

Sarah jerked her gaze to the crimson necklaces circling the girl's throat. In the midst of the beads lay a gleam of gold. As she danced nearer, the gleam took on a familiar oval shape dangling from a familiar gold chain. The force of a blow rocketed through Sarah.

It was her locket. The locket Reginald had given her.

Dumbfounded, she watched the girl shake her hips and glide away, stepping lithely out of the crowd. With one last, serpentine twist of her dark arm, she beckoned to Damien and then disappeared behind one of the huts.

"Excuse me," he said. Without so much as a glance at Sarah, he rose and followed the dancer.

Sarah's mouth dropped open. Damien had traded her precious locket for more than clothing and food.

And now he was going back for more.

Hot with fury, she sprang to her feet and stalked after the couple. She shouldn't be angry. She shouldn't be hurt. She shouldn't feel this unladylike urge to throttle a man who wasn't fit to kiss her toes. Let him go off with his whore. The two deserved each other.

Yet she couldn't sit still, not while the woman wore *her* locket.

At the outskirts of the village, a dirt track wended downward past a thicket of towering rhododendrons and ended at a lush expanse of potato fields and rice paddies. Damien and the dancer stood just beyond the bushy trees.

His back was turned, and Sarah could discern only the low rumble of his voice. The dancer smiled coyly as he dipped his hand inside her bodice. She pressed herself to him like a cat rubbing against its master's leg.

He took hold of her shoulders and pushed her

to arm's length. The dancer again thrust herself at him. He shook his head emphatically and released her, then strode off alone, toward the wild reaches of the valley beyond the fields. The woman stomped her foot and minced away to a hut at the edge of the village.

Her anger ebbing into confusion, Sarah leaned against the stone wall. So he hadn't left to make love to the woman. The purpose of their exchange mystified her.

And where had he gone? Perhaps he wanted her to believe he was seeing another woman. Perhaps he wanted to foster the image of a tomcat who roamed from one feline to another, giving only his body and never his heart.

Sarah compressed her lips. She was reading too much into his actions. The deception would serve him little purpose, for she already believed him faithless. But, by heaven, he would pay for trading her locket to a whore. As she slowly walked back to the troupe of dancers, she vowed to make him recover the piece. The moment he returned, she would take him to task.

Nearly an hour passed before Damien came strutting back. Propping Kit against her shoulder, she stood and coldly regarded him. "I should like a word with you."

He keenly studied her, as if gauging her mood. "I'd like a word with you, too," he countered. "But not here. It's time to head home." He reached for the baby. "I'll carry Kit."

"My, you're offering to do the nanny's job. Or do you mean to deduct a guinea from my wage?"

He looked inordinately pleased by her acid tone. "It means I like to hold my son."

"What about your camera?"

"Two of the village men will deliver it and the glass plates tomorrow."

She and Damien took their leave of the newlyweds and hiked in silence up the steep track.

Her sandals crunching twigs blown down in a recent storm, she wondered what Damien had to say to her. Likely more of his insults. A nightjar cried harshly in the valley below. As the violet mist of evening unfurled over the hillside, they entered the hut. The walk had lulled Kit to sleep, and Damien went into the bedroom to put the baby in his makeshift cradle.

Sarah lit an oil lamp. When he came out, the light cast his serious face into golden illumination.

"Sarah, I wanted to say—"

"Damien, I should like to know—"

They stopped. She frowned.

He swept a mock bow. "Ladies first."

She tightly clasped her hands. "Now you do have me curious. It isn't like you to act the gentleman. Especially when you lie as easily as you bow."

His chuckle held an odd edge of embarrassment. "The relic of an old governess who kept me on the straight and narrow. Or at least she tried to."

Questions about his boyhood sprang to Sarah's tongue, but she forced her mind from questions he probably wouldn't answer. "Why did you go off with that dancer?"

"Umi?" He swaggered to the desk and perched on the edge. "I shouldn't think you'd want to know about *her.*"

"Don't make assumptions about me. I don't want the sordid details, but I should like my question answered."

"As you wish. Umi and I had some business to transact. I doubt a lady like you would care to hear the intimate details." Self-satisfaction tilted his mouth, and he peered closely at her, as if relishing her reaction.

"Indeed." She removed her veil and let the

wisp of silk drift to the table. "I saw you put your hand into her bodice."

He blinked. "You followed us?"

"Of course." Sarah folded her arms. "After all, she was wearing *my* locket."

"Oh . . . hell." Caught off guard, Damien rubbed his hand over his hair. This wasn't going the way he'd intended. He'd meant to test Sarah's feelings by seeing if he could make her jealous. But she looked cold and calm. Too calm for a woman who professed to love him. "I didn't think you'd noticed."

"How could I fail to notice when she was dangling her bosom in your face?"

Maybe there *was* hope. "Ah. Beautifully rounded breasts, at that."

Sarah lifted her slim shoulders in an impatient shrug. "I want my locket back, Damien. Even if you have to do slave labor to earn the money to redeem it. Work out a trade with her. And you'd best be quick about it. In fact, tomorrow would do nicely."

God. She still pined for Reggie. Hot and heavy emotion dragging at his heart, Damien said, "You won't have to wait."

"Pardon?"

He dug in his tunic pocket and extended his hand. "Here."

Her lips parted as she gazed at the gold oval and chain draping his scarred palm. Sweeping closer, she snatched up the locket, and her fingers brushed his. Heat closed his groin in an iron claw.

She drilled him with a frown of suspicion. "How did you manage to get it with no money? Wait." She held up a hand. "I don't think I want to know."

"I wasn't exactly honest with you," he admitted.

"You never are."

Regret knotted his throat. With the jerky move-

ments of a doomed man on his way to the gal-
lows, he reached to the shelf behind him and
picked up a carved wooden box. He opened it
and displayed the stash of silver rupees within.

She clutched the locket to her breast and sank
onto the settee. Bitterness narrowed her eyes.
"Aha. This was another of your lies."

He nodded slowly. "Yes."

"But why? You knew how dear this locket was
to me."

He clenched his hands. Lies leaped to his lips.
Yet honesty might be his only redemption.
"Sarah, I don't know quite how to put this—"

"Try being truthful for once in your life."

"Just give me a chance—"

"I've given you plenty of chances."

"Will you give me one more?" He took a deep
breath and humbled himself. "Please?"

She eyed him with a hint of irony. "Perhaps.
Since you ask so politely."

"Thank you." He peered downward and
mumbled to the lacing of his sandals, "I sold the
locket because I was jealous."

A cricket creaked into the silence. "Jealous?"
Incredulity lifted her voice. "You were jealous of
Reginald?"

Damien gave her a cautious look from beneath
his lashes. Perched on the edge of her seat, she
looked skeptical and all too desirable. He wanted
to undress her, to feast his eyes on her creamy
skin and womanly curves. He wanted to wrap
himself in the warmth of her love.

"Damien, answer me."

God, he hated confessions. "I don't know why
you find it difficult to believe," he said. "Reggie
is everything you admire in a man—noble, honorable, perfect. Every time you told me so, you
rubbed that locket. As if you were caressing your
lover."

She tilted her head, her eyebrows arched in

surprise. "That hardly gave you the right to take it."

He had to make her understand. "For God's sake, you must have compared me to him ten times a day and found me sorely lacking. The gentleman and the rogue. I was hoping you'd forget him if you took off the damned trinket."

Her lips curled, she regarded him with the disgust she might afford a dung beetle. "Do you think I'm so shallow I'd confuse a piece of jewelry with love?"

"Yes. I suppose I did." He wet his dry lips. "I haven't had much experience with love."

"And then did you expect me to think of *you* instead? Is that when you decided to seduce me?"

The chill in her tone swept over him like winter frost. He shifted on the hard desk. "No, I didn't have any definite plan."

"Oh, so the seduction was spontaneous? You were swept away by my allure?"

The memory of their tryst in the temple ached inside him. "Yes."

She rose. "If you can't speak the truth, there's no point in prolonging this discussion."

"It *is* the truth." He spread his palms wide. "Sarah, I didn't intend to seduce you. God knows, it was the last thing in the world I meant to do."

"How relieved I am to hear that. I'm not at all surprised, given your opinion of me. If you'll excuse me, I'm rather tired." Pivoting sharply, she walked toward the bedroom.

Oh, God. Now he'd hurt her pride again.

He crossed the room in three strides and caught her arm. The smoothness of her skin burned through him, settling like a fever in his groin. He wanted to kiss away her stiff expression, to see her features soften with ecstasy. He wanted to hear her say, *I love you.*

"Wait," he said, his voice rough with panic. If

she left now, he might never raise the courage to voice the yearning that had been chafing him for a fortnight. "Stay and listen a moment. What I said came out all wrong."

"Then say what you mean."

"I'm trying to. This isn't easy for me."

"And it's easy for me to stand here and listen to you belittle me? Save your insults for your next conquest." She curled her fingers around the gold, as if it were her dearest possession. It probably was. "Knowing you took my locket under false pretenses was the last straw."

"I'm sorry." Seizing the piece, he stepped behind her and stared down at the plait of blond hair as thick as his arm. He wanted to kiss the tender nape of her neck, to brush his lips over the fine wisps sprinkling her skin. His trembling fingers reached beneath the braid and fastened the locket. "I admit I shouldn't have talked you into giving me the damned thing," he said gruffly. "It was wicked of me."

"Yes, it was. And you needn't curse."

Her certainty discouraged him. Yet as he came around in front of her, he glimpsed in her eyes a wounded sadness and sensed in her rigid muscles a resistance to his closeness, as if she, too, fought the fires of attraction. "But I recovered the locket, didn't I?" He touched her cheek, smooth as satin beneath his fingertips. "Don't be angry at me, Sarah."

"I'm not angry. I'd merely like to be alone."

"Not yet. Not until I finish what I have to say." *Not until I earn the miracle of your smile again.* In desperation, he backed her to the wall and bracketed her with his arms. Her warmth conquered his heart like an invading army.

Before she could duck away, he said swiftly, "I know I'm not worthy of you, not in the way Reggie is. He would never have used you so shabbily in the temple. Hell, he would never have taken you there in the first place. I'm sorry for the awful things I said to you, Sarah."

She regarded him through the golden veil of her eyelashes. "Are you sorry you made love to me?"

"God, no. But you have every right to hate me."

"I don't hate you, Damien."

His throat caught. "You don't?"

"No. Although I do hate the way you behave at times."

"What about the other times? How do you feel toward me then?"

She tilted her head back against the wall and gravely regarded him. "I've been frank with you before. But there'll be no more one-sided candor. It's your turn to be honest. First you tell me how *you* feel."

Cold sweat dewed his brow. He had to open his heart. She would accept no less. "I want to. I swear I do."

"Then you can start by helping me better understand why you push away anyone who tries to get near you."

Her statement closed around him like the jaws of a trap. "I just don't want anyone . . . or rather, I don't want *you* to delude yourself into thinking I'm suitable for a woman like you."

"I'll be the judge of that. I should like to hear more about your upbringing."

He tensed. "Why?"

"Because that's where your problems started. That's when you became afraid to love."

The old defensive wall surged inside him. He let his arms drop to his sides. "I already told you about the fire. What more do you want me to say?"

"Tell me about your father's death."

The urge to run gripped him. He forced himself to stand still. "It's best left forgotten."

She touched his wrist, not with the caress of a lover, but with the commiseration of a friend. "Tell me, Damien. For once in your life, stop closing out the past. Talk to me."

He hesitated. She stood waiting, a vision of womanhood, the gold locket gleaming against her softly wrapped breasts. He admired her determination to understand him when he scarcely understood himself. Though he couldn't give Sarah the security and love she deserved, he could at least give her honesty. For the first time in his life, he could place his trust in another person.

"All right, I'll tell you. But only if you promise you'll not breathe a word of what I say to a living soul."

She looked annoyed. "I would never betray your confidence."

"I know," he said quickly. Unable to bear her scrutiny, he walked to the window. A gust of wind cooled his sweaty brow. The lonely hoot of an owl drifted from the mysterious darkness and shrouded him in the shadows of memory. "It happened on a summer night, a balmy night like tonight, when I was eighteen. I'd been staying at our town house in London, but I came back to my father's estate in Kent because it was Christopher's nineteenth birthday.

"I'd brought Christopher a present—a tin drum from the American Revolutionary War. I'd searched it out in a curio shop to add to his collection. You see, even though he was nineteen, he still played with toys." Guilt rose in him, and he risked a glance at Sarah. She leaned against the wall; her clear blue eyes and impartial expression encouraged him.

"Go on," she said.

"I . . . arrived too late for the celebration." He paused, his throat burning with the bilious memory of the duchess's glower. "No, that's not true. Mother hadn't invited me."

Sarah walked toward him. "Why would she be so cruel as to exclude you from a family gathering?"

Tears stung his eyes. Damien turned to the window lest she spy the weakness. "She couldn't bear to look at me and remember *my* cruelty. As soon as I walked in the door, she walked out."

"I'd love to speak my mind to her—" Sarah exhaled a loud sigh. "But tell me about your father."

"When I came in that evening, he was lolling in a chair in the drawing room. The parlor maid and Bromley—the butler—helped him upstairs. Father had been drinking quite a lot, you see."

"Because of the celebration?"

Damien snorted. "My father didn't need a celebration to get drunk. The fifth Duke of Lamborough had his first glass of brandy before he got out of bed each morning. On his good days, he only polished off an entire decanter. On his bad days, he was stone drunk by noon. Of course, Christopher and I didn't see much of him. He spent most of his time at his club."

"Perhaps the duchess drove him to drink."

"Mother?" The idea astonished Damien. "No, she tolerated his drinking when a lot of wives would have nagged him."

"Perhaps he needed nagging. He was neglecting his sons."

Damien shrugged away the observation. "You don't understand."

"Then make me understand."

"I'm trying. We were alone in the drawing room when Christopher opened his gift." His brother's whoop of delight, the joy on his fair face, still haunted Damien.

"Did he like it?"

"Yes. He pounded out a quick rhythm—he has a surprising knack for music. Then he ran upstairs to show Mother, but she was dressing. So he went to find Father.''

Damien breathed in the cool night air, spiced with Sarah's feminine musk. Oh, God. If only he'd guided his brother away. If only he hadn't succumbed to the need to indulge Christopher.

She touched his arm. ''What happened then?''

''He knocked, but no one answered. Before I could stop him, he opened the door and dashed inside. Father wasn't in his bed, but the balcony doors were open, and Christopher darted outside. I was right behind him.'' He paused. ''We found Father there, along with the parlor maid. Her skirt was hiked to her waist, and his hand was between her legs.''

He looked for disgust on Sarah's face and found only sad perception. ''I'm so sorry for you,'' she murmured. ''No child should have to see his father behave in so vile a manner.''

Damien swallowed a queer lump. ''It was harder on Christopher than on me. Father could scarcely tolerate his imbecile heir. Thank God my brother never understood why Father ignored him.'' Drawing a breath, he gazed down at his clenched fists.

''Finish the story,'' Sarah said gently.

''Christopher was such an innocent he didn't even notice the indiscretion going on in front of him. I tried to pull him away, but he started tap-tapping on his drum. Father was drunk and disagreeable, furious at being caught. He shoved Christopher.'' The old horror clotted in Damien's belly. He braced his hands on the windowframe and saw the awful scene unfold in his mind like a succession of stark photographs.

''And then?''

''Then Christopher impulsively pushed back. He might be a child in his head, but he has a man's strength. Father toppled over the balcony

and fell to the flagstones of the terrace. His neck
was broken.''

Tears smarted in Sarah's eyes. Damien's head
was bowed, and his hands gripped the sill so hard
his scars were white as snow. Seized by a pure
impulse to comfort him, she pressed herself
against his arm, laying her head on his shoulder.
He rested his brow against her hair for a too-brief
moment.

''So,'' she said, ''you've suffered the blame all
these years, Damien. Why?''

''To protect Christopher. I was afraid if word
got out, his actions might be misconstrued as
murder.'' He turned fully to her, and his dark
eyes glittered. ''I was afraid the authorities might
toss him into a madhouse.''

''Surely your mother knew the truth.''

''No. I told Christopher what to say, that I'd
argued with Father and he'd stumbled, that was
all. It was simple. He didn't truly comprehend
what had happened, anyway.''

''But your mother accused you of murder.''

Harsh shadows played over his face. ''Yes. She
was hysterical, shaken by Father's death. Unfor-
tunately some of the servants overheard her, and
that's how the rumor started.''

The unfairness rankled Sarah. ''What about the
parlor maid? Didn't she speak up in your defense?''

''I paid her to verify my version, that it was a
tragic accident. I set her up in a cottage in Corn-
wall and threatened to break her neck if she so
much as uttered my brother's name.''

Sarah shivered. From the hardness in his voice,
she feared he meant the threat. ''Were there no
other witnesses?''

''None. I've never told a single soul but you.''

The magnitude of his trust settled around her
like a warm embrace. Hope took wing inside her,

but she caged the errant emotion. "What a frightful secret to carry around for so many years."

"Perhaps." His voice lowered to a raspy pitch. "But it was the least I could do for my brother. I made him what he is."

Anger at his self-abasement swelled in her. "It's a gross injustice, that's what it is. Certainly you needn't announce it in *The London Times*, but at least your mother should hear the real story."

"What purpose would that serve? It's easier for me to take the blame. In her eyes, I couldn't have sunk any lower than I already had. One more sin on my black soul didn't matter."

Sarah resisted the urge to shake him. "But it's wrong. How can you simply accept your mother's denunciation of you?"

Shrugging, he picked up a *bidi* from a tray on the desk. After lighting it at the lamp, he propped his elbow on the sill. "She's found happiness with me living thousands of miles away. She dotes on Christopher, so I let her go on thinking the best of him."

"And what about her second son? You deserved to be nurtured and loved by your mother, Damien. Every child does. She denied you a normal upbringing."

He swung toward her, his jaw tight. "I told you before, I ruined her life. And my brother's."

"She ruined her entire family by being cruel and vindictive. And to appease her, you've sacrificed your peace of mind, your home in England, not to mention your ability to love."

He shook his head. "Don't read too much into the estrangement, Sarah."

"I will, indeed. I have a stake in this, you know. Because of her, you can't open your heart to me."

His dark gaze riveted to hers, and the deep longing there spread like a balm over her battered emotions. The fragrant smoke of his *bidi* wafted to her. Lifting his hand, he touched her cheek as if in apology. "I know. But I can't simply forget what I did to my brother."

"Of course you can't. I only want you to forgive the five-year-old boy who made a terrible mistake. If someday Kit were to accidentally set your house on fire or cause injury to someone, would you persecute him? Would you deny him your love for the rest of his life?"

Damien opened his mouth and then closed it. His brow lowered in thoughtful perplexity. He drew on his *bidi* and exhaled a puff of smoke that trailed like a gossamer ghost out the window. "You know damned well I wouldn't."

"Precisely my point."

He glowered for another moment. Then a grin made him look more youthful and handsome. "You're quite the debater, Sarah Faulkner. Have you ever thought of writing a newspaper column?"

His teasing took the sting out of her anger. She smiled back. "I am vexed with you, Damien Coleridge," she quipped, half in humor and half in true vexation. "I do wish you would stop taking responsibility for your mother's brutality. It's her failure, not yours."

Was Sarah right? A chink opened inside Damien, a crack in the armor around his emotions. Enough to give him the glimpse of light at the end of a cold, lonely tunnel. He ached to move toward the radiance, yet the effort bathed him in sweat. "I wish I could believe you."

"You *can* believe." Sarah perched her hands on her hips in the guise of a prim nanny. A beautiful nanny he wanted to undress, to spend hours relearning her body, rounded and soft in all the right places. And to hear her murmuring words of love.

"You have a lot of unfinished business in England," she went on. "It isn't fair to cut off Kit from his family. Or to risk his being denied his rightful place as your heir, and heir to the duke-dom.''

The prospect iced Damien's palms. Oh, God. Did he dare go back? To hide his shaking hands, he crushed the *bidi* and flung it out the window. "I'll think about it."

"Please do. You'll never be at peace with your-self until you come to terms with your past. Go home and face your mother. Show her that you've become a good man in spite of her poor exam-ple."

He forced a laugh. "Me, a good man? I'm the one you called a scoundrel and a liar."

"You are. But you're also sensitive and gener-ous. If you'd cease acting so gruff and callous, people would see your better half."

Her words filled his empty chest with a surge of hope and gave him the courage to ask the ques-tion that had gnawed at him for the past fort-night. "Does that mean you still . . . care for me?"

"I thought we agreed you'd tell me your feel-ings first."

Her steady gaze snared him. He didn't know what to say. He didn't know how to find the words to describe his powerful desire for her, his confused swings from elation to despair, the ag-ony of yearning he hid inside emotions so tender they were unmanly.

She stood watching him, her arms crossed over the gentle mound of her bosom. Her eyes were the blue of an unclouded sky; her teeth worried her lower lip. She reminded him of a wounded bird, valiantly awaiting the strike of the hawk. In a stunning flash, he realized she was as fearful as he, and the knowledge settled in his belly like a sweet ache.

He wanted to crush her to him and kiss away her questions as he'd done before. Yet he couldn't. This time, the decision he would put to her must arise from her mind as well as her body.

Gathering her hands in his, he searched for the right words. "You're like a fire in my heart, Sarah Faulkner. A fire that scares me so much I tried my damnedest to put it out. All those days I spent in my darkroom, I wasn't working. I was thinking about you. About how much I want you and need you."

"And?" she whispered.

"And I can't offer you any pledges. I can't even offer you security."

"What are you saying, Damien?"

He took a deep, shaky breath and looked straight into her lovely face. "Sarah, I want you to be my mistress."

Chapter 19

Sarah heard his resonant voice through a cloud of yearning so thick she wanted to surrender to the lure of his arms and forget her scruples in the sweet oblivion of physical passion. Every inch of her body felt soft and ready for him, from the ache in her breasts to the pulsations deep in her belly. Flustered, she managed to shake her head.

"You don't know what you ask of me," she said. "I've always dreamed about marrying someday. About living in my own home. About having a husband and a family to love."

"I know," he said heavily. "I can only love you with my body. I don't know any other way. But I *can* give you companionship . . . and the phenomenal pleasure we found in the temple."

His candid eyes crumbled her qualms, so that she struggled to remember the pain of loving him. "You pushed me away—"

"I won't do it again. I swear I won't." His hands tightened around hers, then drifted slowly up her arms, as if he, too, fought the urge to lock her in an embrace. "I need you, Sarah. My body needs you, and my mind does, too."

"And your heart?" she couldn't help murmuring.

"I haven't a heart to give." He touched his warm brow to hers, his hands gently kneading

334

her shoulders. "That's honest, Sarah. I can't fulfill your dreams now. I don't know if I ever can. But we can share moments many people never have."

"But what if . . . I were to become pregnant?"

"You won't. I bought something else from Umi."

"What?"

Pulling back, he dug in his pocket and extended his hand to her. In his palm lay an object rather like a sausage casing. "This."

Sarah gazed askance at it. "What is it?"

"A sheath. It catches a man's seed and keeps the woman's womb from quickening."

She reddened with awareness. The method seemed so cold-blooded. With heart-wrenching perception, she realized that one of the natural gifts of sexual intimacy was a child conceived in love.

But Damien didn't offer his love.

And she wanted him so badly she could think of little save the rapture shining like a star within her reach.

She reminded herself of all the reasons he was wrong for her. The thought of enduring hateful gossip, of branding herself an outcast by people she respected, probably Reginald, too, made her quake inside. Yet after having survived a bloody mutiny, she knew that life was too short to fret over possible consequences. Her fiancé might be dead, and the British Raj as well. Someday she might return to England and spend the rest of her life caring for other people's children. Better she should savor this radiant promise of joy while she could. And she'd be accused of being Damien's mistress anyway, so why not reap the benefits?

"You'll have to agree to one condition," she said. "If and when we return to English society, our affair will end."

Damien hesitated for an instant. "I understand

completely." He gathered her to him and nuzzled her hair. She reveled in the strength of his arms, inhaled his exciting masculine scent. He added softly, "I have a condition, too."

"What?"

He drew back to touch the locket between her breasts. "That you put this aside for now."

Her heart in her throat, her eyes linked to his, she reached around and unfastened the clasp. Without speaking, she dropped the locket on the windowsill. The tiny click of metal faded into charged silence.

His face gentled. "Will you tell me how you feel now, Sarah? Please?"

His voice was deep and thick with yearning. That he would ask, rather than demand, convinced her of his sincerity. Past and future melted away, leaving only the golden present, a suspended interlude in the mountains of India.

She cradled his firm jaw in her hands. "Yes. Yes. I love you, Damien."

He smiled. Reckless and giddy, she smiled back.

A look of stark desire descended over him, a look that made her tremble, a look that submerged her in sultry adoration. They moved toward each other, and her mouth tingled from the warm and wonderful caress of his lips, his arms so taut around her that he lifted her from the ground. He deepened the kiss, his mouth undulating over hers and filling her with his heat. Scarred hands skimmed over her skin, exploring her most sensitive places until her head spun and she melted into boneless surrender.

No longer could she bank the flames ignited on their day in the temple. A firestorm of passion consumed her, and her hands glided over him, seeking the rigidity of muscle and the hardness of need. She relished his warm skin, tangy with sweat, and the feel of his thick hair, sliding through her fingers.

He unwrapped her sari and let it drift to the floor in a lavender-blue puddle. His clothing dropped away, too, and he walked her backward to the hearth, guiding her down onto the tiger-skin rug.

"Guess what I want now?" he said against her mouth.

"A cup of tea? A *chupatty*? A—"

His mouth trapped her teasing words and transformed them into incoherent gasps. "Imp. I want this."

And then he drove inside her and there was no more need for talk, only the groans and murmurs of mindless pleasure. She clung tightly to him and fancied their bodies soaring in unison, their hearts and souls joining on a glorious ride to the stars.

Long, shuddering moments later, the fire within burned to white ash, and she opened her eyes to the satisfaction of his smile. "Now would you like your cup of tea?" she asked demurely.

He brushed his lips against hers. "I'd rather drink the champagne of your kisses."

"This from a man who professes to lack any talent for eloquence, who describes his writing as 'dry and detestably dull'?"

He shifted against her, his chest grazing her breasts, his hips rekindling her fire. "Eloquence of the body is an entirely different matter, Miss Faulkner. Would you care for another demonstration?"

His silky words enticed her. "The evening is still young. And we've plenty of time. Will you sleep with me tonight?"

He went still, tension in the arms bracketing her, his brown eyes probing. "What if we disturb Kit?"

"Your son will never know." Wondering at the uneasiness she sensed in Damien, she kissed the bronze column of his throat and the strong pulse beating there. "I, however, plan to disturb you for hours."

"Sarah."

She moved her lips to his chin and tasted skin bristly with beard. "Mmm?"

"I've never slept all night beside a woman before."

Not even Shivina? Sarah swallowed the startled question. They had no past and no future, only the golden present. As she gazed into his uncertain eyes, tenderness welled within her. How many other joys had he missed? "You were my first," she murmured. "Now I have the honor of being yours."

That night began an idyll that seemed more like a vivid dream to Sarah than simple reality. She steadfastly refused to consider the consequences of their affair. It was easier to drift through days lazy with friendship and nights ripe with passion. Between bouts of monsoon showers, they explored the countryside and talked over the problems of the Raj. They scrutinized Damien's notes and organized his photographs into a cohesive book. He showed her a picture he'd taken of her asleep, with Kit cuddled in her arms.

Yet Sarah wanted more than political debates and professional discussions. She wanted to reach within him and probe the vulnerable feelings he hid from the world. As the days passed, Damien delighted her more and more with tidbits from his past.

She learned he'd attended Eton, only to be tossed out his second year after having been caught smoking in the chapel. He learned she'd been educated at home by her mother, who had worked as a governess before falling madly in love with the younger son of a baron.

One day, sitting on the veranda while the rain

poured down in sheets, Sarah spoke of her own happy childhood in the hopes of nudging Damien toward a reconciliation with his past. "We had very few possessions," she said, "because Papa was cut off without a penny. He labored as a clerk in a counting house. Yet I remember our little home in Chelsea ringing with laughter. I remember that every Saturday evening he indulged my love of sweets by bringing apple tarts or gingerbread men or the biggest trifle he could afford."

Catching a raindrop and rubbing it between his fingers, Damien said, "Did he ever go back?"

"Back where?"

"To see his parents."

"Actually, yes." She grimaced. "Papa took me to call on them when I was nine, at their estate in Surrey. They were stuffy folk who spent the afternoon reading biblical passages and complaining about disobedient children. They never forgave him for marrying beneath him, but Papa accepted that. He loved Mama and me too much to let their prejudice spoil our happiness. He learned to set his feelings free and to be happy with the man he was."

"How did you end up living in India with your aunt and uncle?"

Sadness caught Sarah's throat. "Papa died of a lung infection when I was ten. A year later, Mama succumbed to consumption. But she carried on contentedly even through a painful illness, for the memory of Papa's love sustained her."

Rain drummed on the veranda roof. Damien watched her with dark intensity. "You want a family like that again."

"Yes," she said fiercely, wishing she could replace his wretched memories with her own happy ones. "It was wonderful."

He took her hand and turned his gaze to the green, rain-washed hillside. "I haven't any memories like that. Mine tend to be like that Christmas

Eve when I was seven . . .'' He pressed his lips together.

The pain in his voice roused her sympathy. ''Damien, if you want to talk about it, I'm always ready to listen.''

Sighing, he turned back to her. ''I would like to tell you. I sketched a picture of my mother sitting on a garden bench, with Christopher and me at her feet. It was my Christmas gift to her.'' A faraway bitterness tinged his expression. ''I was supposed to be in bed, but I was so anxious to see her reaction that I brought the picture downstairs. I thought she'd finally love me. But she was so angry at me for interrupting her music party that she hauled me into the drawing room.'' He paused.

''What did she do?'' Sarah prompted.

Tightening his fingers around hers, he looked down at their clasped hands. ''Mother called my work idealized drivel. She reminded me of what I'd done to Christopher and said she rued the day she gave birth to me. Then she hurled the drawing into the fire.''

Fury burned inside Sarah. ''How horrible! Surely you can't excuse her for *that*.''

He frowned moodily. ''I hardly know what to think anymore. When I remember something like that, the little boy in me wants to take all the blame. Yet if I step back and view her as a stranger, sometimes I wonder . . .''

Sarah held back the condemnation she wanted to shower on the dowager. It was enough that Damien was beginning to see his mother through the eyes of an adult. The decision to return to England had to be his. Only he could acknowledge her cruelty. And only then could he open himself to love.

Until that time, Sarah knew, she must satisfy herself with his growing trust in her and with the hot exhilaration of his lovemaking.

And exhilarate her he did. As soon as Batan left each evening, it was all they could do to eat dinner. He had only to give Sarah that special look or slide his plundering hand toward her bodice, and she fell into his arms. One by one, they tried all the positions described in *The Kama Sutra*. Often they ended up laughing together and eating cold curry at midnight.

When Kit awakened in the predawn darkness, Damien always rose to milk the goat, and then he lay beside her while she fed the baby. Sometimes the three of them fell asleep together. And sometimes after Sarah had settled the slumbering baby back into his cradle, Damien would still be awake, waiting for her in bed.

One memorable night, he crooked a finger and whispered, "Come here."

Assuming the posture of a slave, she knelt beside the charpoy. "What is your wish, O Great Master?"

"Pleasure me."

She did. Languidly and enticingly. And afterward, he set himself to the task of worshipping at the shrine of her body. Their coupling carried them both to soul-trembling heights.

But far sweeter to Sarah than the ecstasies of the flesh was the quiet joy of awakening in his arms each morning, of seeing the first rays of light wash over his tender smile, of watching him bring his son into bed so they could cuddle together as a family.

With all her heart, Sarah hungered for her own baby. She wanted to feel it kick inside her and know the delight of nestling a newborn to her breast. A baby born of her love for Damien.

But he never spoke of love. He never spoke of a future beyond their idyllic hillside retreat. Until one day in late September, when the air grew crisp and cool, and the leaves began to turn gold and bronze on the wooded slopes.

Returning from an errand in the village, Damien drew Sarah into his darkroom, closed the door, and lit a lantern. Yellow light bloomed over the stacks of glass-plated photographs and the row of chemical bottles. When he turned to her, the gravity on his features struck at her heart. "It's safe to return to Meerut," he said.

The news staggered her with joy. Home! She was going home! Then despair closed in. They must abandon their mountain hideaway. Home was the circle of Damien's arms. "What's happened?" she asked. "Have the English put down the rebellion?"

"Not yet, but the tide has turned. A few weeks ago, British forces recaptured Delhi. They took Bahadur Shah prisoner. With one of their ringleaders gone, I'm afraid it's the beginning of the end for the mutineers."

"Yet there's still fighting going on?" Sarah ventured, hating herself for the sick hope within her. She wanted no more deaths . . . yet she desperately sought an excuse to put off their departure.

"The fighting is confined to the stations far to the east of Meerut," he said.

"Perhaps it's safer to remain here until we're sure."

Damien stood moodily watching her, his fists clenching and unclenching, as if he fought an inner battle. "We can't stay," he said at last. "It's time to go back. Once the snows start, we'll be stranded here for the winter."

She pressed herself to his muscled body. "Would that be so very dreadful?"

He grasped her shoulders. Torment dragged at the corners of his mouth. "Sarah, this is no life for you. You're too proud a woman to stay with a scoundrel like me—"

"You're not a scoundrel."

"Let's not debate that again. You should go

back to English society, where you belong. It was your idea to end the affair when we left here.''

"Of course," she said, her heart hollow. "Because of the gossip.''

"People might whisper, but they'll have no proof of any wrongdoing. These are unusual circumstances. Many an Englishwoman must have been forced to take refuge in strange households, unchaperoned for days, even months. Hell, you'll probably be welcomed home a heroine.''

Rather than encouraging her, the possibility dismayed her. A heroine . . . without Damien at her side. "What about our book?''

"You've done wonders with the text. I need only to replace some of the photographs that burned in the caravan. When I come back here next summer, I'll put everything together and then submit the book to a publisher.''

His self-reliance embittered her. "You have the future so neatly mapped out, don't you? You must have been planning this for weeks.''

He pulled her into a fierce embrace, and hope went winging through her heart. If only he could admit he felt more than mere desire for her; if only they could abide here forever.

"It's going to be hell to say good-bye," Damien murmured, "but it has to be done.'' He extracted himself and stepped back. "There's another reason I can't stay here. I've decided to return to England. I'm going to make my mother accept Kit as my heir.''

Flabbergasted, Sarah blinked. She'd finally convinced him. So why did she feel so saddened? "I'll go with you.''

"As my mistress? Sarah, be honest with yourself. You're a conventional woman at heart. Don't think I haven't been aware of you longing for a family and a man who could love you. I can't give you what you want. You knew that from the start.''

His words hurt, and she struck back instantly. "You don't care for me. You can't care for anyone but yourself."

"That's a damned lie." He abruptly slammed his fist on the table. Glass bottles clanged against metal trays. Then silence reigned. When he lifted his head, his eyes were stark with pain. "I do care, by God. Enough to take you back to Meerut, to Reginald and your dreams."

"You yourself said he might be dead. Perhaps everyone there is dead. Perhaps there's no life for me to go back to."

"No more than fifty people died there. You owe it to yourself to find out if you have any friends and family left. And you have too much honor to live in defiance of social mores."

I can never love you. I will never, ever marry you.

Confusion tangled her heart into a painful knot. She thought of sharing a comfortable life with Reginald, of enjoying the status of a doctor's wife. Then she thought of being Damien's mistress, of walking into church and suffering the scorn of women and men alike, of seeing people turn their backs on her. And if ever she had a child of her own, he would be branded a bastard and taunted by the other children.

Bleak reality crept over her like a winter wind. Yet the prospect of giving up Damien and Kit shuddered through her with equal force. She had known their time together would one day come to this cruel end. Or perhaps her true anguish lay in the fact that she had hoped he would fall in love with her.

And he hadn't.

She pressed her hands to her temples. "Damien, I don't know what to think. I don't know what I want anymore."

"There's nothing more to think about." He ran his fingers through his hair, mussing the black strands into the style of a rogue. "We've a long journey ahead of us. I'd like to leave at first light."

"If that makes you happy." She couldn't stop bitterness from seeping into her tone.

"Sarah, I'm sorry. You can't imagine how I wish I could be the man of your dreams."

The gentle regret in his voice only deepened her anger and agony. "You might have been," she said. "If only you'd tried."

With the remnants of her spirit, she lifted her chin and marched to the door. She paused to fling one last, clever gibe, but the desolation on his hard, aristocratic face stopped her cold. He was hurting, too. Because he'd been brutally honest with himself and with her. From the ashes of her heart rose a hot spiral of yearning, a yearning to comfort him, a yearning she dared not indulge.

Her throat aching with unspoken words of love, she turned and walked out.

Chapter 20

❧❧❧

On a cool October afternoon, three emotion-
ally devastating weeks later, she and Damien rode in a bullock cart past the Meerut
bazaar. With the goat tethered in the back of the
cart and Kit perched in the crook of her arm,
Sarah felt a rush of bittersweet nostalgia. Except
for a few burned-out buildings here and there,
the mutiny might never have raged only months
earlier. Vendors hawked their wares on the road-
side or beneath the shade of canvas awnings.
Beggar children in filthy rags beseeched alms from
the passersby. Men haggled over the price of
gourds, women over the cost of gold bangles. She
even spied a British soldier examining a saddle at
the leather worker's stall.

The heavy scents of spices and excrement, the
bright colors and the gabble of voices, flooded her
senses and resurrected the memory of walking
through a mob to rescue Shivina from the fakir.
Sarah clutched the side of the swaying cart. Weary
and heartsore, she yearned for the peace of the
hills, for the log hut warmed by the fires of all-
consuming love.

But the man who rode beside her might have
been a stranger, a dark-eyed native who would
blend with the crowd in the market.

Damien guided the bullock past the tin-roofed

temple where, nearly six months ago, she had informed him of his baby's imminent arrival. Sarah's throat caught. So much had happened since then. Shivina had died. Sarah had survived a bloody rebellion. She had learned the way of life of the Indians and the joys of motherhood. She had fallen in love with a man who kept an unbreachable wall around his heart.

Her troubled gaze drifted to the tiny shrine. In the gloom of the arched doorway stood a priest. Black eyes in a ghostly pale face peered at her. Tangled locks framed bony features. Despite the sun beating on her back, she felt his gaze crawl over her skin like the legs of a centipede.

She blinked hard. With a twitch of his saffron robe, the priest melted into the shadows of the sanctuary. She released a breath. The fakir was dead; Damien had seen to that.

"What is it?" he asked.

Only then did she realize she was clutching his arm. She relaxed her hand and let it fall to the wooden seat. "Nothing."

"Something frightened you," he persisted. "What?"

He knew her so well. "A priest," she admitted. "He was staring at us from the temple, that's all." She looked down at her dusty sari and walnut-stained arms. "Perhaps he saw through our disguises and hated us."

"I doubt it, but anything's possible. The natives have more reason than ever to hate the English." Damien frowned at the rutted road. "It's a damned shame the Indians failed to gain freedom from the foreign devils. They'd be better off without us."

The dull clopping of hooves filled the silence. In their sympathy for the natives, at least, she and Damien found accord. "Maybe our book will make the English see the Indians as a sovereign people," Sarah said.

"If it at least makes them think beyond their sanctimonious imperialism, we'll have accomplished something."

British soldiers drilled on the distant parade ground, where eighty-five native cavalrymen had once been sentenced. If only she'd spoken out . . . But she must accept her mistakes of the past and focus on her future.

The Union Jack fluttered from a flagpole, and sunlight glinted off the steeple of the Anglican church. The familiar sights bolstered Sarah's spirits as much as the blackened ruins of bungalows and barracks saddened her. The destruction was greater here in the English sector of Meerut. She suddenly realized they were heading away from the officers' homes along the Mall.

"Where are we going?"

"To regimental headquarters, to find your uncle. On our way back we'll stop at the hospital and ask after Reginald." Damien nodded at the small, whitewashed building they were nearing. "Unless you'd prefer to see about your fiancé first."

Her pulse fluttered. His turban and tunic covered by a thin coating of dust, his jaw bristly with several weeks' black growth, Damien looked as disreputable as a *badmash*, the antithesis of a girl's romantic fancies. Yet longing ached in Sarah's heart, and she renounced the futile feeling. He couldn't give her the life and love she craved.

"I'll see Reginald first," she stated.

With a flick of his long switch, Damien signaled the bullock to halt. He turned to her, his expression guarded. "Sarah, you'd best prepare yourself. He suffered a grave injury to his leg. He might very well have died from the wound. What will you do then?"

Would you keep me with you?

She swallowed the errant question. "I'll find my uncle. Or seek out friends."

Resolutely she swung her gaze to the smoke-blackened walls of the hospital and the freshly thatched veranda encircling it. Orderlies and servants strolled through the open front doors. A *mali* worked a scraggly patch of garden near the entryway.

The notion of going inside jangled her nerves. Her arms tightened around Kit; he squirmed and babbled a protest.

A man walked out of the infirmary, his gait slow, his progress aided by the ivory-topped cane in his hand. Sunshine illuminated the refined features she knew so well and gleamed over his fair hair before he clapped on a topi.

"Reginald," she breathed.

A great weight of fear lifted from her heart. In its place swirled a sea of relief and joy. And yet beneath the bright waters churned a dark undercurrent of apprehension and sorrow. She forced herself to look at Damien. "I can't take Kit with me."

He tucked the wriggling baby into the cradle of his arm. "There you go, son. Tell Sarah good-bye now. You'll ride with me to the Central Hotel."

Dismay flooded her. "Won't you wait here?"

"No." Damien aimed his stony gaze at the road. "You and Reggie have a lot to discuss. And I have to prepare for my voyage. I'll start interviewing ayahs in the morning."

"But . . ." The enormity of his words inundated her. He was leaving her. Kit was leaving her, too. Tears swam in her eyes, and she brushed a kiss over the infant's velvety cheek. "I'll come by as soon as I've spoken with Reginald. Kit will be wanting his bottle soon—"

"You needn't trouble yourself. I can manage my son for one night."

"But—"

"Look, don't worry about us. We'll manage just fine."

He held the baby with the ease of paternal love and tenderness. Pride and privation wrenched her. She'd taught Damien to be a father. He really didn't need her anymore.

She glanced toward the hospital. A syce guided a horse-drawn *palka-ghari* toward Reginald. Afraid to miss him, she grasped the bundle of her belongings and climbed down from the cart.

"I have to go." She paused. Damien's mouth was set in a strict line. Swallowing hard, she turned away.

"Sarah."

She spun back, her gaze flying to his disreputably handsome face. "Yes?"

"Did you remember the bank draft?"

"Yes. It's right here." She patted her waist, where the paper was secured in a pouch, and then hesitated. "Good-bye, Damien."

"Good-bye," he said gruffly.

If only he would change his mind and call her back. If only he could love her. Tears burned behind her eyes. She swung away before he could spy the moisture.

"Sarah?"

She whirled again. "What is it?"

"Give my regards to Reggie. He's a good man. But I guess I don't have to tell you that."

He snapped the switch, and the bullock plodded away. Her heart beating in her throat, she stood by the road. Her tears made his image glimmer in the sunlight like an archangel etched in gold.

Absurd, she thought. Damien could never be mistaken for an angel.

Reginald moved to the carriage and placed his black satchel on the floorboard.

She hurried down the path, the olive-green silk of her sari fluttering. For so many days her mind had shied away from this moment, the moment she would settle her future. The moment she would once again see the man who could make her dreams come true.

"Wait!" she called. "Don't go."

Reginald flicked a glance at her. One sandy brow arched in genteel dismissal. Then he braced his hand on his cane and, with the other, grasped the side handle of the carriage in preparation to climb inside.

Suddenly Sarah saw herself through his eyes, a nondescript Hindu woman with a veil draping her black hair, her skin as brown as a walnut and her garb gritty with travel dust. She halted a few yards from him. She was conscious of the dirt smooth and warm beneath her bare feet, as warm as the twinge of resentment within her.

"Reginald, don't you recognize me?"

He pivoted sharply, using the cane for balance. His widened blue eyes swept her from head to toe. "Sarah?"

"Yes, it's me."

"Sarah, my pet," he breathed. "I can scarcely believe . . ."

He limped quickly forward. Anticipating his embrace, she met him halfway. But he merely grasped her hand. "Thank heaven, you're alive! After so many months, I feared the worst." Warm and fervid, his gaze studied her. "It's no wonder I failed to recognize my proper English Sarah inside this outlandish attire."

"It was too dangerous to travel as an Englishwoman." His affectionate regard assuaged her bruised spirits. "Oh, how I've missed you."

She pressed her cheek to his shoulder. His heart thrummed against her breasts. His scent of bay rum enveloped her, so gentlemanly compared to Damien's bold male essence.

"Hold me," she murmured. "Hold me close and kiss me."

She anticipated the rise of passion, but Reginald stepped back. To her surprise, his fair features bore a flush of embarrassment. He glanced around at the groom, who stood impassively by the carriage, and then at the hospital, where people filed in and out.

"I missed you, too, darling," he said in a hushed tone. "But we can hardly hold a reunion here. A public place isn't the appropriate setting for displays of affection."

Irritation squelched her elation. "It's a reunion neither of us believed would happen," she pointed out. "Surely people will overlook a lapse in decorum."

"Here, now, my pet." A grin lent a boyish handsomeness to his face. "Let's not spoil our reunion with a quarrel. Come, sit in my carriage. A lady shouldn't stand in the burning sun."

She started to say that she no longer felt like a lady, that her sun-browned complexion hardly required protection. But he was only being considerate. "Thank you," she murmured.

She took his proffered arm and let him lead her to the *palka-ghari*. His painstaking pace tugged at her sympathy. At the carriage, she stopped and set her bundle on the floorboard. "Let me give you a hand in," she said.

"Nonsense. I'm not an invalid."

She dared not trample his dignity, although appearances seemed absurd when she was more able-bodied than he. She grasped his hand, accepted the polite fiction of his help, and climbed inside. There she forced herself to sit still in the shade of the wicker hood while he struggled to follow. Sweat dewed his brow, but he managed to swing himself onto the leather seat. Breathing hard, he propped his stiff leg before him.

The syce moved toward the driver's seat, but Reginald motioned the servant away. "We've the privacy to talk now," he told her. "I should like to hear everything that's happened to you."

She hesitated. How could she relate the events

of the past months without mentioning the rapture she'd found in Damien's arms? "First tell me about you. What happened to your leg?"

Reginald frowned. "That was a dreadful night. I tried to keep the mutineers from taking the magazine. But I had an ill-timed encounter with the sword of a *badmash*."

"You're a hero, then."

He chuckled. "Better you should call Damien Coleridge the hero. Had it not been for his lordship, I wouldn't have lived to tell the tale."

"Pardon?"

"When I fell, he came to my rescue. He saved me from a pack of rebels who surely would have cut my throat."

Astonished, Sarah looked quickly toward the road, but the cart had vanished. Passionate pride glowed in her. How like Damien not to tell her the part of the tale that would make her see him in a favorable light.

"I never knew," she murmured.

"And I never properly thanked him," Reginald said. "For all his reputation as a bounder, the chap has his own brand of honor."

"Yes," she said softly. "That I know."

Reginald gave her a curious frown. "Tell me how you escaped Meerut."

The awful memories poured over her. Swallowing hard, she related her drive past the bazaar, the death of her aunt, and her own ill-fated rush to save Shivina. "Damien took Kit and me to his hut in the hills. That's where we spent the summer months."

"You . . . had no chaperon?"

She gazed down at her hands in her lap. Against her will, she recalled a vivid image of her fingers caressing Damien's naked body. "How could I? There were no English people for miles."

A crow cawed from a plumbago bush near the hospital veranda. Reginald put his hand on her

forearm. "Praise God you survived when so
many women were killed. I spent several nerve-
racking days trapped in a hospital bed and fearing
you'd met the same fate as your poor aunt Violet."

Sarah tipped her head toward him. "But I sent
a message to Patel."

"So I learned. As soon as I was able, I sent for
him, and he showed me the note."

"And Uncle John? Did he come, too?"

"No." His expression somber, Reginald stroked
her wrist. "Some of his sepoys turned on him
that first night. He died valiantly."

Although she'd braced herself for the news, a
well of sadness opened inside her. "How I'll miss
them both," she said on a sigh. "Pompous Uncle
John and silly Aunt Violet."

Reginald stared keenly at her. "It isn't like you
to speak ill of the dead."

"Please don't think I'm belittling my aunt and
uncle," Sarah hastened to explain. "They were
both so very dear to me. And yet they were the
epitome of English society, forever imposing their
own strict values on the natives and believing
themselves superior to the people whose country
they were guests in."

"You've changed," Reginald said, his sandy
eyebrows lifting. "I never knew you to be quite
so liberal with your opinions."

"There's a lot you didn't know about me."
Taking a shaky breath, she knew she could speak
nothing less than the truth. "I have a confession.
For the past year, I've been writing essays under
the name of I. M. Vexed."

His jaw dropped. As if thunderstruck, he sat
back. "You? Impossible!"

"Writing anonymously was the only way I
thought I could express my opinions."

"But everyone believed the editorials were
written by a man." He looked her up and down,

as if trying to reconcile himself to her new image. "We discussed one at your uncle's dinner party before the mutiny. You never let on that you'd ever read the piece."

"I was afraid to speak out. But I was wrong. I ought to have told you . . . and everyone. For that I'm sorry."

Reginald shook his head. "I can't say that I'm pleased to hear this about my fiancée."

I would have cheered you on. Damien's respect for her work gave Sarah the courage to hold her head high. "Gender needn't stop a person from asserting her beliefs."

"Be that as it may, I trust you'll be too busy in the future being my wife to continue your unladylike hobby."

She sat up straight. "Why should I give up my writing?"

Smiling, Reginald took her hand in his. "Here, my pet, don't get your dander up. We've more important things to settle. Now that your aunt and uncle are gone, we needn't wait to wed. You'll need a place to live and a man to take care of you."

The proposal shook her. Yet wasn't this what she wanted, the summit of her dreams? Gazing at him, she felt only exasperated affection, for the rapport they'd once shared had vanished like a flame snuffed by the wind. She'd grown away from him.

With the suddenness of shutters opening to admit light into a darkened room, she knew that more than her appearance had changed. Reginald no longer recognized the woman inside, the woman who could care for a baby as well as kill a mutineer, the woman who could strive against injustice as well as surrender to the fires of physical love.

He had never really known her. Because she had never acknowledged her own strengths.

Through Damien, she had freed a great passion in herself, the passion to openly embrace causes, the passion to give all of herself to the man she loved. And with the painful joy of her awakening, she knew she could never accept any less.

She gently squeezed Reginald's hand, then released it. "You suggest the impossible. I'm afraid I can't marry you."

He pursed his lips. "I realize you've been gone for months with a scoundrel. People might whisper, but I trust you, Sarah. I won't even ask any more questions of you. If we behave as if nothing untoward happened, eventually everyone else will, too."

He knew. Ever the gentleman, he would pretend not to see the stark reality. Tenderness softened her heart. She ached for an easy way to say what must be said. Yet misleading him seemed even more cruel. "Darling Reginald." She paused, her throat dry with the knowledge that she could never turn back. Taking a breath, she said, "Damien and I have been lovers."

Reginald's spine went as straight as his cane. His blue eyes revealed the starkness of shock. "I see."

"Not for the world would I deliberately hurt you, but I can't act as if nothing has changed. And I won't give Damien up." Saying it aloud filled her with elation.

"So why hasn't the bastard married you?"

The sharp question pierced the bubble of her high spirits. "We don't need a legal document to prove our love for each other."

"Balderdash," he snapped. "The knave is using you. I should think a woman with your backbone wouldn't stand for that."

Trembling with pain, she bit her lip. "Thank you for your concern, but that's between Damien and me." She reached up and removed the locket, laying it on the seat between them. "This is yours."

He stared down at the piece for a moment, then picked it up and dropped it in his pocket. He motioned to the syce, who clambered into the driver's seat.

"Where may I take you?" Reginald said.

His return to polite gentility, even in the face of extreme distress, bathed her in sorrow for what might have been. She was refusing the security he offered. She was renouncing public acceptance. She was rejecting the conventional role of a wife. Because now she had an unconventional love, a love too luminous to be dimmed by censure or public opinion.

A deep yearning pulled at her. She must make Damien see that they shared a love too precious to abandon.

"To the Central Hotel," she said in a firm, clear voice.

The short ride seemed interminable. Offering no conversation, Reginald gazed stolidly ahead, and Sarah decided she had said enough. At last the two-story, thatch-roofed building loomed into view. To her surprise, he leaned over and kissed her cheek. "I wish you the best, Sarah. If ever you need me . . ."

"Thank you." She held his warm hand for a moment, looked into the dear features of a friend, and fought against tears. "Good-bye."

Bundle in hand, she slipped down from the *palka-ghari* and went into the hotel. The foyer was shabby, with peeling pea-green wallpaper and threadbare floor mats. In the center of the room two natives squatted, talking in low tones. Near the stairs lay a sleeping man, undisturbed by the fly crawling along his stubbly jaw. The vagrant looked as broad of build as Damien.

But not nearly as handsome. Her stomach fluttered with anticipation. She went to the front desk and rang the tiny bell. A Eurasian clerk smelling of jasmine hair tonic sauntered from a back room. "Mr. Damien Coleridge's room, please."

The clerk looked down his thin nose at her and left no doubt that he dismissed her as a whore. A flush burned her cheeks, but she stood firm until he said, "One-sixteen," and pointed down a hall.

His prejudice left a sour taste in her mouth. Was this what she would endure as Damien's mistress, the rudeness of servants, the ugly stares of people?

She wanted to run. Instead, she walked with the modest gait of a lady down the musty corridor. She found the room at the end of the wing and knocked softly.

The door opened. His hair rumpled and his chest bare, his powerful form outlined by the shuttered light of late afternoon, Damien stood staring at her. He clutched an empty milk bottle. Vulnerability softened his features and melted the misgivings from her soul.

She smiled. "Aren't you going to invite me in?"

He stepped aside and put down the bottle. "I thought you weren't coming back."

"I told you I would." She glanced around the small, dim chamber. "Where's Kit?"

"He just fell asleep." Damien waved a hand to a bed draped in white mosquito netting. Neat rolls of clothing formed a barrier around the baby's small shape. "What about Reginald?"

"In a moment," she said in a hushed tone. She dropped her bundle and moved to the bed. The baby's long lashes lay closed, and his thumb was stuck in his mouth. A flood of love inundated her. She'd made the right choice. "Kit will be crawling soon. We'll need to be careful so he doesn't fall out of bed."

Damien came to her side. "For God's sake," he said in a harsh whisper, "answer me, dammit. Where's Reginald?"

"I imagine he went back to his bungalow."

"But why didn't you go with him?"

Tilting her head back, she studied his tormented features. Now she could see beyond his rugged male beauty to the strength of character that had developed from years of hardship and the unguarded need of a man too wounded to risk his heart. "I didn't go with Reginald because I'm not marrying him."

His eyes narrowed, Damien gripped his fists like a knight ready to joust a rival. "So he guessed about us?" he asked. "By God, are you saying that bastard dared to insult you?"

She curled her fingers around his scarred fist and gently rubbed at the tension in his knuckles. "Are you saying you would mind if he had?"

"Of course I'd mind. You're too fine a lady to be insulted."

His fierceness made her smile. "I'm glad you think well of me. Because I told him you and I are lovers."

For a moment the only sound was the quiet flap of the punkah undulating overhead. Damien touched her cheek. "I don't understand, Sarah. Why would you give up your dream?"

"Maybe I have a new dream. You."

Beneath hers, his fingers tightened. "I can't give you a proper home, a place with roots like you've always wanted."

"As long as we're together, I *am* home." She paused, sorting through her thoughts. "When I spoke with Reginald, I realized he could only give me the outer trappings of happiness. I wouldn't have been happy inside."

"And love? I can't give you that, either." Damien's voice was husky and hesitant.

"Shall I leave, then?" she asked. "Do you want me to walk out that door and never come back?"

The hard edge to his features crumbled, revealing the softness of yearning. "Walk out that door," he murmured, "and you'll take my heart with you."

Joy wreathed her. It was the closest he'd come to admitting the depth of his feelings. She slid her hands up his bare arms and to his chest, where the strong beating of his heart played against her palm. "Then I'll take my chances with you, Damien. I want to help you with your books. I want to accompany you and Kit to England. I want to be there when you see your mother again."

Shifting restlessly, he grasped her shoulders, kneading gently. "That might not be wise."

"Why not?"

"Because Mother might . . ."

Sarah tilted her head. "Might what?"

His gaze shifted to the shuttered windows. "She might tell you things about me. Things that will make you hate me."

She took his jaw in her hands and brought his gaze back. "For mercy's sake. Do you think I'm so shallow? That vexes me."

He grinned. "You are so easily vexed."

"I am when you denigrate yourself. Nothing your mother can say will take away my love for you."

His face sobered. "You're always so certain. How can you love a man who can't honor and cherish you as you deserve?"

The agony within him brought her to a keen perception of how precious he was to her. "Oh, Damien," she whispered. "You've cherished me quite well for the past few months. You can give me so much if only you'd let yourself. So long as we're together, I don't care what the world thinks."

"You need a husband—"

"Then be one to me. If not in name, then with your body and mind and soul."

She boldly pressed her mouth to his and glided her hands over hard-honed muscle and sunbrowned skin. His arms surrounded her, touching her greedily, as if her soft flesh were sustenance for his soul. His tongue plunged between her lips, and she tasted the tender ferocity of a starving man, a ferocity that fed her own desperate yearnings.

His fingers delved beneath her sari, parting the garment and plying her nipples. The banked ardor within her flared to vivid brilliance. Her breasts felt heavy, her woman's place weighted with the hot pulsebeat of passion. Yet greater than her physical desire was the ache to merge their hearts forever, to forge a bond strong enough to last a lifetime, to make Damien need her so much he could never, ever let her go.

She brought her hand downward, over the hair-roughened flatness of his belly to his dhoti. She worked the knot free until the loincloth fell away, and her fingers stroked the rock-hard length of him.

Gasping, he surged against her. "God, Sarah. What you do to me . . ."

The urge to rouse him to new heights throbbed like a reckless drumbeat through her veins. If she couldn't have his heart, she would secure him to her with the velvet chains of passion. She would give him a memory that would burn in his soul forever.

"I mean to do more," she whispered. "Much more."

Sinking to her knees, she adored him with her mouth, caressing places both soft and hard, smooth and rough. His fingers brushed over her hair as if to stop her; then, with a moan of submission, he encouraged her to pleasure him. His groans brought the glow of primal glory to her, the feminine delight that she had the power to claim the surrender of this potent man.

In the moment when his swift bursts of breath told her that he teetered on the brink of release,

Sarah reached for his wrists and tugged him down to lie with her on the rush matting.

He pulled back, gasping. "The sheath—it's in the knapsack."

She was swept by the unreasoning urge to nurture his seed within her womb, the seed of a man she loved with all her heart. "I need you now, Damien. Come into me."

Opening her legs in unashamed invitation, she enticed him onto her. His dark eyes and taut features betrayed an inner struggle; then he moaned low in his chest and glided into her, filling her to perfection, igniting her blood in a flash of white-hot wildfire. He pressed against her, caressing her with his body until an inarticulate cry of joy rose in her throat. Ecstasy rolled through her like the stormy swell of a tidal wave, drowning her fervor in the pure waters of bodily bliss.

When they could breathe again, Damien murmured in her ear, "I don't recall reading about that technique in *The Kama Sutra*."

Stretching her arms, Sarah smiled. "Perhaps you inspire my creativity."

"You inspire a hell of a lot more than creativity in me." He sat up and raked his hand through his hair, mussing the already disheveled strands. "Oh, God, we took a risk. What would we do with another baby?"

"We would love him—or her—the same way we love Kit."

The punkah swished softly in the silence. Through the dimness of the room, his moody gaze met hers. "To tell you the truth, Sarah, I'm afraid. I worry about whether or not I'll be a good father to Kit. I don't need to fail another child as well."

"You've been an exemplary father. You're fair, loving, and devoted to him. And you're even honest about your feelings."

His rueful grin flashed through the shadows. "So I. M. Vexed reformed me after all."

He rubbed her calf in an absent gesture of affection that warmed her more than flowery compliments or false words of love. She sat up, curved her bare feet beneath her, and took his scarred hands in hers. "I meant what I said earlier. I want to go to England with you."

He clenched her fingers. "Sarah, there's nothing on God's earth I want more," he said in a low growl of torment. "But I can't ask you to give up your standing in society."

"You didn't ask. I decided." Aware of a trembly ache, she raised her chin. "You're the man of my choice . . . the man of my heart."

Their eyes locked for an eternal moment. Tenderness and longing gentled his features and wrapped Sarah's heart in the silken bonds of affection. If his attachment to her wasn't precisely love, she thought, then his feelings might grow and deepen with time.

Without moving his gaze, he lifted her hand to his mouth and kissed her palm. "You're quite a woman, Sarah Faulkner."

"You're quite a man, Damien Coleridge. We make a fine pair."

"I wish I could be so sure." Yearning thickened his voice. "I've always thought of myself as a loner. I never envisioned needing a woman as much as I need you. It frightens me."

"You needn't be frightened of something that can only bring you happiness."

"Perhaps that's it," he said slowly. "What have I ever done to deserve the happiness we've shared?"

"Oh, for mercy's sake." Anger gripped Sarah. "Stop seeing yourself through your mother's eyes. You're not a devil, Damien. You're a wonderful, sensitive man with no more faults than any one of us."

He rubbed his brow for a moment, then stood and began to dress, his naked form as strong and beautiful as a living statue of Shiva. "Will you stay here with Kit?" he asked. "I need to go out for a short while."

"Why?"

"My legal documents burned in the caravan. I want to see about acquiring proof of my marriage to Shivina and also Kit's birth record." Damien paused, his expression troubled. "And you've given me a lot to think about. I need to mull things over."

"Of course," she murmured.

Sarah watched him pull on his sandals. He gazed at her again, and she had the odd, unsettling impression he was imprinting her on his memory. Then he went out and quietly closed the door.

She leaned her back against the bed, the rush mat prickly beneath her. He had taken a giant leap in acknowledging his feelings, yet she wanted more. What if he decided he couldn't risk opening his heart to her? What if he refused to let her go to England with him?

Pain burrowed inside her. She would survive, as she'd survived the awful adversities of the past months. Sarah knew now that she possessed the confidence and the courage to withstand the petty dictates of society, a lesson she'd learned from the rich experiences of knowing Damien.

Aching in body and soul, she rewrapped her sari, lifted the mosquito netting, and lay down beside Kit. He shifted position and sighed, and his small presence comforted her. She closed her eyes, and the pressure inside her melted into a mist of weariness.

A noise awakened her. Rising on her elbow, Sarah blinked at the dimness of dusk. She touched the baby and he squirmed, sucking hard on his thumb. Ruefully she acknowledged that she'd let him sleep too long; now he'd be awake late into the evening.

Beyond the white gauze netting, gray shadows shrouded the room. What had she heard?

A black shape moved against the gloom. A scratching sounded; then she saw a muted light. Her heart warmed. Groggy, she yawned and stretched. "Damien? I'm so glad you're back."

A figure walked to the foot of the bedstead. His arm lifted, and a lantern blazed high. She squinted against the sudden radiance. The hazy form materialized into a yellow-draped body and a fanatic brown face framed by long, oily locks.

The fakir.

Gasping, Sarah sat bolt upright. Her fingers clenched the bedcovers. "You're dead."

His cackle of laughter rang out. "Thou only believed it so. We, the blessed of Kali, know the art of appearing lifeless."

She remembered the yogi she'd once thought dead on the steps of the bazaar temple. But he had only slowed his breathing . . .

The fakir had been injured so dreadfully. Yet now he stood before her. Fear slithered like a deadly cobra inside her. "Why have you come here?"

"To finish my ordained mission. For months I wielded my sword in Delhi for Bahadur Shah. I slew many *feringhis*, but never enough to cleanse India of the pollution. When the city fell to the foreign devils, Kali sent me back to Meerut, to wait at her shrine."

Shuddering, she recalled the priest she'd seen in the shadows of the bazaar temple. "So that really *was* you."

His grimace of a smile revealed yellowed teeth. "Thy coming hast opened my eyes. I now know the mission the goddess sent me to complete. The son of a *feringhi* duke will serve the cause of the holy rebellion."

Damien? She wondered what he meant, but the thought fled as the fakir moved slowly around the side of the bed. "First," he said, "I will destroy the product of a Hindu woman's shame."

Kit! He meant to kill the baby.

Horror put her in motion. She threw back the mosquito netting and snatched up the only weapon in sight, a candlestick from the bamboo bedtable. Then she hurled herself between him and the baby.

"Get out!" she screamed.

She swung at him. He leaped nimbly back.

"*Feringhi* she-devil!" he roared. "Thou hast interfered twice, but never again."

He lifted the lamp high. Yellow light bathed his ash-streaked features. In a startling movement, he dashed the lantern to the floor. Glass tinkled. Flames whooshed up the coverlet and licked at the netting.

Sarah screamed again. Dropping the candlestick, she scooped up the baby and rolled for the other side of the bed.

Her limbs tangled in gauze. She tore frantically at the weblike netting. Smoke choked her lungs. In the grips of a sluggish nightmare, she heard Kit wail, the fire crackle, her own pants of despair.

She broke free. The door. She must find Damien.

She started to run. The back of her head exploded into agony. She felt herself falling into a black pit. With her last bit of strength, she tightened her arms around the baby.

Chapter 21

"I am most humbly sorry, sahib," said the *abdur* stationed at the door. He gazed askance at Damien's native garb. "But I cannot permit you to enter without a subscription card."

Damn the English and their bloody rules, Damien thought glumly. He craved a drink in the worst way.

He frowned past the white-coated servant and into the Meerut Club. In the hour before dinner, a few British officers and their ladies strolled the lamp-lit foyer with its pale columns and banks of green ferns. He was about to turn away when his attention was caught by a familiar, fair-haired man clad in tropical white, who leaned on an ivory cane.

"I'm a guest of Dr. Pemberton-Sykes," Damien said.

Instantly he regretted his impulse. But it was too late, for the *abdur* had left his post and was scurrying to the doctor.

Reginald swung around. His perfect features froze into a rigid mask. He limped toward Damien, then waved away the doorman. "It's quite all right, Malhotra. I know the chap." To Damien, he said in a low tone, "What the devil are you about?"

Damien shrugged. He wondered which of them

felt worse, Reginald for losing Sarah or he himself for being faced with the painful prospect of hurting her. "I wanted a drink. You're the only person here I know."

Reginald glowered. For an instant he looked torn between engaging in a bout of fisticuffs and behaving like a gentleman. His carriage stiff and straight, he wheeled around, using the cane for leverage. "Come along, if you must."

Without looking back, he marched away, favoring his bad leg. Damien ambled behind, unsure of what to say. *Sorry, old boy, but I won the girl. Can't help the fact that she fell in love with me instead of you.* He tried to envision Sarah and Reginald sharing a future, but the image sparked a possessive fury in him. God! How had he ever thought he could let her go?

Only men sat at the wicker tables in the bar. Cigar smoke formed a blue haze in the air. As he joined the doctor at a table near the veranda, Damien was aware of people whispering and eyeing his dhoti and tunic. Hellfire and damnation. He shouldn't have come here. He and this bastion of the Raj fit as well as gunpowder and a lighted match.

Reginald rested his leg on a stool and motioned to a servant. "*Koi-hai,*" he said in an imperious voice. "Bring us two whiskey and sodas."

The man hastened away. Reginald drummed his fingers on the table. "So," he said, his blue eyes keen and caustic, "you've compromised Sarah."

Surprised that the doctor would attack so swiftly, Damien fought the engulfing waters of shame. He took a cheroot from the tray of a passing waiter, lit the tobacco, and drew deeply. He hated feeling obligated to anyone, yet he owed Reginald honesty. "Yes, I have," he admitted. "But I never intended to get involved with your fiancée. I told her she was better off with you."

"Did you, now? Was that before or after you seduced her?"

"As I'd never intended to seduce her, of course it was afterward."

Reginald clenched his fists. "I ought to strike you for that."

Damien forced himself to lounge carelessly in his chair. "Why don't you?"

The doctor glowered, then slowly spread his pale hands. "I'd rather know precisely what your plans are for her."

The demand struck Damien hard. He felt like a boy quaking in the face of parental fury. "I haven't decided."

The servant delivered their drinks. Gripping his glass, Reginald leaned forward and said in a grating undertone, "You'd bloody well better decide, your lordship, and it had better be good." He imbued the title with sarcasm. "This is the nineteenth century, and not a medieval serfdom. You've no right to demand droit du seigneur from a lady like Sarah."

Damien burned to retort that their lovemaking had lasted a hell of a lot longer than one night, that Sarah had wanted it with the same ravenous appetite as he had. But he had no right to cause the doctor any further pain or Sarah any further dishonor.

He quaffed the whiskey in one searing gulp. Before he could speak, Reginald went on furiously. "I'd also like to know how the bloody hell you could marry that Hindu woman and not Sarah."

"Shivina?" Damien was abashed to realize her image had grown hazy. What made Sarah seem so much more vibrant? "I suppose I didn't mind marrying Shivina so much because she was content to stay in the background. She acted . . . more like a servant than a wife."

Reginald's mouth dropped with bitter astonishment. "By God, man, do you regard Sarah as less than a servant, then?"

"Of course not. Sarah is more, much more." Damien toyed with the cheroot and formulated his thoughts. "She's my equal. She can challenge my every sharp remark and throw it right back at me. She's a gentle woman, but concerning something she cares deeply about, she can be as fierce as a tigress." He lifted his gaze to Reginald. "We're writing a book together, did she tell you?"

The doctor shook his fair head. "No."

"She's composed the text, with her usual verve and fire." Damien couldn't stop a proud smile. "It's bound to inflame readers, but I like the idea of forcing people to think. So does she."

Reginald looked pensively toward the veranda. "I've always known Sarah had her own opinions, but I never saw her as a fiery woman. I had no idea until today that she wrote editorials under the nom de plume of I. M. Vexed."

"Don't feel left out. She had me fooled for a long time, too. She has more facets than the Kohinoor diamond."

A frown wrinkled the doctor's brow. With more puzzlement than anger, he gazed at Damien. "If you think so highly of her, why won't you marry her?"

Because I'm terrified. I'm terrified that her love will die. I'm terrified of the moment she'll realize I'm not the man she thinks I am.

As thick and cloying as smoke, fear fogged his mind. Damien stubbed out the cheroot in an ashtray. "Maybe I would marry her," he said, "if I had a fraction of your honor."

Reginald gave an ungentlemanly snort. "Good God, man, you risked your life to rescue me from a bloodthirsty mob. I spent weeks in the hospital healing myself when I ought to have been healing others. I never properly thanked you for putting yourself in peril to help me."

Damien shifted, uneasy with the praise. "No thanks needed. I only did what anyone would have done."

"Perhaps valor is in the eye of the beholder," Reginald mused. Pain etched his fine mouth. "I can't understand your uncertainty, but don't let Sarah go. She's a good woman who needs you . . . I could see it in her eyes today."

Damien admired the effort it took for the doctor to relinquish his claim on her. He admired it, because he wouldn't have been half so gracious. Because he loved her, too.

Like a photograph in a developing tray, the realization came into sharp focus. Now he knew why he craved her esteem, and why he suffered the paralyzing dread of losing her. The notion of binding himself to her forever no longer appalled him, for now he knew his heart was already intrinsically tied to hers. Closing his life to Sarah would bring loneliness and despair. Marrying her would open a new world of possibilities.

You can give me so much if only you'd let yourself. Her soft words filtered through his mind. He could stay here like a coward and drink himself into oblivion. Or he could take the risk of going back and pledging his future to her.

"You'll excuse me now, old chap," said Reginald, levering himself to his feet.

"I'll walk out with you."

Damien slowed his eager steps to accommodate Reginald's pace. As they went out into the street, an acrid reek drifted through the cool evening air. The scent of fire stirred the old gut-churning apprehension in Damien.

"Something's burning," said the doctor, wrinkling his nose. "Brings back foul memories of last May."

Damien peered down the street. A pall of smoke, darker than the dusk air, hung over the buildings beyond the corner. A faint orange glow lit the underside of the cloud.

His chest tightened with the force of an awful premonition. "The hotel is burning."

"How do you know—"

Damien didn't hear the rest. He dashed through the stream of humanity clogging the road. Turning the corner, he leaped nimbly to avoid the hooves of a carriage horse and looked ahead. Terror burned a path to his heart.

Fire engulfed one end of the hotel. The end containing the room where he'd left the two people he loved.

He pushed his way through the swarm. The eerie radiance of flames lit the night. Men and women milled in panic. A mother shrieked for her children. In a futile gesture, the hotel clerk splashed a bucket of water on the fire.

Damien couldn't see Sarah and Kit anywhere. With a sudden, sickening certainty, he knew they were inside the conflagration.

He started toward the door. Someone latched onto his arm. Over the din, Reginald shouted, "Are you mad? You can't go in there."

"I have to find Sarah and Kit."

Damien jerked away and ran to the open door. The foyer was not yet ablaze, but thick black smoke clotted the air. Yanking off his tunic, he used the cloth to cover his nose and mouth. He stumbled toward the hall and felt his way along the hot wall. At the end of the corridor, fire leaped and crackled. Memory suffocated him. The horrified cries of his brother echoed in Damien's mind.

His stomach lurched. He wanted to turn and flee. He steeled his nerves. This time he wouldn't let himself fail. He couldn't. Even if he died trying.

The furnacelike heat battered him, yet his palms felt as cold as death. He forced himself to keep going. One hand over the other, then over again, until he neared the fire. Sarah. Kit. Their beloved faces flashed in his mind, brighter than the blaze. Oh, God. They couldn't perish. He had to get them out.

The roar of the fire deafened him. His scalp felt singed, his skin seared. His lungs hurt from the smoke. Flames rimmed the doorframe. It was a scene from hell, a scene from his darkest nightmare. Panic threatened to paralyze him. Without giving himself a second to think, he hurled himself inside the inferno.

He descended into Hades.

Orange-yellow light tinted the room. On the floor, Sarah lay curled in a fetal posture around the squirming baby. At her feet squatted the fakir, his bony hands upraised, his black eyes aglow. His singsong prayers pierced the clamor of the fire.

In one swift lunge, Damien thrust the fakir aside. The holy man howled as he fell back against the flaming bed. Damien snatched up his son, then hauled Sarah to her feet. Swaying, she groped for the baby.

Her lips formed Kit's name, though Damien couldn't hear it. He allowed himself a blessed instant of joy that they were alive. His arm around her waist, he surged toward the doorway, pressing her face to his shoulder to shield her. In the hall, the heat lessened somewhat. He nearly collided with someone in the smoke-darkened corridor.

Coughing, Reginald gripped Sarah's arm. "Is there anyone else?" he shouted.

Damien started to shake his head. Claws dug into his neck. Pain sped down his spine. A sudden weight staggered him. The fakir had leaped onto his back.

Sarah screamed. Damien thrust the baby at her. "Get the hell out!"

"I can't leave you," she cried.

She started toward him. Reginald dragged her away. They vanished into the black bowels of smoke.

The talons gripped with fiendish force. Needles of torment invaded Damien's neck. He reached back and found the bony wrists. He started to squeeze, but an agonizing pressure burst behind his ears.

The flames spun. He plunged into darkness.

"He can't be dead. He just can't be."

Sarah's voice choked. Her throat stung from tears and smoke. The back of her head throbbed like a diabolic drum. She pressed her cheek to Reginald's chest and tried to will away the dread rising like a black vulture inside her. Each breath caused a pain as much as the soul as of the body.

As she had a hundred times over the past three hours, she turned her gaze to the glowing ruins of the hotel. The stench of charred timbers and ash hung in the night air. People wandered about, men poking at the hot wreckage and women bewailing the loss of their loved ones.

Sarah couldn't let herself grieve so. Not while there was a chance . . .

"I wish I could reassure you," Reginald murmured, his voice as raw and hoarse as hers. "But I'm afraid Damien couldn't have survived the blaze."

He gently stroked her hair, but the comforting gesture failed to halt the frenzied swell of horror and grief. She pulled back and gripped his soot-smudged lapels. "He might have escaped another way." Desperate hope spiraled in her. "Perhaps there was an exit at the end of the hall."

"We would have seen him by now. You know he would have come straightaway to find you."

"Unless he was injured. Oh, dear God, he could be lying hurt somewhere—"

"I checked the hospital. Only a woman and a few children with minor burns were admitted. Come now, you're distraught—"

"Maybe the fakir took him somewhere." A horrid memory played through her fevered mind. "He said, 'The son of a *feringhi* duke will serve the cause of the holy rebellion.' "

"The fakir?" Leaning heavily on his cane, Reginald stared at her. "Do you mean the madman who set the fire and attacked his lordship?"

"Yes." Wringing her hands, she paced with jerky steps. "That must be what happened. Reginald, we've got to find them. You must help me—"

"I can't bear to see you like this." He took hold of her arm and held her still. Through the night shadows, his cinder-streaked face wore a troubled frown. "You must accept the fact that Damien is dead."

A tremor seized her, but she fought it off. "I don't believe it! I won't believe it until I see his charred bones for myself." Yanking herself away, she ran to the gutted hotel.

"Sarah, wait!"

She stepped over the remains of a wall and into the ashes. Heat seared the soles of her feet. She cried out and jumped back, thudding into Reginald.

He caught her close. "For heaven's sake! Did you burn yourself?"

She shook her head, but he stooped to look at the bottoms of her feet in the uncertain light, then straightened. "You appear to be all right. Darling, try to get a grip on yourself. The wreckage is still smoldering. It'll cool by morning, and I'll send Ali Khan to search for the remains."

The remains. She felt herself sliding down, down, down toward blackness. Damien was dead. He was *dead*.

The flare of hope vanished, leaving her adrift

in a vast uncharted darkness. Grief burst in her heart and inundated her in a hot gush of agony. Weak and shaking, she pressed her hands to her face and dimly felt the wet smear of tears. On some distant level she felt Reginald draw her close. The pain plunged her in an abyss so deep that no comfort could reach her. Only the spasmodic sobs convulsing her chest proved she was still alive.

Gradually she grew aware of Reginald murmuring in her ear. "Poor Sarah. Please don't weep. I wish I could help you. If I could, I'd bring him back for you."

She struggled to extricate herself from the well of sorrow. "He . . . was so terribly afraid of fire," she said, her voice muffled against Reginald's jacket. "But he came inside anyway. He came for me and for Kit. And then he died in the most horrible way possible. Oh, dear God, I can't bear it."

"You must, my pet. He would want you to go on."

"He was so embittered by the past. I wanted to marry him, but . . . he couldn't love me."

"He did. Yes, he did love you. He told me so himself."

Lifting her head, she viewed Reginald through tear-blurred eyes. His words dangled like a lifeline above her. "When?"

"We . . . ran into each other at the club this evening. I'm sure he was intending to ask you to marry him."

He gazed toward the ruined hotel. She wondered if he was lying to console her. She desperately wanted to believe him. "W-was he truly?"

"Yes, indeed." Reginald patted her back. "I'm sure of it."

The revelation both cheered and crushed her. To think they'd been so close to happiness, only to have it burn away like fire on the wind. Hot tears rolled down her cheeks. "I wanted to go to England with him. He meant to . . . face his family and present Kit as his heir. Merciful God, the poor baby is an orphan now. What shall I do about him?"

"Kit will be fine—Ali Khan's wife is taking good care of him at my bungalow." Reginald handed her a folded handkerchief. "Come now, my pet, dry your eyes. Come back with me and I'll fix you a draught. The morning is soon enough to decide what to do with the boy."

She wiped sooty tears with the white cloth. Bright as a flame, a thought flashed inside her. "I've decided," she said. "I'm going to take Kit back to England myself."

"There's no need to rush into a decision tonight. You've suffered a terrible shock. You need to rest."

Resolve glimmered like a beacon in the darkness of her soul. "I've made up my mind," she said. "I'm going. It's what Damien would want me to do."

His face a pale blur in the gloom, Reginald gazed at her. "I've been given a medical discharge," he said slowly. "I was only staying in Meerut until I found out what happened to you. So we might as well travel to England together."

"I'd like that. I'm glad we can still be friends."

"Now you're to get in bed and stay there, doctor's orders. You've endured more than any lady ought to endure in a lifetime. You'll need to keep strong for Kit's sake."

Reginald put his arm around her and guided her away. Anguish and exhaustion drenched her. She swallowed against the thickness in her throat. Tears wouldn't bring Damien back. Reginald was right, she must think of Kit.

He was all she had left of Damien.

He had nothing left but the pain.
His head clanged with monotonous regularity.

His hands and feet refused to move. His mouth tasted the foul denseness of a rag.

A dreamlike dread burned in his soul. He'd fulfilled Mother's prophecy. He'd died and gone to hell. He was a demon, damned to darkness for all eternity.

But hell surely didn't smell like incense.

You're not a devil, Damien. Soft and certain, the voice echoed through the torment and bathed him in light. Sarah.

He opened his eyes to stygian blackness. The cloying aroma of sandalwood and the reek of ashes tainted the air. He concentrated on clearing the cloud from his brain. This couldn't be hell. Hell was a fiery inferno. A hotel room aflame.

With the impact of a gunshot, memory slammed into him.

Sarah and Kit! Had they gotten out alive?

Hell was not knowing.

Blinking hard, Damien peered into the gloom. The fakir. Somehow he had survived Damien's deathly blow the night of the mutiny. The fakir had brought him here. He couldn't fathom how or why. He recalled the madman clinging with inhuman strength, then agonizing pain and nothing more.

A terrible thought tumbled through his mind. Sarah must believe him dead. At this moment she might be weeping with grief. If she and Kit had survived.

He should have known better than to reach for happiness. Perhaps they were better off without a miserable wretch like him. Reginald would take care of them.

Damien threw off the shroud of bleak thoughts. He wasn't a devil. Sarah was right; his mother was wrong. Oh, God! He'd never see his son grow up. He'd never have the chance to tell Sarah he loved her.

The need transcended physical pain. He yanked hard, but the bonds held his wrists imprisoned. He was sitting, his back to a hard wall. Twisting his head to the left, he spied a horizontal glimmer several yards away. A door?

He tried to wriggle closer. His leg struck something in the darkness. Metal crashed and clanged. He must have knocked over a stack of pots.

As the clamor died, another sound drifted to him. A faint tinkling, like a wind chime stirred by a breeze. Or someone rattling the string of brass bells at the entrance to a Hindu shrine.

A shrine. Incense. The fakir.

His mind leaped from fact to fact like stepping-stones leading him across a turbulent river. He must be in the back room of a temple. Perhaps the bazaar temple, where Sarah had seen a priest watching their arrival into Meerut. This place was a temple dedicated to Shiva and his wife, Parvati. Parvati, whose evil incarnation was Kali.

Confusion roiled in Damien's brain. Kali was worshipped by the outlawed thugees, men who strangled innocent people to appease the goddess's bloodlust. Did the fakir mean to sacrifice him?

A tiny click sounded. Brightness blinded Damien. Squinting, he ducked his head. Brass incense pots were scattered on the stone floor. As his eyes adjusted, he saw the fakir looming in the doorway, a lighted torch in his ash-grayed hand.

With ferocious strength, Damien strained against the ropes. *Bastard! I'll kill you for hurting Sarah. I'll throw you to the vultures for keeping me from her and Kit!*

The words reverberated through his brain. The gag permitted only a low rumble of fury in his throat.

"So thou has awakened at last," said the fakir. "Calm thyself. Thou shalt live, *feringhi* devil, at least for a time. Thy miserable life shall serve a greater purpose.''

His voice rattled through the small storeroom. He closed the door, and the lock clicked into place.

Impotent anger and black despair clashed within Damien. He damned himself for falling into a trap.

The trap that kept him from the son he'd come to cherish and the only woman he'd ever loved.

Chapter 22

A frosty December wind buffeted Sarah. A decidedly English chill invaded her bones. Shivering, she gripped the frog fastening of her hood and tilted her head back. The three-story town house was built of stark red brick. Gray stone laced the tall windows, and four Corinthian columns supported a lofty portico.

Number Twenty-six, Hanover Square. The London residence of the Duke and Duchess of Lamborough. And Blanche Coleridge, the dowager duchess. Damien's mother.

The sense of purpose that had brought Sarah halfway around the world abruptly deserted her. She wanted to turn and flee. Merciful God, what if the dowager took Kit from her?

Looking toward the hired hack waiting at the curbstone, she saw Reginald rub a circle in the frosted window. His lips formed an encouraging smile. He'd held her tight when the charred bones of a man the size of Damien had been found among the dozen people burned in the hotel. Reginald had assisted her in arranging the burial. He'd been wonderful on the long voyage, a father to Kit and a friend to her. Perched on his lap, the baby pressed his alert face to the window. He looked so like Damien that Sarah's throat squeezed tight. No, the dowager wouldn't want

Damien's son. But she'd be forced to acknowledge him as the heir.

With renewed resolve, Sarah took a chilly breath, mounted the steps, and grasped the brass knocker. Her firm rap resounded. The door opened smoothly on oiled hinges. A portly man in the pristine black garb of a butler looked down his ruddy nose at her. White cherub curls crowned the orb of his face.

"May I be of assistance, madam?" His cultured tone daunted her, but only for a moment. This must be Bromley, Damien's sole ally in the household.

"I should like to speak with the dowager duchess."

A slight frown furrowed his brow. "Her Grace isn't accepting callers today. If you would care to leave your card . . ."

"I'm sure she'll see me." Sarah's chest tightened. "What I have to say concerns her son Damien."

Bromley's bushy brows lifted in startlement. "Lord Damien? Do come in, madam . . ."

"Miss Sarah Faulkner. I'm afraid I haven't a calling card. I've come straight from India."

The butler ushered her inside and took her cloak and gloves, then showed her to a drawing room. He surreptitiously glanced over her gown of untrimmed gray velvet and her blond hair drawn into a love knot at her neck. Curiosity gleamed in his pale blue eyes, but he merely said, "Please make yourself comfortable, Miss Faulkner. I shall see if Her Grace is available." Bowing, he went out.

Too nervous to sit, Sarah paced the opulent gold-and-white room, then peered into the foyer. The only sound was the ticktock of a case clock. Silver ribbons draped a Christmas tree. Alabaster statues stood frozen in columned niches. Marble in a checkerboard design of black and snow

gleamed as if no mortal feet had ever desecrated
its perfection. The grand staircase led her gaze
upward to an arched and gilded ceiling and a
chandelier that glistened like an elegant arrangement of ice crystals.

The effect was lovely . . . and very, very cold.

Yearning for the warmth and vitality of India,
Sarah shivered again. She imagined Damien as a
boy in this frigidly formal atmosphere, skipping
down the steps, racing along the echoing corri-
dors, leaping out at Bromley . . .

Despite his atrocious upbringing, Damien had
become a fine man, a man of honor and of sensitivity. Snippets of memory flared like bright
stars inside her.

How I wish I could be the man of your dreams.

But he was. He'd died before he'd learned it
was true. The need to tell him ached like an eternal wound. So many things had been left unsaid.

*I never envisioned needing a woman as much as I
need you.*

Sorrow misted her eyes. Would she ever grow
accustomed to Damien's absence? Would she always turn around and expect to see his smiling
dark eyes, his bold grin beckoning to her?

I worry about whether or not I'll be a good father.

How capable he'd become at caring for Kit, at
delighting in his son. With bittersweet bliss, Sarah
pressed her hand to her belly. Damien hadn't
lived to learn that she nurtured within her womb
the child conceived in their last joyful joining.

She walked to the hearth and rubbed her
hands. The coal blaze warmed her fingers, yet she
still felt chilled. The chimneypiece of pearled marble towered to the ceiling. This must be the fireplace into which the duchess had hurled the
drawing Damien had done as a seven-year-old
boy yearning for his mother's love.

The thought pierced Sarah's grief with the arrow of anger. It was time the dowager faced the truth about her second son.

"Miss Faulkner."

In the doorway stood a woman, thin and snowy-haired, clad in a magnificent aquamarine crinoline. A string of flawless pearls looped her slim white throat. Hardly the formidable dragon Sarah had envisioned, the dowager walked into the room, her steps small and precise, as if she was concentrating on not stumbling.

Hands as pale as parchment lifted a silver lorgnette. She peered at Sarah, looking her up and down. "Kindly state your business. It is quite annoying to have one's schedule disarranged to accommodate uninvited guests."

The numbness left Sarah's tongue. She tightly clasped her hands before her. "Pardon me, Your Grace. I have news of the son you drove away ten years ago."

"Impertinent chit." Blanche shook the lorgnette. "Who are you? His mistress?"

Sarah's cheeks flamed. "I'm someone who cared very deeply for Damien. He certainly had little enough love in his life."

The duchess made a dismissive snort. "Save your sentimental judgments. Give me your report and be gone. What has the boy done now? Been tossed into debtors' prison? Indicted for murder? Or has he sent you here to plead for my forgiveness?"

"Damien is dead."

The golden eyes sharpened. One pencil-thin eyebrow arched. Blanche lowered the lorgnette and walked slowly to a tall window, her face turned to the sumptuous draperies. For a startling instant, Sarah fancied she saw the heaviness of grief slump the dowager's shoulders.

"I always knew that boy would go to an early grave. He was as rash and worthless as my father."

Her rancor in the face of news that would set most mothers to weeping stirred the storm of Sarah's resentment. She stepped toward the dowager. "You've no right to speak of Damien that way. You should be proud of him. He died a hero, saving me and his son from a fire."

The dowager whirled so fast she wobbled. She clutched at the windowsill. "His son?" she said in a strange, wavering croak. "I don't believe it."

Sarah's stomach lurched with uneasiness. "Yes. His name is Christopher, but we call him Kit. Your grandson is waiting with a companion in my carriage."

Blanche stood frozen, her face a mask of icy hauteur. Then she made her way to a gilt table and rang a tiny bell.

Bromley appeared in the doorway. "Yes, Your Grace?"

"Fetch the child from the carriage outside." She waved her lorgnette. "Well, go on. Be quick about it."

Bowing, the butler hastened away.

The dowager swung back to Sarah. "How old is the boy?"

"Nearly eight months."

"He's just a baby, then. Was he born in India?"

"Yes. In Meerut, just before the mutiny began."

Lifting her lorgnette, Blanche again subjected Sarah to a lengthy examination. "And you're the mother? At least you're a comely type. So, did you manage to dupe my son into marriage or not?"

"No, but I—"

"Just as I thought," said the dowager in a scathing tone. "You've come to beg for money. How many pieces of silver will it take to buy your silence?"

Sarah's palm itched to slap the woman. "None.

If you'd allow me a word, I might correct your misconception. Kit isn't mine. His mother was killed in the Indian mutiny. But he is Damien's lawful son and heir.''

''Oh?'' A wealth of mockery enriched the word. ''So you've brought him here out of the goodness of your heart?''

''Yes,'' Sarah said firmly. ''I promised Damien I would care for Kit. And I shall. I know you won't wish to be saddled with him.''

Despite Blanche's hostile stare, Sarah refused to lower her eyes. A thought shook her. The duchess's rigid expression held an echo of Damien in anger, the same hard cheekbones, the same fearless gaze. He'd learned his arrogance at her knee. Only as a man had he learned to open himself to love.

Bromley ushered in Reginald and the baby. Trembling with anxiety, Sarah hurried to them. Kit's chubby face and dark eyes peeped from his winter wrappings. Seeing her, he cooed and smiled. Tendrils of love wreathed her in dismal doubts.

Damien had been right. She shouldn't have brought Kit back to England. Position and privilege couldn't take the place of heart and happiness. Would the dowager accept him?

She unwound his muffler and unbuttoned his tiny sailor coat. Her troubled gaze met Reginald's grave face; then she turned and nearly tumbled over the dowager, who'd moved up behind her. An odd sensitivity touched her thin lips.

''Show me the lad,'' she demanded.

Sarah reluctantly held him quiet for the dowager's inspection. Blanche raised her lorgnette. The brief softness vanished into hard curiosity. ''Why, he has a foreign look about him.'' Still peering at him, she took a step nearer.

Babbling gaily, Kit leaned toward her. His tiny fist closed around her rope of pearls. He yanked

and the necklace broke. The beads flew everywhere, pinging onto the floor, rolling under chairs
and tables. Just as fast, he stuffed one into his
mouth.

"Kit!" Sarah pulled his hand away and stuck
her finger inside his mouth. To her horror, she
couldn't find the orb.

"My pearls!" the duchess wailed. "Bromley!
Find my priceless pearls!"

Even as the butler rushed inside, Sarah hastened to Reginald. "Oh, dear God, he must have
swallowed one. Will he choke?"

The doctor examined the cooing baby. "There's
nothing to worry yourself about. It seems to have
gone down easily enough."

"Nothing to worry about!" exclaimed Blanche.
"Those pearls are a Lamborough family heirloom,
a perfectly matched set."

"And you shall recover all of them." A twinkle
in his blue eyes, Reginald regarded the butler,
scrabbling on the floor for the pearls. "When we
return to the hotel, I shall administer a dose of
castor oil. That should bring the pearl out Kit's
other end."

The duchess wrinkled her aristocratic nose.
"How disgusting. I might have known Damien
would sire an ill-mannered child."

Sarah hugged Kit close, unmindful that he pulled
at her hair. "Don't you dare hold an infant responsible for an accident."

Blanche pivoted toward her. "Who was his
mother?"

Sarah girded herself for battle and said defi-
antly, "She was Damien's wife. Her name was
Shivina."

"Shivina? What sort of name is that for an Englishwoman?"

"She wasn't English. She was a Hindu
woman."

"A Hindoo?" The word rolled like poison off

the duchess's tongue. Her lips formed a curl of shocked disgust. "The child has mixed blood? Take him away. I don't want the boy."

"Fine. Just acknowledge him as heir and I'll raise him. I have copies of the marriage and birth records right here." From her reticule Sarah pulled out both documents, unfolded them, and handed them over for the dowager's inspection.

The papers shook in Blanche's age-mottled hands. "These must be a forgery," she said hoarsely. "I shall summon a constable and have both of you clapped in Newgate."

Leaning on his cane, Reginald came forward. "If I may be permitted to speak, Your Grace. I stood with Sarah as witness to the marriage."

The duchess eyed him as if he were a loathsome spider. "And who might you be?"

"Dr. Reginald Pemberton-Sykes, lately of Her Majesty's services in India."

"Bah. I have only your word on that."

"You may write and verify the records with the Indian registry office," Sarah said. "Lord Canning himself signed the special license."

"Lord Canning." Blanche flung both certificates onto a gilt chair. "He's a weakling, a skirt-chaser like most men. Likely Damien bribed him to sign the document."

"That doesn't make it any less legal and binding," Sarah said.

"Humbug. I shall petition the Queen to annul the marriage."

Alarm jolted Sarah. She mustn't let the dowager cheat Kit out of his inheritance. If only there were a way to ensure his fortune and to take the spiteful woman down a peg in the process.

Could she convince her to accept Kit? By informing her of Damien's innocence in his father's death? It was worth a try.

"Perhaps you'll change your mind," Sarah be-

gan. ''I should like to bring up another matter—''

''Mama!'' A fair-haired man dashed into the
room. A hat and coat were tangled in his arms,
and a red scarf dragged behind him. ''Anne won't
let me go out into the garden.''

Blanche's taut expression eased. ''Please return
to your room, Christopher. I have guests.''
Though her voice was firm, her command held a
note of tenderness.

Sarah's attention sharpened. He was the Duke
of Lamborough, Damien's older brother. Frail in
build, Christopher was a pale shadow of Damien
and a taller version of their mother. His fine-
boned features held an almost feminine softness,
and a pout thrust out his lower lip.

''But I want to go out,'' he said plaintively. ''It
isn't fair . . .'' His voice trailed off as he spied Kit.
''Look, Mama, a baby! Can I touch him?''

Without waiting for approval, he dropped his
coat in a heap on the floor and moved toward
Sarah. His clear blue eyes glowed with delight,
and he brushed a hand over Kit's silky black hair.

He turned his awed face to Sarah. ''What's his
name?''

''He's Christopher, too, but we call him Kit.''

The duke wheeled toward the dowager.
''Mama, just think, the baby has my name. You
said we would get a baby someday.'' A young
woman rushed through the doorway, and he motioned excitedly to her. ''Anne, come here and
see the baby. He has my name!''

Wringing her slender hands, she came forward.
She had chestnut hair and brown eyes, dark
velvet-wing brows, and sweet, if not beautiful
features. She looked cautiously at the dowager.
''I'm so sorry, Your Grace,'' she murmured. ''He
wanted to go into the garden, but it was time for
his medication. When I returned with the pills,
he was gone.''

"Never mind," Blanche said, her keen eyes on
the duke, who chortled when the baby grasped
his finger. "It's more important that Christopher
meet his nephew."

Her calculating expression shot trepidation
through Sarah. Surely the dowager wouldn't
change her mind about wanting Kit . . .

Anne turned wondering eyes to the baby. "His
nephew? And has Damien come back, then?"

"No." Blanche pulled Anne aside and murmured. "He's dead. This is his son."

Shock and curiosity sparkled in Anne's eyes,
but she merely walked to her husband's side and
smiled at the baby, then at Sarah. "May I hold
him, please?"

Sarah hesitated for only an instant. "Of
course."

Anne gathered Kit close and sat on a gold-
striped settee. Christopher trailed after her. "I
want to hold him, too," he said, his expression
turning sulky.

"In a moment," she said. "Babies are very delicate creatures. We must be careful with them,
much more so than with dolls. See how I support
him under the arms? He likes to stand, but I
imagine he can't do it on his own yet."

The duke and duchess bent together, one fair
head and one chestnut. Kit reveled in their attention, babbling his pleasure and batting first at
Anne's yellow hair ribbons, then at Christopher's
watch chain. The duke laughed when the baby
pulled out the timepiece and sucked on the gold
casing.

Anne's gentle devotion to her husband touched
Sarah's heart. What a sadness that a child had
never come from the marriage. The greatest joy
in her own life was knowing that, come summer,
she would bear Damien's baby.

The dowager stood by the hearth and watched
her son. The chilly arrogance of her age-worn fea-

tures had given way to the slackness of despair, the hopeless love of a mother for a damaged and blameless child.

The resentment inside Sarah melted into pity. The feeling surprised her and dulled the edge of her fury. So Blanche was capable of a mother's love, albeit an obsessive love focused on her elder son. Sarah felt a sudden reluctance to blame the old duke's death on Christopher. Yet how could she let Blanche go on believing falsehoods about Damien? How could she let Kit bear the taint of a father who'd supposedly committed patricide?

The dowager glided to Sarah. "The child will stay here," she said in an undertone that the others couldn't hear. "I shall dispatch a footman to fetch his things." She picked up the silver bell from the table.

"Don't," said Sarah in panic. Dear God, she couldn't settle Kit under the wing of a woman who had despised his father. The dowager only wanted him as a plaything for Christopher. "I never meant to leave Kit here," she said in a strident whisper.

"You forget yourself, Miss Faulkner. The boy is my grandson."

Unflinching, Sarah met the dowager's icy glare. "That may be the unfortunate truth, but I shall protect him from you for as long as I can."

"Listen to me, you impertinent—"

"No, you listen." Fear made her bold. "Damien entrusted his son to my care. His last wish was to secure Kit's position as his heir. That acknowledgment is all I require. I can't trust you to give Kit the love he needs."

"How dare you speak to me in so insolent a manner?"

"I dare because I know how brutal you can be. You'll call Kit the spawn of the devil. You'll make a defenseless boy suffer your hatred just as you made Damien suffer."

Her gaze wavered, then sharpened on Sarah. From close up, every wrinkle on her face showed through a thin layer of powder. "Damien was born wicked. Even as a baby, he pulled my hair and wailed to high heaven—"

"He was a fine man and a brilliant photographer." Swallowing tears, Sarah recalled the priceless pictures of India, the chronicle of a country as it would never be again. Someday, she vowed, she would return and finish the book for him. "But you were too selfish and cruel to see his goodness."

Leaving the dowager with her mouth agape, Sarah marched toward the duke and duchess. She strove for a gentler tone. "I'm afraid we must be going now."

"So soon?" said Anne, her smile dying.

Christopher sprang up. "But I haven't shown him my toys yet. Please, couldn't he stay?"

"Perhaps another time." Sarah gathered Kit tight against her shoulder. "We're staying at Mrs. Goodson's Boardinghouse in Chelsea. I should be happy to bring him by to visit."

"Please do," Anne said, rising to join Sarah and Reginald at the door. She gave Kit a wistful glance and touched his hair. "I'd love to have a baby in the house."

The dowager moved toward them like a dragon seeking prey. Her eyes were slitted at Sarah, her parchment hands gripped at her sides. "My solicitor will be contacting you."

The ominous words settled like stones in Sarah's stomach. She picked up the marriage and birth certificates and secured them in her reticule. She had a reprieve, only because Blanche wouldn't make a scene in front of her son. But there was no doubt in Sarah's mind that the dowager meant to take Kit. And if ever Christopher tired of the baby, she would wreak destruction on Damien's son.

In helpless frustration, Sarah despaired of protecting Kit. She had no legal right to keep him.

When they were settled in the hired carriage, Kit peeping out the window at the passing sights, Reginald murmured, "The dowager looked furious. Whatever were you two murmuring about in the corner?"

"I'm afraid I lost my temper and gave her a piece of my mind. She wants to keep Kit as a toy for Christopher."

The clopping of the horse filled the silence. A thoughtful frown furrowed Reginald's brow. "Speaking of the duke, I was intrigued by his condition. You said his mental deficiency was caused by a fire?"

"Yes." During the long voyage to England, Sarah had told Reginald the bare bones of the story. "He was six years old when he was locked inside a cupboard during a fire."

"Odd," Reginald mused, drumming his fingers on the knob of his cane. "I've never heard of a trauma having so permanent and dramatic an effect on the mind. However . . ."

"Yes?"

"Back in medical school, I saw a woman whose mental state was similar to Christopher's. She'd been deprived of air for a brief time during birth. She seemed only a bit slow as a baby, but the extent of her impairment became clear as she grew older."

Stunned, Sarah sat back in the rocking carriage. She hugged Kit so hard he squalled. She loosened her grip and absently patted his back. "Do you really think something other than the fire could have caused Christopher's affliction?"

"It's possible." Reginald shrugged. "Only the doctor who attended the birth could tell us if Christopher suffered oxygen deprivation."

Fury consumed Sarah. Blanche might have made Damien shoulder yet another unjust burden of guilt. "We'll find him, then. Will you help me, please?"

Reginald leaned forward and patted her head. "I would if I could, Sarah. But that was nearly thirty years ago. How could we even know where to look?"

The seed of a plan took root inside her. She would both protect Kit's rights and shield him from the dowager's sharp tongue. She smiled. "I have an idea."

The Christmas wreath at Number Fifteen, Milford Lane, drooped in the icy drizzle. The chill seeped past Sarah's thick merino cloak and into her bones. The dismal weather made her glad she'd had the sense to leave Kit napping at the boardinghouse in the care of the warmhearted Mrs. Goodson.

Reginald eyed the rundown building before them. "Are you sure this is the right place?"

"Yes," Sarah said. "Bromley was certain this is the address of the doctor who delivered Christopher."

Reginald knocked. After a moment, a petite woman garbed in sober black opened the door. Her upswept ebony hair and pale cheeks gave her an ethereal quality, as if she'd floated forth from the mists of a fable. "May I help you?"

"We're here to see Dr. Finch," said Reginald.

Her thickly lashed gray eyes misted. Sadness curved her lips downward. "I'm afraid that's impossible. He passed away six months ago."

Sarah aimed a frown of frustration at Reginald. But his eyes were focused on the woman. "I'm so very sorry," he murmured. "Was he . . . someone dear to you?"

"He was my father."

"I see. Perhaps you might help us, then."

She considered him doubtfully. "I'd be happy

to refer you to another physician. Perhaps Dr. Cunningham on Holles Street—''

''Thank you, but I'm a physician myself, Dr. Reginald Pemberton-Sykes. This is my friend, Miss Sarah Faulkner. We were hoping you might have retained your father's records.''

''Why, yes.'' The woman laced her fingers together. ''I haven't yet had the heart to clear out his office.''

''Then perhaps you wouldn't mind another medical man glancing through the files, Miss Finch.'' He paused, a bemused smile on his face. ''It is Miss, isn't it?''

A hint of roses tinted her cheeks. ''I'm Miss Lily Finch.'' She hesitated only a moment before adding, ''Please, come inside. You must think me ill-mannered to leave you standing out in the rain.''

They entered a shadowed hall. The air smelled of lemon wax, freshly baked bread, and Miss Finch's faint lilac scent.

''Does this matter concern a patient?'' she asked.

''Yes,'' Sarah said. ''A patient your father treated many years ago. I do hope he kept files so far back.''

''Of course. Papa was an excellent recordkeeper. This way, please.'' Miss Finch led them down the passageway, past a meagerly furnished sitting room. She opened a door and ushered them into a dim, musty office. Going to the window, she drew back the checkered curtain, then turned her attention to the coal scuttle by the hearth. ''Empty,'' she murmured. ''I'll see if there's any left in the kitchen.'' She glided to the door.

''Lily.'' Above his starched collar, a dull flush suffused Reginald's neck. ''Forgive me for being so bold, but what a pretty name.''

She laughed, a tinkling brightness in the dingy room. ''Papa always said if I had to suffer the surname of a silly bird, I deserved to be called after his favorite flower.''

As if enraptured, they smiled at one another. Sarah watched in dawning amazement. She had never before witnessed two people so taken with each other on the first meeting. Her heart caught in bittersweet agony. She and Damien had struck sparks at their first encounter, on that long-ago day in the caravan.

Lily tilted her head at Reginald. ''Might I inquire the name of the patient you're looking for?''

''The dowager Duchess of Lamborough and her firstborn son.''

The serenity fled the perfect oval of her face. Like an infuriated fairy queen, she drew herself up and glared at him. ''You might have said so from the start. You aren't welcome here. I must ask you to leave.''

Sarah's interest sharpened. ''You've some complaint against the dowager?''

''She ruined Papa's practice, that's what. I was only a baby at the time, but he said she denounced him as a charlatan. Because of her wicked attack, he lost all of his aristocratic patients. We were forced to subsist on what he could eke out from treating the poor.''

Sarah exchanged a glance with Reginald. ''Then perhaps you *can* help us,'' she told Lily. ''And in the process, we shall absolve your father's good name.''

Snowflakes swirled through the frosty air. Bundled like a tiny Buddha, Kit slept in Sarah's arms. She pressed her cheek to the carriage window and peered into the traffic clogging the cobblestoned streets of Mayfair. The wreaths and holly adorning the elegant town houses awakened the throb of a familiar pain. It was Christmas Eve, the day when Blanche had burned Damien's precious drawing some twenty years ago. Sarah wished she'd had the chance to help him replace that awful remembrance with the bright joy of a shared Christmas.

Today she had a gift to give his memory. Three days ago, in the yellowed files of Dr. Finch, she and Reginald had found the proof she needed. Now, with the other testimony they had accumulated, she could vindicate Damien.

She searched her soul for triumph and found only the hollow heartache that had plagued her across the Indian Ocean, through the Suez and Cairo, and to the wintry shores of England. The sense of homecoming she'd expected had eluded her. Home was a log hut in the Himalayan foothills, warmed by the blaze of a love so bright and strong it would shine in her heart forever.

Drawing a breath of cold air, she cuddled Kit against her cloak. Her grief subsided into a sea of tenderness. Her gloved fingers twisted the end of his scarf. She had gathered her evidence only just in time. This very morning, the notice to surrender Kit had arrived from Drury and Lumm, the solicitors retained by the dowager.

Across the swaying carriage, Reginald cleared his throat. "Perhaps we shouldn't shatter Her Grace's illusions on a holiday."

"I have no other choice," Sarah said quietly, gazing down at Kit's adorably chubby face. "I can't let another day go by with this little boy's future weighing on my mind."

"She does have the right of a blood relation to take him from you."

Sarah suffered a moment's doubt; then she hardened her resolve. "I know, but at least I'll clear Damien's name, for Kit's sake and for the sake of my own baby."

Reginald studied the ivory-topped cane propped against his elegantly attired leg. He lifted his gaze to her. "Sarah, your child needs a father.

I want you to know that my offer of marriage still stands.''

Affection brought tears to her eyes. She studied his classic features beneath the silk top hat, his erect posture and broad shoulders framed by a charcoal greatcoat. She had come to depend on his devoted companionship. ''You've been a marvelous friend, and more understanding than any woman could ever hope for. But I could never ask you to raise another man's child.''

''You haven't asked. I've offered.''

''Out of kindness and honor.'' She felt a moment's regret that she couldn't love him as she'd loved Damien. ''I'm grieving for Damien. I will grieve until I die. You deserve a wife who can give you all of her heart, not just a portion. A woman like Lily Finch.''

He colored, and a smile touched his mouth. ''She was rather lovely, wasn't she?''

''Lovely and intelligent, the perfect wife for a doctor. Perhaps you ought to pay her a Christmas call.''

''Perhaps I shall.''

Sarah bit her lip. ''And you needn't worry about me. I've the five hundred pounds from Damien and a small inheritance from my uncle, enough to support me and the baby. We'll stay here in London so I can visit Kit.''

Pensiveness lit Reginald's face. ''I've been thinking about opening a practice in Chelsea. So I'll be here, too, whenever you need me.''

''I'd like that,'' she murmured.

The carriage jolted to a halt. Lamborough House loomed through a mist of snowflakes. Like a battery of butterflies, nervous anticipation took wing in Sarah's stomach. She calmed herself with the reminder that she held all the aces. History would not repeat itself; Blanche Coleridge would not practice her high-handed manipulation on Damien's son.

Ten minutes later, armored by the evidence in her reticule and a strong sense of purpose, Sarah watched the dowager walk into the drawing room. She wore a severely cut gown of green velvet stamped with red holly berries, the effect frigid rather than festive. Her gait was studied and careful, her chin tipped at a proud angle.

"I'll have no interruptions," she told Bromley, who nodded and shut the doors. She looked at Sarah. "I see you received the summons," she said without preamble. "You were instructed to surrender the child at my solicitor's office after Boxing Day, not invade my home during the holidays."

Sarah's heart wrenched. "And I see you haven't the good grace to wear mourning for Damien." Anger boiled inside her, but she kept her voice modulated. "You didn't even want Kit for Christmas. That proves how little esteem you afford him. And that's precisely why you and I must talk."

"I have nothing to say to you."

"Then you may simply listen, for I will be happy to do enough speaking for both of us."

The dowager narrowed her eyes. A huff of displeasure escaped her.

Holding Kit, Reginald stepped forward. "One moment," he said, fishing inside the pocket of his checkered waistcoat. "I believe this belongs to you, Your Grace."

Extending his palm, he revealed a single lustrous pearl.

Revulsion pinched the dowager's lips. "Leave it there," she said, jerking her hand at a gold dish on a table. "I should turn the disgusting lot of you into the gutter where you belong."

"But you won't dare," said Reginald.

"Yes," added Sarah, "not when you hear what we have discovered."

Blanche clenched her lorgnette like a weapon.

"It's high time you told me what you were about, miss. No doubt you mean to threaten to inform society that I have a half-caste grandson. How much money will you try to extort from me?"

"Not a penny." Sarah quieted her hammering heart. "This is about Kit and his rights as heir to the dukedom. He deserves all the privileges of his birth. But I'll leave him here in your care only if you agree to several conditions."

"Why, you presumptuous—"

"First of all, I shall choose his nanny." She ticked off the items on her fingers. "Second, I will live here with him until he is properly settled in. Third, I will have your permission in writing to visit him whenever I like. And last, I must be assured he'll not suffer from your poisonous tongue."

Scarlet color washed the dowager's cheeks. "You presume to impugn my character—"

"Should I ever learn you've so much as given him a cross look, I shall disclose your secrets to every newspaper in England."

"My secrets?" Blanche scoffed. "I have nothing to hide from the likes of you."

"What about the fact that Christopher has been slow since birth?"

Blanche wilted into a chair of gold brocade. "That's a vile lie. When my precious little boy was only six, Damien locked him in a cupboard—" She clamped her lips shut and glared.

"I know about the fire," Sarah said. "Damien told me everything. You convinced him he'd destroyed his brother's mind. But he didn't. And I can prove it."

"No," the duchess said firmly. "You can't. You may take your fraudulent claims and leave my house." Yet her shoulders lost their starch, and her bosom rose and fell in agitation.

Sarah reached into her reticule and brought out a sheaf of papers. "I wrote out a copy of Dr.

Finch's record. He reports that Christopher stopped breathing at birth and had to be revived.''

''No . . .'' Her voice was a thin, dry note. ''That isn't true.''

''We also found Christopher's former nanny in Dorset. I have her signed testimony that he was two before he learned to walk. He was three before he even spoke a word—''

''Stop it!'' The dowager dug her nails into the fine silk of the chair arms. ''Nanny Smaltrot lied. My son was perfect in every way until Damien destroyed him!''

''Miss Smaltrot has no cause to lie. She said you commanded her to keep silent on the matter. Out of loyalty, she obeyed.'' Going to the table beside the duchess, Sarah laid down all but one paper.

Blanche's eyes flitted away from the documents. Her lips were gray, bloodless. ''You must have bribed her—''

''No,'' Reginald broke in from his stance by the door, ''it was seeing this little lad here that convinced Miss Smaltrot to speak out. She couldn't bear to let his father's name be blackened any longer.''

''You,'' the duchess railed. ''You're a charlatan. Just as all doctors are.'' Despite her fierce words, she sat crouched in a boneless huddle.

Sarah fought a surge of pity. The last document described the circumstances surrounding the old duke's death and proved that Christopher had unwittingly murdered his father. Despite Blanche's beastly behavior toward her second son, she loved Christopher. The prospect of crushing her delusions was daunting.

The dowager had tried to destroy Damien. And she might also try to destroy his son.

Yet Sarah hesitated. Did that give her the right to respond with the same cruelty?

The drawing room doors opened with an inelegant clatter. Bromley came in, his cheeks ghostly pale, his expression stupefied. ''Your Grace—''

''I gave orders we were not to be disturbed.'' Her imperious voice held only a slight quaver. She half rose from the chair. ''Or is it Christopher? Has something happened to him?''

''N-no, Your Grace. I-I don't quite know how to say this—''

A movement behind him drew Sarah's gaze. A man stood there, tall and broad-shouldered, clad in the dark vested suit of a gentleman.

He strode past the butler and into the room. Her disbelieving gaze swept his powerful, godlike form. She must be dreaming, fantasizing. But she blinked and he was still there, his dark eyes smiling, his bold grin beckoning to her.

A small moan of euphoria burst from her throat. On wobbly legs she ran to meet him.

''Damien!''

Chapter 23

Holding Sarah again wrapped Damien in a splendor so pure it surpassed the peak of physical pleasure.

His arms found their home around her slim body. At last he held his English rose, perfect and prickly, delicate and indomitable. His eyes brimmed with tears, and he pressed his face to the crown of her hair. She smelled of sweetness and sunlight. Their lips joined in a hard and hungry kiss.

The fervor of her response banished the nightmarish weeks of fear and loneliness, and the torment that she might have changed her mind about loving him. Sarah was a part of him, as vital to his body as eating and breathing, as essential to his soul as labor and love.

She drew back and touched his cheek, his chin, his chest. She laughed and cried at once. "Oh, Damien. You're alive. *You're alive!*"

"And glad of it."

"But what happened? Where have you been? Your charred bones were in the wreckage of the fire—"

"You found some other poor soul who only resembled me," Damien said. "The fakir struck me. I blacked out, and when I came to, I was bound and gagged in the bazaar temple."

She framed his neck in her soft palms. "But why, Damien? Why did he abduct you?"

"To exchange an English noble for the imprisoned rebel leader, Bahadur Shah. The fakir held me for a week before I tricked him and escaped. Then the English executed him." Blown apart by a cannon, the fakir had been reduced to bloody bits. Damien turned his mind from the grisly details and focused on Sarah. "I was devastated when Reginald's manservant said you'd both already left India."

"Merciful God." She seized his hands and kissed them. "If only I'd known, I'd have waited an eternity."

Someone coughed. Lifting his eyes, he saw Bromley beaming and Reginald smiling. The doctor held Kit. Damien's chest squeezed tight. The baby regarded him with alert dark eyes, then waved his arms and grinned, revealing two new teeth. "Kit . . ."

"Isn't he handsome?" Sarah said, smiling indulgently. "He looks more and more like you every day."

As Damien gathered the baby close, the awesome bond he felt for this small, wriggly bundle again brought the burn of tears to his eyes. To think he'd once feared being a father. Now he had enough love in his heart to embrace the whole world. "I've missed you, son."

Looking over the baby's head, Damien caught an intense, wordless exchange between Sarah and Reginald. His fear returned in full force. Had she married Reginald after all? No, praise God, neither she nor the doctor wore a wedding ring.

"Shall I entertain Kit for a few hours?" Reginald said. "There was a display of toy animals at a shop on Regent Street. Then we'll return to Mrs. Goodson's."

"Thank you," Sarah murmured. "That would be kind of you."

His chest taut, Damien watched the doctor and Kit depart. Bromley bowed and closed the doors.

How close were she and Reginald? Damien wondered. He wasn't sure he could face knowing right now. He'd speak to her later.

He could delay no longer. His throat dried and his palms dampened. Slowly he turned to his mother.

She sat erect in her favorite chair by the hearth, her hands rigid on the brocade arms. Against his will, the old feelings rose in him, the shame, the inadequacy, the pain. He forced himself to view her as Sarah did. *You deserved to be nurtured and loved by your mother.*

She'd grown old in ten years, her posture shrunken and her skin wrinkled, her blond hair gone white as snow. He couldn't recall her needing the lorgnette she now gripped.

Gray-faced, she stared as if viewing a ghost. Her lips were parted, her expression startled. She rose and squared her shoulders. Her face hardened into a familiar mask of hauteur.

"How dare you come back here," she said. "I thought we were done with you."

He wanted to run. He wanted to hide. He almost gagged on a clot of panic. Sarah's warm hand enveloped his cold one. The memory of her words flitted through his mind: *You'll never be at peace with yourself until you come to terms with your past.*

He coolly returned his mother's stare. "I'm sorry my presence still disturbs you," he said. "I was looking for Kit and Sarah. I had to be sure you hadn't hurt them."

The dowager snorted. "I, hurt *them?* I was kind enough to offer a home to that poor, half-breed child you sired. I can give him far more than your lowborn mistress can afford."

Surprise and anger churned in him. Gripping

Sarah's hand, he fought for equilibrium. "But Sarah can give Kit something you can't. Love."

"Love? I'm amazed you know the sentiment."

"It took me years, but I learned from Sarah what you should have taught me." Against all reason, a flicker of hope flared in him. "And I'm amazed you'd welcome my son into your house, Mother. Why would you?"

Her gaze strayed, but only for an instant. "Like it or not, he's a Lamborough. I felt a duty to my kin."

"That isn't true." Fierce as a tigress, Sarah rounded on Damien. "Christopher took a fancy to Kit. That's the sole reason she wanted your son here, to entertain the duke."

Damien's heart lurched. Hating himself for feeling disappointment, he said flatly, "I see."

"Do you?" Her face bleak, his mother took a step toward him. "You've no inkling, either of you, of how dreadful it is for me to look at my son every day and know the fine man he might have been. When I find a way to please him, I seize it!"

"Even if it means using an innocent baby as a plaything?" Damien shot back.

She shook the lorgnette. "You always did begrudge your brother any scrap of happiness. How easily you've forgotten your debt to him."

Damien sweated beneath a shroud of guilt. *To appease her, you've sacrificed your peace of mind, your home in England, and your ability to love.* The nightmare of pain and confusion lifted. He met his mother's accusing eyes. "The fire was a tragedy," he said. "I'll always be sorry for that. But I won't spend the rest of my life atoning for a mistake I made as a five-year-old."

Sarah clasped his arm. The zeal blazing in her blue eyes confounded him. "You won't have to, Damien. You never caused Christopher any harm." Swinging back to the dowager, she snapped, "Tell him."

To Damien's astonishment, his mother crumpled into the chair. Her shoulders drooped into the same defeated posture he'd spied upon entering the room.

"I refuse to repeat your lies." Her voice quivered oddly.

"Then I'll speak the truth." Sarah went to the table beside the dowager and gathered several papers. Returning, she held them out to him. "These affidavits prove that Christopher was dull-witted since his birth. You're blameless, Damien. You didn't bring about his handicap."

He took the papers into his trembling hands. One was a copy of Dr. Finch's medical record, the other a letter from Nanny Smaltrot. He read both carefully, then in disbelief read them again. The hearth fire crackled in the silence. He was aware of Sarah standing close by, of the faint scratch of his mother's nails on the chair arms.

Comprehension curled warmly around him. From the mist of memory came the recollection of many doctors examining Christopher even before the fire. He really hadn't harmed his brother. The darkness fled Damien's soul, and he felt clean and unblemished, as good as he felt standing on a mountaintop in India, as good as he felt while making love to Sarah.

His mother sat hunched like an old woman. Talons of betrayal dug into him. "Why did you lie to me, Mother?" he asked, his voice grating. "Why did you mislead an innocent boy?"

"You weren't innocent. You nearly frightened poor Christopher to death."

"It was an accident. I never intended to hurt him."

"Don't lie to me, young man." She pushed herself upright, the lorgnette dangling from its ribbon around her neck. "You were always defiant and wayward, the very image of my father. I had to crush your wildness so you wouldn't turn out as wicked as he.''

Damien shook his head in bafflement. ''Grandfather died when I was only a baby. He had no influence over me.''

''You inherited his bad blood. You gave me trouble from the day you came squalling into the world. You're cocky and headstrong. You even look like Papa.'' She turned to glower into the fire. ''He made his fortune at the gambling tables. He ended up dying in a duel to defend the honor of one of his whores.''

Damien was still puzzled. ''Do you begrudge the fact that he left me his money?''

She whirled. Agony and anger deepened the gold of her eyes. ''The money be damned,'' she burst out. ''I hated him. He was a hard, cruel devil who abandoned me and my mother when I was only eleven years old.'' Her words choked off.

An inkling of perception touched Damien. ''But I'm a different person. I'm not to blame for the faults of your father.''

She threw back her head; her aristocratic nostrils flared. ''You're different, all right. You and Christopher are as opposite as good and evil. That's why you were always jealous of him.''

Damien's heart pounded from the effort to keep his emotions in check. ''Of course I was jealous. He had your love. I could never please you.''

''Because you're a devil!'' Her palm hit the table and rattled a porcelain dish. ''Christopher should have been whole, not you. I wish you'd died in that fire.''

Sarah gasped. The hellish nightmare of memory reared in Damien; his mother's ugly words hung in the air like the stink of sulfur. The urge to toss back a demonic retort rose so high in his throat he could taste its bitterness. In his mind he heard Sarah's voice: *You've spent your entire life living up to her image of you.*

He scoured himself of darkness and focused on Sarah. Instantly his heart lightened. Her eyes radiated her shining faith in him. By the fierceness of her expression, he knew she would leap to his defense should he ask it of her. But God! Did she see him as only another injustice to be righted? Would she leave him and move on to another crusade?

"But I didn't die," he said slowly, keeping his gaze on Sarah. "I lived to sire a fine son. And I found a wonderful woman who sees the good in me." Knowing she'd come here to fight for his son filled Damien with pride. "Though God alone can fathom where she found the patience to put up with me."

"For a while," Sarah murmured, "you didn't give me a choice."

Her smile enveloped him in courage and contentment. He caressed her cheek, her skin pure and silken to his scars. Reluctantly he turned back to his mother.

As if the outburst had vented all of her steam, she sat wilted in the chair. Tears dripped down her cheeks and made little runnels in her face powder. Pity stirred within him. All those lost years of his childhood, she'd been punishing not him but her own father. And she had become like the very parent she despised.

But whatever the reason, she'd had no right to persecute him.

"I did a lot of thinking on the voyage to England, Mother," Damien said. "I spent days battling anger at you for denying me your love. And grieving for the happy family we might have been."

She attempted to sit straight. "You can't imagine the trials I've endured, having a son like

Christopher. No doctor could cure him. They gave him potions and possets, but nothing worked."

"And so you punished me."

She glared with self-righteous dignity. "I never struck you. I could have many a time, but I restrained myself."

"Yes, you only struck at my heart." Damien shook his head in irony. "I grew up feeling unloved, abandoned by my own parents. I needed your affection every bit as much as my brother did."

"See? You were always a selfish boy. I gave you fine clothes, sent you to the best schools, but you never appreciated it." Her wrinkled fingers twisted a handkerchief. "Christopher was always the perfect little gentleman. I just couldn't let myself believe . . ."

"That he was slow since birth? Admit it, Mother."

"He was improving!" She dabbed furiously at her eyes. "But after you set the fire, his condition deteriorated. You made him worse. It wasn't fair that you could excel at mathematics and art and the classics, while Christopher could barely read a primer."

At one time Damien would have apologized; now her need to make excuses saddened him. Beset by her own demons, his mother would never change. "You keep trying to turn all your ills back to me. But no more. You should have accepted me for what I was—just an ordinary boy who craved a mother's love."

"You're evil," she insisted. "Everyone knew so. You murdered your own father."

Beside him, Sarah took a small step forward, her fingers tense around her reticule. Damien sent her a frown and prayed she would support his version of the truth. Not even to exonerate himself could he implicate Christopher. "No, I didn't kill Father. He fell because he was drunk."

"Nonsense. You yourself confessed you'd argued with him—"

"I only said that because I knew you wanted to believe the worst of me. The truth is, Christopher and I caught him seducing the parlor maid. Father was so shocked by our discovery, he took a misstep and tumbled over the balcony. It was a tragic accident, nothing more."

"You're lying, just as you always do. Christopher would have told me the truth. He lacks your facility for falsehoods."

"He didn't grasp what happened. But it's high time you knew that I won't be the scapegoat for every dreadful event that tarnished your sterling life."

Her shoulders slumped a fraction. "I never meant you harm. I tried to make you a better man."

"I became a better man in spite of you, Mother, not because of you. But I doubt you'll ever see beyond your own blind interests."

"You ungrateful child! How can you say such cruel things to me? And how can you lie to me about Ambrose's death?" Her voice broke in a sob. Putting her face in her hands, she wept.

The strident sound made Damien's belly clench. Like a wax figure in the sun, she drooped in the chair. God, he'd never seen her weep before. Not even when his brother suffered a spell of illness. Conciliatory words crowded Damien's throat. He'd done this to her. He'd made her miserable.

He was about to step toward her when Sarah slipped her hand into his. The slight shake of her head brought the light of comprehension to him; his mother was manipulating him again, this time with tears.

The drawing room doors burst open. Christopher rushed inside. He glanced worriedly at Damien, then hastened to kneel before his mother. "Mama, don't cry. Please, don't cry. I was listening at the keyhole, and Damien's telling the truth. He didn't push Papa. I did.''

She lifted her ravaged face. The aristocratic elegance slipped away and her skin went pasty gray, her fine mouth slack with shock. ''No . . .''

''I pushed him because he wouldn't listen to me play my drum.'' Christopher's lips quivered and his eyes glossed with tears. ''But I never meant to hurt him. I'm so sorry, Mama.''

''Why didn't you tell me?'' she whispered.

''Because Damien told me I must never tell. He said he was going away, so it didn't matter that you blamed him.''

He laid his head in her lap. Her age-mottled hands trembled as she stroked his fair hair. Her anguished gaze lifted to Damien. The stark realization of his innocence haunted her golden eyes. But she said nothing.

Regret saddened Damien. He acknowledged in his heart that he'd hoped to hear her relent. Yet even in the face of overwhelming evidence, she could not reach out to him.

That was her shortcoming, not his. The thought cleansed his soul. With Sarah beside him, he could accept his mother's flaws and focus on the people who were important to him.

He walked across the Aubusson rug and touched his brother's shoulder. ''Chris. You haven't welcomed me home.''

Christopher sprang up. In a display of natural exuberance, he opened his arms. Damien pulled his brother close, absorbed his warmth, and breathed in his soap-clean scent. Deep and unending, a river of love coursed through him. For the first time, he could embrace his brother without guilt and shame.

Christopher let go. ''You aren't cross with me for telling our secret, are you?''

Damien smiled. ''No, I'm not cross.''

The tears vanished and his brother's face lit up.

Excitement glistened over the serene features of an angel. "You were always so sad before," he said, as if they'd parted only yesterday instead of ten long years ago. "But you look happy now. Is it because you have a baby?"

"Yes. Now I have Kit . . . and Sarah, too."

Damien looked at her, and the deep, abiding love in his eyes bathed Sarah in the splendor of hope. She listened abstractedly as he answered his brother's questions about India, as he painted vivid pictures of elephants and tigers, snake charmers and sword swallowers. Though the brothers shared the same high brow and cheekbones, they were a pleasing contrast, Damien as deep and dark as the night, Christopher as pure and golden as sunshine. Joy and pride danced inside her. Though Christopher was the duke, she privately thought Damien the nobler of the two. At last he had slain the dragons of his past.

Blanche Coleridge sat limply, watching her sons. The silk of the chair arms lay shredded beneath her nails. Firelight caught the wetness of tears on her wrinkled cheeks, but she made no attempt to repair the damage. Reluctant sympathy touched Sarah. How sad that the dowager had refused to love a man as wonderful as her second son.

"I have to be going now," Damien told his brother.

"Not yet," said Christopher, pouting. "You haven't played with me in ever so long. I have a whole collection of new drums."

"I'll come back after Christmas to see all your presents."

The prospect brightened Christopher. "Bring baby Kit. He's my namesake, you know."

"I know." Damien smiled briefly; then his face sobered as he looked beyond his brother. "Goodbye, Mother."

Touching Sarah's arm, he guided her to the

door. "Wait," Blanche called in a quavering voice. "Will you be staying in London?"

His muscles tensed. He turned. "That depends," he murmured. "On certain unfinished business."

He gave Sarah a fierce and unfathomable look. She met his gaze squarely. Whatever unfinished business lay between them, they would settle. The prospect of being alone with the man she loved made her sway with giddiness. The moment they walked out of the drawing room, a brilliant bubble seemed to enclose them in the promise of joys to come.

Wreathed in dreamlike anticipation, she waited as he wrapped the cloak around her, clapped a fond hand on Bromley's shoulder, and walked outside. Icy snowflakes pricked her face, yet the cold invigorated her. Damien slid his arm around her waist, as if he couldn't bear to be separated from her.

He ushered her into a hansom cab at the curb, spoke briefly to the high-seated driver, then climbed in beside her. The small interior formed a private cocoon. The scent of leather and snow blended with his unique male essence. The carriage rocked and started down the street.

Their eyes met and married. Their bodies surged together. Against her breast, his heart pounded in harmony with hers like the mesmeric beating of drums. He brushed back her hood and cradled his cool hands around her neck. His thumbs traced the dainty line of her jaw. His brown eyes, alight with flecks of gold, seemed to absorb her into himself. "Saraswati," he murmured. "How I've missed you."

The pet name brought back radiant memories of making love beneath the hot Indian sun. On a sigh of joy, she twined her arms around his neck and lifted her mouth to his cold, snow-kissed lips. A delicious shiver passed through her, and the chill swiftly transformed into a searing flame. Abandoning herself to sensual pleasures long denied, she slipped her arms inside his greatcoat and relearned the hardness of muscles and the smooth, tapering strength of his chest. The bold familiarity of his caresses ringed her in enchantment.

"Oh, Damien," she murmured against the pulse thrumming in his throat, "I never imagined I'd find you again. You're the finest Christmas gift I could ever wish for."

He drew back. Their breaths mingled in a tiny cloud, and the jolting of the carriage matched the tremor of excitement in her blood. Vulnerability blazed in his eyes. "Sweet Sarah," he said on a husky note of yearning. "You do still want me, then?"

She tilted her head in surprise. "Of course. Why would you ever doubt my feelings?"

"I saw how close you and Reginald have grown. You've spent the past couple of months with him. If the two of you have come to an agreement . . ."

She couldn't help a teasing smile. "We have, indeed."

Beneath her fingers, his chest tensed. "And?"

"Dear me, I don't quite know how to say this."

"Dammit, Sarah, don't torture me."

She kissed his furrowed brow. "There's no need to use foul language, darling. Reginald and I have agreed to be friends."

Damien blew out a breath. "I'll never be a gentleman like him," he warned.

"Thank heaven," she said, moving her lips to the faint black stubble on his cheek. "I prefer a scoundrel who'll ravish me in an erotic shrine."

Tenderness softened the hard curve of his mouth. He cocked a black eyebrow. "Suppose I'm not a scoundrel anymore? Suppose I decide to settle down and take a wife?"

Her heart melted into a puddle of yearning. "Did you have a particular woman in mind?"

"Since you ask . . . yes." As he spoke, he rained kisses over her face. "She's clever enough to write a book. She's brave enough to trek through a country at war. She's patient enough to forgive a man's sins and make him see his own strengths. And in addition to the admirable qualities of her character, she has the body of a goddess."

Sarah's pulse beat in her throat. "I am vexed. Where will you find such a model of womanhood?"

"Right here, praise God." Damien rubbed his thumbs over the tendrils of hair at her temples. He looked into her eyes, his own eyes dark with longing. His voice deepening to a gruff pitch, he murmured, "Sarah, will you be my wife?"

Her soul soared at the words she'd never thought to hear him speak. "Yes. Yes, I love you."

"I love you, too."

Tears prickled her eyes. "Oh, Damien. You once said you were incapable of love."

"You make me capable of anything. I had a lot of time to think during those dark hours when the fakir held me captive—"

"It's a miracle you didn't die in the fire," she said in an outburst of emotion. "You faced down your worst fear to save me and Kit. I knew then how much honor and love you hid in your heart."

"Because you taught me how to love." A deep current of mingled adoration and desire flowed from him. "Sarah, my greatest wish is to have a family with you. I want our home to ring with laughter. I want us to have children together, brothers and sisters for Kit."

Smiling, she settled his large palm over her belly. "Your wish will be granted sooner than you think."

The clatter of hooves filled the cab. A wondering glint entered his gaze. "Do you mean . . . ?"

"Yes. Our last time together, we created a baby. We'll have a son or daughter come summer."

His fiercely noble features gentled, and he looked at her with his heart in his eyes. He brought her hand to his lips and kissed her palm. "Now you've given *me* the finest Christmas gift," he whispered.

"At last you'll have the chance to see how close and happy a family can be." The thought of his lonely childhood sobered her. "I was proud of how you stood up to your mother. You didn't let her demons swallow you. You showed her what a fine, good man you are."

"Now I can see she's more to be pitied than feared. Thanks to you, I can visit my brother without feeling ashamed." He kissed Sarah on the nose. "My lovely crusader. You stood at my side and gave me confidence."

"Mmm." With a sultry sigh, she pressed herself to his lean body. Her fingers curved around the bulge in his trousers. "I hope I inspire more than confidence in you."

He sucked in a breath. His hand enclosed hers, his scars smooth and firm as he gently shaped her fingers around him. "Sarah . . . Sarah . . . it's been so long . . ."

She rubbed the length of him. "It's always rather long," she teased, her own loins alive with a sweet, unbearable ache.

"Imp." He grinned even as his jaw flexed with the effort to retain control. "I'll make you pay for vexing me so."

"Will you?" she dared. "Do tell me how."

"First I'm going to take off all your clothes . . ." The cab swayed to a halt. He kissed her forehead. "Hold that thought."

Reluctantly she banked the fires within herself. Damien helped her down to the curbstone in front of a town house built of honey-colored stone. Snowflakes drifted thickly from the gray sky. As he paid the driver, she stood huddled in her cloak and wrapped in the warmth of Damien's love.

He took her hand and drew her up the marble steps to a door bright with brass fittings and adorned with a great Christmas wreath. Without knocking, he ushered her inside.

Candles in wall sconces lit an airy foyer. The scents of evergreen, beeswax, and gingerbread enriched the air. To one side stretched a drawing room decorated in warm blues and creams, and to the other, a library filled with comfortable chairs and rows of books.

"Whose house is this?" she asked.

"Mine. I wanted to bring you to a real home."

She looked at Damien with amazed awe. "How long have you been in London?"

He grinned. "Two days. Money and position can be assets. You convinced me of that."

She took a long breath and released it. "I'm glad you've stopped running from your past."

"The only place I want to run," he said, scooping her into his arms, "is upstairs, to the master suite."

His powerful muscles flexed around her. Sarah caught a dizzying glimpse of gilt-framed pictures and a rich mahogany balustrade. She clung to his neck and pressed her cheek to the firm strength of his chest. His quick footfalls echoed the eager beating of her heart. She felt as if she were floating on air, buoyed by magic.

At the head of the stairs, he shouldered open a door and carried her into a cozy chamber. A tiger-skin rug lay before the hearth, where a fire leaped merrily. Candlelight lent an intimate aura to the cane furniture and exotic wall hangings. Brass vases and ivory carvings abounded. Beside a tester bed draped in indigo silk, Damien let her down, her breasts sliding against his chest, her feet meeting the thick Kashmiri carpet.

"You've re-created India," she breathed.

"Do you like it?"

She twirled. "It's wonderful."

"Stand still." His arms came around her from behind. Without further ado, he unfastened her cloak and tossed it over a chair. Then he set to work on the pearl buttons down the back of her gown. "I much preferred you in a sari," he grumbled. "All this trussing is hell on a hungry man."

She laughed. "It's hell on a famished woman, too."

"Good God," he muttered. "Now you're cursing like me. I really have led you astray."

"Mmm," she sighed as he kissed the nape of her neck. "Astray into the garden of paradise."

He tugged off her gown, and his palms cupped her corseted breasts, his warmth seeping through the boned material. Her loins flooded with heat, and she burned with need for the man who had at last found the courage to open his scarred heart to her. Turning, she met his kiss with her own and then fumbled with the unfamiliar garb of a gentleman. Laughing, they took turns stripping each other of corset and jacket, chemise and waistcoat, underdrawers and trousers. At last he lay beside her on the bed, the silk cool to her fevered flesh.

With murmurs and sighs of delight, they rediscovered the joys of an idyll begun in the Himalayan hills. She touched his magnificent naked form, found the thin scar left by a mutineer's knife, let her hands roam over skin bronzed by the Indian sun. He combed his fingers through tawny hair once dyed black, caressed features once hidden by a gossamer veil, let his hand slide over her abdomen, where their child thrived.

"Love me," Damien whispered.

"Always," Sarah murmured.

She opened herself to him with abandon. Passion brought them surging together, their bodies melding in perfect rhythm, their lips joining in a heartfelt kiss as they celebrated a love that had arisen from the ashes of a bloody mutiny, a love that had brought them halfway around the globe. The splendor burst upon them, raining them in perfect pleasure, blazing as bright as fire across the firmament.

As the sweet-sharp pulsebeats faded, Sarah relaxed. His body covered hers, and she felt their heartbeats slow. His mouth warm against her ear, he murmured, "*Ananda* . . ."

"Perfect bliss," she translated. She moved sinuously beneath him. "My sentiments precisely."

Damien propped himself on his elbow and smiled. "Damn. And to think I once believed you prudish."

"I was." She tracked her fingertips up his furred chest. "Until I met a rogue who forced me out of the trappings of a lady."

A wicked twinkle gleamed in his eyes. "Ah, so you admit I corrupted you."

"Opened my eyes is more to the point. You unveiled the passionate woman inside me. You showed me that love is more precious than girlish dreams and ladylike behavior."

"And you taught me that my emotional armor was more prison than protection." Damien laced their fingers, his scarred and long, hers smooth and dainty. "Now I can give you your dream, Sarah. A loving husband, a big family, a secure home."

"I know you can."

"Of course, if you don't like this house, we'll choose another."

His desire to please touched her heart; his willingness to give up his own dreams washed her in tenderness. "But what about your work?" she asked. "What about the photographs you still need to take for our book?"

"I can make do with what I have. I love you, Sarah. You're a ray of sunshine in my life. Our happiness and our being together matter more to me than anything else."

A joyous laugh bubbled from her. "Then make me happy. Let's return to India. I want to travel with you, raise our children in exotic places, go on great adventures with the man I love."

His dark features lit with yearning. "Are you sure you don't need a proper home?"

Misty-eyed, she hugged him. "Oh, Damien. We can make a home anywhere so long as we're together."

Now that you've enjoyed
Barbara Dawson Smith's
FIRE ON THE WIND,
sample another of Avon Books'
Romantic Treasures—
DANCE OF DECEPTION
by Suzannah Davis

During an uneasy pause in the Napoleanic Wars, an enig-matic man of mystery, Bryce Darcy Cormick, captivates the lovely and spirited Genevieve Maples . . .

"Do you wish for company, or should I leave you to your solitude?"

Genevieve looked over her shoulder at Darcy. "You know, I've almost become accustomed to your creep-ing up on me like that."

He grinned. "Miss Maples, I do not creep."

"On the contrary, you creep very well for a man of your size, rather like one of those African lions one sees in the zoological exhibit at the Tower of London. Although I was thankful for your talent this morning, it's extremely disconcerting in polite company."

"I'll make an effort to stumble over my feet when-ever I approach you from now on."

She turned her face back toward the water, attempt-ing a cool façade to mask the sudden erratic tendencies of her heart. "I'd appreciate the warning."

He moved to her side, surveying the little stream

and the dappling of light and shadow under the willows. "A pretty scene."

"Mmm. I'd like to sketch it. But I'd add a boat there." She pointed. "And maybe a little boy with a fishing pole just on that stone."

"Ah. Someone to ride in the boat."

"Certainly not!" Her smile turned impish, and she shot him a sideways glance. "My little boy is much too young for boating. But he may take his string of trout home to his proud mother. Perhaps I'll even draw her, waiting on that hill over there."

"And where is the father of this fortunate lad?" asked Darcy, playing her game.

"Working hard in the fields, thinking about his family and a fish dinner!" she said with a laugh.

"Are you artist enough to bring such a delightful fantasy to life?"

"Would that I were so fortunate," she murmured obliquely. Shaking off the phantasm, she steered away from personal revelations by taking up business concerns. "In all the confusion, you haven't had a chance to learn our lines."

"I thought you meant me to audition for your grandfather."

"After what you did this morning? Grandpapa is totally besotted by your bravery and heroism. You may spout Lord Byron's new poetry instead of your part for all he cares. However, *I* expect you to know your lines. Now, while we've a moment, let me explain the story . . ."

For the next few minutes, behind the screen of willows, Genevieve explained the melodrama's plot, Darcy's action and stage cues, and had him repeat the few lines required of him. To her dismay, his declamation was wooden and inept, his actions awkward, even comical. For a man with as much innate self-assurance as Darcy, she found this turn of events astonishing.

"Not very good, is it?" Darcy asked after a particularly ear-wrenching rendition of his final line. "You'd better concentrate on finding someone else for King Harold."

"No, no. Maybe comedy is your strength, but I'm sure you can do this," Genevieve hastened to reassure him. Groaning to herself, she knew she'd never find another replacement in time. She simply had to work with the King Harold she had. "You're just tense, that's all. Maybe if you moved around some . . . Here, let's review the sword fight."

Reaching up into the tree, she snapped off a willow branch and passed it to him. "Use this as the sword. Now, here's what you do . . ."

But Darcy seemed even more awkward than ever, slicing the air with his branch and jumping about like an overgrown bullfrog.

"No, not like that!" Genevieve snapped at last. "How came a soldier to know so little of swordsmanship?"

"I served in the calvary. Ask me to ride a horse."

"Never mind! Do it as I showed you, Darcy."

Slipping off his coat, he tossed it onto a handy branch. Blotting his perspiring face on the sleeve of his open-throated shirt, he grinned apologetically. "I'm trying, Little General. If you could show me once more. . . ?"

Genevieve set aside her bonnet, then positioned herself at his side, showing him the footwork, stretching out her arm along his much longer, brawnier one, using her body as a shadow of his to keep him on track. With her back to his front, arm outstretched, she was entirely too conscious of the rocklike solidity of his physique, the crisp sprinkling of dark chest hair revealed by the vee of his shirt, and the musky scent of virile male sweat. She tried to concentrate on his movements, but it seemed that she could feel the heat of his body straight through her muslin gown and petticoats. And still he did not improve.

"You're making this much harder than it has to be," she insisted.

"That, my dear Genny, is a matter of opinion," he said in a strangled voice.

Puzzled, Genevieve took a moment to realize the full impact of his innuendo. With an affronted gasp, she whirled in his arms, her face ablaze. "You vulgar, uncouth—"

He kept her from jerking away by placing a hand on her waist and curling his sword arm around her back. "I'll remind you that I'm not the one who started pressing herself against me like a cat in heat in full view of the countryside.''

She blinked in realization. ''You—you merely pretended to be so clumsy, didn't you? I'll give you credit. You're a much better actor than I thought.''

He inclined his head in gracious acceptance of her accolade. ''I owe everything to my teacher.''

''I was merely trying to help you!'' she spluttered.

''And I wouldn't be much of a man if I didn't enjoy it, would I, Genny?'' He growled, wicked amusement lighting the fire in his blue eyes.

''Unhand me immediately, you lout!'' Mortified, she would not dignify this conversation by struggling. ''I'm no ha'penny harlot for you to insult as you will.''

''Why is it insulting to know that I find you desirable? What greater compliment can a man pay a woman?''

Her color went from rose to crimson at his frankness. ''This isn't seemly,'' she croaked. ''Let me go. Someone will see.''

He sighed but obediently loosened his hold, letting one hand slip under the chestnut curls piled at her nape. Her involuntarily wince made him swear.

''By God, the bastard did hurt you!'' He pushed her hair back to reveal a line of purplish bruises, then lightly traced the welts with a fingertip, cursing under his breath all the while.

''They're not bad,'' Genevieve said, shaking by the savagery of his expression and by the pleasure-pain of his brief caress on her tender skin. The hairs on her arms quivered. ''Darcy? It's all right. I'll heal.''

His thumb came up under her chin, lifting her face so that he could see himself reflected in the forest-colored depths of her eyes. ''Forgiveness for the enemy, is that it, General, but none for me?''

''We're not enemies,'' she answered, breathless and dizzy.

''I hope to hell not. If we weren't standing out in the middle of a public field, I'd kiss you until you believed it, too.''

''Why did you kiss me before?'' she whispered.

"What man in his right mind wouldn't?"

"What?"

He shook his head, his lips twisting in a wry, self-deprecating smile. "You have no idea what your mouth does to a man, do you? It makes promises without ever saying a word. That's why I kissed you, to see what those promises taste like. You're addictive, Genny. One taste, and a man may never be able to get enough. You'd have been safer if you'd slapped me silly and yelled for help."

Bemused by his speech, she answered with guileless honesty. "I didn't want to."

He sucked in a breath, and the thumb that had been stroking her throat went completely still. "It's dangerous for you to say things like that to me."

"I have a feeling we're both very dangerous people," she murmured.

"Are you willing to find out?"

Genevieve smiled to herself. Ah, he was good! Seducing her with words and the heat in his beautiful blue eyes. But beyond that, there was a loneliness in him that called to something kindred in her. Could she believe in that promise? Or was she merely pretending, drawing another pretty fantasy out of thin air because all of a sudden her life seemed so empty? It was crazy and unreasonable, this sudden infatuation with a stranger, yet perhaps they'd have time to get to know each other if he stayed with the company. They could take it slow . . . if it wasn't already too late for that.

Smiling, she took his hand from her throat, then folded her slender fingers around his lean, brown ones. "Perhaps we should try being friends first, Darcy."

"So cautious!" he teased.

"Just practical. No doubt you've used your charming ways to woo many an unwary lady to your bed. I could ill afford to make such a mistake."

Laughter rumbled deep in his chest. "Mistake, is it? Now you insult me! But once in my bed you'll find how wrong you are."

"Rogue! You assume too much."

"Do I, Genny?" he asked quietly, his gaze suddenly intense.